Praise for *Dust Child*

"Achingly honest and ultimately hopeful; essential reading for US audiences." —*Library Journal* (starred review)

"Powerful and deeply empathetic. A heartbreaking tale of lost ideals, human devotion, and hard-won redemption. *Dust Child* establishes Nguyễn Phan Quế Mai as one of our finest observers of the devastating consequences of war, and proves, once more, her ability to captivate readers and lure them into Việt Nam's rich and poignant history." —Viet Thanh Nguyen, Pulitzer Prize–winning author of *The Sympathizer* and *The Committed*

"Intricate and ingenious . . . Vividly drawn." —*The Washington Post*

"*Dust Child* is satisfying, lyrical, and deeply empathetic. Nguyễn Phan Quế Mai is a born storyteller." —Gabrielle Zevin, *New York Times* bestselling author of *Tomorrow, and Tomorrow, and Tomorrow*

"*Dust Child* takes on the difficult subject of Amerasians left behind once the American military fled its own misadventures in Southeast Asia. Look for a reception akin to Min Jin Lee's bestselling *Pachinko*." —*Los Angeles Times*

"In this sweeping, decades-spanning saga, Phong, a half-Black, half-Vietnamese man, searches for the parents who abandoned him while Dan, a war veteran, returns to Vietnam to contend with secrets from his past."   —*The New York Times Book Review*

"Dazzling. Sharply drawn and hauntingly beautiful."
    —Elif Shafak, author of *The Island of Missing Trees*

"From the author of the bestselling book *The Mountains Sing* comes this epic story of those who lived through the Việt Nam conflict or were otherwise deeply affected by it decades later."   —*Ms.* magazine

"Rewarding . . . with a cinematic clarity."   —*Publishers Weekly*

"Scenes of past and present Việt Nam come alive in these pages, drawing you into the lives of a handful of characters who become like your family, and in whose stories lies the heartbreaking story of Việt Nam's complicated relationship with America. With her generous heart and unmatched ability to write across languages and cultures, Quế Mai is the perfect guide for the wounded who search for home and healing."
    —Thi Bui, award-winning author of *The Best We Could Do*

"A worthy and affecting story that is long overdue."
    —*San Francisco Chronicle*

"Both intimate and universal, *Dust Child* is a plea for peace—and a powerful reminder that every person is more than their worst decision."
    —Apple Books

"This moving novel deals with the legacies of shame and trauma—both carried and passed on—by young women who fought in no war, but were battle-scarred just the same."   —Amazon Book Review

"Inherited trauma, intense secrets, and inside looks characterize this lyrical novel by a bold talent." —*Good Morning America*

"*Dust Child* is at once empathetic, devastating, and upbeat, burnished with Quế Mai's stunning signature prose."
—WGBH Boston Public Radio

"As an adopted Amerasian orphan from the Vietnam War growing up in America, *Dust Child* is more than a book to me; it is much-needed reconciliation and healing."
—Trần Văn Kirk (Kellerhals), director of *Intersections*, winner of Best Inspirational Film at the 2022 Cannes World Film Festival

"*Dust Child* offers a fresh, compassionate lens on Vietnam."
—KPBS Radio

"Nguyễn Phan Quế Mai shows us the capacity we hold to confront our pasts, for the purpose of life is not to remain intact, but to break open, to let loss be a guide, to face the echoes of longing. In *Dust Child*, rupture leads to emotional richness, and pain creates the pathways worth walking. I truly cannot wait for the rest of the world to celebrate this book."
—Chanel Miller, *New York Times* bestselling author of *Know My Name*

"Quế Mai adeptly balances these contemporary narratives with Phong's early experiences and the wartime story of sisters Trang and Quỳnh . . . There are no clear heroes or villains here as characters' actions and choices are shaped by their circumstances and the war's legacy."
—*Booklist*

"Spanning the arc of the Vietnam War and its lingering traumas, *Dust Child* brings together an unforgettable cast of characters . . . [and] deftly explores the ways we both inherit trauma and redefine our own paths forward. A family epic to remember."   *—Chicago Review of Books*

"An exquisite novel . . . It is one of the many pleasures of *Dust Child* that despite its portrayal of suffering and difficulty, the novel is also infused with joy. Whether writing of Phong's courtship of the singer Bình and their eventual marriage, or Kim's love of poetry, or vibrant street scenes from the cities, Nguyễn beautifully summons the daily lives of her characters . . . In telling their stories over a lifetime, she gives each of the characters opportunities to inhabit their full humanity, and chances to learn and change."   *—The Boston Globe*

"With a poet's gift for language and a psychologist's eye for the tender, error-prone hearts of mankind, Nguyễn Phan Quế Mai weaves a web of impossible choices, inescapable circumstance, and searing loss, set to the backdrop of a war that changed everything . . . A heartbreaking, beautifully told, utterly unique story of love, loss, and longing that speaks to the very heart of the human experience."
—Kristin Harmel, *New York Times* bestselling
author of *The Forest of Vanishing Stars*

"*Dust Child* is a result of years of Nguyễn Phan Quế Mai's research, and a fervent attempt to acknowledge the lives and experiences of these children, all coupled with a compassion that's unique to her alone."
—Book Riot

"Poignantly written, *Dust Child* is a must-read."
—Diasporic Vietnamese Artists Network (DVAN)

"Nguyễn Phan Quế Mai is one of the most unique storytellers of our time. She creates plots which are Dickensian in their breadth and mastery, while bravely probing the complex emotional challenges of living in a modern world full of disruption and displacement. In *Dust Child*, Quế Mai displays the same tenderness and compassion for her characters, hard-earned understanding of human trauma, and poetically evocative language that made her debut novel *The Mountains Sing* an international bestseller beloved around the world."

—Natalie Jenner, internationally bestselling
author of *The Jane Austen Society*

"Through compelling multilayered fiction, Nguyễn intimately humanizes war's victims, regardless of nationalities . . . Nguyễn deftly wields her own polyglot talents to reclaim lives too long overlooked."

—*Shelf Awareness*

"The sons and daughters of American soldiers and their Vietnamese girlfriends who exhibited African American and European features were shunned by Vietnam's monoethnic society during and after the war. Nguyễn Phan Quế Mai writes of some of these 'dust children' with complexity and heart. This is a powerful and moving story, brilliantly told."

—Robert Mason, *New York Times* bestselling
author of *Chickenhawk*

"Masterful . . . this newest addition into the Vietnamese literary canon should not be missed." —*US-Vietnam Review*

"A compelling written tale that deals with an important aspect of the Vietnam War that is not often available to American readers . . . Riveting." —Vietnam Veterans of America (VVA)

"An insightful, engrossing novel."   —*California Review of Books*

"In her riveting successor to *The Mountains Sing*, Nguyễn Phan Quế Mai has masterfully captured the toll of war and its aftermath on a Black Amerasian, an outcast in the country of his birth; on an American vet, haunted and seeking redemption; and on two Vietnamese sisters, forced by economic hardship into circumstances they could not have foreseen. Nguyễn creates, in her luminous prose, a gripping and nuanced narrative of men and women caught in the web of war and its aftermath."
        —Steven DeBonis, author of *Children of the Enemy: Oral Histories of Vietnamese Amerasians and Their Mothers*

"An engrossing story of Amerasians born to the Vietnamese women and American GIs during the time of the Vietnam War. Told from three points of view with emotion and skill, these intersecting stories will stay with you."   —BookTrib

"With great compassion, with a firm conviction in the redeeming power of love and forgiveness, and with the consummate skill of a great storyteller, Nguyễn Phan Quế Mai weaves us into the lives, past and present, of those called 'the dust of life'—the ostracized, mixed-race children of American soldiers; their mothers, compelled by war into prostitution; and their fathers, the GIs who abandoned them and yet remained haunted by them."
        —Wayne Karlin, author of *Wandering Souls: Journeys with the Dead and the Living in Viet Nam*

"A poignant and suspenseful saga marked by family secrets and generational trauma."   —BookBub

INTERNATIONAL PRAISE

"A powerful novel that reflects on the catastrophic legacy that wars leave to future generations." —*Elle* (Italy)

"By addressing consequences of the American presence during the Vietnam War, this blistering novel illumines the resulting fractured lives of families." —*Toronto Star*

"The intimate care for every character is phenomenally beautiful." —*Women's Weekly* (Australia)

"*Dust Child* has the great power to show soldiers as men, lovers, fathers; and bar girls as sisters, fiancées, mothers. In the end what really marks the characters, what makes them good or evil, brave or coward[ly], is not the role they played in the battlefield or the darkness of prostitution, but how they act in front of the universal responsibility toward future generations." —*La Lettura* (Italy)

"*Dust Child* stays with you. There is something so deeply sincere, even guileless, about it, a genuine sympathy and compassion that somehow subverts the usual expectations and rules of fiction." —*New Zealand Listener*

"An informative story . . . Timely and poignant."   —TripFiction

"The author saw the wounds of her country and then learned to see the ones hidden in the hearts of the people. And once she saw that pain she decided to write about it and, when possible, to heal it."

—*Sette* (Italy)

"A poetic saga that deftly examines oft-marginalized elements of war, race, trauma, and healing, *Dust Child* transports readers to Vietnam to witness the powerful role of compassion in the wake of humankind's efforts to inflict great harm on itself."   —Saigoneer

"Writing for reconciliation, Nguyễn Phan Quế Mai bridges divides."

—*Southeast Asia Globe*

"Quế Mai is a skilled storyteller, and her lyrical turn of phrase reflects her characters' backgrounds as well as their emotions . . . The compassionate treatment of her characters, insights into the period, and eloquent prose are impressive."   —*Financial Times*

"Notable for its boundless compassion for all the characters, from young, brutalized US soldiers to the girls who pretend to love them and the dust children left behind."   —*The Times*

"Beautifully crafted . . . A masterful display of Quế Mai's capacity to evoke compassion through her lyrical prose."   —*The Irish Times*

"A warm, touching family drama."   —*Femina* magazine (Sweden)

"One of the most important works of historical fiction in recent times."

—Sofia Akel, founder of the Free Books Campaign

DUST
CHILD

ALSO BY NGUYỄN PHAN QUẾ MAI

The Mountains Sing

The Secret of Hoa Sen

DUST
CHILD

a novel

NGUYỄN PHAN QUẾ MAI

ALGONQUIN BOOKS OF CHAPEL HILL 2024

Published by
Algonquin Books of Chapel Hill
Post Office Box 2225
Chapel Hill, North Carolina 27515-2225

an imprint of Workman Publishing
a division of Hachette Book Group, Inc.
1290 Avenue of the Americas
New York, New York 10104

The Algonquin Books of Chapel Hill name and logo are
registered trademarks of Hachette Book Group, Inc.

Design by Steve Godwin.

The publisher is not responsible for websites
(or their content) that are not owned by the publisher.

LIBRARY OF CONGRESS CATALOGING-IN-PUBLICATION DATA
Names: Nguyễn, Phan Quế Mai, [date]– author.
Title: Dust child : a novel / Nguyễn Phan Quế Mai.
Description: First edition. | Chapel Hill, North Carolina : Algonquin Books of
Chapel Hill, 2023. | Summary: "An American GI, two Vietnamese bargirls, and an
Amerasian man are forced to make decisions during and after the Viet Nam War
that will reverberate throughout one another's lives"— Provided by publisher.
Identifiers: LCCN 2022044978 | ISBN 9781643752754 (hardcover) |
ISBN 9781643753751 (ebook)
Subjects: LCSH: Children of military personnel—Vietnam—
Fiction. | Amerasians—Vietnam—Fiction. | Vietnam War, 1961–1975—
Children—Fiction. | Abandoned children—Vietnam—Fiction. |
Vietnamese Americans—Fiction. | Families—Vietnam—Fiction. |
Vietnam—History—20th century—Fiction.
Classification: LCC PR9560.9.N45 | DDC 813/.54—dc23
LC record available at https://lccn.loc.gov/2022044978

ISBN 978-1-64375-578-6 (paperback)

10 9 8 7 6 5 4 3 2 1
First Paperback Edition

For Amerasians and their family members who shared with me
their personal stories and who inspire me with their courage.
For the millions of men, women, and children who were pulled
into the vortex of the Việt Nam War. For anyone whose life has
been touched by violence. May our world see more compassion
and peace.

CONTENTS

During the Việt Nam War, tens of thousands of children were born into relationships between American soldiers and Vietnamese women. Tragic circumstances separated most of these Amerasian children from their fathers and, later, their mothers. Many have not found each other again.

DUST
CHILD

Child of the Enemy

Hồ Chí Minh City, 2016

"Life is a boat," Sister Nhã, the Catholic nun who had raised Phong, once told him. "When you depart from your first anchor—your mother's womb—you will be pulled away by unexpected currents. If you can fill your boat with enough hope, enough self-belief, enough compassion, and enough curiosity, you will be ready to weather all the storms of life."

As Phong sat waiting at the American Consulate, he felt the weight of hope in his hands—his visa application, and those of his wife Bình, his son Tài, and his daughter Diễm.

Around him, many Vietnamese were waiting in chairs or in lines for their turn to speak with one of the visa officers who sat at counters behind glass windows. Some Vietnamese cast curious glances toward Phong and he felt the heat of their eyes. "Half-breed," he imagined them whispering. Throughout his life, he had been called the dust of life, bastard, Black American imperialist, child of the enemy. These labels had been flung at him when he was younger with such ferocity that they had burrowed deep within him, refusing to let go. When he was a child living in the Lâm Đồng New Economic Zone with Sister Nhã, he once filled a large bucket with water and soap, climbed inside, and rubbed his skin with a sponge gourd to scrub the black off it. He was bleeding by the time Sister Nhã found him. He wondered why he had to be born an Amerasian.

"Don't worry, be confident and you'll do well, anh," Bình whispered, reaching for him, the calluses on her palm brushing against his arm. Phong nodded, smiled nervously, and took his wife's hand into his. This hand had cooked for him, washed his clothes, and helped to mend the broken patches of his life. This hand had held him and his children, danced with them, yielded new seasons on their rice field. He loved this hand and its calluses, as he did every part of Bình. He had to fulfill his promise to bring Bình to America. Away from the rubbish dumps where she worked, collecting plastic, paper, and metals.

Sitting next to Bình, Tài and Diễm waved at him. At fourteen and twelve years old, they were nearly as tall as their mother. They'd both inherited Bình's large eyes and her radiant smile. Their skin color and curly hair had come from him. "Remember that you are beautiful," he'd told them as they got ready for the five-hour bus ride here. He'd often said that to them, knowing how they were often looked at with disdain by the Vietnamese, who almost always preferred fair skin.

Tài returned to his book, his crooked glasses sliding down the bridge of his nose, the metal frame held together by pieces of tape. Phong reminded himself to talk with his neighbors again and offer a higher price to rent their paddy field. He would grow mung beans for the New Year, the harvest of which would enable him to buy new glasses for Tài and a dress for Diễm. Diễm was wearing Tài's old clothes; the pants were too short, revealing her ankles.

At a counter in front of Phong, an American visa officer was giving a young woman a blue sheet of paper. Phong knew the color well. Blue meant non-approval. As the woman left the counter, something like panic rose up in Phong.

He tried to recall the interview practice sessions he'd had with his family. He had carved the right answers into his memory the way carpenters carved birds and flowers into wood, but now his mind was blank.

"Number forty-five, counter three," the loudspeaker called.

"That's us," Bình said. As Phong made his way toward the counter together with his wife and children, he told himself to be calm. As long as he had his family, he would not let himself be intimidated. He would fight for the chance to give Bình, Tài, and Diễm a better life.

Phong nodded his greeting at the visa officer, who looked just like the American women in movies he'd seen: blond hair, white skin, high-bridged nose. The woman didn't acknowledge him, her eyes on the computer. Phong studied the machine, wondering what mysteries it held. When he got to America, he would work hard and buy a computer for Tài and Diễm. His children had taken him to town, to an internet café, to show him how computers worked. They said perhaps one day he could send words to his parents via the internet. But would he ever have that chance? He didn't even know if his parents were dead or alive.

The visa officer turned to him.

"Gút mó-ninh," Phong said, hoping he'd pronounced "good morning" correctly. Years ago, he'd learned some basic English, but his knowledge of the language had disappeared like droplets of rain evaporating during a drought. "Chào bà," he added, not wanting the American to think that he was fluent in her language.

"Cho xem hộ chiếu," she said.

Her Vietnamese was good, but her Northern accent bothered Phong. It reminded him of the Communist officers who had beaten him at the reeducation camps in the mountains almost thirty years ago.

He carefully took their passports from a folder and eased them into the box under the glass window. He and his wife had given Quang, the visa agent, all their savings to get these passports made and their visa applications completed and submitted. Quang had convinced them that in America, they wouldn't have to worry about money: a monthly allowance from the government would help them survive.

The woman went through the documents, typing on the computer. She turned away and called someone. A young Vietnamese woman appeared, talking to her in English. Phong cocked his head but the sounds were slippery fish that darted away so quickly, he couldn't catch a single one.

"What's going on?" Bình whispered. Phong placed his palm on his wife's back, knowing it would help calm her. Bình had been so nervous about missing this interview, she'd insisted that they catch the bus from their hometown, Bạc Liêu, the day before and wait outside the consulate at four o'clock this morning.

The Vietnamese woman looked at him. "Uncle Nguyễn Tấn Phong, you're applying for a visa under the Amerasian Homecoming Act?"

How nice that she'd addressed him with a respectful title and given him hope by stating the name of the program he was applying for. Homecoming! The word was sacred, the sound of it fluttering in his heart. He was entitled to go home, to his fatherland. Heat gathered at the back of his eyes. And how nice the woman referred to "Amerasian" as "trẻ lai." Phong had never felt comfortable when people called him "con lai," since *con* means "children," "small," or "animal." He was no animal.

"Yes, Miss," he said.

"You'll be interviewed by another officer. In the room over there." She pointed toward his right. "The rest of your family should take a seat and wait outside."

Bình leaned forward. "My husband can't read. Can I please accompany him?"

"I'll be there to help," the woman said as she walked away.

The room was spacious, lit by fluorescent lights. It had no window and Phong felt sorry for anyone who had to work here. His home wasn't much, but it was rich with fresh air. Air that rushed through open windows all year round, bringing with it the scent of flowers and bird songs.

The person he felt sorry for happened to be a plump, white man who sat behind a square brown desk, dressed in a blue shirt with matching blue tie.

The woman stood next to the desk, and Phong sat down on a chair opposite it. On the wall to his right was a large picture of Mr. Obama. A few years ago, Phong's children had rushed home, calling him to come along. They ran toward their neighbors' house, stood outside the fence, and peered through the open window to watch the TV reporting about Mr. Obama becoming the first Black president of the United States. "America is the nation of immigrants," Mr. Obama was saying as people around him cheered.

For years Phong had wanted to go to America, but at that moment getting there became his life's mission. A country that voted for a Black president had to be better than here, where Black people were sometimes called mọi—"uncivilized" or "savage." Once, an owner of a food stall had laughed at him when he applied for a job as a dishwasher. "Look at your skin," she sneered. "My customers would run away because they'd think you make the dishes dirtier."

Behind the table, the visa officer picked up a passport. "Nguyen Tan Phong," he called. He'd left out all the rising and falling tones in Phong's full name and when he said it, the name meant "a dissolved gust of wind," and not "strength from thousands of gusts of wind," as Sister Nhã had intended it to be when she'd named him.

Phong rose to his feet. The man started to tell him something. Phong tried to catch the sounds but once again, they wafted away from him.

"Raise your hand and swear that you are a mixed race person of American descent and that you won't lie," the Vietnamese woman interpreted.

Quang, the agent, had prepared Phong for this. He raised his hands.

"I swear that I'm a trẻ lai. I swear that I don't lie and that everything I say today is the truth."

"How do you know for sure that you are an Amerasian?" the man asked via the woman's translation.

"Sir, the color of my skin . . . Since I was little, I was called Black American."

"But you could also be of Khmer descent?"

"No, Sir. Khmer mothers had no reason to abandon their children. I was . . . I grew up in an orphanage."

"You have proof that you are the child of a U.S. serviceman, then?"

"I don't know who my parents are, Sir. I'm an Amerasian, Sir. Khmer people are short. I'm one meter eighty. And my beard . . . Sir . . . Khmer men don't have beards like this." He touched his thick hair, which ran from his ears to his chin, covering most of his cheeks. Even though the itching was sometimes unbearable, Quang had insisted that he let his beard grow for at least two weeks before the interview.

"Did you previously apply for an immigrant visa with our consulate?"

Phong blinked. Damn it. Quang had told him they wouldn't dig it up.

"Did you previously apply for an immigration visa to the United States?" the officer repeated.

"I . . . I can't remember." Phong gripped the folder of documents. Sweat dampened his palms.

"You can't?" The white man shook his head. "Then let me refresh your memory. Your visa form says this is your first time applying, but . . . I have here your previous application." He held up a paper.

A cold feeling slithered down Phong's spine. The paper had turned yellow, but he recognized the young man in the photo attached to it. It was him, back when he thought he'd found himself a good family. It was him, looking eager and full of hope. Just before Mr. Khuất had snapped that picture, he'd wiped away a tear of happiness from his face.

"This is your former visa application, isn't it?" the white man asked.

Phong rubbed his sweaty palms against his pants. "Yes, Sir . . . It was many years ago."

"More than twenty years. Tell me, why weren't you granted a visa at that time?"

Phong studied the desk's surface. Smooth and shiny like a mirror. The person who made it did a fine job. If Phong could go to America, he'd learn to perfect his craft as a carpenter. He'd use his monthly allowance to buy the wood needed to build all types of furniture, to be able to send his children to the best schools. He loved the smell of cut lumber and the feeling of accomplishing something. He'd heard that in America people could achieve whatever dreams they had.

If he revealed the truth, he'd never get to go to his dreamland. "I don't know why I didn't get a visa, Sir. I guess . . . I didn't have all the papers."

The man shook his head. "We didn't ask for a lot of papers at that time. Immigrant visas were granted for Amerasians based on their looks. Your facial features alone could have gotten you a visa. Tell me the real reason."

Phong's throat was dry. He wished he could snatch the yellowish paper out of the man's hand and tear it up. Tear up the crook Khuất's writing on it.

The man frowned. "You might think that we don't know . . . but according to our records, you tried to bring other people along last time. You claimed strangers as your family members."

The words nailed Phong to the ground. He couldn't move. Couldn't lift his head.

"Uncle Phong, you need to say something. Explain yourself," the Vietnamese woman said.

Phong clutched the folder of documents against his chest. The ache for his wife and children throbbed inside of him. He had to fight for his right to bring them to America. "Sir . . . I'm illiterate. The Khuấts prepared those documents. They promised to help me in America if I brought them along. I was young and foolish, Sir, but at that time, many Amerasians were doing the same thing."

A lump welled up in his throat.

"By trying to bring nonfamily members along, you took advantage of our government's goodwill. You broke the law." The man looked him in the eye. "For us to reconsider your visa application, you need to show us solid proof. Facial features are no longer enough."

"Proof . . . Sir, what kind of proof?"

"Proof that you are in fact the child of an American serviceman. The military service records of your American father, for example, and matching DNA results of you and him."

"DNA?" Phong asked. The word didn't sound Vietnamese. Perhaps the woman hadn't translated it correctly.

"There's a type of test called a DNA test," the woman said. "It can tell who your biological parents are."

Phong had talked to many people about finding his parents but no one had ever mentioned DNA testing. He was about to ask where he could take the test when the man added, "If you have an American father, your father and you need to find each other, then you two submit the results of your DNA tests to show that you're related."

"You say that I need to find my father first, Sir? If you let me go to America, I can find him." He knew America was a large country, but he'd also heard that everything was possible in America.

The foreigner reached for a blue sheet of paper.

"Sir . . . my children don't have friends at school. Kids in our neighborhood don't talk to them. They have no chance here. Please . . ." Phong showed the man a photo of his children, taken in front of their home. Tài and Diễm were smiling shyly, their heads tilted toward each other. It wasn't completely true that they didn't have friends, but Phong had to make his plea more convincing.

The man ignored the photo. He signed the blue paper and gave it to Phong. As Phong stared at the many printed words, he winced and turned away. Sister Nhã had tried to teach him to read, but written words only brought him fear. He closed his eyes, shook his head and gave the woman the paper. "Please, what does this say?"

She cleared her throat. "The U.S. Consulate in Hồ Chí Minh City regretfully informs you that, after a personal interview, your application for admission to the Amerasian program has not met the criteria identified in Section 584 of Public Law 100-202, amended by Public Law 101-167, Public Law 101-513, and Public Law 101-649, the Amerasian Homecoming Act. If at any stage in the future, you are able to submit new evidence to support your claim to Amerasian status, your case will be reviewed. To qualify for an Amerasian visa, you must prove to the Consular Officer that your father was in fact a U.S. soldier. Being of mixed ancestry in itself does not automatically make you qualified."

The woman returned the paper to Phong.

"The fact that you falsified your application might disqualify you for any future application," the man said. "I'm not sure about your chances . . . but in the case that you have proof, send it to us. Goodbye."

Goodbye? No, not yet. Phong stepped forward. "Sir, I'm sorry I made a mistake, but I'm a different person now—"

The man held up his hand. "Once you have proof, send it to us. Goodbye."

Returning to the Land of Fear

Hồ Chí Minh City, 2016

"Ladies and gentlemen, as we start our descent, please make sure your seat belt is securely fastened and all carry-on luggage is stowed underneath the seat in front of you or in the overhead compartments."

Dan took a deep breath and pressed his nose against the cold window, looking down.

"See anything?" Linda asked, leaning over.

"Too cloudy," Dan sat back to give his wife a better view.

"We'll be there before you know it." She smiled, squeezing his hand.

Dan nodded and kissed Linda's hair. Its peach scent gave him comfort. He couldn't have done this without her. He had sworn he would never return to this place.

The plane rumbled through a thick bed of clouds. Linda flipped through the glossy pages of the Việt Nam Airlines *Heritage* in-flight magazine, scrutinizing photos of lavish villas built on top of lush hills, surrounded by white sandy beaches and rolling blue oceans. They'd both grown up in small, cramped homes, and he understood her obsession with beautiful houses, a mindset that had led her to become a real estate agent. Instead of just chasing money, though, Linda often searched out people or projects who'd help veterans with down payments on new homes. Or affordable places for vets to rent. Việt Nam vets. Afghan vets. Iraq vets. "Too many are homeless," she'd told him. He loved her for that.

Outside, clouds still surrounded the plane, closing in. Their darkness stirred something deep inside of Dan. The old fear. His body tensed. He eyed the emergency exit. Two steps away. One step if he leapt.

At the airport, he had approached the check-in supervisor. "Please, I need to sit by the emergency exit."

"Excuse me, Sir?"

He showed his disabled veteran card. Still, the manager shook his head. "All seats next to the emergency exits have been taken."

He moved closer to the guy, whispering through gritted teeth, "Listen, I need to be close to the exit or I can't fly."

He was glad he fought for it and the exit was in front of him, not behind him.

He took a deep breath, telling himself to calm down. After a few long inhales and exhales, he saw clearly how ridiculous it'd been, the whole scene he'd made about the exit. Why was he always playing the stereotypical deranged vet? What was he going to do, kick out the door and jump out of the plane mid-flight?

He was putting on his headset, wanting to listen to some soothing music, when the plane lurched. Passengers around him murmured. The chair underneath him seemed to have disappeared and he threw his head back, hands gripping the armrests. The Airbus was losing altitude. Too fast. Heat surged through his body. The plane made a thundering sound when it bucked in the turbulence. The cabin shook violently.

The captain spoke over the loudspeaker, advising passengers to fasten their seatbelts.

The plane continued its violent shaking.

Inside of Dan, the old fear twisted, a serpent coiling and uncoiling.

He closed his eyes and suddenly he was back in the cockpit of his wartime helicopter, the clouds outside replaced by Vietnamese canopy jungle. The jungle was swirling wildly around the windshield. "We've only got about a foot and a half tail rotor clearance on the right," Hardesty was screaming into his headset. Flashes of AK-47 fire blazed from the forest floor. Rappa returned fire with his M-60, his shoulders shaking. AK-47 bullets were hitting the aircraft. A hole appeared in the plexiglass just above Dan's head. "Receiving heavy fire. Nine o'clock! Heavy fire! Nine o'clock! On the north perimeter!" McNair yelled into the VHF, the copilot's voice high and panicky and then softening. "Dan?" A hand patted his cheek. "You okay?"

He opened his eyes. Some passengers were laughing in relief. The turbulence had passed. Dan blinked, his face hot with anger and embarrassment.

He shook his head, trying to chase away the images of his crew. But they were alive in his mind: his door gunner, Ed Rappa, making the sign of the cross, kissing the ground after their every mission; his crew chief, Neil Hardesty, chewing gum with his mouth open; his copilot, Reggie McNair, checking for the lucky, hole-filled socks he always wore when flying. Dan wished he could tell them he was sorry.

Why had they died while he survived? He'd asked himself that question countless times during the last forty-seven years.

"Hey . . . you need your pills?" The lines on Linda's forehead deepened. He had added many more years to her appearance during their forty-five years of marriage. His rages that quickly gave way to uncontrolled weeping. His blackouts. His nightmares. The ghosts of his war.

"I'm okay, thanks." Tears welled in his eyes. He wrapped his arm around Linda, pulled her to him. She was his rock.

"Your pills are right here if you want them." She gestured at her handbag on the floor under the seat in front of her.

He nodded, looked out of the window, yearning to see the ground. He wished for nothing more than to get off this plane. A long time ago, he'd loved the thrill of flying, the sense of immense freedom and unlimited possibility.

At nineteen, he joined the army and applied to be a pilot even though he didn't think he had much of a chance. Many of his friends had either been drafted or had gotten their notices, so it was just a matter of time before he'd get called up anyway. And he'd figured that going into the army would give him the chance to travel, as well as the opportunity to attend college after his enlistment. When a letter arrived, telling him to get ready for eight weeks of basic training, a month of advanced infantry training, and then nine months of flight training, he'd shouted with joy so loudly that his mom dropped the colander filled with pasta she was making for dinner. She asked him what was wrong and he read the letter to her. He told her he'd taken many aptitude tests and to his surprise he'd passed. The recruitment officer had said the army urgently needed helicopter pilots in Việt Nam, but he'd thought there'd be many people applying.

When his mom said that she didn't want him to go, that he could be killed, he told her not to worry, that God would keep him safe. Like many nineteen-year-olds he thought he was invincible. It had taken him about a month in Việt Nam to lose that illusion. He was only twenty-three when he left the army, but he felt sixty. The knowledge of death had robbed him of his youth.

An announcement came from the plane's loudspeaker. The female voice spoke Vietnamese. He closed his eyes, concentrating on its rise and fall. So lyrical, it sounded like a song. Like the lullabies Kim used to sing to him.

Something sounded familiar. "Xin vui lòng." Did that mean "please"? Before this trip, he'd tried to reacquaint himself with the language, but it didn't seem to help much.

Linda unzipped her bag, took out a jar of cream, lathered it onto her face. She put on pink lipstick. Her favorite color. She was turning sixty-six this year, but whenever he looked at her, he could still see the woman he'd fallen in love with. They'd gone to the same high school, and he'd started to notice her during his junior year. He could still picture her racing up the basketball court, her face red with determination, her tanned legs flying as she dove for a ball. He'd always been glad his younger sister Marianne was on the team. Going to Marianne's games gave him a chance to watch Linda.

"Enough," Linda had told him several months ago, after he'd wept watching the news about the wars in Iraq and Afghanistan. "In fact, more than enough, baby. We went way past 'enough' years ago." She showed him the commission check she'd received from selling a condo. "With this money, I want us to go and deal with your issues, once and for all."

We went way past "enough" years ago. She didn't need to say this trip would determine if their marriage would survive; he sensed it in her voice. He knew she deserved to be happier, yet he also knew it'd be hell to be back. All his bad memories would come alive. But he owed it to Linda to face his ghosts. They were engaged by the time he left for Việt Nam and she was waiting for him when he returned. She'd stayed with him in spite of everything. But what if she knew the truth about Việt Nam? And about Kim?

He took his passport from Linda's handbag and went through the pages. His fingers began to tremble. "Where the hell is it?"

"What?"

"The visa."

She showed him the page with a brilliant red stamp. "See? Still here and still valid."

He shook his head. Việt Nam unnerved him in ways he couldn't control.

"Oh, I nearly forgot." Linda winked as she pulled a twenty-dollar bill out of her purse, slid it between the pages of his passport. She explained that her Vietnamese friends Duy and Như told her to do it. They hadn't been back to Việt Nam, saying that they'd lost their country to the Communists, but apparently they knew.

Duy and Như went to church with Linda, the same church that had gathered blankets, clothes, toys, and food for Vietnamese refugees when they'd first arrived as "boat people" in the late 1970s. Linda saw them every week at mass, but Dan hadn't gone in years. Việt Nam had made him believe that God had little power over a world that was so in love with war.

As much as he loved his wife, Dan wondered if it was a mistake to take this trip with her. The year before, Bill and Doug had asked him to join them when they went back. He just couldn't do it. Now he realized it might have been better to return with his veteran friends. They'd understand his emotions, his fears. Now that he was about to arrive, he was sure he hadn't prepared enough for the trip. He'd visited the Seattle Public Library and his local bookstore and brought home piles of books written by Vietnamese writers. Over the years, he'd read books by American veterans, to try to understand his experiences, to know he wasn't alone. Still, Vietnamese literature opened his eyes. The book that had affected him the most was *The Sorrow of War* by Bảo Ninh, his former enemy. Reading it was like looking into a distorted mirror. He could easily have been Kiên, the Northern Vietnamese veteran in the novel. The title said it all. When he told his vet friends, they were surprised he chose books written by people who had once tried to kill them. Whom they had once tried to kill. But he needed to understand the people he'd dehumanized during the war. In searching for their humanity he was trying to regain his own.

During the first few years after he got back, Linda had tried to ask him about the war, how it'd been and what he'd seen. He told her he didn't want to talk about it. Then one summer night in 1983, he'd dreamt about the Việt Cộng attacking him. Several VC jumped him.

He was wrestling with a man, strangling him, when he heard Linda coughing and choking. He woke up to see his hands clenched around her neck.

Linda would have left him if he hadn't phoned a psychiatrist the following morning to make an appointment. Until that incident he'd refused to see a shrink because he hadn't wanted to be diagnosed with any mental health issue that could lead to him losing rights, even getting his driver's license taken away. Dr. Barnes had pointed out to him that he wasn't the only veteran with problems and then asked him to attend what he mysteriously called Group 031, a name intended to protect the anonymity of its members. Dan appreciated that nondescript name; he didn't want others to know he was attending a PTSD group. That was where he met Bill and Doug. After a lot of counseling and meetings with the group, he felt better, but for years Linda wouldn't sleep in the same bed with him.

In their joint sessions with Dr. Barnes, Linda had learned a few things about his time in the war—but not the most important things. Not about Kim. Not about his dead crew members. Not about the schoolkids whose blood he had watched seep into the earth. On his best days, Dan had even been able to convince himself that none of it had ever happened.

Recently, through a veteran spouse support group, Linda had become friends with Dr. Edith Hoh, herself the wife of a Việt Nam vet. Dr. E., Linda called her. Linda insisted that they see her before this trip. At the meeting, Hoh was encouraging. She said she'd visited Việt Nam with her husband and it helped. She asked them to discuss their feelings and their expectations for the trip. She advised them to give themselves time to process their emotions once they arrived and not to rush into too many activities. She wrote her home phone number on her business card. "Call me in case there's a crisis," she said. "It doesn't matter how late or early it is, just call."

The plane continued its steep descent and once the clouds cleared, Dan peered down. Rice fields. It had been a lifetime, but those fields hadn't lost their emerald color. When the sunlight hit the checkerboard mirrors of water-submerged paddies, they still glinted like knives. And those rivers that slithered through all that green still looked like venomous snakes.

Linda sneaked a look. "Oh, so pretty."

Sài Gòn, now Hồ Chí Minh City, gradually came into view. Once familiar like the palm of his hand, the city's skyline had become totally strange, punctuated by tall buildings gleaming with glass, and streets clogged with traffic.

"Look at all those high-rises." Linda's voice was full of excitement.

He wanted to tell her about the columns of smoke that used to fill the sky, the whistling sound of rockets as they approached the city, the flares that lit up the night, the street beggars who'd lost arms and legs, but he feared bringing up the memories.

He craned his body, looking for the sight of Tân Sơn Nhứt Airport, now called Tân Sơn Nhất, where he'd been stationed, at first just ferrying big shots and celebrities on what could be regarded basically as sightseeing jaunts. "Many are called but few are chosen, young Warrant Officer," the First Sergeant had told him. "You were first in your class and look good in photos, just the way they like it. Be grateful." One time he'd even flown a well-known Hollywood star out to a firebase. His aircraft commander and the other crew members were awestruck. But he found the presence of the visiting actor reinforced the odd sense he was having of playacting, being in some movie about the war rather than the real thing. While he was grateful not to be in combat, he also felt guilty and a need to test himself under fire. He thought that was the whole point of being there.

Eventually he was assigned as pilot and aircraft commander to the company's slick platoon. Flying his Huey, a Bell UH-1D/H helicopter, he'd engaged in combat assaults and resupply missions, carrying rations, ammo, or live soldiers in, and sometimes dead or broken soldiers out. He had no way of knowing how those missions would change his life forever.

Tân Sơn Nhất Airport spread out before his eyes. It looked unfamiliar, and a weight lifted from his chest. The place had changed. He shouldn't worry so much. He was just a tourist now. A flabby American with a fanny pack accompanied by a woman with a selfie stick. No one needed to know he was a vet.

As he watched a flight attendant across from him lean back in her seat and adjust her áo dài, he was again flooded with memories. Kim had often worn the same type of dress, with a high collar and soft cloth flowing from her neck down to her knees. One day many years ago, he had admired her in her white áo dài getting ready for a Buddhist ceremony at a neighborhood pagoda. They'd just moved into the apartment he rented for her. She was standing by the window, her hand moving the comb down her river of hair. He was on the bed, astonished at the irony of his host country: the beauty and grace amid the horror.

"We're here. Yay!" Linda said as the plane rolled to a stop. Dan squeezed his forehead. He'd tried to erase Kim from his life. He'd burned all her pictures. He'd tried to convince himself that she was just a dream, a ghost. But she had remained stubbornly real in his memories, and now she was rushing to him as he returned to the city where they'd met.

Again, he saw her beautiful eighteen-year-old face. Her brown eyes. Her tears.

An Impossible Choice

Phú Mỹ Village, Kiên Giang Province, March 1969

Trang lifted the hoe's wooden handle high, swinging it down with all her might. As she drove it into the field with a phập sound, breaking away a large chunk of earth, a sharp pain dug into her right palm. Her blisters must have burst. She clenched her teeth.

A few meters away, her seventeen-year-old sister, Quỳnh, bent low, uprooting wild grass. Her face was hidden under her nón lá conical hat. One year younger than Trang, Quỳnh had failed to pass the tú tài exam, just like Trang, and was unable to obtain her high school diploma. Trang had always believed her younger sister would pass, but everyone knew that only about a third of all students would make it through each year.

Trang longed for a breeze, but heat clung to her like a second layer of skin. Her shoulders ached. Four rice seasons ago, when she'd started working full-time in her family's fields, she'd thought the constant pains in her body were caused by a serious illness, probably cancer. When she told Hiếu, the boy she adored, he laughed, saying that if they had a buffalo to plow their land, their bodies wouldn't have to suffer. Hiếu knew because he'd also become a rice farmer.

Trang and her younger sister had been working since sunrise, but more than half of the field was still filled with wild grass that they had to uproot and clear away. Then they'd have to scoop water into the field and plow the soil again and again, until it became loose and aerated, ready to receive rice seedlings.

When the shortness of her shadow told Trang it was nearly noon, she picked up a dry bottle gourd and poured water into her mouth. She gave Quỳnh some. "Still so much to do."

"We'll get there." Quỳnh wiped sweat from her long, tan neck. "Có công mài sắt có ngày nên kim."

Trang nodded. There was so much wisdom in the proverb Quỳnh had quoted: Persistence turns a bar of iron into a needle.

Quỳnh squinted her eyes against the sunlight. "Last night, once again, I dreamt that we were attacked by helicopters. Right here!" She scanned the fields that stretched out to the green rim of their village. The scene was almost empty, except for a few farmers bending low above the soil. A flock of storks rose up, their white, fluttering wings resembling mourning headbands.

"Remember the most important thing? If they come, stand still. Don't run." Trang watched Quỳnh drink. She'd been praying to Buddha for protection. A few days ago, American soldiers had pursued some VC suspects through the fields of a neighboring village. Rumors had it that American helicopters had shot three farmers.

"Ha, if something happens close by, I bet you'll be so scared, you'll pee in your pants, chị Hai." Quỳnh finished the water and picked up her hoe. She called Trang "sister number two," even though Trang was the eldest sibling. People in their region believed that evil spirits often went after the eldest children, hence the traditions of calling the first child "second."

Trang didn't know how she'd react if troops stormed their field. She'd managed to survive her encounters with helicopters. Some of them had flown so low that the wind they generated threatened to fling her through the air like a leaf. But she didn't dare duck. She'd stood there, surrounded by swirling dust, her eyes tightly closed, her prayers silenced by her sealed lips. Her parents had taught her many survival lessons, one of which had to do with helicopters: they shot and killed anyone that ran.

"Buddha will watch over us. Live or die, Heaven will decide," Trang told Quỳnh, then stepped up onto the field's bank. Grass tickled her feet, chasing away the worries that had clouded her mind. A grasshopper sprang up, disappearing into a clump of touch-me-not plants. The plants' leaves curled up in an instant, leaving their purple flowers open like delicate cotton balls. She wondered if it was a farmer who'd first given the plant its name: cây mắc cỡ—the sensitive plant.

Quỳnh wiped her feet against the grass. Her cheeks were pink. Strands of hair that had freed themselves from her ponytail framed her oval face. Trang felt a pang of jealousy. How did Quỳnh always manage to look so pretty? She had so many admirers.

"Má really needs to cook more rice. I can't work hungry like this." Quỳnh slipped on her plastic sandal.

Trang's stomach rumbled. The night before, her mother had eaten less than half her usual amount, saying that she was full. Quỳnh scraped and scraped the rice pot with a spoon, but there were no grains left. Later on, as Trang went out to the water well to wash the dishes, she saw her mother standing in their front yard, completely still as if Heaven had planted her into the earth, staring across the yard at their former brick home. The home they'd lost.

Trang and Quỳnh left the field. Along the village road, thatched houses stood silent under tree shadows. Several farmers were carrying baskets, their footsteps quickening under the noon heat. A group of soldiers from the Army of the Republic of Việt Nam, the ARVN, passed them, and Trang was thankful for the sight of their rifles. Less than twenty kilometers away, the VC guerrillas had gained partial control of some villages.

At school, she'd been taught that the aggression of Hồ Chí Minh and the Communists had caused the war. But she knew the seeds of the conflict had been sown many years prior, when France occupied Việt Nam. It was Hồ Chí Minh who defeated the French and now his government was controlling the North.

In the South where she lived, the Việt Nam Cộng Hòa government and its army, the ARVN, were in charge, and American troops were also supposed to help protect them. But the VC—Northern Communists who had infiltrated the South and Southerners who supported Hồ Chí Minh—were lurking everywhere. They might be men in black clothing carrying guns, or innocent-looking girls with hand grenades under their shirts.

She didn't understand why people had to fight but the war seemed to be getting worse. The Americans, who supported the Southern government, had been bombing the North. Revenge would surely follow. The thought made the hoe feel heavier on her shoulder.

She followed Quỳnh, her eyes fixed on her sister's long hair, the same hair she'd woven into thick ropes as they sat in the shade of their banana plants, waiting for their father's return.

◈

Four years earlier, when he was drafted into the ARVN, their father brought home two baby banana plants to grow in the garden.

"I'll be back the day they bear fruit." He scooped water with a coconut bowl, pouring it onto the soil.

Trang clung to her father's strong, muscled arm. "Please . . . don't go, Ba."

"You know he has to." Quỳnh pushed Trang away. "Don't you dare cry. Your tears will bring him bad luck."

Their father dropped the bowl and pulled his girls into his arms. "I'll be fighting alongside the most well-trained soldiers in the world. They've been sent here all the way from America, imagine that! They have advanced weapons, and they'll keep me safe. Don't you worry."

During the following months, Trang begged the banana plants to grow fast. She fed them the buffalo-dung compost their mother had prepared for the rice plants. She and Quỳnh jumped up and down, clapping their hands when the first plant flowered. The second plant followed soon after. The flowers grew huge and hung like the red lanterns that filled their village during the Mid-Autumn Festival. Layers of the lanterns opened and fell away, revealing rows of bananas. Every day after school, Trang and Quỳnh would sit under the bananas, looking out at the gate. To pass the time, they wove each other's hair.

New banana plants grew, replacing the old ones. One rainy day, Trang came home and saw her mother sitting next to a strange-looking man. His face was haggard, half-covered by a rough beard, his eyes tired and distant. When the man whispered her name, Trang dropped her bamboo basket, scattering the white so đũa—vegetable hummingbird flowers she'd picked for their sour soup.

Trang's father was physically whole, but he no longer laughed. He didn't want to talk about what he'd seen or done. Later, she would find out that he'd been released from the army because of his mental issues.

◇

"Do you think it'll rain soon? It's so hot," Trang asked Quỳnh, who walked ahead of her. Quỳnh shifted her hoe onto the opposite shoulder and looked up. "Oh, is that Hân?"

Trang squinted. From the opposite direction, a cyclist was leaning forward, pedaling hard, pulling a cart on which Hân and her mother sat. Hân used to be Trang's best friend. A year before, she'd left their village for Sài Gòn, for a job her uncle had helped her find with an

American company. She sent so much money home, her mother had built a brick house.

"Hide." Trang tugged her sister's arm, looking around for a bush. Hân was a rich girl now, she shouldn't see them in ragged peasant clothes carrying mud-caked hoes on their shoulders.

Quỳnh broke free. "Chị Hân, chị Hân," she called toward the bicycle rickshaw. "When did you get back?"

The rickshaw screeched to a stop. Hân looked glamorous in a flow-ered shirt and silky black pants. "Oh, hello . . . Did you two just come back from work?"

Trang nodded, wishing she could disappear into the crack of earth next to her feet.

"Chào cô," Quỳnh greeted Hân's mother, who smiled at them.

"Má, you go on home." Hân jumped down from the rickshaw.

"Don't forget your grandma is coming for lunch," called Hân's mother as the rickshaw drove away.

"You look good, Sister . . . much chubbier." Quỳnh eyed Hân up and down.

"Oh, not good to be chubby." Hân patted her stomach.

"How come?" Quỳnh asked.

"In Sài Gòn it's trendy to be skinny." Hân laughed.

Trang shook her head. How could it be? Being chubby meant being rich. Only poor people were skinny.

Quỳnh, Hân, and Trang made their way toward a trứng cá—a Panama berry tree—which stood tall on the village road, its branches reaching out like a mother hen spreading her wings to protect her chicks. From the green canopy dangled hundreds of tiny fruit, some of them red, ripe like tiny stars. Each was packed with perfumed sweet-ness, Trang knew. She wanted to roll up her pants, swing herself onto a branch, and keep climbing until she could reach them.

Hân tiptoed, then jumped, but could only grab a pink fruit, half-ripe. She popped it into her mouth. "So . . . how are things with you?"

Quỳnh and Trang dropped their hoes. Quỳnh hopped onto a low branch, her feet dangling.

"So-so . . ." Trang took off her nón lá, fanning herself and her friend. The conical hat, woven from palm leaves and bamboo sticks, was a gift from her mother. Trang had stitched her name in red thread onto the inside of the hat, together with the opening verse of Nguyễn Du's *The Tale of Kiều*: "A hundred years—in this life span on earth/ talent and destiny are apt to feud."

"I met a couple of our friends this morning . . . They told me some people were at your home yesterday, shouting?" Hân asked.

Trang bit her lip. Why were her friends gossiping like this?

"Our lenders," said Quỳnh, "they can go to hell."

"Yeah, they can fucking go to hell!" Trang spat out her words. It actually felt good to swear. The lenders had started coming to their home last year, when her parents' childhood friend ran away with the money they'd lent him. The man disappeared with not just her parents' life savings but an amount equal to hundreds of gold taels that they'd borrowed and loaned out to earn a difference in interest rates. The lenders had been polite at first, but over time they'd lost their patience. Couldn't they see that her parents were victims and had no means of repaying them?

Hân signed. "My mother told me about the con man who cheated your family. Apparently he convinced many people about a so-called lucrative partnership with a bank. I hope the police will catch him."

"He's been gone for more than a year now, I'm not sure the police are still looking. And the lenders, they're threatening to take away our field and our home, not that it's worth much." Quỳnh picked a fruit and threw it so hard it bounced across the road.

Trang thought about the long trips her mother had made with the other victims to search for the con man. The last time her mother returned, she'd banged her head against the rock-hard clay jar that stored their water and said that she wanted to kill herself for her mistake.

"I know how hard you two have tried to find a job," Hân lowered her voice, "but have you looked beyond our province?" She waited for some villagers to pass before continuing, "I'm telling you this because you're my friends. . . . You two could make money in Sài Gòn."

"But you have your uncle there, we know no one." Trang gazed at Hân's hair. Why did she have it cut so short? And her skin, she'd done something with it, it was so fair it glowed.

"You don't need to know anyone." Hân smiled. "You just need to look . . . you know . . . pretty. Both of you are beautiful. I'm sure you'll do very well."

"But do what exactly?" Quỳnh asked.

"Drink Sài Gòn Tea." Hân laughed.

"Tea?" Quỳnh jumped down from the branch.

"Yeah . . . Sit in a bar, drink Sài Gòn Tea and earn good money."

"Bar? What's that?" Trang asked.

"Oh, a place where they sell liquor to American soldiers. We call them GIs."

Trang shuddered. How could Hân suggest that they drink with those foreign men? Some of them had blood on their hands. Blood that often haunted Trang in her dreams.

Hân scanned their surroundings. The village road was empty, yet she still whispered. "You swear not to tell anyone? Not even a ghost?"

Quỳnh and Trang nodded.

"My job . . . it's not with an American company. I work in a bar. I go there, drink Sài Gòn Tea and earn money."

Trang brought her palm to her mouth. "But I thought your uncle—"

"He found me a good job, right? Wrong! I gave him some gifts so he would keep my secret. A distant cousin had done the same and told me." Hân winked.

"The rest of your family, they know?" Quỳnh asked.

"Certainly not. You're the only ones I've told."

Trang stared at Hân. If people in the village found out, they'd surely call her "me Mỹ," a prostitute for Americans. Here, women were never allowed to drink with men, even at parties.

And what would Hiếu think if Trang drank with American men? The night before, in the moonlight, Hiếu had reached for her hand. The warmth of his touch had sent her fleeing from him.

"Look, it's not as bad as it sounds," said Hân. "I don't have to work under the hot sun, and I earn about fifteen thousand đồng per week."

"Get out of here! Sister Trang and I only made twice that much from the entire planting season last year," Quỳnh gasped.

"I know." Hân nodded. "You're prettier than me, so I'm sure you'll make more."

"We're not prettier than you. And I don't think we can do it, you know . . . work at the liquor place." Trang shook her head. Her mother had taught her and Quỳnh the four virtues of a good Vietnamese woman: hard work, beauty, refined speech, and excellent conduct. For sure she wouldn't allow them to drink with men.

"Didn't you hear her?" Quỳnh turned to Trang. "Your friend is making fifteen thousand đồng per week. Imagine if we earn half of that. We could help Ba and Má repay their debts."

Hân nodded. "With the money I'm sending home, my Má can take care of herself and my siblings better."

Trang recalled how Hân's mother had fainted during her husband's funeral. He'd gone away a soldier and come back a corpse. But she looked so well now. Trang wished she could do the same thing for her mother. And for Quỳnh.

"See? It's only Sài Gòn Tea." Quỳnh pulled Trang's arm then turned to Hân. "It's tea that you drink, right?"

"It's mostly tea . . . Trust me, you'll do fine."

"What do you mean 'it's mostly tea'?" Trang asked.

"I mean it's only tea." Hân waved her hand. "Listen . . . if you want to help your parents, think about what I've said. The bar where I work, they're looking for new girls."

Quỳnh pinched Trang. "This opportunity is gold, chị Hai."

Trang shook her head. "Our parents, they wouldn't let us work there."

"You think my mother would?" Hân smirked. "She'll never find out, that's for sure. But with this damned war getting worse and worse, we need to save some money . . . for the future, you know." She lifted her wrist. Her golden watch dazzled Trang. "I need to go. Grandma must be waiting."

"Xe lôi, xe lôi," Hân shouted toward an approaching rickshaw and turned back, whispering: "If you want to know more, come to my house tonight. And remember: not a word to anyone."

"Sure. See you tonight," Quỳnh said, as if she was the older sister who could make decisions for the two of them.

Hân climbed onto the rickshaw. The driver jingled the bell and started pedaling, pulling her away. Trang stood under the tree's shadow, watching the flowers on Hân's shirt blaze like flames on the village road. She'd dreamt about Sài Gòn, the big city with prestigious universities and office jobs. But this was different. She couldn't imagine bars and American "GIs."

"She looks happy and she's rich. We can be like her." Quỳnh stared at the cracks on her feet and at her toenails, yellowish due to their long and frequent contact with muddy soil. She reached for the hoe and resumed their long walk home.

◈

"VỀ RỒI ĐÓ HẢ? Nước chanh đó, uống đi con!" Their mother called, telling them to drink the fresh lemonade she'd made, as soon as Trang and Quỳnh stepped inside. They'd washed themselves at the well in the garden, and water droplets still lingered on Trang's face, arms, and legs. She savored their cool kisses.

She squinted her eyes to find her mother squatting in the corner of their hut, cooking.

"What's for lunch, Má?" Quỳnh downed a full glass of lemonade.

"You asked for this last night." Their mother held up a piece of golden rice crust.

Quỳnh took it, crunched it between her teeth. "Delicious!"

Trang's mouth watered at the sound of chewing. She loved how her mother could command the flames of her stove and her clay pot to turn her rice into different textures: crusty rice to be enjoyed with fried shallots; tender rice to be eaten with dry fish; soft, melt-in-your-mouth rice to be devoured with tiny shrimps caught in streams and ponds and cooked with fish sauce and pepper.

"Trang, I can't stop looking at this. You're so talented." From his bamboo bed, her father held up a notebook, a broad smile lighting up his gaunt face.

"Where did you find that, Ba?" Trang reached for her drawings of the human body. Biology was her favorite subject. She'd always wanted to be a doctor.

"Your mother was looking for scrap paper to sell . . ."

"When your father saw your notebook, he insisted on making frames for your drawings and hanging them up." Trang's mother put steaming bowls of rice and spinach onto a bamboo tray.

Trang looked around at the dried coconut leaves that made up the walls of her home. If her drawings were to be hung, they'd look much better in the brick house her parents had been forced to sell to pay off some of their debts.

"Mr. Ánh visited today. These are from him." Her father gave Trang a stack of paper. Exercises for tú tài exams. Trang nodded and felt grateful toward her former teacher. Like her parents, he believed Trang and her sister were still capable of passing the exams and continuing on to college.

"We'll practice tonight, Ba." Trang flipped through the exercises. Most students had private tutors. She and Quỳnh had to try extra hard but their bodies were always drained of energy by the time they lit their coconut oil lamps and sat down at their bed to study.

She checked the bandages on her father's legs. The war was so cruel: it had spared him during his years as a soldier but found him later in the town market when he was buying seedlings for the new planting season. Mortars exploded near him, killing dozens of people. Pieces of shrapnel were still buried deep in his legs and he'd need more operations. Medical treatments were free for veterans, but with Ba bedridden, a few months of salary payment provided by the ARVN upon his release from the army was a grain of salt in the ocean of their debts. He had no pension at all.

◈

BACK AT THEIR FIELD, Quỳnh launched her hoe into the earth. "I want to go to Sài Gòn. I want to be like Hân."

Trang threw a lump of grass onto the field's bank. "I'm not sure it's a good idea." She sensed her best friend had changed; there was something mysterious about her.

"So you want to stay here and rot on this rice field?"

When Trang couldn't answer, Quỳnh dropped her hoe. "Those nasty lenders have threatened violence, chị Hai. On top of that, they're bringing our parents to court. I've heard the judges will likely order our parents to pay interest on the loans. Backdated until last year. If we can't pay, our parents will be thrown into prison!"

Tears stung Trang's eyes. A few months ago, she'd told her parents that they could pack up and disappear, like their debtor had. But both her Ba and Má shook their heads. They were Buddhists and wouldn't cheat. Besides, where would they go and how would they survive?

"I hear what you're saying," Trang told her younger sister, "but I don't want to become a me Mỹ."

"Yeah, you're afraid of being called an American whore, but it's you who cry when the lenders shout at our parents. . . . I don't care what you decide, I'm leaving."

Trang looked at her sister, her feet sunk into the soil, sweat streaming down her face. "I'm the oldest child . . ." She sighed. "It's my duty to help Ba and Má. I'll go. You stay."

"If one of us is to leave for the big city, it should be me." Quỳnh gave her hoe a hard kick. "I'm the one who can't wait to get out of here."

"I can't let you go alone. Sài Gòn is a dangerous city, em."

"And you think it's safe here?" Quỳnh pointed in the direction where gunshots were echoing. "We might actually survive this war if we go to Sài Gòn, chị Hai. With so many Americans there, the VC won't dare to make trouble. Come with me!"

"But we can't leave Ba and Má—" As Trang debated with herself, she felt as if she was making an impossible choice.

"Shouldn't grown-ups be able to take care of themselves? And don't forget it's them who got us into this mess." Quỳnh picked up her hoe, swinging it down so fast she narrowly missed her own foot.

❖

THAT EVENING, Trang stood in Hân's garden, eyes wide, listening to stories about Sài Gòn: its movie theaters packed with fashionable people, its wide boulevards filled with American cars, its French-style villas cleaned and dusted by teams of servants from the countryside, and its American men. "Those men who return from the battlefields are so wrecked," Hân whispered, "we just need to make them laugh, and they'll fill our pockets with American dollars."

"American dollars. That's what we need." Quỳnh grinned, rubbing her palms.

"The good thing is that we don't use our real names at work," Hân giggled. "I call myself Mai, and I tell others I'm from Cà Mau."

"That's so cool." Quỳnh clapped. "A fake name, I like that!"

"A name easy for Americans, with a flat tone, like Lan, Mai, Hoa. Or you could pick an American name. Suzy, Tina . . ."

"That doesn't sound bad at all." Trang admitted. "But do you feel safe in Sài Gòn?"

"Are you kidding me? It's the safest place right now. I live near Tân Sơn Nhứt Airbase. It's so well protected, a VC would pee in his pants if he got close."

"Tell us more about the bar—"

"Dinner's ready!" Hân's mother poked her head out of the open window. "Trang, Quỳnh... come eat with us."

"Thanks, Auntie, but we need to go home," Trang answered with a smile. From where she stood, she could see a beautiful sofa and a radio. When would she be able to buy such things for her parents?

"Wait." Quỳnh reached for Hân's arm. "I'm going to Sài Gòn with you. When will you leave?"

"Five o'clock in the morning, the day after tomorrow. From the bus station." Hân turned to Trang. "I know you're worried, but there are tens of thousands of girls like me there."

Trang bit her lip. In *The Tale of Kiều*, the beginning verse of which she had stitched onto the inside of her hat, Kiều sacrificed her own happiness to help her parents and younger siblings. Kiều's struggle and courage were so remarkable that countless people, including Trang, memorized sections of the 3,254 verses about her life. Could Trang be half as brave as Kiều?

Sài Gòn sounded exciting. Trang wanted to see the paved streets and the movie theaters. She'd pick a new name and no one would find out. "If we don't like the work, we can leave at any time?"

"You got that right." Hân nodded.

Walking home with Quỳnh, Trang agreed that both of them would give Sài Gòn a try. They passed Hiếu's house and her heartbeat quickened. She poked her head over the fence, hoping to see him, but also fearing that he was there.

"Let's go." Quỳnh pulled her away.

"Should I tell him?" Trang whispered.

"Don't be so dumb, he'll change your mind."

Hiếu's square face, tall nose, and full lips filled Trang's mind. She wondered what it'd be like to kiss him.

She didn't know how Hiếu felt about her, so a few months ago, when her mother and Quỳnh took her father to the hospital, Trang dressed up in her best clothes and solemnly said a prayer while holding *The Tale of Kiều* high above her head. Her right thumb opened to a page of the book and when she looked, it pointed at the passage starting with line 3095, which said:

> It's priceless, chastity—by nuptial torch,
> am I to blush for what I'll offer you?
> Misfortune struck me—since that day the flower
> fell prey to bees and butterflies, ate shame.
> For so long lashed by rain and swept by wind
> a flower's bound to fade, a moon to wane.

After reading the passage, Trang had clutched her chest and cried out. Many people around her believed in the fortune-telling magic of this epic poem, but she no longer wanted to. She didn't know what this prediction for her future meant, but it sounded grim.

She knew, though, that virginity was everything. In her village, if a girl didn't bleed on her wedding night, her husband had the right to walk out of the marriage, leaving the girl and her parents ashamed for the rest of their lives.

She didn't like the idea of being around American men, but Hân appeared to be happy. In Sài Gòn she and Quỳnh would be drinking tea, nothing else. No man would be allowed to touch them.

They passed their former home. Its brick walls gleamed in the sun. Trang had loved every corner of this house: the cool, spacious living room where she'd played hopscotch with Quỳnh; the bedroom where her hammock dangled between her bed and the window; the kitchen filled with the aroma of her mother's cooking. She had to help her parents get their house back.

❖

QUỲNH WANTED TO tell their parents right away that they were leaving, but Trang needed one more day to think. She still had questions. The next evening, they went to Hân's house again.

When they returned home, thunder tore open the sky. Heaven dumped torrents of rain onto their two-room hut. Trang ran to the wooden cabinet—their most valuable possession. Inside were her tú tài practice papers and her beloved books: *The Tale of Kiều*, *The Tale of Lục Vân Tiên*, *The Tale of Phạm Công and Cúc Hoa*, all of them novels written in the lục bát poetic form, alternating lines of six and eight syllables. The cabinet had already been covered by a raincoat, but she wrapped it in another layer of plastic. Then she passed Quỳnh bowls and buckets. They arranged them around the house, catching the water that leaked through the roof.

Trang looked at her father, who was on his bed, staring up at their family altar. His hands were clenched into fists. He was in pain, but didn't utter a sound. Sitting next to him, their mother was mending Quỳnh's shirt, which Quỳnh had torn while climbing their guava tree. Trang thought about the many years her mother had tended the field, taken care of her daughters, cooked, and cleaned. She'd been the pillar for her injured husband to lean on. A proverb said that rough seas make better seamen, but Trang knew wars made tougher women. Despite the challenges, her mother had always been determined that her two daughters be brought up properly. "Just like your banana plants, you need good soil," she'd said. "And your soil is your education."

Her parents had embedded their dreams and hopes in the names they'd given their daughters: Quỳnh was a rare flower that bloomed only at night—the night-blooming cereus; its white petals radiated a beautiful, pure scent. Trang meant "graceful, gentle, virtuous."

Trang and her sister had wanted a virtuous life filled with knowledge. They'd sat underneath their mosquito net each night studying long after all the other oil lamps in their village had been extinguished. Each morning they got up before any rooster threw its song into the darkness. How unfair that the war had disrupted their chance for a better education.

Quỳnh elbowed Trang. "You tell them about us leaving. You're the older one."

"No, you should. You're the smart one," Trang said.

Quỳnh shook her head but cleared her throat. "Ba, Má . . . remember our friend Hân? The one working in Sài Gòn? Well . . . she helped us find a job. Chị Hai and I are leaving for the city."

"What kind of a job?" Their mother looked up.

"Secretaries for an American company," Trang said. Hân had given her the idea.

"But Sài Gòn . . . it's too far away." Their mother put down the shirt.

"Just 250 kilometers, Má," Quỳnh said. "We can be home in a few hours on the bus. We'll visit as often as we can. And our salaries will be good."

Their mother looked at their father, as if begging him to stop the girls.

Their father turned. His eyes were tired, his skin as pale as paper. "I remember Hân, she used to come by, but not since a long while. Why would she help you find a job?"

"Because she's my best friend," Trang said. "She visits her mother often, and we just saw her."

The lines on her mother's face deepened. "I don't want to talk bad about anybody, but some neighbors have been whispering about Hân. A young woman like her, earning quite a bit of money in Sài Gòn . . ."

"People are jealous." Quỳnh laughed. "Hân earns well because she's smart. She can speak English as fast as the wind." She wiped her hands and reached into her pocket. "Here, see for yourself."

Quỳnh showed their parents a photo of Hân in her long pants and long-sleeved shirt, sitting in a whitewashed room behind a desk. Several Vietnamese people stood behind her. An older American man wearing a suit towered above them, smiling. Hân's mother displayed a larger version of the same photo, in her newly painted living room.

"Will you two be working here as well? What sort of an office is it?" Their father scrutinized the photo.

"We'll be working at another office. For an American shipping company," said Quỳnh.

"I don't like the idea of you being around American men," their mother said. "I've seen some of the things they've done around here."

Their father coughed. "Not all American soldiers are bad. Some of my former comrades were actually kind."

Trang recalled the occasions when American soldiers had distributed sweets to the children in her village. Once she'd seen two soldiers teach a kid how to ride a bike. As each soldier ran along each side of the bike, cheering the kid on, she realized they were just young boys themselves.

"We won't be around American men, actually," said Quỳnh. "The boss in our office is a woman, the rest of the team is Vietnamese."

"As long as our girls work in an office, it should be fine. American companies are known for being professional," their father said.

"Please, don't worry." Quỳnh massaged their mother's shoulder. "Chị Hai and I won't have time to make trouble. We'll have to learn lots of new things."

"But the war is spreading." Their mother sighed. "I don't want you out of my sight."

"Má, if the Communists reach Sài Gòn, we'll run home," Trang said, though she wasn't convinced herself.

"Má, please," said Quỳnh. "We can't just sit still and watch the lenders coming every day to threaten you. We'll be careful." She turned to their father. "Ba, you know Sài Gòn, tell Má we'll be fine."

He looked away. "I wish I could go and work instead."

Their mother reached for his hand. "You've done your part. If you leave, who'll keep me company, huh?"

"Má is right," Quỳnh said. "We need you home, Ba. As for chị Hai and me? We can overturn buffalos." She flexed her arm muscles, then laughed. "Don't worry, please . . . Haven't you taught us that young birds leave their nest when they've grown enough feathers? We need to see the world and will take care of each other. And we'll be staying with Hân and her friends."

Trang's father said nothing. That meant he agreed.

Trang gave her mother an envelope swollen with money. "We'll return this to Hân when we get our first salaries. Her bus is leaving tomorrow morning. We'll be joining her."

Her mother put down the envelope. She picked up the shirt but didn't start to sew. She stared at it. After a long while, she stood up, stepped toward the altar. She lit three sticks of incense, bent her head, and offered silent prayers to Buddha and their ancestors. With incense sticks in her hands, Trang knelt down.

When she finished her prayer, she joined her sister by her father's bed. "Come on, Ba," said Quỳnh. "Help us practice English. We need it for our job." They'd learned English at school, but Trang hadn't spoken it in so long, and English was one of her worst subjects.

"Let's see . . . What do you say when you greet your American boss for the first time?"

"Hế lô," Quỳnh said.

"Hế lô is too casual. Say 'hao đu du đu.'"

"Hao đu du đu," Quỳnh and Trang said in one voice.

"How about 'My parents send their thanks'?"

"No need." Quỳnh waved her hands. "We need to practice more useful words." She tapped at her forehead. "Words like salary, bonus, hungry, thirsty . . ."

"Sá-la-ri, bố-nợs, hắng-ri, thớt-sờ-ti . . ." their father said.

Quỳnh and Trang repeated the words after him.

"That's good, but for 'thớt-sờ-ti,' you need to say the 'th' better. Stick out your tongue and blow on it." He showed them.

Quỳnh and Trang followed what their father did. The next thing they knew, they were clutching their stomachs, doubled up with laughter.

A Bird Finding Its Nest

Lâm Đồng–Hồ Chí Minh City, 1984–1993

Phong was on his knees, digging a patch of elephant grass. His twelve-year-old arms were as thin as firewood sticks. The sun punished him with its boiling heat but he didn't care. He swore he'd just seen the shiny head of a large cricket. Holding a twig, he dug furiously. Kids in the neighborhood were staging a cricket-fighting contest that night. They wouldn't let him participate, but his crickets would fight among themselves.

Behind him was a sagging hut where he and Sister Nhã lived. When they were driven out of the orphanage a few years earlier and up into this village in the mountainous province of Lâm Đồng, Sister Nhã had hired local men with whom she worked, cutting down tree branches, bamboos, and rattan leaves to build the hut. It sat far away from the other huts that had been erected by the men, women, and children who had been chased out of their homes. Considered "bad elements of the society" by the Communist government, they were meant to settle here in the New Economic Zone to cultivate new land, to grow their own food.

"Phong ơi," Sister Nhã called from inside the hut.

He ignored her. She'd been ill for a few weeks. She'd stopped going to the field, and he was secretly glad because it meant he didn't have to work either.

"Phong ơi, come inside. We need to talk."

"You want me to brew your herbal medicine again, Dì?" he called back, calling the Catholic nun "Auntie" the way he'd been taught. "Later!"

"Please . . . Dì xin con."

Sister Nhã rarely begged him. He shook his head but dropped the twig and wiped his hands against his shorts.

The hut was cool, darkish, and pungent with the bittersweet smell of medicine. Sister Nhã was a thin shadow on the bamboo bed. Her hands were clutching her stomach the way she'd been doing frequently in the past months. She'd lost a great deal of weight. It annoyed him that she wasn't sleeping much at night and instead stayed up holding her rosary and praying.

"I only have a minute." He put the paper box that caged his crickets on the floor. He counted the brown insects again. Only three. He needed a few more. As he straightened his back, his eyes adjusted to the dimness. Sister Nhã was as pale as a hovering spirit.

He felt her forehead with the back of his hand. She didn't have a fever; she was cold and sweaty.

"Does your stomach hurt, Dì?" He gazed at her hollowed face. She hadn't been eating much. She'd cooked sweet potatoes that morning but just sat watching as he devoured them.

She reached for his arm. "You've been a good boy, Phong. You're my beautiful son."

No one had ever told him he was beautiful, except for Sister Nhã.

He walked to the back of the hut. Next to the stove, which was just a hole dug into the ground, he knelt down, lifted a pot blackened with soot, and poured water into a cup. There had been days when he and Sister Nhã played cards and whoever won would get to decorate the loser's face with soot. He'd laughed so hard as he gave Sister Nhã different types of mustaches. Sister Nhã almost always let him win. Her laughter had risen up alongside his, high and free, filling the belly of their hut as the soot filled the wrinkles on her face.

He wished he could make her laugh again. For months Sister Nhã had been drinking the stewed liquid of roots and tree bark sold by a blind man at their neighborhood market, but it didn't seem to help. Perhaps if they had money to go to a doctor, she'd get better.

He gulped down the water, filled the cup again, and helped Sister Nhã sit up. She drank a few sips, shook her head, and lay down again. He was about to go outside when she clutched his hand.

"Phong . . . I hope that you'll have more than a few minutes for me today. I'm going to tell you a story . . . You have to remember the details, to be able to find your parents."

His parents? He'd often asked about them but Sister Nhã had always said she didn't know them. She never talked about her own life, either, as if she harbored some terrible secrets. Why did she decide to tell him now?

He chose the sturdier of their two rickety bamboo stools and sat next to the bed.

Sister Nhã smiled at him. "I'll tell you the story part by part. Can you then repeat it for me?"

A "no" was forming in his mouth. Was she trying to teach him how to read words? He hated words. Kids who knew how to read and write were monstrous; they hit him and called him all types of names. There had been evenings when Sister Nhã gave him a notebook and a pen. He'd thrown the pen against the wall and the notebook onto the floor. His body ached from the day's work on the field and all he wanted to do was sleep or play outside. Once, frustrated, Sister Nhã had shouted at him. He screamed back, kicked the notebook. Her slap landed on his cheek so hard his vision filled with fireflies. When he burst out crying, she held him tight, sobbing, apologizing, saying that he needed a proper teacher. She didn't know that the idea of a school made him shudder; his bullies would be there, waiting for him.

Sister Nhã untangled a dry leaf from his hair. She placed it gently next to her pillow, as if not wanting to break the already brittle leaf.

She held on to his arm. "Darling, without your parents' names and pictures, your story is all you have. And your story begins with me."

He nodded. Finally she was going to tell him about herself. He'd always wanted to know why she loved him even though other people despised him.

"I was born a Catholic," Sister Nhã began. "As a young girl, I wanted to serve God. So instead of getting married, I became a nun and worked at Phú Long Orphanage. In Hóc Môn. On the outskirts of Sài Gòn." She looked at him. "Now . . . what's the orphanage's name and where is it?"

"Phú Long Orphanage. In Hóc Môn," he said.

"Yes, you clever boy! At the orphanage, together with two other nuns, I took care of Amerasians like you as well as Vietnamese children. Some were orphans. Some still had parents but they were too poor to raise them. Some children had been separated from their parents during bombing raids."

He nodded. He hoped his parents hadn't died.

"At the orphanage, there were many things to do but I was happy. My life had a purpose. One spring night after I'd gone to bed and slept for a few hours, I heard a baby crying. The sound was weak, and not from inside the orphanage. I rose from my bed and got my flashlight.

"It was a pitch-black night. There was no moon, no stars, just the wind howling above my head. I shivered in the cool air and shone my light toward the orphanage gate, where the crying came from. Occasionally mothers would leave their babies there." She looked at him.

He repeated what she had just told him.

She nodded, clutched her stomach. She winced but continued. "As I got closer to the gate, the crying became louder and more desperate. I unlatched the bolt. The metal door creaked as I pulled it open. I stepped outside. I looked around but didn't see any sign of a baby. I paused and listened more carefully. The sound was coming from somewhere in midair. *Oa, oa, oa.*"

Hair stood up on his arms and on the back of his neck. "The baby was crying from midair?"

"Yes . . . In front of the orphanage stood an ancient Bodhi tree, with hundreds of hanging roots. This tree is a symbol of Buddhism and even though the founder of our orphanage was Catholic, she insisted that we take care of it to show that people of all religions can live in harmony. That night, I saw a bag dangling from one of the Bodhi's branches. A sedge bag! The crying was coming from there. I rushed to the bag and lowered it. Reaching inside, I felt a baby. Wrapped in a blue blanket, it was as small as a cat, and trembling."

Phong trembled, too, as he recounted the details, reminding himself he had to remember them, to be able to find his parents.

"Inside the orphanage, I unwrapped the baby," Sister Nhã continued. "A beautiful boy! There was a big birthmark on the right side of his chest. The mother had left nothing else in the bag. No clothes, no address, no name, no birth certificate."

Sister Nhã lifted Phong's shirt. Twice the size of his palm, his birthmark was dark as burnt firewood. He'd tried to rub it off, but it was getting even darker.

"Remember, my child, your birthmark will help you find your mother. Your mother will remember it. When someone claims that you are her son, you must ask . . . you must ask if there's any birthmark on your body."

Phong nodded, his face tingling at the thought of his mother looking for him. When he found his parents, kids in the village would stop taunting him. They'd no longer sing made-up songs about a bastard named Phong born to a prostitute.

Sister Nhã caressed his face. "You arrived at the gate of Phú Long Orphanage in February 1972 as a newborn. Please . . . never forget." She fumbled inside her pillow and gave him an envelope. "Keep this safe. It has two letters. One with your life story. The other . . . is for your mother. I've described what a wonderful person you are, and thanked her for entrusting you to me."

"Don't you think she might be dead?" The words escaped his mouth before he could catch them and hold them back.

"I know she's alive. I can feel it."

"But why a letter, Dì? Can't you tell her yourself when we find her?"

"Phong . . ." Sister Nhã wiped beads of sweat from her upper lip with her trembling hand.

"Nothing is going to happen to you, is it?" He stared at her. Half her hair had gone white, her cheekbones protruded. He hoped she wouldn't be put into a coffin. He'd seen coffins, carried by men and followed by women and children who wore white banners on their heads, wailing.

"Phong . . ." Sister Nhã pushed herself up. "Mr. Thông the healer said that I have a large lump inside my stomach and it's growing."

"He means you'll have a baby?"

"No, it's not like that." She chuckled and ruffled his hair. "Oh, I adore your innocence, your everything."

He beamed at her laughter. "I won't forget, Dì. . . . Phú Long Orphanage. A sedge bag. Branch of a Bodhi tree. You found me in February 1972 and gave me the name Phong." He paused. "Dì, did anyone ever come looking for me?"

Sadness flickered across Sister Nhã's face, then disappeared, almost too quickly for Phong to catch it. "I'm sorry, Son. But wherever your parents are, they must be thinking about you."

"They don't want me. They threw me away, Dì!"

"Please . . . don't think like that. The fact that you were put inside a bag and hung on the tree branch showed that the person who'd brought you to me cared about you very much. And the war . . . it was terrible."

"My father . . . you think he's American? People called me Mỹ đen all the time. I hate it."

"Your father must be a beautiful man. You have his skin, his hair." She untangled his curls. "When I sold postcards in Sài Gòn . . . to raise money for our orphanage, quite a few Black soldiers bought from me. Some told me to keep the change. Your father could have been one of them, Phong."

"They were that nice? What did they look like?"

"Most of them were very young. Some had the same skin color as you, some were much darker. Some were friendly toward me, but others suspected that I was a Communist in disguise and that I could be hiding a hand grenade under my clothing. They pointed their guns at me or told me to go away. They were just boys, you know . . . Boys who were scared of the war as much as I was."

He tried to imagine his father, but any image that came to his mind was blurry, as if concealed by layers of mist. He'd been hoping that his father was a nice man but he wasn't sure now.

Sister Nhã opened another envelope and gave him two pictures. One showed a large Bodhi tree and the gate of Phú Long Orphanage. In the second photo, three women and a group of children stood, beaming at him. "That's you," she said, pointing at a tiny boy. Phong studied the picture. How happy he'd looked. Sister Nhã, too. Dressed in her headscarf and long robe, she appeared so young and full of life. He wished they would all come back to the orphanage and be a family again.

He spotted Miếng in the photo and wondered whether she would ever come back. Sister Nhã had brought Miếng along from the orphanage too. When she was fifteen, Miếng ran away with a married man, taking all of the savings Sister Nhã had buried under the bed.

"Do you know where they are now?" He pointed at the people in the picture, squinting as he tried to recall a face or a name, but nothing. He'd just been a three-year-old baby when he was ripped away from the safe cocoon of the orphanage.

"Some of the children should be with their relatives," Sister Nhã said. "Before Sài Gòn collapsed, we didn't have any money left so I wrote to mothers who had left their children with us. We also put up notices for adoptions."

As young as Phong was, he understood that Sister Nhã had no way of contacting his relatives, and Vietnamese families didn't want to adopt Black children anyway. He and Miếng were two Black kids from the orphanage.

"The other nuns went back to their families, but I came here so the three of us could stay together." Sister Nhã's eyes were distant. "I hadn't done any farming before in my life, so I had a lot to learn."

"I am sorry you are stuck with me, Dì."

"Don't ever say that." Sister Nhã's voice was stern. "You're the best thing that ever happened to me. You're God's gift."

Phong wiped a tear from his eye. God must be real for someone as kind as Sister Nhã to exist.

He filled the cup again and insisted that Sister Nhã finish it. He told himself he had to take care of her better.

"Dì . . ." he cleared his throat. "There's something I don't understand . . . I get it that everyone around us here is having a hard time, but why do so many people hate us?"

"Oh, they don't hate us, Son." Sister Nhã looked at the pictures again, her eyes lit up with nostalgia. Then she carefully returned the pictures to the envelope. "The authorities associate us with the enemy, so people who are not Christian stay away from us to avoid trouble. If our neighbors get upset at us, it's because they need to take their anger out on someone. Some of them used to have privileged lives, living in villas, owning cars. All of a sudden everything they had was taken away, they were branded capitalists, and had to leave their homes." She explained that the war had ended nine years earlier, but the fighting hadn't stopped: the government had been sending people to reeducation camps and New Economic Zones, to turn remnants of the old regime into good citizens. The terrible embargo imposed by the U.S. made life extra-difficult and people resentful.

Phong didn't understand everything his guardian was saying but he recalled how loud their closest neighbors—a mother and her two daughters—had screeched when they found leeches clinging to their calves after returning from the field. He would never forget those women's sullen faces later that night as they squatted on the ground in the common hall alongside Sister Nhã and everyone else to sing songs praising the new government. During such meetings, while he was being bitten by mosquitoes, government officials passion-ately preached about everyone's responsibility to rebuild the country through their labor, how they had to fight Việt Nam's food shortage by farming empty lands, how evil the American imperialists were. Such speeches, together with daily radio broadcasts about the American transgressions, instilled in Phong a sense of guilt, a constant reminder that he was born out of a wrongful act. He was sure that such speeches and broadcasts made his neighbors avoid him more.

Sister Nhã sighed. "You see, we should always look past people's actions and try to understand their reasons. Your parents . . . they must have had reasons to be apart from you. I hope their circumstances have changed, and they can now take care of you."

"But how will I find them, Dì?"

"God will show you the way." The nun lifted her rosary off her head and placed it around his neck. "Put yourself in God's love."

He touched the shiny wooden beads, his guardian's most precious belonging. He could lose the chain or break it when climbing trees. "I can't, Dì . . ."

"From now on, you wear it. God will protect you. Don't forget to pray every day, my son."

◆

PHONG HAD ALWAYS thought that Sister Nhã loved him too much to leave him alone in the world, so when she died he hung on to her so tight his neighbors had to disentangle them and pull him away. "Dì," he screamed as the nun's body—wrapped in a straw mat—was being lowered into a freshly dug rectangular hole. He launched himself toward her as the neighbors held him back. He did not want to let the ground swallow his Dì and take her away from him. She would be too cold under the dark earth; they hadn't been able to afford a coffin.

It rained hard and long after Sister Nhã's burial. As Phong howled, thunder rumbled in the distance. As he beat his fists against the bed that he and his guardian once shared, lightning flashed, tearing the dark sky into a million pieces.

Once Phong's tears had dried and everything became quiet, he learned the weight and depth of sorrow. He understood the true meaning of loneliness; it ate at his core the way termites ground away their meager furniture.

He set up an altar for Sister Nhã, lit a small candle, prayed to God to bring her soul to heaven, and to keep him safe on earth. He asked if he should try to escape; he had nothing left, his only hope was to find his parents. His neighbors had given him some food but he knew they would soon return to their own struggles. Several days later, Sister Nhã appeared in his dream. "Go back to the orphanage," she told him. "Perhaps your mother has returned to look for you."

He thought he wouldn't be able to leave, but he managed. Perhaps the guards took pity on him and ignored it when they saw him slip away. He saw no pity, though, on the faces of the people at a bustling market he ventured into after a day of walking. Some ruffled his curly hair and pulled his ear. Some laughed at him, chanting, "Mỹ lai, Mỹ lai, mười hai lỗ đít," calling him an Amerasian with twelve assholes. One man kicked him for no reason and told him, "Hey you, Black American. You lost the war, why don't you fucking go home?"

People had said these things to him before, but Sister Nhã had always been there to shield him from their venomous words. Without her, those insults felt like knives that slashed him open. A deep anger within him grew, like a flame that burned strong, its heat making him fearless. He started stealing: some peanuts, an apple, an orange, an egg—which he ate raw. That night, as he sank his tired body into a pile of dry rice straw a seller had left behind, he recalled how Sister Nhã had made animals out of straw for him to play, how she'd woven a straw hat for him, and the many meals she'd cooked with straws. His tears mingled with the faint scent of the rice harvest, and he promised Sister Nhã he would survive, for both himself, and for her. He brought her rosary chain and letters to his face, inhaled her love, and repeated in his head the story she'd told him.

The next day, he succeeded at pickpocketing. He held the money tight in his palm and ran from the market, his victim—the man who'd kicked him—chasing. Phong's sandals had been broken and he was barefoot. As pebbles dug into his skin, the pain made him more determined. He ran faster.

After a long while, he slowed down. No soul was in sight. Only trees and birds that sang for him their comforting words. He let their songs lead him forward. He found a highway where a truck driver gave him a lift to Hóc Môn. As he stood in front of the Phú Long Orphanage, he gazed at the Bodhi tree, at its many branches and hanging roots. He imagined his mother reaching up, tying a sedge bag onto a branch. He heard his own cries as his mother walked away, not looking back.

The orphanage had been taken over by the army and the sight of soldiers made him shrink back like a snail withdrawing into its shell. But he gathered his courage and lingered outside, hoping he might run into his mother. It took him nearly a week to realize how ridiculous he was: he didn't even know what his mother looked like.

He wandered to Sài Gòn and became a bụi đời, the dust of life. He hated the term, for it referred to all homeless people, as if to erase them of their own identities. Many bụi đời he knew were Amerasians. Like them, Phong slept on the street, fought for food, and stole. He joined a gang. After years of living wild like this, he broke into a house and took a bicycle. He was caught and sent to a reeducation camp high up in the mountains of Lâm Đồng.

On his first day at the camp, he was told that he was cặn bã xã hội—dreg of society that had to be reeducated by hard labor. Several Amerasians were in the camp with him, and others were criminals or former soldiers who had fought against the Communists. There were harsh rules they all had to follow. Anyone who tried to escape would be shot.

By now, at fifteen, he no longer looked like a child. His skin had been roasted even darker by the sun, his arms were muscled, his hair thick and curly. He was expected to work as much as an adult. Together with the others, he cut down trees, hoed, and dug, turning dry and rocky areas into cultivable fields able to grow manioc and sweet potatoes. His stomach constantly moaned for food, too greedy for the single bowl of rice and the few strings of vegetables that he received at each meal. Around him, people collapsed, dying from the different illnesses that swept through the camp. He caught malaria a few times and was lucky to survive.

Working on the land made him miss Sister Nhã even more. He felt he'd failed her by living life the way he had. He no longer prayed and had lost her rosary chain, her letters, as well as the pictures she'd given him. Gone were the beacons that would lead him to his parents. He swore that if he was given another chance, he would lead a good life, a life worthy of his guardian's love and faith in him; he would try harder to blend into the Vietnamese society; he would stay away from gangs and troublemakers.

Released from the reeducation camp at seventeen, he walked to the closest city, Đà Lạt, and chose its streets to be his home. The cooler weather here suited him, as well as the lonely lakes and rolling hills covered in pine trees. He felt closer to his father staying here, as Đà Lạt used to be the holiday resort for the French and the Americans. He honored his promise to Sister Nhã's soul by earning his meals instead of stealing them. He shined people's shoes, collected recyclable garbage to sell, sold cigarettes and soft drinks, and worked as a porter and laborer. He slept in parks and on pavements until a year later, when a long-distance bus driver recruited him as a helper. At last he earned enough money to move into a small room that he shared with four other men.

He spent the next two years dangling his body out of the racing bus, calling out to potential customers, pulling them on board. Two years fighting against thieves who blended in with travelers. Two years helping the driver and his customers smuggle goods by hiding them above, under, and inside the bus. Two years carrying bags of rice, corn, manioc, and sweet potatoes heavier than his own body. He didn't mind the hard work, but watching families travel together tore at his heart. In their union, he saw himself as a solitary bird without feathers or a nest, unable to fly and having nowhere to return to. He observed the mothers around him, wondering what it would take for them to abandon their own child. He watched the women who were old enough to be his mother, asking silently if he had been a part of their life.

His buses made frequent trips to the Mekong Delta and occasionally to other cities. One morning, he was leaving the bus station in Hồ Chí Minh City, heading for his favorite coffee shop, his twenty-year-old body exhausted, when he heard a voice, "Phong ơi, Phong." He swirled around, stunned at the sound of his name. He'd grown used to being nameless. He was no longer a bụi đời—the dust of life—for he could rent a room; but his boss and his roommates all called him Mỹ đen—Black American. The only people who called him by his name were other Amerasians, but he hadn't seen any of them for a long while. Some of them were still gangsters, and he'd been staying away from them to avoid trouble, and to focus on his plan. He had decided that once he had enough money, he'd buy a patch of land, and grow his own food. During his years with Sister Nhã, he'd realized that plants and nature always offered him comfort, and were in fact kinder than most people.

"Phong ơi!" The sound of his name swam to him again through the clinking bells of cyclos and the rumblings of buses that were making their way into the station. He blinked, shielded his eyes against sunlight with his palm. The person who called was a middle-aged woman. She avoided a bicycle and hurried toward him.

"Phong . . ." She continued to call, her voice pitched, as if she was breathless.

"How do you know my name?" He stared at her as she got closer. Her skin was fair, her hair permed, and a pair of gold earrings dangled from her ears. She looked too glamorous to be hanging out at a bus station.

She grabbed him by the arm. "My son . . ." She pulled him into her and buried her face into his chest. "Má xin lỗi con, Phong ơi," her voice trembled. She'd called herself Mother, offered her apologies. When she looked up at him, tears had filled her eyes. "I . . . I gave you away when you were a baby. I am so, so sorry."

Her words sounded as if they had traveled from another world, so far away that they'd lost their meaning when they reached him. "Cô . . . cô vừa nói gì?" He asked what she'd just said, addressing her as Auntie. He stepped away from her, looking her up and down. She was around forty years old. Old enough to be his mother.

"Too many people here." She dabbed her eyes with a handkerchief and gestured toward those who were staring at them from the sidewalk and eateries. "Come with me and I'll show you something. Then you'll believe me." She turned, waved for a cyclo.

"You just said you're my mother?" He wanted to shake her until she told him the truth.

"Yes. That's right, Son." She pulled his arm and climbed onto the cyclo. He clambered in after her.

She gave an address to the cyclo driver who craned forward and peddled them along.

"If you're my mother, where did you leave me? In front of what orphanage?" He asked, breathless. If she answered Phú Long, he'd ask about his birthmark. He wondered how she'd known his bus schedule. Had she been waiting at the station for a long time, to be able to talk to him?

"Shhh." She cried again, blowing her nose into her handkerchief. "Wait until you see the things I want to show you, Son. Then you'll understand."

He was impatient but the woman buried her face into her palm. Her shoulders shook. Her suppressed cries stirred something deep inside of Phong. The high walls that he'd erected to protect himself started crumbling, leaving him bare. The woman reached for his hand and her warmth permeated his fingers; the warmth he'd dreamt of during the countless nights these past eight years, cold wind his only company. The tremors of the woman's body traveled to his, and he shuddered. Something buckled, and the tears he'd held back for years broke. They rolled down his face, stinging his eyes, blurring his vision. He had thought he would never forgive his mother, but at that moment he decided if the woman could prove that she was his Má, he would help her overcome the ghosts of her past, so that they could build a future together.

The cyclo screeched to a stop. They'd arrived in front of a two-story house. A middle-aged man opened the gate, beaming, inviting him inside. As he sat on a wooden sofa, the man whispered to the woman and gave her a thick envelope. Phong stood up when she turned and hurried out to the street.

"Má . . ." Without thinking, the word "Mother" tumbled out of his mouth.

The woman disappeared behind the gate.

The man smiled at him. "Sit down, Phong. I know your favorite drink and I've prepared it for you." He stirred a glass and the smell of coffee mixed with sweetened condensed milk filled Phong with an intense thirst.

He stepped away. "Who's that woman and who the hell are you?"

"Relax, Son. My name is Khuất. Welcome to our home." The man gestured toward the high walls decorated with large paintings, the solid wooden furniture, the motorbike. Phong's eyes lingered on a grand altar with the statue of Jesus Christ.

The man poured tea into his egg-shaped cup. "That woman, forget about her . . . She has no relation to you. Whatever she said was just her way to convince you to come here. You want to hear the truth? I'm not related to you, either. But my wife and I, we want you to be our son. We asked that woman to find you and bring you here."

The muscles in Phong's stomach clenched. How foolish of him to let the woman trick him with her reptilian cá sấu tears. Oh, he wanted to find her, shake her, and shout at her. She must have spied on him as he visited the coffee shop near the bus station. How cruel of her to have played on his deep yearning for his mother's love.

Phong headed for the door. If he hurried, he would make it back before his bus returned to Đà Lạt.

During the next many years, Phong would often reflect on this moment and wish he had walked away. What happened next would change his entire life.

"Can't you just stop and listen to what I have to say first?" The man stepped toward Phong and gave him a faded photograph. "My friend . . . His name was Phi-líp, but I called him Thằng Khờ because he was so naïve about the war."

Phong stared at the foreign man in the photo. A Black soldier who stood on the bank of a rice field, a metal helmet on his head, a gun in his hand.

"He was very kind to me." Mr. Khuất's voice trembled. "He saved my life, but the fucking war killed him. . . . That's why I need to help a Black person, to honor him. I know about the discrimination people like you have been facing and I detest it." Mr. Khuất lowered his voice. "Phong . . . I've asked many people about you. You've been through a lot, and you work hard. I like that. You see . . . I'm looking for a young man to adopt. My wife and I . . . we tried for years, but she could only bear us two daughters. And you know what our old proverb says. Nhất nam viết hữu, thập nữ viết vô—a son is a child, ten daughters equal none. Our daughters will belong to their husbands' families once they marry . . ."

"You want to adopt me?" It was the most ridiculous thing Phong had heard; he had to laugh. "And how do you even know my name?"

"Haven't you heard the saying 'Có tiền mua tiên cũng được'? We can buy everything with money, even fairies." Mr. Khuất winked. "I have eyes and ears at the bus station and around town. I've looked into many cases of boys like you and know you'll be a good fit for our family. Now, it's up to you to decide, but once you walk out that door, I won't ever want to see you again. I have several people on my list and any one of them would die to have a chance to live with us. The chosen person will have his own room upstairs. A bedroom of your own, imagine that. You could eat all your meals with us. There would be no need for you to work anymore."

"But có đi có lại. What would I need to do in return? Clean your house, be your servant?"

"No . . . nothing like that." Mr. Khuất chuckled. "Just be good company, that's all I ask. As for the cooking and cleaning, you won't even have to lift your little finger. My wife is excellent at it. So what do you say, eh? Don't you want to give this a try? Stay for a couple of days, enjoy our home and hospitality. If you don't like it, you can leave."

Phong wanted to leave right then. He didn't believe Mr. Khuất's story about his Black friend, but he wasn't sure he even cared. The idea of a bed, and his own room, was too tempting. He couldn't help comparing this spacious house to the stuffiness of his shared room, so small that he and his roommates had to roll up their sleeping straw mats during the day to make space for them to move around. Their toilet was a hole dug in the small backyard. Whenever Phong lay down to sleep, he would smell the stench of shit and hear the buzzing of flies.

He looked at the iced coffee which Mr. Khuất had placed on the table in front of him, and his thirst begged him to take a sip. When he was still debating what to do, a middle-aged woman descended the staircase, smiling broadly. As she told him how happy she was to meet him, he noticed that she was wearing a rosary chain around her neck. Like Sister Nhã.

The rosary chain and the altar made him stay. He felt he had come to the home of God and God would help protect him.

That night, Mrs. Khuất welcomed Phong with a sumptuous dinner. Her two daughters, one older than Phong and the other younger, didn't say much, even though Mr. Khuất kept urging them to talk. Phong was given a room on the second floor, furnished with a wooden bed three times the size of his straw mat. It was the first time he had ever slept on a mattress. He wasn't used to its softness, though, so during the night he got a pillow and moved down to the floor, where the cool tiles felt like home against his naked back. In the morning, he grinned from ear to ear as he practiced aiming his pee at the gleaming belly of the white Western toilet. Later, he stood in the shower, his eyes closed as the warm droplets poured down on him. For the first time in his life, he didn't have to scoop up water from a bucket to wash himself.

Phong thought he would stay only one day or two—to find out more about the Khuẩts and their real reasons for bringing him here—but the comfort of their home felt like the embrace of the mother he'd always wanted. The ways Mrs. Khuất took care of him reminded him of Sister Nhã. She cooked for him every day and bought him new clothes. She washed and ironed his pants and shirts. As he admired himself—a well-dressed young man—in the mirror, he felt grateful. He tried to help with household chores but she told him he only needed to clean his room.

Mr. Khuất went to work during the day and his daughters to school, and Phong felt as if the house belonged to him. There was a video cassette player in his room, together with more than twenty movies. These movies took Phong to America—a country of magnificent landscapes, modern cities, horse-galloping cowboys, and girls so beautiful that they visited him while he slept. He longed to set foot in America, if only once in his life.

On the fifth night of Phong's stay, when he was contemplating going back to the bus station to send a message to his boss, Mr. Khuất came into his room, waving sheets of papers in his hand. "Phong, guess what? By pure chance, I've just discovered your luck! Amerasians like you can now immigrate to America."

Phong sat up in his bed. The night before, he'd dreamt about kissing an American girl. Her neck smelled of roses, unlike the sweat of the girls he'd been with.

"It's complicated and expensive to put together your paperwork, but I'll help you take care of it." Mr. Khuất explained that to be able to leave, Phong needed to apply first for a passport and an exit permit from the Vietnamese authorities, then an entry visa into the U.S. He patted Phong's shoulder. "Life in America is good, but it won't be easy at first. You'll need a family to take care of you. You'll need someone who is fluent in English, like me, to help you." He smiled at Phong. "If you want, we can all go, as a family. American people are kind, you see? They sympathize with people like you. Their government approved something called the Amerasian Homecoming Act, which allows Amerasians to bring families along."

"But we aren't family." Phong walked away from the bed. He'd been dazzled by the chance to immigrate to America, but now his mind was clear, like the sky after a hard rain: this family had brought him here to use him as their ticket to go to America. They'd let him watch American films to tempt him. He knew plenty of people who were desperate to leave; some had fled in fishing boats, entrusting their lives to the rolling waves of the big oceans. He'd once thought about joining them, but had no gold to pay for such a trip.

"Don't you worry," said Mr. Khuất. "The truth is that some Vietnamese families adopted Amerasians years ago, and they have been able to go to America under the Amerasian Homecoming Act. And I know people who have just gotten together with con lai like you and left together. We won't be the first."

Phong couldn't believe what he was hearing. How could he go along with such serious lies that this family had adopted him? He'd had enough troubles with the authorities. Besides, he'd promised Sister Nhã that he would live an honest life.

Mr. Khuất pushed a small silk bag into Phong's hand. "Three rings. That's one and a half gold tael! For you to buy whatever you need to prepare for our trip to America. When we get there, I'll give you more."

Phong looked into the bag. The gold rings met his eyes. Sister Nhã had saved all her life and everything she had was worth less than two rings.

"See how well I take care of you?" Mr. Khuất beamed. "As I said, the paperwork won't be easy, but I know people. . . They can help register you, backdated, into our family book, so it looks like you were adopted into our family a long time ago."

Phong shook his head. He would need to lie to the authorities who might beat him and imprison him. He opened his mouth. "But—"

"There's no 'but,' Phong. Remember, you're entitled to bring family members along. You are a child of America and Americans want you home." Mr. Khuất gestured around the room. "Look at this beautiful house. I earned it with my clever mind. I work as a private English teacher now, but during the war I made my fortune by supplying sandbags to the American army. I know how Americans think. I walk with my wooden sandals in their stomachs, as our proverb says. I know them inside out. I've studied their rules, and I wouldn't propose for us to go to America if it wasn't feasible." He squeezed Phong's shoulders. "Aren't you excited that we'll all have a new beginning in America? That we can officially be a family? That I can help you there with my English?"

"But you have everything here. Why leave?"

"I can't begin to tell you what the Communists did to us since the fall of Sài Gòn." A frown deepened on Mr. Khuất's forehead. "They took away our savings in the banks. They nationalized our factory and stole our other houses. Things are going to get worse, and I can't let my daughters live under such oppression. All we want is to live in freedom. Would you help us, Son?" Mr. Khuất started calling Phong "Son," as if it was the most natural thing.

When Phong didn't answer, the man sighed. "Just hold on to the gold while you think about it. And don't forget, in America we'll help you find your father. We'll continue to be your family. You don't have to be alone ever again."

That night, instead of sleeping, Phong stood next to the window, looking up to the black sky, the gold in the nest of his palm. If he'd had such fortune before, he could have saved Sister Nhã.

He couldn't believe that from a child of dust he had been turned into a person of gold. "You are a child of America and Americans want you home." The words of Mr. Khuất rang in his ears. Even if the man had lied time and time again, Phong wanted to believe in these words.

The next morning, Phong headed to the 30/4 Reunification Park, where many Amerasians hung out. He hadn't been there for years and the park was emptier than he remembered. It took him a while to find several trẻ lai. They told him that it was true: trẻ lai could now go to America based on their non-Vietnamese features. As many mothers of trẻ lai had abandoned them or destroyed their papers out of fear of punishment from the Communists, trẻ lai could claim anyone as their family and bring them along.

Two of Phong's friends, who were older than him, had already been approached by rich families who wanted them to marry their daughters and bring the whole family to America. Those his age or younger had received offers to be adopted by families. The people he talked to warned Phong that even though it was possible for them to leave, the paperwork could take years. Procedures were complicated, fees expensive, bribes had to be paid, and too many people were applying. For an illiterate, penniless person like Phong, it would almost be impossible, unless he found those who could help.

His friends told him that the gold offered by Mr. Khuất was too little, and that he should ask for more or find a different family. Five taels of gold in advance would be the market price.

Walking back to the Khuấts' house, Phong saw people sleeping on the streets, beggars stretching their palms, pleading to passersby. Boys his age bent their backs low in the sun, shining shoes for rich men. He didn't want to be homeless ever again. Here was his chance to leave for a better future and he had to grab it. He couldn't do it on his own, and Mr. Khuất seemed to know how to get him to America.

That night, Phong told Mr. Khuất his friends were getting five taels of gold. The man said "I'll give you another ring, for two taels in advance, then three taels when we get there," and Phong nodded.

During the next months, Mr. Khuất worked hard in preparing Phong and his family for the exit permit interview and entry visa interview. He staged scenes for their family photos which he brought to Chợ Lớn Market in the Chinese Quarters. A week later, he showed Phong the same photos, now faded, as if they had been taken years ago.

Mr. Khuất also wrote down many possible questions and answers about them being a family and demanded everyone to learn them by heart. He ran practice sessions with Phong. The man was determined not to fail and his confidence calmed Phong's anxiety.

Once their exit permit applications had been submitted, Phong kept himself busy with new exercise routines: he ran up and down the staircase and did pushups; he lifted weights, using blocks of bricks. And he found himself a job: stringing bamboo curtains for a cooperative. As he squatted on the floor of his room, piercing the cut-up bamboo pieces with thin metal wire then connecting them into long strings, he imagined the homes where his curtains would travel to. Homes filled with good conversations and laughter. He was determined to build a home like that for himself. He'd started calling Mrs. Khuất and Mr.

Khuất "Mother" and "Father" so that he would pretend better in the interviews, but didn't feel comfortable with it. As much as he yearned to have parents, parenthood couldn't be bought with money. It had to be earned and proven over time, and it certainly couldn't be based on lies.

But he lied and passed the exit permit interview.

On the day of their American visa interviews, Phong was called in first, then Mr. Khuất, and finally Mrs. Khuất. The visa officer was friendly toward Phong, and he thought he did very well.

That night, loud noises woke Phong up. He tiptoed downstairs toward Mr. and Mrs. Khuất's room. They were arguing. By eavesdropping, he learned that when the visa officer had challenged some answers from Mrs. Khuất, she got frightened and broke down.

"You're a foolish woman," shouted Mr. Khuất.

"All of his questions, they made me feel like a criminal." Mrs. Khuất wailed.

"Now you'll make us rot in this hellhole. Damn you!"

"How can you commit to such a serious lie when you are a Catholic? Don't you think God will judge you?"

"God knows that I need to get us and our daughters out of this shithole. He will not judge."

The shouting got louder. Phong covered his ears. Back in his bed, he lay awake until the morning. He hoped they'd stop fighting. He felt sorry for Mrs. Khuất.

He thought Mrs. Khuất cared for him, too, but the day they learned that their visa applications failed, she told him to return the gold rings, pack his things and leave. Her eyes were as cold as those of the fish she'd often brought home and butchered for dinner.

"It's not my fault, I did my best," Phong told Mr. Khuất, who was sitting at the table, reading a newspaper.

The man turned the page and kept reading.

Phong trembled with rage. His dream of going to America had just been shattered. He went upstairs to collect his clothes. Standing next to the window, he looked into the silk bag. The four gold rings gleamed their promise under sunlight. He'd taken them to a gold shop to check if they were real; he knew the Khuấts were cheaters. "It's pure gold, twenty-four karat," the goldsmith had announced, then asked, "Where did you steal these? Want to sell them to me? Best price in town."

Now, Phong dropped the silk bag into the chest pocket of his T-shirt. The Khuấts had paid him so that he'd lie on their behalf, which he had done to his best ability. He'd fulfilled his part of the deal.

Downstairs, he headed for the door, only to see it blocked. Mr. Khuất stood there, a large wooden stick in his hands. "Return us the gold," the man pointed his weapon at Phong. "You only had one task to do, to convince those American people, but you failed. Yes, you did! "

"You destroyed my chance for a better life, and now you blame me?" Phong slung the strap of his bag over his shoulder and rolled up the sleeves of his T-shirt to show off his muscular upper arms. "You said you had asked many people about me, yes? So you must know that I love to teach those I hate some lessons."

The Heat of Sài Gòn

Hồ Chí Minh City, 2016

Dan picked up Linda's suitcase and followed her out of the airport. He was surprised nobody had given him trouble. The immigration officer didn't take the money Linda had slid into his passport, and no one had inspected their belongings.

A few feet from the exit, he paused. Too many people were standing outside. Once, in a dream, he was walking somewhere in the Mekong Delta when a man ran behind him and stabbed him in the back with a knife, shouting, "Return my wife and my children to me!" The man bore the same face as a farmer he'd seen kneeling and howling outside a burning home.

Linda turned. She smiled, stretched out her hand. She'd seen him pace their living room during the nights before their departure. He reached for her, tethered himself to her fingers.

Outside, all the people were looking past him, searching for arriving passengers, babies and flowers clutched to their chests. Several guards stood casually in dark green uniforms. None of them had weapons. The heaviness in his chest eased.

"Where's our guide?" Linda stood on tiptoes to look further, then pulled Dan forward. She waved to a man who'd emerged from the crowd, holding up a sign that read MR. DANIEL ASHLAND & MRS. LINDA ASHLAND.

The man smiled, lowered the sign, hurried toward them. He was slim and looked fit, and it was difficult to guess his age. A big scar cut across his left cheek. "You can trust him," Duy had told Linda. "He's an old friend, my former comrade. An experienced tour guide, too."

The man extended his arm. "I am Thiên. Welcome to Sài Gòn!"

"Thanks for picking us up, Mr. Thien." Linda beamed. She'd followed her friends' advice and addressed Thiên with a respectful title.

Darkness had fallen. A strong wind blew, ushering the smell of rain forward. Thiên waved for a taxi. In the car he handed them each a business card. "This has my mobile number. If you get lost, you call me. You call me anytime you need."

Dan put the card into his breast pocket, telling himself there'd be no way he would let Linda out of his sight. Especially here.

Thiên gave Linda a copy of the itinerary, explaining their two-day program in the city before leaving for the Mekong Delta.

When they had planned the trip, Linda had suggested that they experience Việt Nam beyond the war. No visits to war museums or to the popular Củ Chi tunnels where tourists got a glimpse into the lives of Communist soldiers living underground during the war. Dan couldn't agree more.

Linda had read the itinerary so often, she must have memorized it. Still, she switched the light on and studied the pages as if it were the first time she'd seen them. "Looks good," she announced happily before putting them into her handbag.

Thiên gave Linda a small bottle. "Mosquito repellent. My wife made it herself, from lemongrass. She has a small shop. Please . . . spray your arms and legs every day as you go out. It's rainy season, so there's dengue fever."

"Thank you so much," said Linda, beaming. "By the way . . . Duy and Như sent some medicine for your mother. It's in my suitcase."

"Ah, they're so kind. I wish I listened to them and tried to go to America. Too much corruption here. Little freedom of speech."

"How bad is the corruption, Mr. Thien?"

As Thiên and Linda gossiped about local politics, Dan listened to the rain hammering onto the car. It had often rained like this. He'd been frightened of it, but Kim had said rain was her music. She would lie with him in bed, humming, her naked body a beautiful brown next to his white skin as raindrops tapped onto the windows of their apartment.

The street was almost empty. Through the thick curtain of rain, he saw two moving figures. A woman was pulling a child's hand. They were running.

During the last time that he saw Kim, she had clutched his wrist tightly, telling him she was pregnant, and that she wasn't lying.

He sank deeper into the seat, pressed down by the weight of guilt. He hoped Kim and the child had survived the war.

And he hoped Linda would forgive him, if he ever got up the courage to tell her. During the first year of his return, he had often thought about confessing his affair to Linda. But he feared she would leave him.

Linda centered him. He'd realized how loyal she'd been to him on the day of his return to Seattle from his one-year tour in Việt Nam. He had no memory of stepping off the plane, only of being suddenly in the arrival hall with a group of soldiers, all of whom, like him, looked dazed in their khaki Class A uniforms decorated by rows of ribbons, and silver pilot or aircrew wings or combat infantry badges on their chests. A crowd of people stood outside, Linda and his mom among them. Linda was rushing to him when someone shouted, "Look at those fuckers." A woman and a man spat in his direction. "Baby killers!" someone shouted, "How many kids did you kill? And how many women?" As his mom started crying, he stood there, stunned. The people screaming at him weren't carrying banners or signs. They looked like anyone waiting for loved ones. His countrymen.

"I'm sorry, honey," Linda said later as she drove him and his mother home. Her knuckles were white as she gripped the steering wheel. "Those people . . . they're just ignorant. A bunch of rich, spoiled brats who'll never be forced to really risk their own asses. Regardless of how I feel about the war, I can never resent you or anyone else who has to fight it. You did what you thought you were supposed to do at the risk of your own life. You're a man of honor, Dan. Don't let anybody tell you otherwise."

A man of honor. He clung to her words, as if her saying it could make it true.

"She's right." His mom reached toward the front seat for his arm, her eyes welling up with tears. "I'm proud of you son. I'm glad, so glad you made it home."

He had a month's leave before reporting to new duties at Fort Wolters, Texas. In the weeks after his return, as demonstrations against the war raged around town, Linda stayed by his side, defending him ferociously when anyone put down veterans. They were working-class kids who had no choice, she would say. "If Dan hadn't gone, someone would have to go in his place," she told her friends. It took her three weeks to confess to Dan, as if admitting to an affair, that she'd been to several anti-war demonstrations. At some level, she felt her protest was a betrayal of him. He told her he was proud she'd gone; he would join her if she decided to go again. She never did when he was around. Perhaps a part of her remained disturbed and embarrassed that he'd been in the war. She told her friends and acquaintances that his only job had been to conduct search and rescue missions, and that he'd risked his life to save others. She truly believed that he hadn't killed any civilians.

He never corrected her. If he let her define him, it would give him something to live up to.

Their marriage had survived because she considered him an honorable man.

"Mr. Thien . . ." Linda leaned forward in the taxi, her voice cheerful, "when we're done with the city tour tomorrow, could you take me to the hairdresser my friend Jenna went to? She was there a few months ago and said the service was excellent and the price so cheap."

"Everything here cheap for Americans," said Thiên. "Madam also wants new clothes? I know good tailors."

"Yes, but I'd like to go to the tailor Jenna recommended. He did such a great job."

Jenna was a member of the veteran spouse support group Linda attended. She had visited Việt Nam with her husband and said the trip was better than any doctor, better than any medicine.

Outside, as their taxi approached the center of town, groups of people stood on the pavement, squeezing themselves into the narrow spaces under the eaves of houses and buildings. Several raced by on motorbikes, their heads covered by rain ponchos. Dan tried to look at their faces but everything was a blur. Would he recognize Kim if he saw her? Probably not. Years had passed and she'd look very different. Or she might be dead.

A cell phone rang. Thiên picked it up, speaking rapidly. Once the call was done, he turned around. "My granddaughter. She got nine out of ten in her math test."

"What a clever girl," said Linda. "How old is she?"

"Eight, Madam. I have a son and one granddaughter. How about you?"

Silence filled the taxi. "We don't have any children," Linda said finally.

"Oh, sorry, Madam. . . . Sorry I asked."

Dan reached for Linda's hand, intertwining his fingers with hers, hoping she'd feel comforted. What a pity they'd never been able to have children. By the time they considered adoption, Linda said she was too old to handle a young kid. He should have tried to change her mind, assure her how much he would help, and that she would make a great mother. She had no siblings, and with his only sister living in Australia and deliberately out of touch, sometimes he wished for a bigger family.

Perhaps Linda would never forgive him for the child he'd had with Kim. It would mock their failure to have children.

The rain's drumming eased, then disappeared. A motorbike passed the taxi, carrying two adults and two children squeezed between them. On another motorbike a young woman embraced her lover, laughing with him. He and Linda had looked like that before the war, inseparable, laughter spilling out of them as naturally as the air they breathed. The war had robbed them of their youth, their pure joy.

Linda rolled down the window. The wind rushed in, carrying with it the fresh smell of rain.

A boy who sat behind a motorbike waved. "Hello! How ah you?" he called toward their taxi.

"Oh, hello there." Linda waved back, smiling.

"I am fine, thank you. And you?" The boy beamed as the taxi sped away from his bike.

"People here are so friendly." Linda responded to another child's wave.

"Because you are nice. To unfriendly people, we can be nasty." Thiên laughed. "We have a saying . . . hmm . . . I hope I can translate this . . . When go with Buddha, we wear Buddhist robes, when we see ghosts, we wear clothes made of paper."

"It sounds good, but what does it mean?" Linda asked.

"In the company of Buddha, wear Buddhist robes, in the company of ghosts, wear ghost clothes?" Dan offered a translation.

"We make a perfect team!" Thiên clapped his hands.

The taxi turned onto a big boulevard lined with trees and lit up by streetlights. Dan was amazed to see all the fancy shops, recognizing international luxury brand names. Even under the hands of the

Communists, Sài Gòn looked rich. There were hardly any homeless people sleeping on the pavement, unlike Seattle. It was incredible how he'd been brainwashed about Communism, its danger to humanity. During his military training, he'd been told about the domino theory, that if one country fell to Communism, others would follow and Communism would take over the world.

How naïve he'd been about the war. In fact, he'd known nothing about Việt Nam when he signed up for the service. He had imagined the country as an exotic place. Although it was 1968 and the anti-war movement had already started, he'd been too distracted with problems at home to pay attention. And secretly he'd dreamt of being a hero. Heroes were born out of wars and there he was, feeling proud he would join one of the most powerful armies in the world to rescue the pitiful Vietnamese from the savage Communists. But his reading later about Việt Nam taught him that the Vietnamese didn't need pity. They had fought courageously for independence against the Chinese, the Mongolians, the French, and the Japanese.

It had taken him years of such reading to understand that he'd been sent to Việt Nam to save it from the Vietnamese, and saving the Vietnamese meant killing them. By the millions. Learning all this made him angry, made him drink, but it also made him nod at the truths his reading kept revealing. There was one book that made him scream in outrage and throw it against a wall—the one by Robert MacNamara. He still remembered the eleven reasons the former Secretary of Defense gave for America failing in Việt Nam, among them "our profound ignorance of the history, culture and politics of the people."

Not just ignorant, they'd been arrogant and racist. General Westmoreland, former commander of U.S. forces in Việt Nam, had said: "The Oriental doesn't put the same high price on life as does a Westerner. Life is plentiful. Life is cheap in the Orient." Dan shook his head. If Westmoreland had met Kim, what would he say to Kim's love for life and the many things she'd done for her family? Would he be able to look Kim in the eyes and tell her that life was cheap for Vietnamese?

"Here we are. Majestic Hotel!" Thiên announced as the taxi pulled to a stop.

Dan hesitated at the sight of people and motorbikes outside; then he took a deep breath, pulled his backpack onto his shoulder, and stepped out.

Hotel Majestic looked as magnificent as ever, with its domed glass windows, its elaborate entrance where a guard stood. Painted a pale yellow, the building now had a bright red Communist flag flying above its name. He gazed at the rooftop, recalling that it had one of the best views of the city. He had to take Linda up there, tell her tales about the foreign journalists who used to hang out at the rooftop bar during the war.

To the right, Tự Do—the Street of Freedom, now called Đồng Khởi—the Street of Uprising—stretched out before his eyes, lit up by colorful lights. Were some of the bars still there? During his final month here, he'd been a frequent customer. The girls had been younger than Kim, undemanding and not pregnant.

"This hotel was built by a Chinese Vietnamese businessman in 1925," Thiên gestured toward the Majestic. "His Chinese name was Hui Bon Hoa, but we called him Uncle Hỏa. He was once Sài Gòn's richest man. His family constructed thousands of buildings, including the current Fine Arts Museum."

"That's amazing," Linda said. "And how interesting that this hotel looks just like some of the buildings I saw in Paris." Linda tilted her head, looking up to the lit windows of the higher floors.

As Linda mentioned French architecture, Dan thought about the terrible things the French had done to the Vietnamese. They'd colonized the country for decades, divided its people, caused the First Indochina War, which killed hundreds of thousands of people. Then he noticed how Linda's innocent words had instantly snapped his mind to the subject of French colonialism. That was the thing about being here.

In America he could pretend that world history had nothing to do with his life. But as soon as he stepped back into the hot air of Việt Nam, he knew that notion was bullshit.

A young bellhop in a white suit rushed to them, whisking their suitcases away. Dan and Linda walked to the entrance, where a guard bent his body as he opened the door for them. Dan bowed in return. He didn't like how some other Western guests ignored the doorman, behaving as if they, like the architecture, hadn't changed since the old French colonizers.

Inside, the air was cool and smelled of rose perfume. Linda gasped at the impressive entrance hall. At the long counter to the left, two receptionists looked stunning in their áo dàis. Dan searched their faces. They were young enough to be his grandchildren but had no Caucasian features.

As Linda and Thiên checked in, Dan walked to the glass window and gazed out at the road, studying the faces of those who passed.

Linda arrived at his side. "Our room is on the highest possible floor. River view!" She gave him one of their two key cards.

"See you in half an hour . . . for dinner," Thiên said.

Upstairs, the bellhop opened the door to their spacious, air-conditioned room. The bed looked luxurious, covered by a white duvet on which rose petals had been scattered. Dan felt a pang of guilt. They could never afford this type of hotel back home.

A lacquer vase stood on the dressing table, filled with red roses. Kim had often decorated their apartment with fresh flowers. She'd always gone on about how cheap they were, harvested during the night, brought into the city by farmers all the way from the countryside. She'd talked about those farmers with such tenderness and he knew she'd have preferred to be working on her rice field instead of at the Hollywood Bar.

Linda took off her shoes and stepped across the room toward the glass panel of a large window. "Look at this view!" The Sài Gòn River was a dark snake dotted by ships lit up with lights. Between the river and the hotel was a large road filled with motorbikes traveling in opposite directions.

At the door, Dan gave a five-dollar tip to the bellhop, whose face brightened as if he'd just earned a hundred bucks. Dan bolted the door, securing it with the metal chain. He relatched the window that faced the river as well as the glass door that led to a small balcony.

At home, he was always the last to go to bed. He couldn't sleep without double-checking all the doors and windows. When they bought the house more than ten years ago, the first thing he did was install an automatic alarm system. But in his nightmares, the VC could always disable it.

Sitting on the bed, Linda studied her red and swollen knees. "I couldn't sleep on the planes at all, could you?"

He shook his head, reached into her handbag for the tube of Bengay. He brushed the hem of her dress high up onto her thighs and felt a stir of desire. It had been months since they last made love. His nerves before the trip hadn't helped.

He lathered a layer of the medicine onto her knees and massaged them. "Make sure you drink enough water. The last thing we want is you getting sick."

As Linda took out her phone and snapped picture after picture of the view, Dan rested his head on a pillow. He wanted to close his eyes for a minute, but on the wall opposite the bed was an oil painting of children in a field of flowers. The children were running toward him, laughing. An image of Kim, pregnant, flashed in his mind. Was the child he'd had with Kim a boy or a girl? Had his child been forced to run for its life from the Communists' revenge? His child. It was the first time he allowed himself to use those words. His child.

A long time ago, when his sister Marianne left home leaving only a note saying that they were not to look for her or contact her ever again, he had sworn to his mother that he would be a good father. Marianne had blamed them both for enabling the abuse she'd suffered at the hands of his dad, a drunk who often hit his wife and two children. But at least his dad had been there for him throughout his childhood, had brought food home and kept a roof over their heads, had helped send him to school.

He feared he had turned out worse than his father. What kind of person was he to have walked away from his own child, from his pregnant girlfriend?

Being here was pushing him toward the course of action he'd been thinking about since agreeing to go on this trip. He should look for Kim. He should try to find out what had happened to his child. If his child had survived, he or she would be forty-six this year. He might already have grandchildren. Maybe even great grandchildren. They might be here somewhere, within his reach.

He had to find them.

Sài Gòn Tea

Sài Gòn, 1969

Trang stepped off the shuddering bus at Xa Cảng Miền Tây Station. Around her, passengers streamed out of different vehicles, their shoulders drooping like withered leaves. Unlike them, she wasn't tired. Her eyes were open wide, watching. Quỳnh's were, too. The station was in the outskirts of Sài Gòn, surrounded by ricefields, and to venture into the city, they took two other local buses, then a cyclo. The cyclo seat was too small for the three of them, so Quỳnh sat on Trang's lap, holding their bag of clothes and several of her books.

"Trương Minh Ký Street," Hân told the driver, who leaned forward, powering the cart attached behind his bike. His arms were wiry but muscular. Trang's father used to have arms like those. Arms that had carried her to school, picked fruits high up on trees for her, hoed, and watered, and harvested. She had to do well at her job, send money home to free her parents from their debts, and allow her father to get the treatments he needed so he could walk and his arms could once again be the pillars of her family.

She held on to the cyclo's steel frame as cars, motorbikes, and xe lam—three-wheeled mini buses—rushed past. She wondered who got to live inside the brick houses that lined the road. She admired the graceful áo dài dresses worn by the women walking on the pavements, and gasped at those wearing short, revealing miniskirts. Her mouth watered at the sight of colorfully decorated street stalls that sold all types of food, from noodle soup to desserts.

She searched for the con man. Perhaps here in Sài Gòn, she and Quỳnh could find him. They'd agreed that if they spotted him, Trang would follow him and Quỳnh would run and get the police.

A truck filled with foreign soldiers approached. They looked young and relaxed, very different from the men she'd seen patrolling her village. They flashed their smiles at the women, calling out something, laughing.

Hân called back something, and the men roared with laughter, clapping their hands.

"They say we're beautiful girls." Hân giggled as the truck sped away.

"What did you say?" Quỳnh asked.

"That they're sexy boys."

"Get out of here." Quỳnh thumped Hân's shoulder. "If you're not careful, they might kidnap us and take us to America."

"Oh, I wish." Hân continued to laugh.

Trang gestured toward a group of Vietnamese military police in green fatigues and steel helmets. "They come to your bar, too?"

Hân shook her head. "They go to their own. Our bar is only for white men. Sometimes Black men come to ours, but it's very rare."

"So each group of soldiers has their own territory?" Quỳnh asked.

"You're so clever." Hân knocked her curled finger against Quỳnh's head.

They passed a school. A group of girls dressed in white áo dài and matching white pants chased each other around a phượng tree whose flowers bloomed like red flames against the blue sky. Trang closed her eyes, wishing she could go back to her life as an innocent student. She promised herself that she would, once she'd earned enough money.

The cyclo chimed its bell as it entered a small alley. Street peddlers knitted their ways through the tiny lanes branching off it, their singsong voices urging people to buy sticky rice, mangoes, and steamed cassava.

Hân lived on the second story of a concrete building. As they removed their shoes, Trang was suddenly conscious of her brown feet and yellowish toenails against the cement floor. Near the entrance stood a small wooden altar where a statue of the Laughing Buddha sat behind a vase of marigolds and a plate of red dragon fruit. The lingering perfume of incense lifted Trang's spirit.

Light poured into the room from a window. Two wooden beds stood on opposite corners and between them hung such beautiful clothes, Trang couldn't take her eyes off them. Three girls were lying on a bed, singing a vọng cổ folk song.

"My roommates," Hân said. "They also work at the bar."

Trang nodded and listened to the vọng cổ soaring and dipping. The girls were good, their voices clear, coated with Mekong Delta accents. Trang knew the lyrics. It was "Lan và Điệp," a tragic love song she'd often sung, swinging in her hammock. Trang wondered why love stories, especially beautiful love stories, had to be sad.

Would her blossoming love for Hiếu meet the same fate?

The girls finished singing and jumped down from the bed. One was tall, another had short hair, and the third girl had a dimple opening like a tiny flower on her right cheek.

"Trang and Quỳnh . . . from my village," Hân told her roommates. "They'll be joining us at the Hollywood."

"First day in Sài Gòn?" the girl with the dimple looked her up and down.

"Yes, Sister." Quỳnh smiled.

"They'll find their own place, but need to make some money first," Hân said. "Do you mind if they stay here for the time being?"

"Here?" The short-haired girl arched her eyebrows.

"Not a problem for me." The tall girl shrugged. "We were new to this city once, and somebody helped us."

"But you'll have to sleep on the floor, we have no space on the beds," the short-haired girl said.

"On this beautiful floor? We'd be glad." Quỳnh beamed. "In return for your help, perhaps we can cook and clean?"

Trang wished she could have her younger sister's quick thinking and confidence.

"Can't say no to that." The girl with the dimple clapped her hands.

The short-haired girl sniffed. "Perhaps something is wrong with my nose . . . but I'm smelling food . . ." She eyed the sedge bag next to Hân's feet.

"Nothing can escape you, can it?" Hân laughed. "My mother wanted to spoil us, again."

They sat on the floor, in a circle. As the stewed cá lóc fish and sticky rice melted in Trang's mouth, she thought about her mother, alone now in their kitchen.

The short-haired girl picked up a piece of fish with her chopsticks. "You know the best thing you can do for yourself while in Sài Gòn?" She turned to Trang. "Find yourself an American boyfriend."

Trang glanced at Quỳnh. There were many things she was not sure about, but she was certain about one thing: she wouldn't want a soldier as a boyfriend. She'd witnessed some soldiers' violent acts and being a soldier made her father miserable.

"American men . . . they can be generous, let me tell you." The tall girl winked. "But beware. Some are big. They might break you." She lowered her voice, and the others burst out laughing.

The girl with the dimple scooped sticky rice into her own bowl. "Your boyfriend doesn't have to be an American. There are some Australians around, too. Any of them will do."

Trang's mouth fell open. Back home, Hân only mentioned Sài Gòn Tea and now—a foreign boyfriend? She was certain she could drink tea, and if she had a boyfriend, it could only be Hiếu.

"Don't move too fast, you're making them dizzy." Hân laughed. "First things first. . . . Time for some training." She turned to Trang and Quỳnh. "Now, listen carefully. When a soldier comes into our bar, he'll want to talk to a beautiful girl like you. To do that, he must buy drinks for him and Sài Gòn Tea for you."

"You get paid by the drinks he buys, so if he doesn't purchase new ones after half an hour for himself and for you, tell him he should. And if he still doesn't, leave him for another guy," the tall girl said.

"Seriously?" Trang stopped chewing.

"Sure," the short-haired girl said. "Flirt with as many soldiers as you want, but not when they're already with another girl."

Trang didn't want to flirt with men. She'd talk to them and drink tea with them, and that's all.

"Got it." Quỳnh sounded enthusiastic. "First, we get the guys to buy us drinks. Second, we don't steal customers from each other."

The tall girl nodded. "In the bar, we drink from this." She held up a tiny glass. "There's no salary, but for each tea you get a man to buy you, you'll get a share, and if he likes you, he'll give you a tip."

"Fantastic." Quỳnh clapped her hands.

"But . . . Sài Gòn Tea is only tea, right?" Trang recalled the hesitation in Hân's voice when she'd explained about the tea.

"Well . . . it's supposed to be tea mixed with whiskey, that's why the price for each glass is so high." Hân giggled. "The soldiers who come to our bar are Americans, and American men are easy to cheat, you see? So there's only tea in our glass. That way, we don't get drunk; we can flirt with many men and get them to buy lots and lots of drinks. The bar makes money and so do we. A win-win situation."

"Hold on," said Quỳnh. "Don't the men find out?"

"Nah, all the liquor that they swallow makes them so distracted, they don't notice." Hân shook her head. "And you also need to flirt, get their full attention so they don't stare at your glass. . . . Hey, don't look so worried. Whiskey and tea have the same brown color. Anyway, some Americans know that we cheat them, but they don't care. They just want to talk to pretty girls. So the prettier you are, the better."

Trang's eyes widened. The idea of cheating Americans sounded dangerous. After all, they were big men who had weapons.

The short-haired girl filled the tiny glass with water. "It's all about acting, really. . . . Be cool and you'll be alright. Just pretend you're drinking whiskey instead of plain tea." She picked up the glass, held her head back, poured the water into her mouth, swallowed, winced, and banged the glass onto the floor.

The girls clapped. The short-haired girl wiped her mouth and filled the glass. Quỳnh's turn. She tossed the water into her mouth, screwed up her face, and let out a big "ah." Watching her, Trang was reminded about the men from her village after they'd swallowed mouthfuls of rice liquor.

Everyone clapped. The glass was again full. Trang thought about standing up, dragging Quỳnh out of the room and telling her to go home. But images of the lenders flickered in her mind. Just a few days before, they'd pushed her crying mother aside and carried off the family's piglets.

Heat rose to Trang's face. She poured the water down her throat and banged the empty glass onto the floor.

"Be more convincing." The girl with the dimple filled the glass. She held it up, took a sip, shuddered, and put it down. She picked it up again, took another sip and clucked her tongue. "This American whiskey is damn good." Her voice slurred and the other girls cheered.

"Now eat up," said the tall girl. "We need to get ready for work soon. You have better things to wear?" She looked Quỳnh and Trang up and down.

Quỳnh eyed Trang. "We're wearing our best clothes."

"Ôi trời ơi." The tall girl exclaimed. "But you look like grannies in those." She stared at Trang's white shirt and black pants.

"There's no way you can come to work with us dressing like this." Hân turned to the other girls. "But we'll help them, right, Sisters?"

The girls nodded, giggling.

As Quỳnh and Trang washed the dishes, Hân checked their shoe and dress sizes. When the dishes were done, short skirts, high-heel shoes, and blouses had already been brought out and laid on the two beds.

"Where did you get these?" Quỳnh fingered a pink dress.

The material appeared so elegant, Trang didn't dare touch it.

"My ex-boyfriend bought it for me, from Australia. He was there for R & R." Hân looked proud.

"What's R & R? Did you get to go to Australia with your boyfriend?" Quỳnh asked.

"R & R means Rest and Relaxation," said the short-haired girl. "American soldiers get to go on holiday once a year. They can choose from many nice places . . . Hawaii, Bangkok, Hong Kong, Tokyo. . . . Your boyfriend can't take you, but he might buy you presents."

Trang shook her head in disbelief. American soldiers could take holiday from the war? Her father had fought alongside American soldiers but she hadn't heard about him getting to go anywhere nice.

"So, you had a boyfriend? Where was he from?" she asked Hân. She wondered what else she didn't know about her best friend.

"Oh, Hân has already forgotten about him." The girl with the dimple flicked her hand. "We change boyfriends like people change shirts. American boyfriends are good for you, really. . . . Just don't take them seriously. Have fun with them and let them buy you things." She winked.

"Try this on." As if trying to switch the topic, Hân gave Trang a blouse the color of young banana leaves. "I had it tailor-made at Chợ Lớn Market. It might fit you."

Quỳnh had already stripped her clothes off and was putting on the pink dress. Trang turned away. She hadn't seen her sister naked before. Their bodies were not to be shown to others.

"Come on, we don't have much time." Hân gave Trang a skirt and pair of shoes.

Trang faced the wall as she unbuttoned her shirt. She hoped nobody was looking. The blouse fit her, but it was so revealing that she had to put her hand in front of her chest.

The girls cheered and clapped as she practiced walking on high heels with Quỳnh.

"American boys will like them. Flowers from the field, ready to be picked," one of the girls said, and the group burst with laughter again.

Trang looked at the blouse and skirt Hân had chosen for her, wishing that they would grow longer, larger.

"Take the clothes off and pack them for the bar," Hân said. "We wear decent clothes on the way to work." She winked.

Following her friend, Trang knelt in front of the altar. She prayed that Buddha would bring her nice customers today. But does Buddha grant bar girls blessings?

As they descended the stairs, Trang smiled at her younger sister and realized Quỳnh was nervous. A droplet of sweat was rolling down her forehead.

"We'll be careful, and we'll be fine." She squeezed Quỳnh's hand. She promised herself to watch over her little sister.

As they crossed two long streets, Trang didn't dare look up. She held her bag of clothes above her face, pretending to shield herself from the sun, fearing someone from her village would recognize her.

Finally, they arrived in front of a door with a big, red sign that read "Hollywood Bar". Trang knew about Hollywood for its films, and she wondered what Hollywood meant. In Vietnamese, a name almost always embodied a message. The name of her village, Phú Mỹ, meant "rich and beautiful," which had been true a long time ago, before the war.

Inside, the air was dark and eerie, packed with the smell of smoke and liquor.

"Wait here," Hân said before disappearing behind a wooden door.

To Trang's left stood tables where fifteen or so girls and ten middle-aged women sat, yawning. Their faces had been painted by makeup, their clothes tight and revealing. Two young men stood behind a counter, washing a pile of glasses. Bottles of different colors and sizes lined the shelves behind them.

The wooden door swung open, and Hân walked out, together with an older woman. Layers of makeup covered the woman's face. Her eyes were sharp, piercing through Trang. An aura of confidence and power emanated from the woman, and Trang knew she was the owner.

"Good afternoon, Madam." Quỳnh bowed. "We beg you for a job. My Elder Sister Trang and I—"

"Come." The madam snatched Trang's hand, pulling her through the door. Trang looked back to make sure Quỳnh was following. They entered a room furnished with a large mirror, a low table, and several armchairs. A taxidermied tiger's head hung on the wall. When Trang caught the animal's cloudy, desperate eyes, a shudder ran down her spine: the eyes resembled those of a VC suspect being held by GIs on a road in her village.

The madam lit up a cigarette. "Speak any English?" She blew out circles of smoke.

"We learned it at school. We just need some time to practice it, Madam," said Quỳnh as Trang tried to suppress her cough.

"You need to be fluent. Learn fast, for this is not a place for the stupid."

From a drawer of her low table, the madam pulled out a pocket-sized English phrase book and gave it to Quỳnh. "I'm lending it to you for now. Go through it with your sister. Learn the phrases by heart."

"Yes, Madam."

"Drink any liquor?"

Quỳnh and Trang looked at each other. They shook their heads.

"Then try . . . when you have to. And listen . . . your job is to charm the men into buying drinks and not let them find out what's in your glass." The madam sucked in another puff of her cigarette. "Because we only employ capable girls, there's a one-week trial period. To pass, you need to meet a quota of six Sài Gòn Tea per night."

Trang felt sweat running down her forehead. Hân had said on average she got customers to buy her ten teas each night.

"Have you picked your nicknames?"

"Yes, Madam. I'll be Lan, and my sister Oanh," Quỳnh said.

"Oanh? That's too difficult for Americans. Kim will do."

"Madam," Trang said, "I like the name Kim . . . but I heard there's already another Kim at the bar?"

"Americans can't get enough of Kim." The woman chuckled. "The other Kim is tall, so you'll be short Kim. Is that set?"

"Dạ." Trang bowed in agreement. Whatever. She wanted to shed herself of the stupid nickname as soon as she stepped out of the bar anyway.

The madam flicked her finger and ash scattered from her cigarette onto the floor. She dropped herself into an armchair. "Our bar is not just a normal bar. It's special..." She took a drag of her cigarette and Trang wondered what "special" really meant.

"I named it Hollywood after the famous filmmaking city in America. . . . Only gorgeous and seductive girls can work here—" As the madam went on preaching, the tiger stared at Trang. Its eyes pleaded with her for help. Trang's vision blurred and she saw the VC suspect looking at her from the dirt road of her village. He was being dragged by American soldiers. He was kicking his legs, screaming. "I'm innocent! I'm not a Việt Cộng . . . Please . . ."

"VC! VC!" An American soldier roared, pointing the gun at the man's chest.

"No, no, no, no . . ." The man cried. "I know nothing about the ambush. I have no idea who killed your comrades. I am—"

A rifle butt cracked his face.

A hand slapped Trang's cheek. "Cheer up. You're not allowed to day-dream about your boyfriend, you hear me?" The madam clucked her tongue. "And remember this, if an American wants to sleep with you, he'll need to buy a ticket from the bar counter, the price depending on the number of hours. Forty percent of what he pays is yours."

"We won't . . . we won't be doing that," Quỳnh said.

The madam laughed, baring her teeth, white as the tiger's. "Every girl who enters this place says that at first. But trust me, you won't be able to hold yourself back." She took another puff of her cigarette, her eyes squinted behind the smoke. "Change into your work clothes upstairs, then go charm the men. Get them to buy you each at least six Sài Gòn Tea, or else you're gone after tonight."

In the stuffy changing room, Trang sat on a chair as Hân applied makeup on her. From what she'd heard from the tiger madam, she feared the Hollywood was both a brothel and a bar. She wanted to leave. But what would she do with her sister in this big city? How would she help her parents repay their debts?

"Open your mouth, just slightly," Hân ordered. "I'm lending you my lipstick, but after today you'll have to buy your own. And cream and face powder."

Trang blinked, her body numb. Out there in the bar, she would be một món hàng, to be examined, chosen or rejected by men. Hiếu's face appeared in her mind. *Why are you doing this?* he asked.

"Done." Hân pushed a mirror forward. A girl on the other side of the glass stared at Trang. She had big eyes and thick, red lips. Her skin glowed under a thick layer of powder. Trang had never worn makeup before and didn't recognize herself.

Her thoughts flowed toward Hiếu. Last night, after the hard rain, he'd come looking for her, but Quỳnh said she wasn't home. Unable to face him, Trang wrote a letter, only to tear it into pieces. She asked her mother to tell Hiếu that she'd gone to Sài Gòn for an office job and would be back soon. Even if he didn't find out the truth, would she have the courage to lie to him, and still be able to look him in the eye?

Trang sighed and looked around. "Where's the toilet?" She hated her habit of needing to go to the bathroom whenever she felt nervous.

"Outside . . . to your right." Hân smeared red color onto Quỳnh's lips. Quỳnh was silent; the meeting with the tiger madam seemed to have thrown a bucketful of cold water onto her soaring spirit.

The room next to the changing room was tiny and smelled of pee. Trang was sure it was the toilet but when she looked, there was no hole in the ground. Instead, a large ceramic bowl rose from the floor. She stood thinking, then took off her shoes, skirt, and underwear. She climbed onto the bowl. With her feet firmly placed on the bowl's ring, she squatted down. Before she could relieve herself, she lost her balance. She jumped down.

She stared at the bowl. Perhaps it was used for face washing after all. Luckily, she hadn't peed in it.

"What took you so long?" Hân snapped when she returned. "I'm doing my best to help you, but if you don't do your part, the madam will kick all of us out."

Trang didn't answer. She gazed at Quỳnh, who appeared like a stranger with so much makeup on. Quỳnh was beautiful enough, she didn't need makeup. She shouldn't be around American soldiers, only in the company of respectful boys like Hiếu.

Trang caressed Quỳnh's shoulder. "Be careful out there, please, em."

Quỳnh nodded and adjusted Trang's skirt. "You stay safe, too, chị Hai."

They held each other's arm, wanting the moment to last, knowing that their lives would never be the same as soon as they set foot into the bar.

As they left the changing room, Trang tapped on Hân's elbow. "Is that the toilet?" Through the half-open door, the white ceramic bowl gleamed.

"Don't tell me you climbed onto it, the way you do with our squatting toilet," Hân said.

Trang felt her face turning red. "Shouldn't I? How else can I pee?"

Hân burst out laughing. She pulled Quỳnh and Trang into the small room and closed the door. "This is an American toilet. To use, you just sit on it, like on a chair. Don't climb onto it or you'll break your neck."

"That's what I just did." Trang giggled. "Oh . . . I'm such a rice farmer."

"Flushing is easy." Hân pressed a round metal button, sending water gushing into the bowl.

Trang's mouth opened. Back at her village, every time she went to the toilet, she had to lug a pail of water all the way from the well. She couldn't help but laugh. "You two head out to the bar first. I have to see for myself how this American wonder works . . ."

Not everything here was bad, after all.

◇

WHEN TRANG STEPPED back into the bar, the lights were on. The room was illuminated in a reddish, misty glow. A strange type of music was playing. Except for the drums and guitar, she didn't recognize the instruments. Several foreign men had appeared and were sitting around a table, drinking and smoking. Some women, Hân included, surrounded the men. Two men were standing, swaying to the music, each with their arms wrapped around a girl.

Quỳnh was at a table by herself, near the entrance. Trang joined her. "American soldiers," Quỳnh said, "we'll drink with them, we'll make money from their tips. Promise me that we won't sleep with them? Promise?"

Trang squeezed Quỳnh's hand and nodded. She should have done a better job at persuading her younger sister to stay home. It should have been her sole responsibility to help her parents.

Trang needed to know if the foreign men carried weapons. She looked them up and down but saw no gun nor hand grenade. But they could be hiding guns inside their clothes.

She cocked her head, listening to conversations from the other table. The sounds were unfamiliar and made no sense. Hân had said the rusty English she'd learned at school hadn't helped her at the beginning, and that it took her a few weeks to understand what was going on.

Trang studied the women around her, wondering about their reasons for working here, whether they were happy, and their future plans. She wanted to get to know each and every one of them, the way she needed to know Hân again.

She faced the entrance, hoping to see new customers coming in, when a voice said, "So, you're the newbies?" Trang turned to see a girl around her age standing with her hands on her hips. Her hair was dyed blond. Her diamond-shaped eyes, full lips, and high-bridged nose made her resemble the celebrated actress Thẩm Thúy Hằng. Her breasts were so huge, they overflowed from the neckline of her white, glittery dress.

"Oh, hello." Trang stood up. "I'm Kim and this is my sister, Lan." The bar names sounded so strange on her lips, she was sure she'd never get used to them.

The girl tossed her chin. "I saw you staring at me. Didn't your parents teach you manners?"

Before Trang could answer, Quỳnh pushed herself between Trang and the girl. "Don't you dare talk about our parents."

"Hey, hey . . ." Hân ran to them. She bowed to the girl. "Elder Sister, forgive me for forgetting to introduce my very good friends to you. It's my mistake, I'm very, very sorry."

As the girl was glaring at Quỳnh, the bell at the door clinked. Trang turned to see a bald man stepping into the bar. The next thing she knew, the blond-haired girl was by the man's side, her arms slung around his neck.

"Who is she?" Trang asked, watching the couple exchange a passionate kiss.

"Tina is her bar name." Hân shrugged. "She's most popular with the men and the owner's favorite. I think she wanted to check you out. Make sure that you aren't competition."

"How can we ever compete with her?" Trang asked.

"Just don't get in her way, okay?" Hân lowered her voice. "Tina had a bad fight with another girl here several weeks ago. The next day, the girl was beaten up by some gangsters from Ông Lãnh Bridge. She's still at the Đồn Đất Hospital."

"And what did the police say?" Quỳnh frowned.

"You think the police care about our problems?" Hân walked away.

The bar was getting crowded. Whenever a man appeared, a flock of girls raced to him, clinging to his body. The man would choose someone and the rest would scatter back to their seats. Tina was surrounded by several men who looked at her as if they wanted to swallow her alive.

"How many boyfriends does she have, and how do we know if someone is already hers?" Trang mumbled.

"We need to get the men to come to us." Quỳnh pulled Trang up. They stood leaning against the bar counter, facing the entrance. Next to Trang, a girl was playing cards with a soldier who rubbed his hand up and down her thigh.

A while later, two men stepped through the door. Brushing away the girls who hung onto them, they headed for the bar. "Here we go. Smile," Quỳnh said, and Trang flashed her biggest grin, her face quivering.

The men ordered their drinks, then eyed the sisters. Trang smiled so hard, she felt as if her face were cracking.

The older man bent down to Trang. "Oát-xì do nêm?" he shouted above the music. His mustache looked like the whiskers of a tiger. His words sounded faintly familiar, but terror was a flood of water that drowned Trang's thoughts. "Du a bíu-ti-phun," the man continued. Trang shrank back, holding on to the chair behind her.

"Hey, relax. He likes you." The girl next to Trang elbowed her.

"Could you help translate what he just told me?" Trang asked.

"Well . . . he said 'What's your name?' and 'You are beautiful.'" The girl turned and told the man something. They both laughed.

The girl winked at Trang. "I asked him to bring you away and give you some pleasure." Glitter twinkled on her half-naked chest.

Next to Trang, Quỳnh was practicing her English with the younger man. Her voice was small, and it melted quickly into the swirling noise.

The mustached man told Trang something, making a drinking gesture.

Trang nodded. "Sài Gòn Tea," she mumbled.

The man's face lifted into a broad smile. He shouted something over the counter. The bartender nodded, hurried away and returned. He gave Trang a small glass, filled with a dark brown liquid and the man a large one in a lighter color. Trang's heartbeat quickened. She had no idea what was in her drink. She hoped it was only tea. If the American caught her, she'd blame it on the bartender.

The man looked into Trang's eyes as he clinked his glass against hers. Trang's lips trembled as she raised the liquid to her mouth. It smelled stale. She took a sip, tasting something bitter, yet it cooled her throat. She winced and pretended to shudder. A few steps away, the tiger madam was flirting with a soldier. She was laughing so hard, her whole body shaking.

The man pulled up a chair and made Trang sit down next to him. One hand around her shoulders, his other hand held his glass, which he lifted to his lips over and over, whispering to himself. At one moment, Trang was sure he was weeping, but when she dared sneak a look, his eyes were dry.

Trang ordered another Sài Gòn Tea, reminding herself to try to take advantage of her first customer. She looked for Quỳnh. There was her younger sister, dancing, moving her body, swinging her hips, tottering on her high heels, just like the girls around her. Where did Quỳnh learn to dance like that? She shouldn't let the man hold her so tight.

Tina approached Trang. "Your sister is ugly as a wild pig." She giggled. Arm-in-arm with a muscle-bound man, she moved to the bar's entrance and disappeared into the night.

Fear, cold as ice, slid down Trang's spine. Tina had chosen Quỳnh and her as enemies. But why?

The mustached man kept drinking, the bartender refilling his glass whenever it was empty. Once Trang had finished three Sài Gòn Teas, he stood up, pulled her to his solid chest, and said something that sounded so tender she wished she could understand it. Then he pushed a bill into her palm.

A red one-dollar note. It wasn't a real American dollar, but a Military Payment Certificate. Trang's father had shown it to her, explaining that American soldiers got paid in MPC and used it for currency. Trang would need to figure out how to change the note into Vietnamese đồng before it expired. She smiled up at the man. "Cám ơn ông." She thanked him, calling him Sir. Given their age difference, she should address him as "Uncle" and call herself "Niece," but perhaps not when she was trying to flirt with him.

As she watched the man stagger toward the door, the bartender tapped on her shoulder. "Keep this safe." He gave her a copy of the bill the man had paid. "Give it to Madam by the end of the night."

She studied it. "But why four Sài Gòn Tea? I only drank three."

"Shh." He winked and rushed to another customer.

A smile blossomed onto Trang's lips. She loved the fact that her countrymen found different ways to make money out of Americans. Americans were so rich anyway, a little cheating wouldn't bring them any harm.

A hand caressed her neck. A tall, white man bent down, his blood-shot eyes staring straight into hers. "Chào em. Em vui không?" His Vietnamese was pretty good.

"Chào anh," she returned his greeting, but didn't answer his question whether she was happy. How could she ever find happiness here? If she had a choice, she'd rather be back in her field, nursing rice seedlings into young plants, spreading a carpet of green onto the barren soil, then, in a few months, harvesting golden seeds packed with the sweet blessings of Mother Earth. As a farmer, she was a creator, an artist.

But she'd been given no choice. She pushed the dollar bill deep into her skirt pocket, then held on to it. She'd send this, all of this, home.

The man leaned closer. "Em đẹp qua." His accents were slightly wrong. As she was about to answer that she wasn't beautiful, he leaned closer, his breath pungent with tobacco and liquor. "You cherry girl?" he asked in Vietnamese.

"What?" she moved away from him.

"Want some private time, just you and me?" He winked.

She walked away, wanting to look for Quỳnh.

"Shouldn't you be entertaining him?" The tiger madam blocked her way, frowning at her.

Trang tilted her chin toward the man. "He's scaring me, Madam."

"No need to be afraid of me, darling." The man reached for her hand, but she stepped back.

"Now, don't you be silly." The tiger madam waved a finger at Trang. "This nice young man just wants to talk to you."

"Talk? But he's suggested a private time."

"And what's wrong with that? You don't even need to go far." The woman smiled but her eyes were cold. "We have private rooms at the back of the bar."

A Flash of Hope

Hồ Chí Minh City, 2016

Outside the American Consulate, the sunlight felt like a blazing fire. Phong walked to the shadow of a tree, but at the sight of two policemen standing guard on the pavement, he quickened his footsteps.

Bình, Tài, and Diễm were behind him. Their sobs were as quiet as soft rain but ravaged him like a storm.

"Đồ vô dụng," Phong scorned himself as useless for disappointing his family.

He headed for the bus station. They had several buses to catch. If they were lucky, they'd be home before midnight. On the spacious Lê Duẩn Boulevard, cars and motorbikes raced past, horns beeping. They crossed the street in the direction of towering buildings, so tall Phong felt as small as an ant.

"That arrogant woman in the consulate ruined our chance," Bình said. "If she'd let me come into the interview . . ."

"Then you'd have gotten us the visa? Are you saying you could've done better than me?" Phong sensed the blame in his wife's voice and felt terrible. He wished she would console him, tell him they'd be fine eventually. She had known about his troubles with visa applications and should understand how difficult this was for him.

"I told you how important this was, yet you didn't prepare enough—"

"Hey, how did it go?" Quang the visa agent shouted from across the road. He navigated the traffic, scurrying toward them, a cigarette between his lips. "Did you get the visa?"

Phong dropped the folder of documents. He gripped Quang's collar. "You told me there would be no problem. You took twelve million đồng from us. That's nearly six hundred American dollars."

"Don't." Bình tore him away from Quang.

"Calm the hell down." Quang spat out the cigarette. "You want them to see you start a fight?" He gestured toward the policemen.

Phong clenched his fists. "I want my money back. At least half of it."

"Are you fucking stupid? Don't you fucking know how difficult it was for me to get an interview for you? They wouldn't have seen you without my help. No refund. Now go home. Once you've saved enough money, call me. We can put together another application. We'll try again."

"You rotten rat. I'll tell the Americans how you cheated me."

"Go on. Do it then." Quang ground the words between his teeth. "I can promise you this much: bring me any trouble and you'll never be able to set foot on American soil."

"Don't you dare threaten us." Tài stepped in between the men. He glared at Quang. "Like my father said, return us half the money!"

"I won't return shit!" Quang spit out his words and walked away.

Bình and Diễm squatted down, gathering their papers. Phong's hands trembled with fury. Quang had taken all of their money. Worse, the man had planted ideas into his head, that a better life was waiting for him and his family.

"You okay, Ba?" Tài reached for his shoulder. "I would've kicked that crook's ass if it wasn't for them." He eyed the policemen.

"I shouldn't have lost my temper." Phong shook his head. His experiences had taught him that street fights would almost always make matters worse. "You shouldn't be like me, Son."

"I'm proud you stood up against that cheater, Ba. Otherwise people like him would keep bullying us."

Tài reminded Phong that there were too many nasty people out there. Just last week at the market, Phong had seen a Vietnamese woman dressed in high heels and a silk dress kick a Khmer street vendor's baskets, sending her vegetables tumbling across the muddy ground. While Phong told the woman off and she yelled back at him, the seller had just bent her head, frantically collecting her water spinach, cucumbers, and tomatoes. She hadn't responded to the Vietnamese woman's accusations that she'd blocked the pathway. In their hometown, too many Khmer were looked down upon because of their darker skin. Having fair skin elevated one's position in Vietnamese society as it signified education and money; the rich and educated didn't have to labor under the sun. Phong understood the frustration of his Khmer friends; they'd told him many tales about the Khmer Empire, which was once prosperous and had encompassed many parts of the Mekong Delta, parts that were taken over by the Vietnamese several centuries ago.

They walked. Phong eyed the long road ahead, his feet heavy, his throat dry, his head aching.

"Nghỉ uống nước chú ơi," from the pavement, a woman called out to him. She was standing next to a steel cart that displayed fresh coconuts and different types of drinks.

"Do you have iced tea, Auntie?" Bình asked the seller.

"Yes, only two thousand đồng per glass."

"Let's take a break, anh," Bình called out to Phong.

Phong sat down on a low plastic chair next to his wife and children.

"Two glasses, please, Auntie," Bình said. "That's four thousand đồng, right?"

"Yeah, as cheap as water ferns."

Bình took out her wallet and paid for the tea. She was the one who saved every penny they earned. Phong didn't remember the last time his wife bought herself new clothes or makeup. If he got to go to America, he'd use his first monthly allowance to buy a good facial cream for Bình, a cream that would soothe the sunburn on her cheeks.

The seller took an ice block from her styrofoam cooler and shattered it with a piece of flat metal. Under her conical hat, her crooked smile revealed several missing teeth. Freckles dotted her wrinkled cheeks. She must have been around sixty-five years old. Old enough to be Phong's mother. Did his mother ever come back to the orphanage to try and find him? Could this woman be his mother?

"You aren't from here, are you?" The woman asked, dropping pieces of ice into two large glasses. Phong hoped for some light of recognition in her gaze, but she didn't even look twice at him.

"We're from Bạc Liêu." Bình fanned herself with a hat she'd taken out of their backpack.

"Ah, the legend of the Bạc Liêu Prince, I remember . . . Was he so rich that when a girlfriend dropped a coin, he burnt ten banknotes to light the dark to look for it?" The woman laughed, pouring tea into the glasses.

"Yes, he did many stupid things like that," Tài said.

"Extravagant spending and his family has almost nothing now." Diễm stole glances at the pack of peanut candies the seller had placed on the small table in front of them. "His mansion now belongs to the government. And one of his sons had to work as a cyclo driver to earn a living."

"Oh dear. But that's life. Đời là lên voi xuống chó."

Phong nodded at the wisdom of the proverb. Life is riding high on an elephant, then low on a dog.

Bình and Diễm reached out for the full glasses. They drank.

The woman wiped her face with the sleeve of her shirt. "The man you were arguing with, he promised to help get you to America?" she asked Phong.

"You know him, Auntie?"

"Everyone around here does." The woman shook her head. "Don't trust him. He makes money from mixed-race people like you, especially those from the countryside."

"He charged us twelve million đồng." Bình sighed. "And the Americans . . . they just said no to our visa application."

"Trời đất ơi! You should have applied by yourself. You didn't need an intermediary. But . . . to be honest, it's very difficult to get to America now without an outsider's help."

"Outsiders?" Phong was sure the woman was talking about some other type of agents, people who'd charge much more than Quang.

"Well . . . there're American men who come back looking for their children. They might be able to help you."

Phong put down the tea. "Men who were here during the war?"

"Yes . . . they were young boys then. They're old now."

"They're coming back?" Tài and Diễm asked in one voice.

"A few of them are. Very few." The woman lit a cigarette and inhaled. Phong studied her through the shifting layers of smoke. Women didn't usually smoke.

Bình gripped Phong's hand. "Anh Phong, your father might be back looking for you."

Phong swallowed. As he grew older, his wish to know his father didn't fade, it intensified. He stared at the glass of tea in his hand. His identity was as murky as the drink. He didn't even know whether his mother had registered a birth certificate for him and what name she'd given him. If he found her, would she tell him the truth about his father? Would she explain the real reasons she'd abandoned him? When Bình decided to marry him, her father had said, "Phong's mother must be a prostitute and his father a killer, why marry him? Family members relate if not in feathers then in wings."

He had to find his parents, to prove his father-in-law wrong, so that Bình would be accepted into her family again.

The drink seller fanned herself with her conical hat. "Now, now . . . I didn't mean to give you hope. As I said, very few American veterans are coming back to look for their lost families. It's a recent thing. I think these veterans . . . they're getting old. They have regrets and want to fix their past mistakes."

"You met them, Auntie?" Bình asked.

"Don't you read the papers?" With the cigarette in her mouth, the woman combed through a stack of papers at the lower level of her cart, pulled out a page from a newspaper, giving it to Bình. "See it for yourself."

Phong leaned over. Avoiding the written words, his eyes stayed fixed on a picture; so faded, it must have been taken a long time ago. A white man, dressed in a military uniform, and a Vietnamese woman, dressed in an áo dài, beamed up at him. They looked young and as glamourous as movie stars.

"The man is searching for his lady friend," Bình said. "It's an advertisement."

"Yes . . . American veterans, if they really want to find their ex-girlfriends or the children they'd had with those girlfriends, they place notices on newspapers and TVs," the drink seller said, blowing smoke from her nose.

Phong smacked his palm against his forehead. He couldn't afford to buy newspapers regularly and had no TV. Still, he should have known. His father could have been back looking for his mother and him.

"The advertisement, what does it say?" he asked his wife.

Bình smiled in embarrassment. She gave the newspaper to their son. "Tài, you read it. I have no idea how to pronounce those foreign words."

"Sure." Tài sat up, clearing his throat. "Tôm Sờ-Mít looks for his lady friend Lan Lan. Lan Lan used to work at Nguyễn Văn Thoại Street. Tôm Sờ-Mít met Lan Lan in 1972 when he was a mechanic at Tân Sơn

Nhứt Airbase. Anyone with news about Lan Lan, please call Mr. Thiên."
Tài continued by reading a mobile number.

Phong looked at Tài, expecting to hear more, but Tài had put the
paper down. "That's it?" Phong asked.

"Yes, Ba."

"It's expensive to place such a notice so one needs to be brief," the
drink seller said. "Trà đá, thuốc lá, chú ơi," she called out to a man who
stopped to buy a couple of loose cigarettes from her.

Phong studied the picture. He saw joy and love in the couple's eyes.
He hoped they would be united with each other soon.

He turned to his son. "Tài . . . tell me the contact number printed in
this ad again." The drink seller had said returning Americans might be
able to help. Phong had to talk to Tom Smith, whose name, when pronounced by Tài, sounded like Tôm Sờ-Mít, which was memorable, as it
meant "a shrimp touches a jackfruit."

"I can tell you," said Diễm, picking up the paper, reading Mr. Thiên's
number aloud.

Thiên meant "Heaven," and perhaps Heaven was sending Phong
light. Phong repeated the phone number, memorizing it. His family often praised Phong for how good he was with numbers. He could
memorize and calculate in his head as smoothly as a silkworm could
thread silk.

"This drink seller . . . she knows a lot," Bình whispered. "Let's stay
and talk to her."

Phong nodded and wrapped his arm around Bình's shoulder, appreciating how determined she was. She always knew how to pick herself
and their family up whenever they were let down. He pulled his kids
into his other arm. When the ground seemed to have crumbled under
him, Tài and Diễm reminded him that they were his strength.

Phong paid for three peanut candies and gave them to his wife
and children. He gestured at the newspaper. "Why do you think the
American man is looking for his lady friend, Auntie?"

The drink seller extinguished her cigarette. "They must have had a child together. I'm quite sure Lan Lan was a bar girl. . . . Nguyễn Văn Thoại, that's the old name of the current Lý Thường Kiệt Street. There were lots of bars there, serving American soldiers during the war."

Phong studied the woman in the photo. He'd been wrong about her, but her face looked pure and innocent. "What do you think about the chance of him finding her?"

"Hmm, it's been more than forty years. The woman might be dead. Or she has a family and doesn't want to be contacted. And Lan Lan, you know anyone by that name?"

Phong shook his head.

"Exactly. Lan Lan doesn't sound right. Perhaps Mai Lan, or Thanh Lan? It's been so long that the American can't even remember."

◈

AFTER THEY FINISHED THEIR TEA, Phong walked a short distance with his wife and children then told them to go home first. He needed to have his DNA test done. The drink seller had given him the business card of a Mr. Lương, saying that the man provided free tests, thanks to the help of Amerasians in the U.S.

"I want to stay!" Diễm said, her eyes fixed on a clothing store across the street.

"I want to know how they do this test on you. It's so exciting!" Tài insisted.

"You can't miss another day of school." Bình shook her head.

"Your mother is right," Phong said. "Your exams are coming up. You're very smart, but you've still got to study." Phong looked at Diễm, whose eyes were brightened with curiosity, and Tài, whose face was filled with resolve, and felt pride gushing through his body. While he couldn't finish grade one, Tài was in eighth grade and Diễm in sixth. He would do everything he could to ensure that they finished high school, and perhaps even enter university.

Bình pulled Phong away from the children so they could talk privately. "You really want to stay a couple of days, anh?" she asked.

"The drink seller said we need help from outsiders, I have to find them." Phong didn't tell Bình, but after the DNA test, he'd go back to the consulate and get some money back from Quang the visa agent. There was no way that crook could walk away like that. And he'd like to talk to the drink seller again. After she'd told him about the DNA test, a group of youngsters had arrived, ordering fresh coconuts and chattering noisily.

"But you don't have enough money to stay on," Bình insisted.

"I'll manage. You know me . . . don't worry."

"Don't do anything illegal, anh Phong—and be careful with your wallet. We have nothing left to help get you out of prison."

"Stop being my mother!" Phong snapped. He had lived in Sài Gòn long enough to know how dangerous this city could be. Still, he wished he had returned earlier. He might have heard about the DNA tests, and about the returning American veterans. His home was 300 kilometers away, half a day by bus, but he felt like it belonged to another world. There, the only news he listened to was from a public radio perched on top of a neighborhood tree. Each morning, a broadcast woke him up exactly at five o'clock. Most news had to do with government leaders visiting this city, that province, or another country.

Tài stepped in between Phong and Bình. "Please . . . don't fight." He shook his head. "I'm so tired of this. Of waiting, of begging others for a chance." The teenager's shoulders sagged as if he was an old man. "I've been thinking . . . that perhaps it's time we stop dreaming about immigrating to America. America has created this illusion that it can rescue everyone, but it has its own problems. It's not like Black people have it so easy there. I'm not sure we would be accepted."

"Ha, trứng mà đòi khôn hơn vịt hả? How can eggs be smarter than ducks?" said Phong. "You haven't seen life, Son. And you can't tell me that all these people inside the consulate waiting for their visas are stupid."

"But they might be applying for business or tourist visas . . ."

"Don't you remember the relatives of our neighbors who came back from America? They are so well-off, so educated. I just want to give you and your sister the same chance," Phong insisted. He'd believed in the American dream all his life, he wasn't ready to let his own son crush it.

"Yes I know . . . and I appreciate it, Ba," Tài sighed. "But I hate to see how trying is affecting you."

"Without trying, we'll never succeed," Bình said.

"You are the egg who wants to be smarter than his parents, the ducks," Diễm told Tài, laughing. "The egg can't be smarter than the ducks, la là lá la la," she sang, running away as Tài tried to catch her.

◇

PHONG STOOD OUTSIDE the Sài Gòn Post Office. He'd just used a public phone to call Mr. Lương, who told him to come for a DNA test the next morning.

On the phone, Phong had reconfirmed that the test was really free. Too many people had tried to cheat him, and too many more had made him empty promises. He needed to be careful, like he should have been with Quang. Just thinking about the visa agent made it hard to breathe.

He had three hundred fifty thousand đồng with him. Bình, Tài and Diễm needed the rest to get home. He pulled his hat lower. He had planned to go home right after the interview and had brought next to nothing with him. He wished he had a long-sleeved shirt to cover his arms, and his razor to shred off the stupid beard. He needed a place to lie down and sleep, but hunger dug its sharp claws into his stomach, and the sun hammered its heat onto his head. The money he had would buy him a good meal and a bus ticket home, but not a room in a cheap hostel. Where would he sleep tonight?

The Sài Gòn Cathedral stood in front of him, its redbrick walls and high domes as majestic as they'd always been. On the stone steps of the entrance, he could still see the body of his twelve-year-old self. The body that knelt, shivering beneath merciful hands. The body that wandered the streets of Sài Gòn, looking for things that could fill his stomach.

Near the cathedral was a café packed with customers who spilled out onto the sidewalk, sitting side by side, sipping their drinks. A man was struggling to unload crates of soft drinks from a parked mini-truck.

Phong approached the man. "Brother, may I help you? Shall I bring these into the shop?" He hoped to earn a tip, or a bottle of drink.

Before the man could answer, a woman rushed out from the café. "My customers are looking . . . Don't let him touch anything. He looks dirty . . . And who knows, he might be a drug addict. A thief."

"Go away," the man said, heaving a crate onto his shoulders and staggering into the café.

The eyes of those people on the sidewalk were fires that burned their marks into Phong, and he felt mortified. He walked away with his nails dug into his palms. If he punched somebody, then he'd still be a man. But Bình was right, it wouldn't be worth it. They wouldn't have the money to get him out of prison.

He should have prepared better for this trip. When the letter from the consulate arrived asking him and his family to come for a visa interview, he was so excited that he forgot what it was like in this city. Bình had suggested that they drain their pond, sell the fish, and bring the money. But he insisted that in a few more months, the fish would be big enough to fetch a good price, sufficient for them to buy new tin sheets for their leaking roof.

He made his way to the cathedral, where the sound of singing voices rose like birds toward the sky. He paced alongside the cathedral's high wall, his hands tracing the rough, red bricks. He'd prayed to God as well as his Vietnamese and American ancestors. If they heard him, they hadn't answered. Still, he said the Hail Mary prayer and thought about the kindness of Sister Nhã.

In front of the church's entrance, a woman sat, a baby in her arms, a small box in front of her. The woman's face was gaunt but unwrinkled.

She was too young to be his mother, but he still stared at her, his eyes lingering on the sickly-looking baby. He could have suffered like this baby if his mother hadn't given him away; he could have spent his earliest years on the street instead of in Sister Nhã's care and warmth.

"Má, where are you? Do you ever think about me?" Words escaped from deep within him, soft as a whisper, bitter like tears.

Facing the Consequences

Hồ Chí Minh City, 2016

Walking with Thiên and Linda to a local restaurant for dinner, Dan noticed a beggar, dressed in tattered clothing, a small child in her arms. She stretched her stick-thin arm toward him, murmuring something. The street light shone onto her face, and in her eyes he saw Kim's desperation. He wanted to give her some money but had no change left. He turned away.

Why was he feeling bad? He'd treated Kim well, hadn't he?

No. He was too old to keep lying to himself that he was the man of honor Linda had wanted to see when she looked at him.

Bánh Mì Như Lan was similar to the eateries Kim used to take him to, only bigger and more crowded. Sitting on a corner of a busy crossroad, it was filled with noise and packed with people. Instead of doors, it had counters selling many types of dry and cooked food. Customers on motorbikes drove right up to the counters to buy food without even turning off their engines. Behind the counters were Formica tables and plastic chairs. Linda wrinkled her nose, eyeing the rubbish scattered on the floor.

Thiên assured them that such a place sold authentic food. He ordered for them and soon the waiter placed the food in front of them: crunchy baguettes stuffed with thinly sliced roasted pork, pate, pickled vegetables, spring onions and coriander; plates of fresh and fried spring rolls; and bowls of steaming noodles.

Dan reached for a baguette but Linda stopped him. She fished her phone out of his backpack. Linda loved taking photos and had to bring her phone everywhere with her. He was glad he'd left his mobile, which he mainly used for work, at home in Seattle. He'd always resisted the ways technology intruded on his private life.

Linda took picture after picture of the food. She'd be posting these soon. "Done!" she said. "Bon appétit."

He picked up a bánh mì, closed his eyes, and inhaled.

"Mmm, this is good," said Linda after she'd bitten into hers.

"When France invaded Việt Nam, they brought bread." Thiên squeezed some lemon into his bowl of noodle soup. "We took the bread and made it better."

Dan chewed slowly, savoring each bite. The bánh mì tasted just as it had in the apartment he'd shared with Kim. Perhaps he could visit their old building, just to see how it had changed. As hard as he tried, though, he couldn't remember the street's name. Nor the name of the road close by the apartment where his favorite bars used to be.

The food was so flavorful, they finished everything. Dan thought he was too full but ended up sharing a fresh coconut and a seven-color dessert made with jelly, beans, and coconut milk with Linda. Thiên devoured another bowl of noodles while talking enthusiastically with Linda about real estate, the ridiculous prices of land, apartments, houses. The Communists had changed the city's name to Hồ Chí Minh, but Thiên kept calling it Sài Gòn. "Fastest way to make money here," he told them, blowing his nose into a paper tissue, "is become friend with important government officials. Or bribe them. They tell you where to buy land."

"So you own land, Mr. Thien?" Linda asked.

"Only a little bit, Madam. None of my friends are important officials, and I hate corruption."

"Me, too." Linda clinked her glass with Thiên's. "By the way, please do call us by our names. Any friend of Duy's is a friend of ours."

"Ah, thank you but I'm used to it. It's my job." Thiên waved his hand.

When the bill came, Linda converted the amount into USD. "Fourteen dollars for the three of us? We can eat here every night," she exclaimed, then took more pictures of the busy counters. "By the way, we need to exchange some money. Should we do it at the hotel?"

"Tomorrow I take you to gold shop. Rate much better."

"You have enough cash to change this for me?" She gave Thiên a ten-dollar note.

"Sure." Thiên handed her some cash, and on their way back to the hotel, Linda gave all of it to the woman beggar. "Buy some nice food for your child, please . . . and bring him home," she told the woman, then studied the face of the sleeping boy, who looked skinny and possibly ill.

As Thiên translated, the woman bowed to Linda, the child clutched tight to her chest. She was too young to be Kim, Dan thought.

At home, Linda volunteered twice a month at a shelter for homeless women. She cooked and served food, organized donation drives, talked to the women, and helped them in any way she could. Dan picked up donated items and took care of the electrical repairs for the shelter, but didn't otherwise involve himself in the women's lives. Their problems—domestic violence, mental health issues, sexual abuse, and drug dependencies—were too much for him to deal with. He admired Linda's strength and compassion.

Perhaps when he found Kim and his child, Linda would help them. Or walk away from him and never come back.

They took another route, passing several open-air bars that thumped with loud music. Excitement bubbled in Dan's chest, as if he was becoming young again. He was about to suggest stopping for a drink when Linda yawned. "Damn, I'm exhausted," she said. "I can't wait to hit that soft bed."

Dan looked around and took in the city's hectic activity. Despite his jet lag, he was full of energy. He had to make the most out of his two days here.

His watch showed 8:45 p.m. when they arrived at the entrance of the Majestic. He really wanted to see the street where Kim's bar used to be.

He hesitated then pulled Linda's arm. "Honey, why don't you go up and sleep. Give your knees a rest. We'll have a long day tomorrow. My headache . . . I need some fresh air. I'll go for a stroll with Mr. Thiên along the river."

He prepared himself for her questions, but she nodded. "Don't take too long. Jenna said the jet lag is terrible. We'd better sleep early."

"Sure." He kissed her on the cheek.

He watched Linda enter the hotel. For a moment, he thought about going after her. He thought about his promise not to let her out of his sight. But the hotel looked secure and well-staffed. Besides, Linda wouldn't go anywhere without him.

"Sir, is your headache bad? You need medicine?" Thiên asked.

"Thank you, my friend." He patted Thiên on the shoulder. "What I need is your help in visiting the street where my favorite bars used to be. But please . . . don't tell Linda, she doesn't need to know."

"Ah . . . of course." Thiên winked. "I can take you to excellent bars with beautiful girls." He edged closer, whispering, "They can dance for you in private. Sexy. Naked. Whatever you want."

"No . . . no, that's not what I have in mind." Dan chuckled, but immediately felt guilty. He cleared his throat. "Hmm . . . I used to hang out with my friends at a street near the airport. I'd like to go there, for memory's sake."

"Street near airport . . . with some bars during war . . ." Thiên tapped his finger against his forehead. "Perhaps Trương Minh Ký Street, now Lê Văn Sỹ? A veteran based at Tân Sơn Nhứt told me he used to go there. Fifteen minute by cyclo I think."

"That's it. That's the place." A cyclo trip used to take Dan fifteen to twenty minutes and cost around 100 piasters, or 25 cents. Taxis were faster but much more expensive. "Do you remember some of the bars' names?" He hoped Thiên would mention the Hollywood.

"I wasn't in Sài Gòn back then. But I heard about two streets with best bars for GIs: Nguyễn Văn Thoại Street, and Tự Do Street over there. Rex Hotel and Continental were also popular."

"I'd like to visit the street near the airport. Would you come with me? We can get a taxi—"

"I have a better idea," Thiên said. "I take you on my motorbike. You give me same amount as taxi fare going there and coming back? Fifteen dollars okay?"

Dan liked the entrepreneurial spirit of Thiên. "I'll pay you tomorrow when I get some change." He looked up, suddenly feeling anxious. Most rooms on the highest floor had their lights on. Linda wouldn't go anywhere without him. She should be safe.

Thiên had parked his bike a short walk away. Dan studied the old Honda. It was half the size of his own Harley back home and one front mirror was missing. He wasn't sure it could carry his weight but Thiên drove with confidence, maneuvering through the dense traffic, humming a song.

Soon, Dan's shoulders relaxed. It was actually pleasant to be on the bike. The heat, which had clung to him, was now easing its grip thanks to the breeze. People who surrounded him with their motorbikes paid him no attention.

Shops lined both sides of the roads, selling all types of goods, from baby clothes to metal products, to stationery. Restaurants were filled with people. It was late, but businesses were still open. One shop seemed to sell electrical supplies. Perhaps he could check it out later.

Maybe he could get some cheap stuff for his radio-building hobby. His former comrades, the few whom he was in contact with, were surprised that he'd become an electrician. They said he could earn better money working as a private helicopter pilot or a flight instructor, but he wanted none of that. He'd returned from Việt Nam with nearly two years left on his enlistment and had been assigned as a flight instructor at Fort Wolters, Texas. But he had nearly crashed a helicopter when he saw one of his students' faces melt into the face of Reggie McNair, his dead co-pilot, and yanked away the controls. The army had grounded him, given him an array of pills to take and, to his relief, changed his medical profile so he could not be sent back to combat. His last months in the army were spent supervising paper work, dazed by his medications and the alcohol with which he self-medicated. After his discharge from the army, he decided to go back to school. His service had earned him a $130-a-month allowance for college under the GI Bill and he'd used it for two years at a community college that offered the vocational training he needed, as well as some English courses where he'd indulged his love of reading. Afterward he went through his apprenticeship, joined a union, and got his electrician's license. He wanted to work with his hands, to solve problems. Being an electrician required good skills and a mind that could visualize the flow of electricity, switches, lines of incoming and outgoing power. With his job, he didn't need to talk too much to people and could dictate his own hours.

"Here we are. Old Trương Minh Ký Street, now Lê Văn Sỹ," Thiên said as they entered a large, busy road.

Dan looked around. No bars, just storefronts that sold cosmetics, clothing, and flowers. "Are you sure this is it?"

"Yes . . . I already took quite a few vets here. It's a long road."

They passed a new-looking church, a pagoda, and a petrol station. These buildings hadn't been there before. More florists, clothing stores, restaurants, tea houses, and hotels. The only thing that resembled a bar was a modern beer garden.

When they passed a railway that cut across the road, Dan tapped Thiên's shoulder. "I remember this. My favorite bar wasn't too far from here. It was called the Hollywood."

Thiên stopped alongside the road. "Let me ask around. Stay with my bike."

As Thiên went into a store, Dan felt something eerie, as if someone was standing behind him, holding up their hands, ready to grasp his neck. He spun around. The traffic was rushing by, ignoring him. He pushed the motorbike up on the sidewalk, toward the narrow wall of a shop. He stood facing the road, his back against the wall.

He waved when Thiên returned. "Any luck?"

"Nobody knows Hollywood Bar."

They traveled up and down the street. Thiên patiently talked to many people but they all shook their heads. Dan didn't see anything familiar. In his nightmares about Việt Nam, nothing had changed. How ridiculous of him to not have anticipated that the old Sài Gòn was gone. The Vietnamese had built themselves a new city. A city that no longer needed to suckle from America.

Dan looked around. Perhaps he could try to locate the apartment instead. "Mr. Thien, I have a good friend. Larry. He used to rent an apartment for his Vietnamese girlfriend around here. He asked me to check the building out, take some pictures for him." It would have been better to tell Thiên the truth since he needed Thiên's help to find Kim, but he had to be careful since Linda was involved. He had to protect his wife.

Thiên looked at him sharply. "You have the address?"

"Larry said it's on a small lane not too far away from the railway."

They drove. Thiên turned into a path that cut into Trương Minh Ký. Dan gazed at the tall, narrow houses lining up on both sides. The street where he'd rented the apartment used to have tamarind trees, and Kim had sometimes picked their fruit to cook delicious sour shrimp soup for him. He couldn't see any trees now. Just concrete, people, shops, and motorbikes.

"Your friend Larry, what's his girlfriend name?" Thiên asked.

"Kim. She worked at a bar."

"Kim was a popular name for bar girls. Not a real name."

"Really?" How stupid of him not to have known. All that time, Kim had used a fake name. What else did she lie about?

After going through many small lanes, Thiên returned to the main road. "Let me ask about the Hollywood Bar once more."

Dan nodded, telling himself he'd give Thiên a generous tip.

Thiên approached a man standing next to a motorbike at the corner of a crossroad. The man seemed startled as he saw Dan. Then he looked at Thiên with such an intense gaze, as if he was about to weep. Thiên and the man exchanged words for a while.

"I feel so bad for that man," said Thiên as he drove Dan away. "He works as a motorbike taxi driver. Like me, he used to be an ARVN soldier and was imprisoned in a reeducation camp. When he was in the camp, his wife left on a boat with his children. He's been waiting for them since. Thirty-eight years, imagine that? When he saw us, he thought his wife had sent us to look for him. He thinks she made it to America and you are her friend." Thiên choked up.

Dan looked back at the man. Thirty-eight years of waiting. More than thirteen thousand days of longing for one's wife and kids, not knowing whether they were dead or alive.

He thought about Kim. Her swollen stomach. Her hands stretching toward him. Her telling him that the child was his. Was she waiting for him?

In front of the beer garden where they stopped, an old man sat, begging. Thiên gave him some money. Inside, Thiên ordered a plate of grilled pork, a glass of fresh beer for himself, and a lemon soda for Dan.

"You don't drink?" Thiên asked.

"Not anymore." Dan had been sober for five and a half years. He'd told his sister but she didn't believe him. Too bad she wasn't able to see it for herself.

He had managed to find Marianne a few years after their mother's death, but she'd refused to come back to Seattle. The memories of it were too much, she'd said. They had talked on the phone a couple of times and he'd driven across the country for four days to see her in Vermont. Things had gone decently at first, but then he'd gotten drunk. She kicked him out of her house, yelling that he was just like their father. She'd since moved to Australia, farther away from him.

Most tables in the beer garden were full, surrounded by men whose faces were flushed from drinking. Some were loudly counting one, two, three in unison before clinking their glasses and downing their drinks in one gulp.

Thiên raised his glass. "Trăm phần trăm. Bottom up!"

They clinked glasses. Dan took a gulp of his soda. Thiên finished his beer in one go. A waitress, dressed in a red dress that was so short that her underwear almost showed, filled Thiên's glass. At the table next to them, a man picked up his guitar. Music floated from his fingers, rising into the air, drowning out all other sounds. Dan wished Linda were here. She would have enjoyed this, seeing how the locals spend their evening.

When the man's singing voice climbed up, dipped, and rose again, Dan shivered. The lyrics sounded familiar, as if coming from the marrow of his memory.

Thiên sang along, then smiled. "I love this song, written by Trịnh Công Sơn. We call him the Bob Dylan of Việt Nam."

"Oh, I remember now. Kim used to sing his songs."

"So you were close to Larry's girlfriend?" Using his chopsticks, Thiên dipped some herbs wrapped around a piece of pork into a bowl of fish sauce, where chopped chili and minced garlic accentuated the amber color.

"I didn't know her actually." Dan forced a laugh. "Larry said his girlfriend adored a songwriter who was regarded as the Bob Dylan of Vietnam." He couldn't tell Thiên this, but Kim used to recite long sections of an epic poem that contained thousands of verses. During their nights together, she'd often sent him to sleep with those verses, or a lullaby, or a Bob Dylan of Việt Nam song.

He found himself comparing Kim and Linda. Unlike Kim, Linda wasn't a reader. He had given her books written by other vets, books in which he could see himself as clearly as if they were mirrors. He hoped they would help Linda understand him better, but she left them on the shelves, unread. She didn't care much about poetry. Once she'd said she didn't understand poetry, nor why people wrote poems. For him, poetry was the language of the soul. Writers could hide their feelings behind fiction, but had to bare their soul to poetry.

Kim would understand what he meant. If he'd met Kim in a world without war, would they have had a chance? He wasn't sure, but he yearned for a partner with whom he could share his love for reading. For him, a conversation about books represented the most intimate discourse. It revealed a person's values, beliefs, fears, and hopes. Experiencing the same books enabled people to travel on similar journeys and brought them closer together. Dan had found that at the book club he and his veteran friends had been treasuring for years.

Was Kim still reading these days, and was she happily married? He hoped so. And he was again gripped by the hope that their child had survived.

Many years ago, while catching the train home from work, he'd found a copy of the *New York Times* on an empty chair nearby. A boy stared at him from one of the pages. Born to a white GI and a Vietnamese woman, the boy had been abandoned during the war. After reading the headline and the first paragraph, he folded up the newspaper, returning it to the seat. He told himself that if Kim had given birth, she would have taken care of their child. A dedicated Buddhist like her wouldn't have given up her own kid. She'd always managed her situation well and overcome many obstacles. And her sister was there to help.

Now, thinking back to the article, a lump rose up in his throat. He turned away and looked out to the road. Kim or his child might be passing by him right now, on one of the many motorbikes and scooters, and he wouldn't even know if it was them.

Once the singer had finished, Dan turned back to the table. "Mr. Thien . . . once I read about kids of American GIs here. The article said they had a difficult time. Is it true?"

"Yes . . . many GI kids were homeless. We called them bụi đời, which means the dust of life. Some GI kids were lucky to make it to America, but not all."

"You know GI kids who are still here? How are they doing now?"

"They're mostly poor. Many didn't have a chance to go to school, so finding jobs is difficult." Thiên took a pack of cigarettes out of his breast pocket. "You smoke? No?" He lit one and inhaled, blowing smoke through his nostrils.

Dan leaned closer across the table. "I have some questions. But . . . the things we discuss tonight . . . please . . . don't tell Linda. Don't mention anything to our common friends Mr. Duy nor his wife. In fact, I'd be grateful if you can keep this to yourself." It was risky to ask Thiên to conceal things from Linda, but he had no choice. On the other hand, Thiên was a vet, he would understand how complicated the war was.

"No problem." Thiên finished his second beer. He snapped his fingers. As the waitress filled his glass, he told her something, which made her flush. She bowed and went to the next table. Dan winced as Thiên leaned back in his chair, his leg on another chair. Dan wondered what type of a person Thiên really was. He had acted like a polite tour guide while on duty, but no longer. There seemed to be two people in Thiên: the compassionate one who'd cried for his former comrade and given money to beggars, and the married man who flirted. But who was Dan to judge? After all, he'd done much worse.

"So . . . what questions you want to ask?" Thiên gulped down his beer.

"Well . . . I told you about Larry. He's a very good friend. He was here from 1969 to 1970. When he left, his girlfriend, Kim . . . she was pregnant. Larry wanted to keep in contact with her but it wasn't possible. And now, with me being here, Larry asked if I could look for her. He wants to keep it confidential . . . He's married, and his wife has no idea."

"Sure. We all have secrets to keep." Thiên took a drag of his cigarette, studying Dan through the smoke. "You have a picture of Kim? Her address? Full name?"

"No . . . not anymore. But Larry remembers that Kim had a sister. Both of them used to work at the Hollywood Bar."

"We already asked about that bar. No luck."

"Perhaps we haven't met the right person . . . You think you could go back tomorrow and ask around for Kim and her sister? The Hollywood Bar was well known. And Larry . . . he wouldn't mind paying for your time."

"But it's difficult. Kim was a popular bar girl name. Her sister may not be a real sister."

"I'm sure that was her real sister, working in the same bar. They were very close. People might remember them. Their father was sick, and Kim wanted to be a doctor."

"You remember what they look like?"

"Well . . . I didn't meet them. But Larry said Kim had long hair, brown skin, and she was slim."

"That could be any bar girl." Thiên chuckled. "You American men . . . you boom-boom bar girls, have children with them, yet you don't know their names or who they really are."

Dan winced. Yes, he didn't know much about Kim, but he did care about her. He appreciated the many things she'd done for him, and the ways she'd tried to save him.

"It's not me who's looking for Kim, Mr. Thien. It's Larry," he said, hating it that he had to lie, but he needed to protect his marriage.

"Whatever." Thiên flicked the ashes of his cigarette on the floor. "Whoever your friend Larry is . . . if he wants to look for Kim, I hope he has good intention. I know men like him who come back here to find our women, only to break their hearts again. Some of you guys are selfish and ignorant. During the war, you used our women for sex, and now some of you use them to be able to feel better, to get rid of your guilt."

Dan blinked, stunned by Thiên's sharp words. "Larry isn't like that, Mr. Thien. He wants to find Kim to meet his responsibility as a father."

"You sure?" Thiên blew smoke out of his nose. "Recently I help an American vet find his girlfriend. After forty-five years. I was happy at first but he made her miserable."

"Why? What happened?"

Thiên sighed. "The guy is insensitive to our culture. He made the woman think he still loved her, then disappeared again. He doesn't want to talk to her now that he knows she is alive. I feel so bad for her. Rejected twice by the same man."

"But why did he want to find her in the first place? Did they have a child together?"

"Yes . . . but the child died when it was a baby."

"I'm sorry to hear that. My friend Larry . . . he's considerate. I know he cares about Kim and won't hurt her again." Dan appreciated Thiên being frank about the consequences. If he found Kim, he had to be clear that he loved his wife, so there would be no misunderstanding. But what if Kim still loved him and his feelings for her returned once he saw her again?

"If you're sure Larry is careful," Thiên rapped his fingers on the table, "then I can help him. I help GIs look for their kids. It's a part of my job on top of being a tour guide."

"Really? How many veterans have you helped? Did many of them find their kids?"

"Quite a few GIs over the last ten years. Some found their women and children, but not many. Work is difficult and needs time."

"Larry doesn't have time. He's getting old, and he's sick."

"Tell Larry to publish notices on newspapers and on TV."

"But that would cost a lot of money, no?"

"Very cheap for Americans. Fifty dollars for a short search notice in a national newspaper."

"That's quite affordable, but I have to ask Larry. As I said, he wants privacy."

"My fee's also very cheap for Americans. Tomorrow night I can go back to Trương Minh Ký Street. I can do many other things to help find Kim. My starting fee is one hundred dollars. If we find Kim, Larry should give me more."

Dan didn't need to think. He gave Thiên a one-hundred-dollar bill. "By the way, Larry said Kim had a small scar above her right eye, caused by a childhood accident."

Thiên took out a small notebook and started writing. "What did your friend Larry do?"

Dan wanted to say Larry was a Marine but Thiên needed the right information. "He was a helicopter pilot."

"So his job was just like yours?"

Linda and her mouth. He'd told her that if Thiên asked, she could say he was a vet, but nothing else. They'd talked frequently before this trip and he wondered what else she'd revealed to Thiên.

Thiên's phone rang. He picked it up, laughing and shouting into it. He turned to Dan. "My cousin. I'm very late for his birthday party."

◈

WHEN THIÊN DROPPED Dan in front of the Majestic Hotel, his wristwatch showed 11:05 p.m. He should go up to the room. He'd been gone too long and Linda could be anxious, if she wasn't sleeping. But all he wanted was to be by himself.

He crossed the street and stood leaning against the railing that ran beside the water. The river was Kim's hair, black, smooth, stretching until eternity. He recalled how she'd caressed his naked body with her hair, how she'd made him laugh, their passionate lovemaking, the meals that they'd shared, the fights that they'd had. Upon reflection, he was shocked at how intensely he'd felt for Kim while being in love with Linda. As if he could love two people at the same time. But were his feelings for Kim love or lust? He wasn't sure, but he was certain it wasn't pure sex. Kim had enabled him to see that Vietnamese people were just like Americans, neither barbaric nor pitiful as his training had taught him.

He gripped the railing. He realized now that what he'd done to Kim was the deepest cause of his regrets. He had to find her and his child. Knowing that they were okay would enable him to make peace with the person he was, with the decisions he'd made. Perhaps he was selfish, like Thiên had said, but he felt certain that Kim would want him to get in touch if she'd had a child with him. If he found her, he'd be respect-ful. He'd try to find the best solution so that he wouldn't hurt Kim nor Linda.

He only had two weeks in Việt Nam and two days in Sài Gòn. He had to make the most out of his time.

What if tomorrow he pretended to be sick? Once Thiên took Linda on the day tour, he'd rent a taxi and go looking for Kim himself. Before that, he'd ask the hotel to let him use their computer; he'd search the internet for the Hollywood Bar. Perhaps Kim and her sister were on Facebook and he could find them somehow.

He shook his head. It wouldn't be fair to Linda. She'd planned for this trip as a vacation but mainly as a kind of geographic therapy for him. Perhaps the right thing to do was to confess, but that could very well ruin their marriage.

The more he thought about it, the heavier his feet became. He doubted he'd be able to find Kim behind Linda's back, and that he could avoid hurting both women at the same time. By finding Kim, he might risk losing Linda and their life together. But by not searching for her, he'd forever be tormented; his trauma would never be healed, and he'd never have a peaceful marriage with Linda.

He sighed.

His room was quiet. All the lights were off, except for the dim glow of a bedside lamp. Linda knew him well: he must have at least one light on.

Standing at the entrance hall, he cocked his head. Linda must be sleeping. He bolted the door, secured it with the metal chain.

He eased his shoes off, opened the bathroom door, closed it behind him and locked it. He sat on the toilet, his palms against his face. Other vets had been returning to Việt Nam for years, looking for their children, but not him. Kim and his child might have been abused and hungry while he'd enjoyed a comfortable life.

"I'm sorry," he whispered. "I'm so sorry."

Tears flowed down his cheeks. He sobbed uncontrollably.

It took a long while for him to calm down. A headache blurred his eyesight. The goddamn wound in his head was giving him trouble again.

He tiptoed toward the bed. He looked for Linda and his mouth opened. She wasn't there.

"Honey," he called.

"Linda." He pulled the duvet away. He checked under the bed and behind the curtains.

"Linda!"

He rushed to the window. The Sài Gòn River was there, a calm black sheet. The street was almost empty. A motorbike zipped by.

He jumped toward the phone, dialed reception. He beat his fist onto the table as the phone rang and rang.

A click at the other end. "Good evening. May I help you?" a girl's voice said.

"Have you seen my wife? Linda . . . Linda Ashland."

"Oh, the lady with blond hair?"

"Yes, for God's sake. Where is she?"

"She was here, Sir. She talked on the phone, but she's just gone upstairs."

Someone rapped at the door.

"Who is it?" he shouted.

"Open the goddamn door!" Linda screamed.

He pulled it open. Linda stood, her face red, her lips quivering.

"Where have you been?" he said. "You freaked the hell out of me. I thought you'd been kidnapped."

She avoided his gaze, stepping inside. Her shoes were on the floor of the entrance hall and she swung her leg, kicking them, sending them flying toward the middle of the room. She grabbed her suitcase.

Behind the Dark Room

Sài Gòn, 1969

Trang took another step back from the soldier. There was no way she'd go to a private room with him.

The tiger madam clicked her tongue. "Now . . . don't be silly. You're lucky he likes you. Look how handsome he is. And how young."

"No, Madam . . . He's drunk."

"She a virgin? A cherry girl?" the soldier asked the tiger madam, swaying to the music. He eyed Trang's chest.

"For sure she is. Fresh from the countryside."

The soldier pulled out some bills. "I want a short time with her."

The tiger madam nudged Trang. "That's a lot of money. Take it. No need to buy a ticket for a short time this time."

"No." Trang took another step back.

"Are you stupid or what?" She grabbed Trang's hand, her long fingernails digging into Trang's skin. "He's one of our best customers.

No one is allowed to make him unhappy." She caressed Trang's cheek. "Come on, beautiful . . . He's impatient. Look, he's already eyeing some other girls."

"Madam, I don't want to."

The woman tried to push the money into Trang's palm. "No need to share with me this time."

Trang pulled her hand away, shaking her head.

"Think you're so good?" the madam hissed. "I thought you wanted to help your parents with their debts."

"I do, but—"

"Well, I won't ask you again. How many customers did you have tonight, huh? One! And he didn't buy many drinks." She signaled toward Quỳnh, who was flirting with another man. "Watch how well your little sister is doing. That's her third customer. She's meeting her quota. It looks like you'll have to go back to your village and she can stay."

The tiger madam returned the money to the soldier. She got on her tiptoes and whispered something into his ear. He shook his head and went to the bar, grabbing a girl by the waist, dancing with her.

Trang found a vacant table, sat down and waited. Her eyes were fixed on the entrance, but no new customers came in. Quỳnh was doing well; her man was buying her one Sài Gòn Tea after another. Trang's chest grew heavy. She couldn't leave her sister alone here. She had to stay, to protect Quỳnh.

When the clock above the entrance showed nine thirty, she bit her lip. She only had one more hour until the bar closed due to the city's curfew. She looked for the tiger madam. "The back room, Madam, is it just for a private chat?"

"You don't have to do anything in there that you don't want to." She then turned toward a bartender, shouting, "They're asking for more drinks. Are you deaf as well as blind?"

When the soldier finished dancing, he returned to Trang and

gestured toward the back room. Trang closed her eyes and nodded, cold sweat dampening her neck.

The back room was dark, lined with sofas and filled with the murmurings of other couples. Trang folded her arms across her chest.

The soldier tapped on a sofa. "Ngôi xuong đi em."

Trang told herself to stay calm as she sat down beside him. If they talked, he wouldn't do anything to her. "Your Vietnamese is good," she said. "Where did you learn? I can help correct your accents."

The soldier inched closer to her. His lips were wet on her cheeks, his breath ripe with the pungent smell of liquor. She pushed him away. "Madam said we only talk."

"Hm, talk? Yes, I like talking, too." His hand was on her thigh, slithering under her skirt.

"No." She tried to stand up. He put his leg across her stomach. He was heavy, and she wanted to scream. But she feared she'd upset the tiger madam.

"Shh." The soldier caressed her face. "We shouldn't disturb other couples."

"Please . . . I don't want to be here."

"Come on, sweetheart, be a good girl." He reached for her shirt.

She tried to get up, but his strong arms held her back.

"You're lucky I'm in a good mood." He chuckled. "Is it your first time with a man? Hmm, your shyness turns me on. Just stay calm. Don't you want your madam to praise you?"

His hand left her body, but his leg was still on her stomach. She felt him fumbling with something and heard a zipping noise.

"Touch me." He reached for her arm, placing it on his chest. He had opened all of his shirt buttons and his chest hair reminded her of the pet monkey her neighbors had kept in their back garden. She shuddered, pulling back.

"Please, sweetheart." He found her fingers and guided them down to his thighs.

"No." She snatched her hand away. Heat rushed to her face. Did she just touch the man's private part?

"Don't be shy, little darlin'," he whispered, breathing hard. Before she had time to react, he wrapped his arm around her, pulling her toward him. He kissed her hard on her lips. She struggled, freeing her mouth but found her face being pinned onto his sweaty chest. She turned to breathe, and in the dimness, saw his hand moving up and down on his sexual organ.

She closed her eyes in disgust. His body tensed up like a rock under hers. He started to moan, whispering American words. Was he calling someone? Was it the name of his girlfriend, for he uttered it with such tenderness?

She bit her lip to stop herself from screaming. She thought about Hiếu, who'd walked her home from school hundreds of times, and later from her home to the rice field. She'd never let him hold her. They'd never kissed. She wanted to be a good girl, the girl who remained a virgin until her wedding night, the girl with the four virtues her Má had taught her.

The man shuddered as something hot and sticky shot toward her face. She turned away, trying to stop herself from vomiting.

◆

TRANG WALKED INTO the night after the bar closed. The street was empty, lit up by lightbulbs suspended from tall metal poles. A wind swept through the air, sending a piece of paper swirling toward the black sky punctured by flares. She wished she could fly up like that piece of paper, above the streetlamps, above the half-moon. Only then could she be alone with all the darkness in the world.

Quỳnh walked in front with the other girls. Trang stayed behind, her head bent. When she had left the back room, she'd gone to the toilet and locked herself inside. After a good cry, she stepped back into the bar. She just sat there staring at Quỳnh as she talked to another man.

Whenever Quỳnh turned, she looked away. She couldn't meet Quỳnh's eyes anymore.

She thought about home and fought back tears. When the problems first started with the lenders, she'd been angry with her parents for having been swayed by the con man. But after reflecting, she saw how her parents had tried all their lives to give her and Quỳnh the best possible opportunities. They had even dreamt about making enough money to send their two daughters overseas to study. That had clearly been a mistake.

Ahead of her, someone had stopped and was waiting for her.

"Our madam said both you and Quỳnh did good tonight," Hân said. "You earned well, so you can stay. Well done!"

"Why didn't you tell me?" Trang gritted her teeth.

"Tell you what?"

"The back room."

"Oh, someone asked you to go there already? You lucky girl."

"You should have told me, Hân."

"Come on, Trang. The back room, we call it the fun room. You go there, have fun with your soldier and get paid. Isn't that a good deal?"

"No, Hân. I don't want to do the things people do there."

"You mean you're better than us?" Hân snorted. "Look . . . I know this is new to you, but boys and girls do these things all the time. We give each other pleasure. Didn't you like it when he touched you?"

Trang looked away. How disgusting that Hân talked like this. She'd thought Hân was innocent. She'd trusted her.

"You didn't let him do anything to you?" Hân gasped. "Well . . . I hope he still paid you. I assume you haven't had a real boyfriend, but soon you'll like it. You know . . . men can give us a good time."

"Hân, please . . ."

"Hey, I'm being honest with you. You should know that these soldiers, they don't just want drinks. They want our bodies. The happier we make them, the more they pay us."

Trang glared at Hân. "I'm not a whore. I don't want to be."

Hân paused in her steps. She opened her mouth and Trang thought harsh words would come rolling out. But Hân shook her head, looking down. The silence felt like a stretched rubber band between them. Hân released it with a deep sigh. She lifted her face. "You can call me a whore, Trang, but I'm proud to be doing this for my family. And these American soldiers, they're here to save us from the savage Communists. Believe it or not, I want to make them happy. So go ahead and call me whatever you like."

Hân turned and quickened her steps, joining the girls ahead of them.

◈

LYING ON THE sedge mat spread on the floor, Trang's body ached. Next to her, Quỳnh was snoring. Trang closed her eyes but images flickered in her mind. Images of the mustached soldier weeping, of the tall soldier moaning, of Tina calling her younger sister an ugly pig, of Hân standing on the street with hunched shoulders. Images of her father reduced to lying in his bed, of her mother bending her back in the rice field, of the lenders charging into her home and taking away anything of value. Images of dead people scattered on the village road after the Tết Offensive, when the Communists launched vicious attacks on the ARVN in her village, images of the VC suspect dangling from the tamarind tree on that bright Sunday morning. These memories filled her vision, then her brain, the pain spreading to her chest. She sat up, panting, her arms squeezing her rib cage.

She had to calm down. She took a deep breath, held it in her lungs and let it roll slowly out. After another inhale and exhale, her heartbeat slowed. She stared out at the balcony. To ease the heat, Hân and her roommates had left the balcony door open, and Sài Gòn's life streamed in. Sounds of a baby crying and a mother humming a lullaby. A dog barked. A rooster crowed. Wheels of a bicycle rolling down the street.

Soft bell of a cyclo. Hurried footsteps of someone, perhaps a street seller. Rumbling of airplanes from Tân Sơn Nhứt Airbase. The hooting of a train that blared then faded into darkness.

A soft rustling from inside the room. She turned. A shadow was rising from the bed to her left, making its way out to the balcony.

She followed, careful not to wake Quỳnh. Outside, the sky was still lit up by flares that exploded and hung in the air for several minutes. Her mother would be thrilled to see so many graceful arcs of light; she'd sewn pillow cases from the flares' white cloth parachutes and made storage boxes out of their aluminum pipes.

The balcony was narrow and cool, dimly lit by a streetlight several meters away. A girl stood, a red dot floating in front of her face.

"I didn't know you smoked," Trang whispered.

Hân turned. "Can't sleep?"

Trang shook her head. "I'm sorry . . . for using that word . . . you know."

"You're right. That's what I am. A whore." Hân took a drag of her cigarette, smoke spiraling out of her mouth.

"May I try?" Trang asked.

"Why? It's bad for you," she said, but gave Trang the cigarette.

Trang tried to imitate Hân. As she inhaled, a bitter taste invaded her tongue, mouth, and throat, she coughed and choked.

Hân laughed, patting her back. "You okay?"

Trang nodded, her eyes teary. Holding the cigarette between her fingers, she stared at its red dot. "Hân, I'm thankful you're helping us earn money. . . . But I didn't expect it to be like this. You said we'd be drinking Sài Gòn Tea only. I hung on to those words and let them take me and my sister here."

"If I'd told you everything, would you have come? Back home, what can you do, huh? You want to waste your life away working in that rice field?" Hân snatched the cigarette from Trang. The red dot blossomed as she inhaled. "I put my job on the line for you and Quỳnh by bringing you to the bar." She blew out a plume of smoke. "But if you want to quit, just go home . . . Leave in the morning if you want to."

Trang swallowed. In addition to the amount she'd given her mother in the envelope, she'd borrowed more from Hân to pay for the bus tickets, the cyclo ride, and dinner last night—a quick bowl of noodle soup on the pavement opposite the bar. "Quỳnh and I counted the money we made. It was good . . . but we'll need a week to pay you back."

"You know . . . you were much better than me at school," Hân said, shaking her head. "You worked so hard, and I always thought you could become whatever you wanted to be."

Trang reached for the cigarette. The second drag tasted less bitter. "If I have money"—she coughed—"I'll be able to study and become whoever I'm destined to be."

"You want to study more?"

"Sure . . . I'd still like to be a doctor." Trang closed her eyes. Her father's doctors had saved his life, but she wished they'd do more to help him walk again, not to mention cure him of his invisible wounds.

She turned to Hân. "I'm fed up with being poor, with being chased by lenders, with not having enough to eat." She stared at the horizon. If she returned home, her future would be buried beneath the rice field's mud. "I'm thinking . . . that perhaps I should give this a try. If I do it well, I might be able to save. And when this war is over, I can go to medical school."

"That's a good plan, Trang . . . or should I call you Kim?"

"Kim doesn't exist outside the bar." Trang ran her fingers along the metal railing. "I need to make money. Tell me how?"

"Ha? Just a moment ago, you wanted to leave." Hân eyed an airplane that thundered above their heads.

"I know, but if I leave, Quỳnh won't join me. As they say, I've thrown my spear, I have to follow its path."

"You won't blame me later?"

"I think I might regret it if I don't give this a try."

Hân shook her head. "Alright . . . as I said, most soldiers want to have fun with us. So here are some tips. If an American soldier asks 'you cherry girl?' he wants to know if you're still a virgin. In that case, you should act shy, cover your face with your hands and pretend you don't know. The more innocent you look, the better chance he'll think that you haven't had sex before. Then he'll pay three dollars for a short time."

"That means going to the back room with him?" Trang thought about the tall American soldier who'd paid her four dollars.

"Right. A long time means going to a private room, or a hotel. In that case, the money is double."

Trang shuddered. A long time must involve real sex.

Hân flicked her cigarette. "Trust me, sex doesn't have to be bad. If you relax, you might enjoy it, you know . . ." Trang blushed to hear the word "sex" spoken out loud. No one had talked to her about it. It was a taboo subject, something she was supposed to find out about after her wedding night.

"As I said, men can make us happy," Hân added, and Trang squirmed, thinking about the hairy chest of the American soldier and the odor rising between his legs.

"For a short-time or long-time, our madam will take sixty percent." Hân blew smoke from her nose. "That's a lot, but we need her. She protects us. You don't want to know how many crazy men are out there . . . Our madam also has to pay bribes to get us each an ID card, for example. Without this special ID, we might be arrested by the police at the bar, or on the street when we go home late at night."

"You're walking on a rope of fire, Hân!"

"Nothing will happen to us, trust me. I heard our bar is protected by giang hồ—thugs who help keep us safe as long as the money flows. Our madam is well connected, and her husband is a high-ranking government official. She seems to like you so don't make her change her mind." Hân threw the cigarette down onto the street below.

"Hang on . . . You said our madam safeguards us. What about the girl who was beaten up by the gangsters?"

"Tina hired those gangsters. That's why our madam did nothing."

Trang bit her lip. Her job was more difficult and dangerous than she'd imagined. "I've been thinking about Quỳnh, you know . . . I don't want her to go into the back room or spend the night with a stranger. She's my little sister . . . And the fact that she confronted Tina last night . . ."

"Let me talk to Tina and make peace among you guys," Hân said. "And about Quỳnh's decisions with the men, don't you think it's her choice? She's smart and seems to know what she's doing."

"She's too young for this. Please . . . help me watch out for her."

Hân nodded.

"Are you not worried about becoming pregnant?" Trang asked. "I was thinking . . . that if I get a child before being married, my parents would die . . ."

" . . . from shame, I know. But there are rubbers. If we can convince the men to use them, we won't get babies."

Trang's eyes widened.

"I only learned how to use them once I got here, of course," Hân said. "If a man puts a rubber onto his thing before he goes into you, you won't get pregnant. And you won't get bad germs from him, either."

"Bad germs?"

"Nasty things that make you itch and hurt down there. . . . But some men . . . they don't like rubbers. If you insist that they put the rubber on, they get angry and won't pay you . . ."

Trang shook her head. "You do these things with men, and you don't worry that your future husband will know?"

"How will he?"

"Well . . . you won't be bleeding on your first night."

Hân giggled. "Don't you know it's quite easy to fake? Chicken blood, for example . . . Men are more stupid than you think." She yawned. "I

mentioned the nurse. She checks on us every two weeks, to make sure
we don't carry yucky germs. Men come to our bar because they know
we're clean."

"She checks the men, too?"

"I wish. . . . Apparently only us girls are supposed to carry diseases."

◈

THE NEXT DAY, Hân asked Trang and Quỳnh to get ready for
work early. She wanted to introduce them to the other bar girls. "Talk
to them before you put on makeup. Let them think you aren't as pretty
as them," Hân said. "And don't forget to tell them you know the rules
and that you won't steal their boyfriends."

On their walk to the bar, Hân said competition among bar girls was
normal, and that each of them had to fight for her own survival. Most
women working at the Hollywood came from the countryside. Some
had brothers or fathers who'd been killed in the war. Some were simply
poor.

Tina wasn't there when they arrived and Trang felt the tightness
in her shoulders ease. While Quỳnh joined a group of women sitting
around a table in the center of the bar, Trang made her way to another
table. She bowed to three women who sat there: two girls around her
age and a woman in her forties who were putting on their makeup.
The older woman pointed at an empty chair and gestured for her to sit
down.

One of the girls introduced herself as Lan, her friend as Trịnh, and
the older woman as Oanh. "So yesterday was your first day, huh?" Lan
said, applying powder to her face. "What a scene you made . . . with the
American who wanted to go to the back room with you . . ."

Trang looked down at the table covered in water stains. She was
afraid she would always be tainted by men who touched her in this bar.

"You look ashamed." Oanh painted a deep red color on her lips. "Are
you ashamed to be here?"

Trang wanted to say yes, but didn't want to offend the women. She asked instead, "Sisters, may I ask how it is for you to work here?"

"I heard you come from a small village like me? Yes? So let me tell you something," Lan said while applying her mascara onto her thick lashes. "I think it's liberating to be here. You have fun, you earn money, and you don't have to labor like a buffalo under the hot sun all day long."

"Before this, I had to cook three times a day." Trịnh pinned a plumeria flower into her long black hair. "My parents and younger brothers bossed me around like I was their servant. They considered me dirt, calling me stupid and useless. But you know what, with the money I bring home these days, they look at me with different eyes. They don't even let me carry my own plate to the kitchen after a meal when I come home for a visit." She laughed.

"Ah, I'm different from these young chicks. I was born and grew up in this city," said Oanh, pushing her bra up so that her breasts would pop out more. "Also, I was no virgin when I started this job. I thought I was too old but it turned out some men liked women with experience." She sprayed some perfume on her right wrist, then rubbed it against her left. "I already have three children with my Vietnamese husband, you see? I wish he could take care of my kids, but he's a drunk, addicted to gambling. The money I earn here feeds, clothes, and sends the children to school. Does my husband have a problem with it? Of course he does, but until he can bring home enough money to give our kids a comfortable life, he'll have to keep his mouth shut."

Trang was astonished at the forthrightness of these women. She wished she could spend the whole afternoon talking to them, but the tall American soldier came back for her. He wanted only her. She spread out a deck of cards and offered to play but he shook his head. By nine o'clock, she counted the amount of tea her customers had bought her: three glasses.

In the back room, she didn't let the tall man take off her clothes, but she touched him down there until he shuddered and moaned. She tried to imagine the act to be liberating and empowering, just like she'd been told earlier, but only bile rose to her throat.

She went to bed with ten American dollars clutched against her chest. The man had given her five dollars tonight, the same amount she would have earned from many days of hard labor.

When she arrived at the bar the next day, the changing room was bustling. At one end, some of the girls were getting dressed, but at the other end a girl was lying on a table, her legs spread wide, her lower body completely naked. An older woman was standing between the girl's thighs, shining a light onto her private parts.

Trang pulled Quỳnh aside. "You sure you're okay with this?"

"Why not?" Quỳnh asked. "Remember dì Vinh from our village? I'd wanted to become a midwife like her, so I used to go past her place. Once I snuck a look behind her curtain and saw her checking a patient, just like that."

"It's not just about this, em. The work here . . ."

"So what do you expect me to do, huh? Run home to Ba and Má and cry?" Quỳnh rolled her eyes.

There was a white cloth covering the table, and when it was her turn to be checked, Trang lowered her naked bottom onto it and shivered.

"Lie down flat on your back," the nurse ordered.

"I haven't been with a man, Auntie." Trang cocked her upper body on her elbows. "Please . . . be careful."

The nurse turned to her metal tray.

Tears burned the back of Trang's eyes; she was a fish on a chopping board waiting to be split open.

"There's no way around it. It won't take a minute. I'll be gentle," said the nurse, her hand halfway into a glove.

Trang shrunk back when the woman reached for her groin. She bit into her shirt collar as the woman held her thigh with one hand, the other reaching inside her.

The pain lingered as she sat at the bar, flirted with men, laughed along with them. She laughed even though she didn't understand what they were saying. The evening dragged on endlessly.

The next afternoon, the police visited the bar. Tina had been found in her rented room, her throat slit open, her body decomposing in the heat. "Vietnamese gangsters," Hân said. "Play with fire and you'll get roasted."

"I think somebody robbed her," another bar girl offered. "She got too many American dollars. It's her fault for showing that she has money."

"Don't speak ill of the dead." Oanh glared at them. "Tina deserves our respect."

"Ha, respect for a bully?" Quỳnh flicked her hair and applied another layer of lipstick.

"Tina was illiterate, you know that?" Oanh shook her head. "Her parents believed that if a girl knew how to read and write, she'd bring trouble upon herself by writing romantic letters to boys. So instead of sending Tina to school, you know where they sent her? To a rich family; she had to work as their house maid. When she was fourteen, Tina was raped by her master. At fifteen, she ran away to Sài Gòn."

"That's why she was fierce. It was her way of defending herself." Trang brought her palm to her chest.

That evening, Trang burned incense for Tina, regretting the fights they'd had. If Tina were alive, she'd have liked to make friends with her. She felt grateful to her parents for ignoring their neighbors' ridicule and sending her to school. There'd been times when the men in her village had told her father that an educated girl would have difficulties finding a husband, that no man would want a woman who was richer in knowledge than him.

Trang became more determined than ever to earn money fast so she could pay her parents' debts and gain her freedom. She agreed to go to the back room with men she knew, men who accepted that she wouldn't let them enter her. She'd touch them until they came. Whenever they asked her for a long time, though, she shook her head. Each dollar would go a long way, but her virginity was her pride.

Trang didn't talk to Quỳnh about the back room but watched out for her little sister. Thankfully, Quỳnh didn't leave the bar to go anywhere; she did well in attracting customers and charming them into buying drinks. Her English was certainly better than Trang's.

After two weeks, they could pay back Hân the money they'd borrowed. After a month, they started sending money home. Trang calculated in her head that it would take over a year to clear their parents' debts.

Trang studied and practiced new English words each day with Quỳnh and her customers. She watched other bar girls and learned tricks to charm the Americans. She winked at them, swayed her body, and let them touch her if they bought enough liquor. She would walk away from a man if he didn't buy enough drinks. She started earning more money from tips.

Each evening, after coming home from work, Trang would scrub herself with a scented soap bar to remove all the filth. Then she would curl up on the floor, next to Quỳnh, with a book. She reread the ones she'd brought from home and devoured new titles that she'd purchased. The stories transported her into another world, purified her. As she traveled into women's tales from ancient times until now, into the lives of the Trưng warrior sisters, the Empress Nam Phương, and the poet Hồ Xuân Hương, she absorbed their strength. And she learned from Quỳnh, who considered their time at the bar as pretense, a performance, and snored like a farmer after a day of hard labor as soon as her head hit the pillow.

After a month and a half, she moved with Quỳnh into a small room they rented with three other girls. They put most of their money aside for their parents but spent some on things they needed for their job: clothes, makeup, shoes, and jewelry. And as an investment for their work, they hired an English teacher.

They studied in the mornings and worked at the bar in the afternoons and evenings. They told each other to imitate the most popular bar girls, and gradually they became popular themselves. More soldiers came in asking for "the sisters." And once Trang was able to command more and more Sài Gòn Tea, the tiger madam stopped bullying her.

Trang smiled when she helped Quỳnh put together money to send home. She wrote a long letter to her parents describing how much Quỳnh and she were enjoying their office job. "Our American boss is very nice to us. She never shouts and she's teaching us English," she wrote. "Please, don't forget to buy good food. We'll send some more in a few weeks to help settle the debts."

When Trang reread the letter, she wondered how she'd become such a good liar. She should have felt bad but strangely her body was as light as a butterfly's wings. Her parents had sacrificed their lives for her and she was proud to return their love. That night, she slept like a rice seedling and woke with new determination sprouting inside her.

After nine weeks away from home, a letter arrived. Trang kissed her mother's writing, her tears falling. Her father's most recent surgery was successful. "He'll be learning how to walk again soon. Can you believe it? It's all thanks to you girls. But we miss you. When will you be able to come back for a visit?"

She hadn't dared give her mother her real address, using Hân's uncle's instead. He lived far away from the bar but had a motorbike. They'd agreed that whenever a letter arrived, he'd deliver it in exchange for one thousand đồng. His job as laborer for a construction project didn't pay much. He'd fought with the ARVN and been injured, some shrapnel still buried inside his lungs.

Trang reread her mother's letter each night before falling asleep. She wanted to catch the bus and go home, yet she feared her parents might be able to sniff the smell of American men on her skin.

She had hoped her mother would mention Hiếu, but nothing. Once, she dreamt that he came to Sài Gòn looking for her. How ridiculous. For sure he'd found another girl. He was his parents' only son and they'd want him to marry soon and produce a boy to keep their family blood running. His name, Hiếu, meant "loyal to parents," after all. From now on, she had to forget about him.

She kept looking out for the mustached man, her first customer. She wanted to know if he was okay because he'd been so sad. Unlike the other soldiers, he didn't force himself on her. The look on his face and the way he talked to himself haunted her.

Around the middle of her third month at work, Trang saw a white man step into the Hollywood Bar, his T-shirt and jeans tight against his youthful body. Through the mist of cigarette smoke, she saw his face and her heart jumped: he was the one who'd accompanied the mustached man.

"I back soon," Trang told her customer, a big-bellied man who was smoking and chatting to another man sitting next to him. The big-bellied man nodded, pinching her bottom as she walked away.

Trang hurried toward the young man, nearly tripping on her high heels. "Your friend, where?" she panted. Standing close to him now, she could see that his eyes were tired; they were moving, looking around the bar, as if searching for someone. Finally, the eyes fell onto hers.

"Your friend, where?" she repeated.

"Huh?"

"Your friend."

"Friend, who?"

"Thì cái ông có râu đó." Frustrated, she uttered in Vietnamese.

He shook his head.

"Your friend, where?" She used her fingers to suggest the existence of a mustache on her face.

"Mustached?" The young man squinted his eyes.

"Yes. Mu-ta. Your friend, mu-ta."

"You mean Jimmy?"

"I know no name. He, mu-ta. He, me." She made a drinking gesture.

"Yeah, I remember. Jimmy talked to you."

"Where Jimmy?"

Before the young man could answer, someone snatched Trang's arm, pulling her backward. She crashed into the fat-bellied man. He gripped her shoulders, turning her around, shouting at her. Words she couldn't understand, except for one: "bitch." Chó cái.

The young man said something and the fat-bellied man screamed at him.

The tiger madam appeared by Trang's side, her face red with anger. "What did I tell you, Kim? Never flirt with two men at the same time. Never!"

"Oh, no, madam . . . I didn't flirt. I was just asking about his friend, that's all." She freed herself from the fat-bellied man, gesturing toward the younger man. "His friend was here during my first night. He had a mustache and—"

"Did he fuck you and stuff you with dollars instead of his sperm?"

Trang stared at the tiger madam, too shocked to utter a single word. But the woman was no longer looking at her. "No fight. Here no fight," she told the two Americans, who paid her no attention. They were busy shouting and pushing against each other.

"Madam." Trang pulled the bar owner's arm. "Please tell them I didn't try to flirt. I only wanted to ask about the mustached man. I was rude to him and I just wanted to apologize."

"Apologize my ass." The woman shook her head but squeezed herself between the two men. She spoke rapidly to them.

It took a while for things to calm down, and a while longer for Trang to comprehend that the mustached man was dead. Shot in the head. Fell facedown in a rice paddy and lifted away by a dustoff—the word the young American soldier used for a medical helicopter. The soldier was standing beside her on the pavement outside the bar, smoking a cigarette, talking too quickly for Hân to translate.

"Got it? Jimmy is gone. He's never coming back. So don't ask me about him again." He flung the cigarette onto the ground, snuffing it with the heel of his boot. He stared at Trang, his eyes blood-red. Before she could answer, he turned and left.

◈

THE NEWS ABOUT the mustached man's death staggered Trang. Before that, she'd thought about American soldiers as men who carried guns, who drank and smoked, who killed and tortured, and who were hungry for sex.

Now, whenever Trang was out on the street, she watched how awkwardly those soldiers moved through Sài Gòn's tropical heat, how they sweated through their thick uniforms, and how they stood out due to the whiteness or blackness of their skin and the bulkiness of their bodies. From her chair at the bar, she saw the distant look in the eyes of experienced soldiers and smelled the fear from brand-new ones. She understood that while these men had come to Việt Nam without their families, they were somehow carrying their parents, friends, and siblings on their backs—just like she was carrying hers.

The more Trang tried to understand the Americans, the more she realized each man was different. Some were kind and gentle, some abusive and violent. And those who'd gone through battles were certainly unpredictable. More than a few times she'd seen fistfights. Once, two men drew their handguns and pointed them at each other. From under a table, she gripped Quỳnh tight as the men's shouts intensified. Her mouth dropped as she saw the tiger madam, in her high heels and miniskirt, step into the narrow space between the two guns, her hands pushing the muzzles toward the ground.

A few days after Trang learned about Jimmy's death, she was practicing new English words with a customer when Quỳnh pulled her shoulder. "Sister, once you're done with work go home first. I'll be there soon," she said quickly, then linked arms with an older soldier, heading for the entrance.

Trang ran after her. "Quỳnh . . . don't."

"I'll be fine." Quỳnh looked up at the man, who bent, kissing her on the lips.

"Sister, it's not safe . . . You don't need to do this."

"Is there a problem?" A voice rose behind Trang's back. The tiger madam.

"I was just saying goodbye to my sister, Madam," Quỳnh said, and the man led her away.

"No!" Trang reached forward.

The tiger madam held her back. "We have rules in this bar. If you have any problems, leave."

"But she's too young, Madam." Trang watched Quỳnh get into a taxi.

"Well, anyone who steps inside the Hollywood is a full adult—"

Trang broke free, running to the car. "Quỳnh, please . . . You don't have to."

"I know what I'm doing, chị Hai. Don't worry." With those words, she shut the door. The taxi sped away from Trang.

◆

AT HER APARTMENT, as Trang waited for her sister's return, the sounds of occasional gunshots, of airplanes taking off and landing, made her more restless. Sài Gòn was becoming more unsafe. Rumors of new uprisings had filled the bar. The Communists had failed in the Tết Offensive but many people believed another big attack was imminent.

Trang suspected that Quỳnh had gone out for a long time tonight because of the news from home. Their parents hadn't mentioned it in their letters, but Hân's mother had told her the court had ordered Trang and Quỳnh's parents to pay a high monthly interest on what they still owed. Trang had expected this, but the news still devastated her. Her family was racing against time.

When the roosters began to crow, Trang heard the creaking of the wooden staircase. She rushed out. A thin figure was climbing the stairs, tangled hair covering her face.

"Little Sister?" Trang asked.

Quỳnh looked up. Her face was red, her eyes puffy.

Trang ran over and took Quỳnh into her arms. "Where did you go? I was so worried."

Quỳnh turned away. Her shoulders shook. Trang hugged Quỳnh tighter, her heart wrenching. Once, when Quỳnh was ten years old, she was bitten by a snake while playing hide-and-seek in the garden. Her mother had carried Quỳnh on her back, running barefoot to their village's health clinic. When the nurse tended to Quỳnh, Trang soaked her mother's shirt with her tears. She promised herself that if her sister lived, she would take better care of her. Now, she had failed not just in that promise, but in her duty to her parents. How she wished her mother was here to right all the wrongs.

"I'm so sorry, em. I'm a terrible sister," she whispered. "I should have stopped you tonight. I shouldn't have let you come here in the first place."

Quỳnh untangled herself from Trang. She sat down on the steps. "Don't blame yourself, chị Hai. You did try to protect me, but I know what I'm doing." She blew her nose.

"If it's because of the court, we can find another way."

"What way, tell me?"

"Perhaps we can borrow from the tiger madam, or Hân . . ."

"You think I haven't tried?" Quỳnh rolled her eyes.

◆

As days passed, the war pressed down on Trang, its horror vivid on the faces of GIs and in the reports of fierce battles featured on newspapers and TV channels.

"The Northern Communists and the VC are coming," Hân told the girls at the Hollywood. "They'll eat babies and rape all the women. When the day arrives, we have to darken our faces with charcoal and make ourselves ugly."

Trang shuddered. By serving American men, she'd become the enemy of the Communists. If they took over Sài Gòn, she'd surely be punished.

"The VC will burn those who've had their hair curled and chop off the fingers of those who've painted their nails," another girl said, and Trang stared down at her red nails.

"Nothing will happen to us," Quỳnh told Trang after they'd gone back to their room. "Before those savages arrive, we'll flee." She reached under her bed, felt around, and pulled out a wad of money. "Just twenty stacks like this, and we won't have to work again." She whacked the dollar bills against her hand. It was all of their savings, hidden in a secret compartment cut into the bedframe. Quỳnh counted the wad each day, adding the money they'd earned the night before. The money was to be sent home the following week.

The next night at the bar, a GI asked Trang for a long time, offering nine dollars instead of six. "I'm going home in two days, and I want you," he said.

She shook her head. As the night went on, she kept staring at her drink. Quỳnh had gone out for a long time. The war was a disease rotting the Southern Republic. She'd heard about recent attacks near her village. She had to go home to her parents soon. She couldn't let Quỳnh carry the entire burden.

When the man approached her again, she studied his appearance. He was an older soldier. His nose was crooked, his face long, his skin punctured by pockmarks. He'd taken her to the back room many times and never forced himself on her. She knew him well enough to trust him a little. After all, what could he do to her? The nurse had poked into her so often down there, she was already as torn as a beggar's clothes.

"Me cherry girl," she told the man. "You want long time? Twenty dollar."

"Get out of here. No girl ever gets that much."

She shrugged.

"You really cherry girl?" he asked.

She nodded. "You know me. I no boom boom."

He licked his lips, staring at her breasts. She pushed her chest closer to him. "You buy long-time ticket six dollar. You give me remain fourteen dollar. You no tell madam."

She put her hand between his legs. His chim was swelling. She gave it a gentle massage.

His breath was hot against her ear. "Alright, you bitch."

After he'd bought a ticket for her time, she made him pay her the additional fourteen dollars. She hid the money inside her clothes in the changing room.

The room he rented was tiny and smelled like a rat's nest. The windows were covered in dust as if they'd never been opened. The mattress was soft and the bedsheet dotted with yellowish stains.

"So . . . am I the lucky guy? You really cherry girl?" On the bed, the man reached for her legs, pulling her to him. She stared at his penis.

"Me afraid," she whispered.

"No need to be, baby." He brought her foot to his mouth, sucking her toes.

"You wait." She fumbled inside her handbag.

"What the hell is this?" He laughed. "I don't want any fucking rubber."

"No condom, no boom boom." She shook her head firmly.

"No . . . sweetheart . . . no. I paid you a lot of money, remember? I'm clean, you don't have to worry."

"I want no American baby. No condom. No boom boom."

"You're unbelievable!" the man said. She thought he'd slap her, but he took the condom and ripped open its package.

When he entered her, Trang let out a big cry. She felt as if someone was slicing into her with a knife. Struggling to breathe, she dug her nails into the mattress.

"No fast, no fast," she begged him, but he had a wild look on his face. He gripped her buttocks, pumping into her furiously. She balled her hands into fists and shut her eyes, biting her lip until it was over.

"Oh man, you were so tight!" The man rolled off her sweaty body, panting. Then he cocked his head, grinning. "Sorry, babe. Couldn't help myself."

She lifted her bottom, staring down. A red patch was spreading on the yellowish sheet, as red as rose petals. The petals which she should have given her husband on their wedding night.

She snatched the blanket, wrapped it around her waist, ran to the bathroom. She turned on the shower, washing herself. The pain throbbed between her legs. She hoped the condom hadn't broken and the man hadn't managed to plant his seeds inside of her.

After she'd dried herself, she stood, shaking. She had no more hope to be with Hiếu. He deserved someone better.

Out in the room, her customer had fallen asleep, his face turned to the door, as if he wanted to be watchful of the VC even in his slumber. Picking up her clothes, she eyed the pair of jeans he'd thrown carelessly onto a chair. A pocket was swollen, a brown leather wallet sticking out. Her heart was in her mouth as she crouched down, reaching for the wallet. It was packed with American bills, real green dollars, not the red MPC dollars. The man must have them because he was going home.

Her roommates, Linh and Hường, had often talked about how much the American government was paying their soldiers. Hundreds of dollars each month. Each monthly payment could buy several motorbikes. How unfair. Trang and Quỳnh had entertained countless soldiers for months, and the money they'd earned couldn't buy a single motorbike.

Holding the wallet in her hand, Trang looked back at the soldier;

he was still snoring. "This is for justice," she thought as she took two five-dollar bills. She wanted more, but feared he'd notice it.

Ten dollars and she couldn't sleep the whole night.

When the American woke up, yawning, she shut her eyes. She focused on keeping her breath rhythmic and her body still. She strained her ears and heard him sit up. Her body tensed at the sounds of his footsteps clicking against the damp tiled floor, of the water tap running, of him peeing. She turned onto her side, curling up like a shrimp, pulling the blanket to cover her body and half of her face. She ruffled her hair, smearing it with her saliva. If she made herself unattractive enough, he wouldn't want her again.

She closed her eyes as the toilet flushed. Sounds of footsteps moving closer to the bed. Silence. He must be standing, looking down on her. She froze as his breath warmed her face, his lips wetted her forehead.

At the jingle of keys, she opened her eyes a crack. The American hummed a song as he picked up his jeans. She thought he'd count his money, but he didn't even glance at the wallet. She closed her eyes and felt his mouth against her ear. "Goodbye, babe. Goodbye, my Vietnam."

After he'd gone, she buried herself under the blanket. Only then did she dare breathe.

◇

FROM THEN ON, if Trang trusted a soldier enough, she agreed to go on a long time with him. If she was with a man who didn't have any weapons with him, she'd check for his wallet. She kept what she'd stolen separately, under her jar of uncooked rice. She had felt powerless before, and now, by saving for her and her sister's studies, she felt she was gaining control of her life.

Taking money from men was her secret—her joy and her revenge toward American soldiers who were stealing her youth and her innocence. If it wasn't for this war, she'd be a happy girl, working hard to become a doctor. If it wasn't for this war, she wouldn't see her sister drifting further and further away from her. These days, Quỳnh didn't want to talk, and whenever they did, their conversations were shallow, as if both of them feared that if they reached down deep enough, they would touch the hearts of their pain.

◈

FIVE MONTHS INTO HER WORK, Trang saw two men stepping through the Hollywood's door. While the older man quickly found himself a girl, the younger one, blond and tall and slim, stayed near the entrance, looking as if he'd come to the wrong place.

A couple of bar girls rushed to him and Trang looked away. She was tired and unwell. Her new high heels hurt. She regretted buying such a cheap pair. She sat by the bar counter, staring at the palm of her right hand. Once, her village's fortune-teller had predicted that she'd marry and have one child. Would anyone want to marry her anymore? For sure it wouldn't be Hiếu. How stupid that she'd dreamt, once again, that he came to Sài Gòn looking for her. Her mother's letters hadn't mentioned him at all. If Hiếu missed her, he'd have sent her a message. By now, he must have guessed that her job had nothing to do with an American company.

The smell of men's cologne drifted into her nose. The blond man was sitting down on the empty chair next to her.

"What would you like to drink?" the bartender asked him.

"Hmm . . . what do you have?"

"Beer, whiskey, cocktail, you name it." The bartender gestured at Trang. "And if you want to talk to this nice lady, you can buy her a Sài Gòn Tea." Then he said something else Trang didn't understand.

The bartender winked at her. "I told him to buy you a tea every half an hour if he wants to talk to you."

She smiled and returned her gaze to her palm. The fortune-teller had also said that her lifeline was short but refused to say what that meant.

"Sài Gòn Tea?" someone said.

She lifted her head. The man was smiling at her.

She nodded.

The bartender placed a glass of beer in front of the man.

"What's your name?" he asked Trang.

"Kim." She drank the tea, shuddering, sticking out her tongue, hoping she looked convincing. Twice, her customers had checked her drinks. One man was so angry, he threatened to report the bar to the police. The tiger madam tried to calm him, and he only softened when Trang agreed to go with him to the back room for free. As for the second customer, she managed to charm him into believing that the bartender had made a mistake. For the rest of the night, though, the customer insisted that the Sài Gòn Tea cocktail be mixed in front of his eyes. Trang became so drunk, she threw up and had to spend the next day in bed.

"What your name?" she asked.

He told her over the noise of the bar.

"Your name Đen?" She smiled. "Đen mean black."

"No black. See?" He pointed at his face. "I am white." He said his name again. Again, his name sounded like Đen to her.

She nodded. "I know. Easy. Đen. Meaning black."

"No black." He laughed, shaking his head. He picked up his glass of beer and drank. When he put it down, the glass was still quite full. He asked the bartender for a pen and paper. He wrote down his name. *Dan.*

She took the pen and wrote her bar name. Kim.

"Where . . . do . . . you . . . come . . . from?" he spoke slowly.

"Bạc Liêu," she lied.

"Bat Liu?" he said.

"No, no Bat Liu. Bạc Liêu."

He opened his mouth and hesitated. "Bat, Bat Liu."

It was her turn to laugh and shake her head.

"My Vietnamese, so bad?" He scratched his head. "You have to help me. What is this called?" He pointed at a chair.

"Ghế," she said.

"Ge?"

"No ge. *Ghế.*"

"Ge, ge . . ."

That whole night, she taught him Vietnamese. His pronunciation was so terrible, she had to giggle. The laughter filled her and lifted her up. Unlike other soldiers, Dan sat a distance from her and didn't once touch her. To keep track of time, he undid his watch and placed it in front of him. Every half an hour, he ordered her a new Sài Gòn Tea. She noticed that he didn't drink much, that he smelled good, not just from the cologne but from a healthy body. Unlike most other men who frequented the bar, he didn't smoke.

When Dan left, she hoped he would come back. He was the only customer so far who'd made her laugh genuinely.

The Tree of Love

Hồ Chí Minh City, 2016

The grass at the 30/4 Reunification Park was wet from the evening rain. A cool wind cut into Phong's face. He took off his shirt and brought it to his nose. Bình had ironed it before their departure to Sài Gòn. He inhaled her touch. He hoped she'd gotten home safely with the children and hadn't run out of money along the way. He wished he had made up with her before saying goodbye, told her he was sorry. But he'd been upset about the visa and how bossy she was. When Bình agreed to marry him, people whispered that she only did it for the chance to migrate to America. They were wrong. He knew she loved him.

He used to believe that he didn't deserve love because his life was cursed. He used to believe that his parents had done something unspeakable and that he was being punished for it. The luck of his life had been meeting Bình. Her faith in him had enabled him to regain his confidence. Yet for years, he'd feared that she was just a beautiful illusion, and he would wake up to find her gone.

If the Khuấts' scheme to use him as a ticket to America had been successful, he might never have met Bình. But she wasn't waiting for him outside the Khuấts' doorstep.

That day many years ago, when the man Khuất blocked his way with a large stick, Phong had taken a fighting stance. He only needed to demonstrate a few high kicks and powerful punches before the man slipped away from his view.

After leaving the Khuấts' house, he'd gone back to the building where the American Consulate people had interviewed him. He asked them to let him reapply for a visa. He was told that once his application was rejected, his chance was small, but he could go to the Amerasian Transit Center to seek help.

Located near Đầm Sen Park, the Transit Center was packed with more than a thousand Amerasians by the time Phong arrived. Built and funded by the American government, it was managed by Vietnamese. The trẻ lai who stayed there had been homeless or came from the countryside. They were either waiting for their visa interviews, for their flights, or for another chance. Everyone's case was different, but all hoped to leave. After registering and answering countless questions from Vietnamese officers, Phong was given food to eat and a room to share with five other boys.

As months passed and his efforts to reapply for a visa failed, his hopes dwindled. Apparently, many trẻ lai had been associated with fake papers and the American government decided to apply strict rules. Phong wasn't sure what these rules were. Visa officers were the ones who decided. Those in the Center often talked about a visa officer known as Mr. Ten Percent, who rejected 90 percent of the visa applications he handled. They hoped to be interviewed by others who appeared to be more generous, but even so, some of them only granted visas to around 30 percent of their cases.

In 1997, the Center was shut down. Phong was twenty-five years old and once again homeless. He'd only worked odd jobs a few times during the last four years, and now he needed full-time employment. He went back to the bus station, only to find no job openings.

Sitting at the bus station for hours, he stared at the people arriving and leaving. Sài Gòn had rejected him like a body rejecting a foreign object. He knew that the Mekong Delta, which he'd visited countless times while working on the long-distance bus, was rich with rice harvests. The perfume of such harvests lingered in his mind and called to him. He got off the bench and hung on to the back of a truck, telling himself he would go as far as the truck would take him. After an entire day of traveling, the truck made its final stop. He jumped down. He was in Bạc Liêu, a small province on the Southern tip of the Mekong Delta. He wandered around. Noticing dark-skinned people like him, he learned that they were ethnically Khmer. They were poor but known to be hardworking. Their skin color made him feel he belonged.

He sold the four gold rings, which he'd sewn into the bottom of his bag during his stay at the American Transit Center. The money was sufficient for him to buy a plot of farmland, on which he built a small house using bamboo and coconut leaves. Once he had a roof over his head, he walked from house to house and told the farmers that he was Khmer, and could help with planting seasons and harvests. He worked hard and saved money. After a few years, he was able to buy an adjacent plot of land, where he planted rice and vegetables.

Bạc Liêu, his new home, was the cradle of cải lương music— Vietnamese folk opera; it was where the master musician Cao Văn Lầu composed his many well-known songs. Phong fell in love with the music because it mirrored life. In each song he saw the struggles and courage of ordinary working people. He realized that he needed music as much as food and air. He started going to cải lương plays in order to lose himself in the music and performances of traveling troupes. He heard Sister Nhã's cries and laughter in the voices of the guitar with its carved fretboard, the moon lute, the pear-shaped lute, the two-string fiddle, the sixteen-string zither, and the monochord. During his first year in Bạc Liêu, he learned much of Cao Văn Lầu's music by heart and started to play the đàn sến, a two-string plucked instrument.

One day, after attending the cải lương play *Phạm Công Cúc Hoa* with his Khmer friends, Phong stayed back with them at the Bạc Liêu Park. The night was dark, dimly lit by a street light. He was on the grass playing his đàn sến when a girl, sitting close by in another group of friends, responded with her singing. Her friends sang, too, but the girl's response stirred something deep inside of Phong. In her voice he could see the rice plants bloom their first flowers; the storks stretching their wings, riding on a sunset; a school of fish dashing through a gushing stream. She breathed hope and life into an ordinary song.

As he was leaving the park, the girl approached him, saying she needed a đàn sến teacher. He recognized her voice instantly. She said her name was Bình, which he loved, since it meant Peace, just like her voice. Bình was short, shorter than his shoulder. In the dim light, he couldn't see her face clearly to know her age. He said he wasn't good enough to be a teacher, but he gave her his address.

He didn't think she would actually show up and was surprised when she came two days later, in the late afternoon while he was working in his small garden. He was afraid she would turn away as the daylight exposed his skin color. But Bình behaved as if he was like her: fair and Vietnamese. She walked barefoot between the rows of corn, okra, and eggplant, complimenting how healthy they looked. She squatted down, touching the emerald lettuce heads and the red tomatoes as if to make sure they were real. "Not just a talented musician, you're a wonderful gardener," she announced.

When she left, he felt something had been born between them, like a seed being sown into fresh soil after the rain. He asked his friends about her and was relieved to find out that she was two years younger than him and unmarried. And she worked as a rice farmer, just like him.

For months afterward, she would visit him, not to learn, but to sing as he played the đàn sến. And to spend time in his garden. In between them, a tree of love started to flourish, gaining new leaves. Full moon after full moon, their music intertwined, growing roots into one another. He revealed his origins to her, and Bình said she admired him even more, knowing how much he'd gone through and how he'd managed to make a life for himself. She ignored the whispers of neighbors and friends. She didn't care that her parents and brother disliked Phong. She told him he was a good man and she trusted him. She'd previously had a boyfriend who was abusive, and in Phong she found the respect that she needed from a man.

Phong had had enough experience with women during his years on the street and in the shelter to know that Bình was sincere.

Their wedding ceremony, hosted by his Khmer friends, was simple but joyful. They sang, laughed, and drank rice wine. That night, on the wedding bed he'd built by himself, Bình kissed his birthmark as she peeled away his clothes. She told him how handsome he was and how attracted she had been to his muscled arms, toned body, and full lips.

Still, when his children were born, he wanted them to have Bình's fair skin, straight hair, and flat nose. He didn't want them to face the prejudice he'd been subject to. But his father's genes refused to fade, remaining alive in his children. Alive in their skin color, their facial features, the texture of their hair.

At least his children could have pure Vietnamese names. Tài meant "talent," fit for a boy, while Diễm meant "elegant," perfect for a girl. He especially liked it that his son had his middle name, Tấn; and Tấn Tài was also the name of his favorite singer: Lê Tấn Tài, whose vọng cổ songs enchanted Phong.

Alone in the 30/4 Reunification Park now, thinking of the woman he had married, the mother of his children, Phong wished he had his đàn sến instrument, so he could pour his emotions into music. He peered across the darkness, toward the Foreign Affairs Bureau. His eyes were moist, thinking about his Amerasian friends who had gathered with him in front of that office, petitioning their cases to anyone who listened. They'd spent many nights here, sleeping side by side, like fish in a clay pot.

Where were his friends now? Did they ever find peace?

◈

THE DNA TEST was faster and easier than Phong had imagined. It didn't involve any blood taking, just the swabbing of the inside of his cheeks. Mr. Lương, who took his sample, worked for a travel agency. He said a laboratory in America would analyze Phong's DNA and register his data with an organization called Family Tree. If any of Phong's relatives, such as his father or mother, had done the same, their DNAs would be matched, and both parties would be informed. Phong learned that Amerasians in the U.S. had been sending free DNA test kits back to Việt Nam to help trẻ lai like him who were left behind.

"Please help pass along my sincere thanks," Phong said, sitting at a table in Mr. Lương's cramped office. "Do you know if many of them have been able to find their fathers?"

"Very few . . . I just read a statistic, that tens of thousands of con lai like you are still looking for their parents," Mr. Lương said, and Phong wished the man would call him "trẻ lai" instead of "con lai."

"For the few con lai that found their parents," Mr. Lương pushed a cup of tea toward Phong, "the ending wasn't always happy. I just want to tell you the truth, so you can prepare yourself."

"Please . . . tell me more." Phong had been in the dark for too long. The world had moved on and left him behind. If he could read and had been able to follow the news, things would have been different.

"Here's a story for you," Mr. Lương poured tea into his cup. "I know this con lai, a beautiful woman . . . around your age. She made it to America. She had her father's address and photos, so she wrote him long letters. No answer. Finally she got up the courage, traveled to his city, and went to his house. She knocked on the door. When a man opened it, she knew that it was him. She told him who she was and you know what happened?"

Phong shook his head.

"The man slammed the door. In her face! He screamed for her to get off his property. He said if she didn't leave right away, he'd call the police for trespassing."

Phong shuddered. The woman had lost her father twice: the first time when he abandoned her, and the second time when he rejected her.

"She had no choice but leave." Mr. Lương shook his head. "She swore never to contact her father again. For years she hoped he'd reach out to her. But nothing."

Mr. Lương refilled his cup. "Sad stuff like that happens, Phong. So don't have high hopes."

Phong drank his tea. If he didn't have hope, not just his hands but his heart would be empty. "Do you know why the father didn't want to accept the daughter in this case?" he asked. Sister Nhã had taught him to always look past people's actions and try to understand their reasons.

Mr. Lương shook his head. "A lot of vets just don't want to accept their kids when they are found. There could be many reasons. For example, some of those men had no idea that they had fathered children in Việt Nam. Or they are traumatized and want nothing to do with their past. Searching for family members is more complicated than people think." He looked at his watch. "Shit . . . I'm running late for a meeting in town." He put Phong's DNA samples into an envelope.

"But if I find my father via DNA testing, it would mean he'd accept me, right? Because he registered his own DNA test?" There were many more questions Phong wanted to ask.

"Maybe. But people do these DNA tests for lots of reasons. And your father doesn't need to do the test himself; you might be able to locate him via the DNA results of one of his relatives, like his siblings or children."

Mr. Lương folded the consent form for Phong's DNA test, which Phong had signed with his finger prints. "Recently an Amerasian here in Sài Gòn found his father this way; his DNA results matched those of his father's sisters. I was happy for him at first, but not for long, because shortly after, he learned that the father had already passed away."

Phong gazed into his empty cup. Filling it now was the possibility that his father, who must be in his sixties or seventies now, had died. Suddenly he was afraid to learn the truth.

The Secret

Hồ Chí Minh City, 2016

D an wanted to scream at Linda but kept his voice down. It was nearly midnight and he had no idea why she was acting like this. His head throbbed, as if reminding him that it could never fully heal from the injuries suffered from the crash. When the medics were airlifting him from that stinking jungle, one of them said it was a miracle he was alive, let alone conscious, after suffering such a serious head injury.

Linda pulled the closet open. She'd hung up all her dresses neatly, as if they were being displayed in a shop, together with a large, white hat she'd ordered online. Now she yanked them from their hangers, dumping the clothes onto the bed. In her pajamas, she looked disheveled.

"What are you doing?" he asked. "You scared the hell out of me by disappearing like that."

She opened the safe and took out her passport.

"Linda." As he raised his voice, pain sprang up inside his brain. "What's going on?"

She threw her clothes into her suitcase.

"Talk to me, damn it!"

"I'm so stupid," she said, tears glistening in her eyes.

"I don't know what you're talking about."

"How did you become such a good liar, huh?" she retorted. "We've come here for a holiday, and you snuck behind my back looking for your ex-girlfriend. Or should I say girlfriends?"

"What ex-girlfriend?" His heart raced. He shouldn't panic. Linda was just guessing.

"How many girls did you sleep with when you were here? How many kids did you father?"

Dan turned away. He tried to think. She'd made a phone call downstairs. Fuck! Thiên must have told her about his search for Kim.

"I should've known from the day you came back." Linda threw her guidebook into her suitcase. "You called her name in your sleep, remember? You called her goddamn name and when I asked you, you said it was your fucking Korean comrade."

"What name?" He threw his arms into the air. "It was a lifetime ago and I don't know why you're bringing this up. And don't forget it was your idea to come here. I didn't want to be back. It was your own damn idea!" He despised himself for blaming Linda, but it was true that he'd said no to this trip. She'd believed it would help him heal and improve their marriage. And now his marriage was in deeper trouble.

She went into the bathroom and slammed the door shut. He heard the tap running and Linda blowing her nose.

He clenched and unclenched his fists. He wanted to punch Thiên in the face.

He dug into his pocket for the guy's business card while reaching for the hotel phone.

"Helloooo." Thiên said after the first ring, his voice almost drowned out by the noises of people cheering and glasses clinking in the background.

"What the hell did you tell Linda?" He kept his voice low so Linda wouldn't hear him.

"Oh, is that . . . Mister . . . Mister . . . Mister . . . Dan?"

"What the fuck did you tell my wife?"

"Oh . . . she was very . . . very upset." Thiên's speech was so slurred Dan had to press the phone tight against his ear to be able to hear him. "She wanted to know where you went. She said if . . . if I didn't tell her everything, she'd hire another tour guide. So I said . . . we tried to find the Hollywood Bar."

"You son of a bitch. You promised to keep things between us." The water was still running in the bathroom, but he watched out for Linda.

"Hey, don't be angry, Mister." Thiên hiccupped. "I told her it's your friend Larry." Men in the background started singing, banging on a table. "I know that it's you and Kim, but I didn't tell her."

Dan slammed the receiver down. For sure Thiên had told Linda on purpose. They'd behaved like the best of friends at dinner. "Selfish and ignorant" were Thiên's exact words when he talked about American vets. Telling Linda was his revenge.

Dan paced back and forth. The humming of the air-conditioning was too loud, rumbling in his head. The pain blurred his eyes. He wanted to lie down, but he needed to convince Linda that he had been faithful to her since Việt Nam.

Linda walked past him. She tossed her toiletries bag into her suitcase, zipping it up. She gathered her shoes, sliding her feet into them.

"Damn it. Can't you just sit down for a minute and talk? Thien told you some bullshit, and you believe him?"

She pulled the suitcase toward the door.

He blocked her way. "Where the hell are you going?"

"I'm getting myself another room. And you know what I hate most in my life? Liars!"

He reached for her shoulders with both hands. "Linda, listen to me. You're the only woman I've loved throughout my life." That was the truth as he knew it.

She stood still, her head bent. "You rented an apartment for Kim, you had a child with her."

He dropped his arms. The realization that Linda knew was so shocking, he felt like blood was being drained from his veins.

A tear slid down Linda's cheek. "You lived with her while you were engaged to me. And all that time, I supported you. Told everybody you were a hero. I stood by you!"

In front of his eyes, the foundation of his marriage was crumbling: Linda's respect for him. He couldn't let it happen. He would tell her the truth at the right time, when she had calmed down. "I don't how what Thien told you, but it's Larry who's looking for Kim. I haven't had the chance to tell you about him. He—"

"Don't you dare lie! If it's someone else's girlfriend you're looking for, there's no reason for you to hide it from me, and for you to weep like a baby. Yes . . . I heard you crying in the bathroom after you came back tonight, and that's why I went downstairs to call Thien. Thien only confirmed what I should have known a long time ago. It's her who made you leave your shoes outside the house, burn incense for your dead comrades, make an altar with a Buddha head. And all the other weird things you did when you first got back. Tell me the truth. Tell me everything or I'll go home tomorrow."

Heat rose to Dan's face. Linda was mocking the rituals that had helped calm him when nothing else could.

She pushed past him.

"Linda, please . . ."

With one hand on the suitcase, her other hand yanked at the door.

Dan hadn't seen Linda this angry for a long time. But he'd made a grave mistake by looking for Kim behind her back. He had to do something before it was too late.

"Honey, wait," he said. "You're right. I am so, so sorry. Kim . . . I spent time with her in Saigon."

◇

LINDA GRABBED A small bottle of Jack Daniel's from the minibar. She half-filled a glass, and threw herself down into the armchair.

Dan got himself a soda water. He should be taking something for his headache but felt he deserved some punishment. He sat on the bed, leaning his tired back against a pillow.

Linda drank her whiskey.

Looking at her, he recalled the day they said goodbye as he left for Việt Nam. "Stay alive and come back to me," she'd whispered, her tears staining his cheek. On the flight to Sài Gòn, he'd kept her picture in his pocket, only to pull it out often, gazing at her beautiful face. He'd believed that as long as he had her photo next to his heart, he'd survive. They'd both been so naïve.

He gazed at the curtain behind Linda. "Saigon was a mess in 1969 when I landed. I'd been trained for twelve months in the States but nothing could prepare me for the war—"

"Cut the crap and tell me how you met her." Linda picked up a red rose from the lacquer vase. She plucked the petals, one by one, throwing them onto the floor.

"I'm trying to explain the circumstances."

"Fuck your war stories. Don't give me that poor-me veteran bullshit."

"I understand you're upset, but I'm not asking for your pity, nor anyone else's. I'm the one who must bear the consequences of my actions. But for you to understand these actions, I need to take you back a bit. Can I?"

She looked away.

He closed his eyes. "We never talked about this, but I came to Vietnam very ignorant . . . and brainwashed. During my training, I was told that we were fighting people that were subhuman. My instructors called the Vietnamese gooks, dinks, slope heads. On my flight here, the guy I sat next to told me not to worry about killing the Vietnamese, that life was cheap for them, that they'd been at war with other countries for hundreds of years. So I didn't care about the Vietnamese at all. I figured they weren't like us." He shook his head. "Two weeks after my arrival, I went out for the first time. That night, I met a girl."

"Where?"

"At a bar . . . She was shy, very different from other bar girls. We started talking and I realized she was just a normal human being. She made me curious about the Vietnamese. During the next few times that we met, she taught me Vietnamese and I tried to teach her English. I found out that she didn't want to be a bar girl, but she had to help her parents pay their debts. Her father was very sick."

He gauged Linda's reaction, hoping she would empathize with Kim's situation.

"So you felt the need to rescue her?" Linda said bitterly. "What a noble reason to betray your fiancée."

"It was she who rescued me. The war . . . it was beyond terrible. Most guys I knew were into drugs and prostitutes. We all had to escape reality sometimes, so we could survive. At first, though, I tried to stay loyal to you. I did try . . . very hard. I was in love with you and committed to you, as I've always been. But you were far away, and I was young and selfish."

"Yes, you were selfish. I bet you destroyed her life, too. How young was she?"

"Eighteen when we met."

"And you got her pregnant? For God's sake." Linda gulped down her whiskey. She got a second mini bottle, poured herself some more.

"Go easy on that stuff, honey—"

"Now I get it." Linda gave out a small laugh. "I get why you didn't send many letters home. And your words, they were so . . . cold. But I thought you were busy with your flight missions, with saving your comrades." She took a breath. "Were you in love with her?"

"How could I be if I couldn't even talk to her properly?" Dan said. "Her English was very basic and my Vietnamese was terrible." He had cared for Kim and felt tenderness. But he had never once thought about leaving Linda for her. And by the end, if he were honest with himself, he had often treated Kim like shit, taken everything out on her as if she were Việt Nam, the war itself.

"Did she know about me?"

"I didn't tell her, and she didn't ask."

"Great." Linda plucked some more petals. They scattered down to her feet, red as blood. "So how long were you together with her?"

"A few months. I was away a lot on missions. The pregnancy . . . I didn't plan for it. I was careful . . . But there were times I was drunk. And I was high . . ."

"Here it goes." Linda lifted her whiskey. "Just blame it on the war."

"I'm not. I'm blaming myself," he said. "I was very irresponsible. When Kim told me she was pregnant, I only thought of myself. My tour was up, I was going home. I cursed her." He choked. He wanted to confess to Linda what he'd really done to Kim but the truth was too horrific, he couldn't do it. He took a deep breath. "So I gave her some money, to help with the baby. A few weeks later, I was shipped back home."

Linda hugged her shoulders with her hands, as if bracing herself for what was to come.

"I honestly don't know what happened to her after that. I didn't contact her, and she didn't have my address. Later, a buddy who returned told me that she'd come to the base asking about me. She was very pregnant then."

Linda leaned against the table, her palm against her mouth.

He crushed the soda can he was holding, absorbing the pain as its sharp edges dug into his palms. "I've lived with this guilt all these years, Linda. I was young and irresponsible. But the thing is . . . many American men stationed in Saigon had girlfriends. And most turned away from those girls once they became pregnant. It was a crazy time. We were selfish, we were scared."

Linda finished her drink. She stepped toward the window, placing her hand against the glass.

He swallowed. "Linda, I've tried to deny it for too many years, but the baby Kim was carrying was mine. My child might be here in this city."

Linda turned to him. Tears zigzagged down her cheeks. "How could you have kept this from me?" Her voice trembled with fury. "During the years I was trying to conceive, you pretended as if you knew nothing about pregnancies. You could have killed that poor woman. Young, pregnant, abandoned by you. What else . . . what else did you lie about?"

◆

DAN LAY ON THE BED, watching Linda sleep. He had been awake the whole night. His headache simmered.

Linda moaned, turned to her side. He held his breath, not wanting to wake her. He'd watched her like this during the many nights when he'd feared sleep. And just like those days, he was afraid of losing her.

Linda hadn't had an easy life: her dad had died in a car accident when she was a toddler, and her mom had to work nonstop to raise her. Her broken childhood and Dan's had been part of their bond. When they got married, he'd promised her mom he'd take good care of Linda. Once again, he'd failed to keep that promise.

Linda stirred, opened her eyes, looked at him, and turned away.

"Good morning," he said.

She shifted her body even farther away from his, and got out of bed. She pulled open the curtains, and sunlight streamed into the room.

"Want some coffee?" Dan said. "I could go downstairs and bring you a cup." At home, he was the one who made coffee for them both in the morning.

Ignoring him, she went into the bathroom. He heard the sound of water running in the shower.

Dan closed his eyes and concentrated on his breathing, hoping to get calm, hoping his headache would ease. The bathroom door opened. Kim emerged, wearing a blouse and a skirt, like the day she'd gone to the zoo with him. Tears were streaming down her face.

Your child here in Sài Gòn, anh Dan, she said. *Your child hungry. Your child need you.*

He wanted to ask for the child's name, whether it was a boy or a girl, but he couldn't open his mouth. He leaned forward to touch her arm, but he felt nothing.

The Oriental does not put the same high price on life as does the Westerner, General Westmoreland said in his ear.

You're a man of honor, Linda said.

Dan opened his eyes. There was no one in front of him.

The bathroom floor was wet, the perfume of soap lingered in the air.

"Linda," he called, searching the room again. His breathing eased at the sight of her suitcase. Her phone was on the bedside table, charging.

Downstairs, the lobby was bustling. A group of Western tourists had just arrived, chatting away next to their pile of luggage.

Thiên walked briskly to him. "Good morning, Sir." He gestured toward the sunlit window. "Fantastic weather. Perfect for day tour."

"Have you seen my wife?"

"She's having breakfast." Thiên pointed toward the hotel restaurant.

"Look, whatever the hell you told her last night, it made her very upset."

"Sorry." Thiên scratched his head. "The party last night . . . too much liquor. And Madam, she really wanted to know where we went. I can't deal with women tears. But I only said your friend Larry is looking for Kim."

"Yeah, but she isn't an idiot."

Thiên smiled. "You shouldn't worry. Wives are like that. Upset one day, okay the next. Wives need to support husbands. We men shouldn't be afraid of wives."

"It's not your goddamn business to preach how I should treat my wife. Don't you dare talk to Linda about Kim again."

The smile on Thiên's face vanished.

The breakfast buffet offered a wide range of hot and cold Vietnamese and Western dishes, but Dan didn't have much of an appetite. Linda had her sunglasses on and didn't talk to him. She'd sometimes given him strong doses of the silent treatment for a day or two, but this felt different. He'd fucked up big-time, and they were in a new country, hit by intense emotions and jet lag.

They finished breakfast quickly and met Thiên outside the hotel. "As on the itinerary, we'll visit the Jade Emperor Pagoda this morning," Thiên said. "It's beautiful, more than one hundred years old. Then we'll go to Chợ Lớn, which means 'big market.'"

"How far away is the pagoda?" asked Linda.

"Twenty minutes by car."

"If you don't mind, I'd like to wander about a little." Linda looked toward the former Street of Freedom, where shops spilled their wares onto pavements.

"Sure."

Linda started walking ahead. Thiên caught up with her. "Straight ahead are important sights which are a part of our itinerary."

As they passed Maxim's restaurant, Dan paused. Back in the old days, this two-story building had been a bustling bar and nightclub. He peered through the glass door. No one was inside, just fancy-looking tables and chairs. On the door was a restaurant menu, the writing too small for him to read. He'd like to come back at lunch or dinner time to have a look inside, see how much the place had changed.

Along the street, he searched the faces of female vendors behind newspaper stands or baskets filled with bread, flowers, fruits.

Shops lined both sides of the road, selling silk, handbags, clothing, lacquer-ware, and souvenirs carved from buffalo horns.

"Lighter from GI. Best quality. You look," a middle-aged woman called out to him. She opened a wooden box and a dozen Zippo lighters gleamed under his eyes. He studied the engravings on their metal covers. One read "Vietnam 71-72 Quang Tri" with the word *fuck* in red ink. Another said:

> We are the unwilling
> Led by the unqualified
> Doing the unnecessary
> For the ungrateful.

Such sarcastic words, but true. True to the low morale he'd seen among many of his comrades and himself. True to the ignorance of his commanders, who had believed they could bomb the Communists into surrender. True to the role of America in the war; they should have let the Vietnamese sort out their problems themselves. True to the treatment veterans like him had received back home.

"You buy, Mister?" The woman said. "Cheap price. Only for you."

"No, thanks," he muttered. He didn't need another reminder of the war.

Ahead of him, a woman ran out of a shop and tugged at Linda's arm. "Áo dài for you, Madam? You will look beautiful. Just like model there. You come in. Cheap price for you. Tailor made. Twenty-four hour."

Linda shook her head and kept on walking.

At the traffic light, he followed Thiên and Linda across the street and entered a small alley. The tall, narrow houses blocked out the sun, making him feel caged in. Electric wiring crisscrossed above his head. The skin on the back of his neck stiffened. He glanced around.

Thiên exchanged words with a white-haired woman who was holding a young boy in her arms while feeding him a golden banana.

Dan studied the woman. Her many wrinkles told him she was in her seventies. Did she work at the airbase, or at a bar? Could she have known Kim?

"She's a friend of my mother," Thiên told Linda as they left the woman.

Dan's mother would be eighty-five this year if she were alive. He had brought the war home and given it to her.

"Children will make things better," she'd told him when he said he was marrying Linda. "So, go and have plenty of babies." He wished he could have given her the joy of having grandchildren.

What would his mom say if she knew he was looking for his child? For sure she'd tell him it was the right thing to do. Perhaps his sister would talk to him once he'd found his kid.

At the sound of running footsteps, his heart raced. A group of children were spilling out of a door to his left, chasing each other, laughing. As they disappeared into a house across the street, he wiped sweat from his face. While returning from the war, he'd been on a layover in California when some kid threw a can into a rubbish bin. He dove onto the airport floor and rolled into a corner.

Still following Thiên and Linda, he left the alley and emerged into the sunlight. The statue of Mother Mary was still there, her peaceful face tilted upward, her hands holding the globe. Behind her, the Sài Gòn Notre-Dame Cathedral stood as if frozen in time. The building still bore the same reddish brick color, its twin towers crowned by white crosses. The same spacious boulevards surrounded the complex. Inside, the air was cool. Linda chose a bench and knelt, her head bent. She must be asking God what to do next. Dan wanted to pray, too; it'd been so long since he believed in any divine help. But as he neared a pew, his eyes caught sight of a woman who sat a few rows ahead. Her hair was black, long, smooth as silk. Like Kim's hair. Kim used to make her own shampoo with some dried pod fruit she grilled on open flames.

"I need some air," he told Thiên, then went outside, down the steps and into the square.

The noise and heat almost knocked him over. It was mid-morning, but the roads were packed with traffic. Too many people honking their horns. He felt the beginnings of a new headache.

"You change money, Mister," a woman waved at him, calling from a roadside café. He shook his head but she hurried toward him. "You have American dollar? Best rate just for you. Twenty thousand đồng one dollar." A conical hat in her hand fluttered in the breeze. He'd once seen the same type of hat next to a motionless woman. The rotor wash of his helicopter had flipped the hat away, revealing the woman's face, scorched and twisted. "Didya see that gook?" Hardesty had yelled through the intercom. "Looks like someone zippoed her face."

"You change money, Mister?" the woman asked.

He blinked, took a deep breath, and nodded. "Where're you from?"

"Trà Vinh. You know where Trà Vinh, Mister?"

"I don't think so . . ." Kim had told him the name of her hometown but there was no way he could remember it. Back in 1969, there'd been plenty of women who offered exchange services, sold drinks, and traded PX goods on the street. Kim could have done the same kind of work after he'd left her. She couldn't have continued to work as a bar girl while visibly pregnant. He remembered again with sickening regret how cruel he had been to her when she'd told him about the pregnancy.

He handed the woman a hundred-dollar bill.

She held the money against sunlight. "Your money no fake?"

"I brought it all the way from America, lady."

"America also fake." The woman grinned, running her fingers along both sides of the bill. She studied it once more. "I have to feed children. I careful." She opened her shoulder bag and handed him four big wads. "Two million đồng."

From the 50,000-VND bills, Hồ Chí Minh beamed at him. Dan stuffed the money into his pockets.

"You no count?" The woman giggled. "I can cheat you."

"I have no doubt." He smiled. It wouldn't be bad if a Vietnamese woman cheated him, he deserved it.

"Careful with money, pickpocket," the woman said, before running toward a group of tourists, her hat flapping on her head.

He turned back to the church. On the entrance steps a beggar was clutching a small child against her chest. He gave the woman some money as Linda and Thiên appeared, heading into the square.

He smiled at Linda. "I exchanged one hundred dollars. We're rich here, millionaires." He handed Linda a wads of bills.

Without a word, she put the money into her handbag, her eyes hidden under her sunglasses. As she turned away from him, he felt anger rising within him. He didn't know what exactly he was angry at. At himself, at the situation, or at his past mistakes. Or at Thiên.

He turned to Thiên, only to see the man shaking his head at him.

"You changed money on the street?" Thiên said. "I'm sure you were cheated. Gold shops much better." Thiên pointed at Dan's swollen breast pocket. "Watch out for pickpoc—"

"Stop telling me what to do!" Dan snapped. "I'm sick of your big mouth."

Thiên's face darkened.

Linda glared at Dan.

Heat rose to Dan's face. How dare Thiên judge the men who'd come back to look for their women and children? Whoever decided to do it was brave. For those who found their women and disappeared again, they must have had their reasons.

"That looks beautiful, Mr. Thien." Linda gestured toward a yellow structure across the road. "What kind of building is it?"

Hiring Thiên had been Linda's decision, and now the guy was her ally.

"That's Sài Gòn Post Office, built in 1886," Thiên answered.

"It looks French, very French," said Linda.

"Yes. It was constructed when Việt Nam was part of French Indochina, originally designed by Gustave Eiffel, whose company built the Eiffel Tower. Later, the building was reconstructed by other French architects."

"Really?" gasped Linda.

Dan studied the arched windows and the intricately decorated façade. He'd seen them during the war but hadn't cared.

"I had no idea," Linda said, taking off her sunglasses, admiring the building. "Gustave Eiffel also co-designed the Statue of Liberty, Mr. Thien."

"I want to see the Statue of Liberty and the Eiffel Tower before I die. But I need a job that pay better."

Dan almost laughed. How clever Thiên was, hinting about a big, fat tip at the end of the tour.

They crossed the road. Dan watched the people streaming in and out of the post office. If Kim was in Sài Gòn, she must come here from time to time.

As Linda approached the stairs leading up to the post office, Thiên signaled Dan to stop. He waited until Linda was out of earshot, then lowered his sunglasses, looking Dan in the eye, his scar twitching. "I think you don't need a guide. If you do, I don't care. Today my last day working for you."

The Danger of Fire

Sài Gòn, 1969

Trang finished her English lesson, cooked, ironed her clothes, ate lunch, and wrote down the words she wanted to say to Dan, yet it was only noon. Over the last two weeks, Dan had returned to her bar three times, and each time he'd sat a short distance from her as he practiced his Vietnamese. Through him, she'd learned new English words. And she learned that she could have normal conversations with someone, conversations that lifted her up and transported her away from the harsh reality of life.

Dan had asked her to meet him again that night at eight o'clock. Arriving at the bar, nervousness prickled her skin. She didn't want him to see her with another soldier, so until eight o'clock, she pretended to be busy. She ran in and out of the bathroom. She joined Quỳnh and her soldier, chatting with them, telling them silly stories. When the tiger madam pulled her aside, asking why she was not receiving customers, she said she was waiting for someone.

"The one from a few nights ago, who can't drink?" The madam smirked. "Don't be such a dreamer. He seems to belong to a good family, and he won't set eyes on you for long."

Trang lowered her gaze, staring at the tiled floor. Her madam was right. With her job, she'd smeared not only herself but her family with filth.

"Snap out of it, will you?" The tiger madam lifted Trang's chin, turning her face toward the bar. "See the guy over there? He looks miserable. Go make him happy."

She took a few steps forward, dreading the moment she had to talk to another stranger.

"Em Kim, em Kim," a voice said.

She swirled around. Dan was standing in front of her, a smile bright on his face.

After they sat down at a table in the corner, Dan showed her what he'd brought along: a map of Việt Nam, a small notebook, and a Vietnamese–English dictionary. He pointed at different locations on the map, North and South, and she taught him how to pronounce their names. She gazed at Bến Hải River, which slashed her country in two, and wondered if she'd ever cross it. The names of the Northern provinces sounded so strange on her tongue, as if they belonged to an imaginary planet. The North mystified her. How did the people there survive the American bombings? Were the Northern Communist soldiers as savage and cannibalistic as the rumors, which referred to them as "ăn lông ở lỗ"—"creatures who eat raw meat and live in caves"—and "đầu trâu mặt ngựa"—"creatures with buffalo heads and horse faces"? During the Tết Offensive the year before, the bodies of those soldiers had filled the river near her home. Some neighbors had gone to check on them. They came back whispering that the men looked like pigs, their bodies swollen, rotting.

Talking to Dan, though, helped her forget about the war and all its troubles. He was trying so hard to learn new words that lines deepened their marks on his young forehead. But his pronunciation was so bad, she kept laughing.

On the first page of the blank notebook, she wrote down the words she'd taught him and the corresponding English meanings. They went over the words again while other couples around them were flirting, kissing, touching each other, or dancing to the music.

She'd never asked another American about his duty in Việt Nam, but she found herself asking Dan. When she couldn't understand him, he fumbled with the pages of the dictionary. Finally, he pointed at a word.

"Fi cong. I'm a pilot, em."

"Fi cong?" She gazed at the Vietnamese translation. "Oh, you mean phi công."

"Yes, fi cong. Pilot."

"You phi công? You too young."

"I'm twenty. Old enough, em." He smiled, flipping the pages. He pointed at another word. "Chuc than. Helicopter. Helicopter pilot."

Again, she couldn't understand him. She looked at the Vietnamese translation. "Oh, you mean trực thăng. You phi công trực thăng?"

"Yes, fi cong chuc than. Helicopter pilot."

She sat frozen, her vision filled with the images of helicopters roaming the sky of her field and village. Their deafening noise. Their gigantic green bodies resembling murderous dragonflies. Soldiers with machine guns standing at their doors. She'd always associated helicopters with violence and death. How could someone as gentle as Dan be connected with helicopters?

"I no like helicopter." She stood up. "They bad." She hadn't cared what other soldiers did, but Dan was different. She wanted to tell him about innocent farmers who'd been shot from the aircraft.

"No . . . I do no bad. Come on, em." Dan also stood up.

"You have gun on helicopter?"

"What?"

"You shoot?"

Dan waved both of his hands. "No. I don't shoot. I'm just a copilot

now. My helicopter transports people. Here . . ." He showed her the
Vietnamese words.

She bit her lip. If he transported people, it shouldn't be bad.

"Hey, don't look so worried." He folded his map. "Let's talk about
something else, something that makes you happy . . . Your family . . .
Tell me about your family."

"Fam . . . ili? I no understand."

He reached for the dictionary, fumbling with the pages, and pointed
at a word. "Za dinh. Family."

"Gia đình?"

"Yes. Your za dinh. Tell me about your za dinh."

It was the first time a foreigner had asked about her family.

"Papa, Mama make rice."

"Make rice?"

"Ya. They work. They make rice."

"Ah, you mean they are farmers?"

"Ya, farmer. My sister, there." She gestured toward Quỳnh, who was
standing at the bar counter, flirting with a man.

"That's your sister? Real sister?"

"Real sister. Same papa, same mama."

"I see . . . Is she younger or older?"

"She baby sister."

"What's her name?"

"Lan." She told him Quỳnh's bar name.

She was glad Dan had brought the dictionary along. It helped her
describe how beautiful her village was: the rice fields that became vel-
vety carpets during the planting season and a sea of rippling golden
waves during the harvesting time; the river that draped its silky body
around the feet of tall bamboo ranges; the ponds that were filled with
blooming purple water lilies all year round.

"Would you like to keep this dictionary?" Dan smiled at her. "It'll
help with your English."

"Really? You not joking?"

"No joking. You keep it."

"I pay you. How much?"

"No, no pay. But you can do something for me."

"What?"

"Translate for me one day when I visit the zoo."

"Hmm?"

"Let's ask our good friend what 'zoo' means." He turned the pages of the dictionary. "Xo thu?"

"Oh, sở thú?"

"Yes, I was told that Saigon has one of the oldest zoos in the world."

He turned the pages again and she learned the names of different animals: elephants, giraffes, hippos, monkeys, tigers, leopards.

"You not afraid of VC at sở thú?" she asked him.

"VC at the zoo? Nah. Don't think so. If any VC goes there, the tigers will eat them. *Grrr.*" He bared his teeth.

She tossed her head back, laughing.

◈

THE NEXT SUNDAY, Dan picked Trang up in the morning. She felt giddy sharing the same seat with him on the small cyclo. For the first time, she was going out with an American in broad daylight. She'd been afraid of being attacked by the VC, but on the ride, Dan's voice calmed her. He pointed at the charming Vespas and the sturdy Honda Dreams, and told her about his motorbike back home in America.

Now that she sat high up on the cyclo, she noticed how many homeless people and beggars there were on the street. They were sleeping on the pavement, some with disfigured faces, others with missing limbs. Most of them must have fled their villages in the Central and Mekong Delta regions, where bombings and mortar strikes had become as frequent as daily meals. She shuddered, thinking about her parents. Her village was safe for now under the protection of the ARVN, yet the situation could change as swiftly as the wind changes direction.

Once they arrived at the zoo, though, her worries became smaller, then disappeared as she walked through the flower-filled park, fed sugarcanes to the elephants, imitated the monkeys' calls, and admired the gigantic hippos as well as the graceful leopards. She didn't really need to translate for Dan as most signs were also in English, but she made him practice Vietnamese. She liked being his teacher. Perhaps she would get better at this and teach Vietnamese to Americans for a living.

She had worn high-heeled shoes so as not to look too short compared to Dan, and her feet hurt from walking. After an hour, he bought her a pair of plastic sandals from a wandering vendor. "You look so cute with those!" He admired her feet. "Seriously, no more need for high-heels." He made the motion of throwing her shoes into a bush and she had to stop him.

"So, you like the zoo?" he asked. They were eating ice cream, their backs against the trunk of an ancient banyan tree.

"I could live here." She inhaled deeply. Sunlight, filtered through the swaying canopy of leaves, jumped rope on her arms. It felt so good to be around Dan, perhaps she could invite him to her home village for the coming New Year. She would show him how to fold banana leaves around sticky rice, mung beans, and pork to turn them into bánh tét, how to climb coconut trees to pick the best fruit to make candied coconut ribbons. In her latest letter, her mother had insisted that both daughters must come home for Tết even though the celebrations were still several months away.

"I could live here, too," Dan said. He studied her, his gaze intense, then turned away. She wondered if he was married, or if he had a girlfriend back home. She'd learned the word "girlfriend" and practiced on her customers, but she'd never asked Dan, perhaps because she didn't want to know the truth.

The zookeeper blew his whistle, announcing, "Sở thú sẽ đóng cửa nửa tiếng nữa."

"They close in thirty minutes," she translated for him.

"We still have time, hurry." He gathered her shoes.

"Hurry for what?"

"Pictures. I saw a street photographer over there."

She raced on the grass with him at her side. She imagined that if she lifted her legs just a little higher, her whole body would float among the clouds. How wonderful to have a day when she didn't have to think about survival, or deal with the greed of men. Dan treated her with respect, and she appreciated it.

"You two make a nice couple." The photographer snapped their picture. "Wait twenty minutes, and it'll be ready."

"Please make two copies." Dan paid for the photos.

When the man handed them the photos, Trang cupped her hand against her mouth: the boy in the photo resembled Dan but the girl looked like somebody else: radiant, beautiful, and full of life.

Dan gave her a photo. "So we won't forget this fun day."

"Never." She held the photo against her chest.

◇

HER ROOM WAS deserted when Dan brought her back. Quỳnh and the other roommates had left for work.

"Oh no, I am late." Trang panicked, imagining the tiger madam's sharp words.

"So . . . this is where you live." Dan stepped into the room. "How many of you sleep here?" To her embarrassment, he looked around. The room was messy, clothes were strewn on the floor and dirty dishes piled high in a bucket.

She didn't want him to pity her. She was about to tell him to leave when a whizzing sound tore through the air. An explosion that sounded like a bomb shook the building.

"Down!" Dan leaped toward her. He pulled her to the floor, shielding her. Another whizzing sound approached, and this time, the mortar exploded even closer. The window shattered, showering glass like rice seeds onto the floor.

She screamed.

"Stay calm, I'm here." His heart trembled against her back. His breath was hot on her hair. His arms gripped her tight.

"Việt Cộng tấn công Tân Sơn Nhứt. Việt Cộng tấn công Tân Sơn Nhứt," somebody was screaming from the street below.

"What did they say?"

"VC attack Tân Sơn Nhứt Airbase."

"Damn." He gripped her tighter.

Silence, then sounds of people crying, calling for each other. Dan sprang up to his feet.

He leapt over the fallen glass and opened the door to the balcony. When she reached him, he was holding on to the railing, watching the columns of smoke twisting toward the sky.

"It looks like our base was hit. I've got to go."

She followed him back inside and to the door. "No! Stay here." She held on to his arm. She wanted to say that it was dangerous out there, and he should remain inside, but couldn't find the English words. She didn't want to lose him to this terrible war. She wanted him to be able to return to his parents, the way she needed to return to hers.

A tear escaped her eye and he paused. He released the door handle and turned. Time seemed to stop moving as he took her face into his hands. His lips were on her eye, kissing her tear away. A long moment passed as he held her against him. She could hear her own heart, beating as frantically as a young bird trying to break free.

When she'd gathered enough courage to lift her chin, he'd moved his face closer. His breath smelled like honey and felt as fresh as early morning sunlight on her skin. He was so close she could see his fine lashes, the irises of his eyes. She shivered as his lips touched hers. Tender, warm, gentle. Like a flower, she opened herself to him. He tasted sweet and fragrant. Other men had kissed her, but for the first time, she felt her body was a đàn tranh instrument, singing under Dan's touch.

She wanted the moment to last forever, but Dan peeled himself from her, apologizing that he must go.

Standing on the balcony, she watched him race from her building down the lane. Then he disappeared from sight.

◈

THE NEXT AFTERNOON, she was wiping a table when Dan arrived. The bar was still quiet. Some girls were chatting among themselves, the rest were putting on makeup. Quỳnh was alone at a table, going through her English phrase book.

"I can't stay long," Dan told her, smiling shyly. "I just came by to say hello." There was a yearning in his eyes, so strong it almost took her breath away. All she wanted to do was reach up to him and taste his mouth again.

But she felt she wasn't entitled to that kiss.

"You should know something." She led him to a table in the corner and turned the pages of the dictionary. He'd treated her with respect, unlike other American men, and she must do the same. She couldn't deceive him.

"Em làm điếm," she said, pointing at a word.

"What?"

"Po-ti-tu," she tried to pronounce the word. She pointed at her chest and at the word *prostitute*. "I dirty, I po-ti-tu. Men pay money. I go with them. My papa sick. I need money. I po-ti-tu. I send money home."

She closed her eyes. If she could return to her village, she'd seek shelter in the shade of the trứng cá tree, the way she and Quỳnh had always done as they walked home from the rice field. If only she had met Dan during the time of her innocence, then she would deserve him.

"I'm sorry," Dan said, "but you are just doing what you need to do to help your family."

She turned away. She would not let herself cry in front of him. In addition to being a prostitute, she was also a thief. But the truth was too bitter for her to admit.

He tried to tell her something but she wouldn't listen. She left the table.

Sitting on the toilet, she cried into her palms. Dan had used his body to shield her from the explosion. He could have died for her. Her books and her mother had taught her about worthiness, and she wasn't worthy of his care and attention.

By the time she returned to the bar, he'd gone and she was sure he wouldn't be back for her. Still, she found herself refusing any offers to go to the back room. She told the men it was her red day.

That night, like the previous night, she could hardly sleep. Dan kept appearing in her mind, as if he was a light and her eyes the switch. She missed his voice, his laughter, the ways he enabled her to relax and be a normal girl. She realized that she needed him in her life. She had to fight for him.

The next evening, she went up to the tiger madam, who stood leaning against the bar counter, counting real American dollars as well as MPC bills.

"Madam," she said when the woman finished, "my frequent customers buy lots of drinks these days. I don't need to go to the back room anymore. No more long time."

"Why? I thought you needed to help your parents?" The woman stuffed the money into her leather handbag and lit a cigarette.

"Yes, I've been helping. My father had another surgery recently. The doctor said he's improving and perhaps he can walk again."

"So?" The woman blew out smoke.

"What I'm saying is that . . . now that I can earn enough money to keep going, I don't want to be alone with men anymore. I speak enough English, and I know how to charm them."

"Is that because of the blond boy? As I told you, don't be such a dreamer!"

"It's just that I can't do it anymore. At least for the time being—"

"Hello, Kim," a voice interrupted her. She turned to see a large man, one of her regular customers.

"Hello." She gave him her automated smile.

"We'll talk later," the tiger madam told Trang. She patted the man on the butt. "You look stronger every day, sweetie." She winked and walked away.

Each moment that Trang waited for Dan was agonizing. She felt she'd made a mistake by telling him the truth. She hardly believed her eyes when he appeared that night, smelling like an exotic, faraway dream.

The music was blasting. Though it had provided Trang with a distraction during the past months, she wished it would vanish. Same for the people around them. She pulled him toward a table at the furthest corner.

"I want to talk . . . about something." Her heart beat so fast she had to bring a palm to her chest.

"I also have things to tell you." He smiled.

She unfolded a piece of paper. She'd written this with the dictionary's help and had practiced reading it over and over. She hoped she wouldn't make a mistake. "Dear Dan . . ." She looked up to check his reaction. "I told my madam I don't want to go into a private room with another man anymore. I want to stay just a bar girl from now on."

He reached for her hand. "You're doing this for me?"

She nodded. Then she shook her head. "No, I do for me."

He gazed into her eyes. "I also wanted to tell you something. I've been thinking . . . I've seen people dying around me. The attack on Tan Son Nhut . . . three of my friends were killed. I'm scared as hell . . . So as long as we both stay alive, I don't care." He kissed her, this time longer, more passionate.

"I dream about you last night," she said after he'd pulled away. She couldn't believe she was confessing her feelings. Where had her mother's teachings gone? As a woman, it was inappropriate of her to reveal her emotions first. If others knew, they'd ridicule her, calling her "cọc đi tìm trâu"—"a tether searching for a buffalo."

"Oh yeah? What happened in your dream?"

"This," she said, pulling him to her.

That evening, he asked about her father's health and the reasons she and Quỳnh had to work at the bar. He apologized to her, though it wasn't his fault.

The next time he came back, he told her his family wasn't rich; he had to support his mom, but he wanted to help her family, too. He gave her an envelope. At first she tried to refuse, but he said it was for her parents. That night, sitting on her bed, she opened his gift. One hundred red dollars. Tears brimmed in her eyes. She gave it to Quỳnh, who knew the black market well and could obtain a better exchange rate than her. She wrote a letter to her parents, telling them how fascinating the zoo was. As she sent the money and the letter home the next morning, she wished she could tell her Ba and Má about Dan. But she knew she had to keep him a secret.

Dan came back the following night and as they kissed, she pressed herself against his body. She wanted to melt into him, become a part of him.

"I want you so bad." He wove his fingers into her hair.

"Me too." She felt herself blushing. She'd dreamt about being naked with him for days. She wanted to hold him closer, feel his heartbeat against her, touch every inch of him. She'd feared sex before, but she trusted Dan. She didn't know the type of hunger that came with love.

The hotel Dan took Trang to was so grand, she admired its high ceiling, exquisite paintings, and spacious lobby. Yet she had to hide her face behind a scarf. She had to be careful, or else gossip would catch fire and travel to her village.

Once they entered the room, she latched the door. She undid her blouse buttons. She had wanted this for herself. She was entitled to this happiness.

As Dan unzipped her skirt, she brought her hand to his chest and felt the blood of his twenty-year-old body rushing through her.

He was tender, passionate, and caring, unlike anything she'd experienced. When she made love to him, every cell of her body became alive, demanding more. She was a đàn tranh, a seventeen-string zither, each string echoing its unique sound as it had found this perfect partner to discover joy with.

The next time they made love, they gave their body parts names, told each other stories which didn't make sense because they didn't know each other's language well enough, held each other close, and laughed out loud.

"I wish you had your own apartment," he said afterward, his finger on the bridge of her nose. "Some of my friends rent apartments for their lady friends, and they said it's very convenient. I mean . . . it's probably cheaper for me to rent you an apartment than these hotel rooms."

She buried her face into his chest, inhaling his scent. People only stayed with each other when they were married. And what if her parents found out?

"I can pay for the rent. We need some furniture."

"Phở nì chờ?"

"Ah, some chairs, a table . . . Perhaps we can buy ourselves a radio, and a TV. What do you think?"

She didn't answer.

"And we need a really, really strong bed." He climbed on top of her.

◆

DURING THE FOLLOWING DAY, she missed him as if he were a part of her body; without him she couldn't function properly. With the war intensifying, life was unpredictable. She could be killed any day.

She'd never had the chance to live for herself, and now she must.

She counted the money she'd stolen from other men and hidden under her rice jar. Fifty-eight dollars. Her education could wait. She'd ask the Tiger Madam for a day off work and go to Sài Gòn Market to buy some decent clothes to wear when going out with Dan. She'd visit Tao Đàn Book Store to buy herself some new books of poetry and love songs. She'd give the rest of the money to Quỳnh and try to convince her once again to stop sleeping with men. Quỳnh had accepted her role as an entertainer—in and out of bed. She didn't have a boyfriend, saying that she'd make better money being free. The last time they talked, Trang had reminded Quỳnh about safety, and Quỳnh had shown her the condoms, and demonstrated her self-defense moves, which their father had taught them many years back. "One more year and we'll be out of here," Quỳnh said, more determined than ever. Any advice Trang told her was water poured on a duck's feathers.

That evening, Dan appeared at the bar and surprised her with a rose.

"When are you done with work, my beloved em?" His tongue was warm on her earlobe.

"Three hour, anh." She felt herself getting wet. Sex with him had been incredible; she had been a dry field thirsting for rain.

"Three hours? But I have to be back to the base by then."

She looked up at him, admiring his blond hair, arched nose, and blue eyes. He was Từ Hải in *The Tale of Kiều*, who rescued Kiều from the wicked madam Tú Bà and her brothel.

"Want to hear some news, em? I asked around and I found a place for us. Want to see it now?"

"Our own place?" She felt as if he'd just proposed marriage to her. Deep down, she believed only married couples lived with each other.

"Yes, it's not too far from here. Can you leave for a short while?"

Dan bought a ticket for a two-hour long-time.

The one-bedroom apartment Dan wanted to rent was on the top floor of a three-story house, nestled in a small lane within walking distance from the bar. It had a back entrance—"For safety," he said. The kitchen was spacious and opened onto a balcony filled with pots of red and yellow moss roses. The bedroom had a double bed, an armchair, and a radio. Instead of a squat toilet, there was a white and gleaming Western one. And instead of a water tap and a bucket for washing, there was a shower.

She ran her hands on the bamboo curtains. They reminded her of home.

"What do you think, em?"

She reached for her bag and opened the dictionary. "Can my sister stay here with me?"

"Not when I am in town, but if I'm away for a few days, she can have sleepovers. I just want our privacy, you know . . . I need to visit you whenever I'm free, and when we can make a lot of noise." He winked.

She withdrew her hand from his. He lifted her chin. "What's wrong?"

"Papa, mama will know . . ."

"They live far away, remember? The back entrance . . . I can come in and out without anyone knowing. And this . . ." He patted on the bed. "Our privacy. Our heaven."

He sealed her lips with a kiss. He pulled her into him, his teeth knocking against her teeth, his chim swelling against her thigh.

◇

QUỲNH FACED THEM as they stepped into the Hollywood. "I need to talk to my sister," said Quỳnh, frowning at Dan.

"Hello." He smiled. "Kim told me about you." He held out his palm.

Quỳnh ignored it. "You wait. I talk to my sister."

She pulled Trang aside. "You're getting serious with him, aren't you? Don't forget, chị Hai, that all Americans will leave us. Just get money from them, but don't give them your heart."

"I can't believe you were so rude to him. You should apologize." Trang searched for Dan with her eyes. He was talking to the bartenders, making them roar with laughter. She turned back to her sister. "Believe it or not, Dan is special. He's kind and gentle. And he really likes me."

"I knew it! You've fallen into his trap. They're all like that at the start, but once they own you, they'll drop their masks. Don't you already know the danger of fire? You'll get burned."

"Come on, Quỳnh . . . Remember how many men I've already talked to, huh? Dan is unlike any of them. And he makes me very happy." She pulled her sister closer. "He just showed me the apartment he wants to rent for us."

"Are you crazy? You want to move in with him?"

"I didn't think I'd ever do this, but yes."

"He'll crush your heart, chị Hai."

"No he won't."

"Why?"

"Because he loves me."

"Did he tell you?"

"He doesn't need to."

"If you like him that much, go on . . . move in with him." Quỳnh pursed her lips. "Just make sure that he pays you a monthly allowance."

"He gave me one hundred red dollars the other day, you haven't forgotten about that, have you?"

"He should give you the same amount every month, and more. He should take you to the military post exchange for you to buy PX goods so you can trade them for profit. If you don't tell him, he'll soon forget."

"I don't want to talk about money with him, em."

"Then what does he want from you? Oh, I know. Your body. And you should want something from him in return: money."

Trang felt hurt and disgusted. Why did both the tiger madam and her sister refuse to think that Dan liked her as a person? She was sure Dan didn't just want her body. He wanted her as a companion. He had cared about her, had sent money to her parents, had taken her to the zoo, had bought her flowers, had really talked to her. He was unlike other Americans.

Quỳnh sighed. "Chị Hai . . . we are just water hyacinth plants floating on a river. Don't let the current pull you down. Protect yourself because nobody else can. And under no circumstance should you allow yourself to get pregnant."

"Pregnant?" Trang chuckled. "You think I am stupid? For sure I won't get pregnant. We're being careful and he knows I don't want a baby." She'd seen Amerasians on the street—the homeless children who'd been abandoned by their parents. Their foreign features made them stand out like thorns in people's eyes.

And she knew the danger of pregnancy like a bird knew the strength of the branch it perched on. The girls at their bar often talked about the abortions they'd had to have: where to go, how much it cost, and how long they had to abstain from sex afterward; the money they lost because of it. Well known at the bar were stories of the two girls who'd died from home abortions and the six who'd given birth to children during the last three years. Of those six mothers, four gave their newborns away before returning to the bar; one actually did go with her baby to America with her boyfriend; no one knew what happened to the remaining girl.

In no case would Trang allow herself to get pregnant.

"You said you wouldn't have an American boyfriend and look at you now." Quỳnh shook her head. "Remember, he'll only be here for a short while and won't bring you to America."

"I don't want to go anywhere. I'll stay near Má and Ba." By now, Trang knew that Americans were rotated on a twelve-month or thirteen-month tour; most would go home after that. Dan would, too, but she hoped he'd extend it, now that they were in love. Perhaps he'd even stay. She hadn't allowed herself to dream, but now that she had Dan, nothing seemed impossible.

"I've heard that people do crazy things once they're in love," Quỳnh smirked. "Don't forget that our parents need money, chị Hai. They don't want a grandchild, fathered by an American soldier."

Trang squared her shoulders. "Look who's acting like an older sibling now, huh? If you must know something: Dan is a pilot. That means
he isn't a normal soldier but an important officer."

"Oh, so you think he's too high up to drop you? The higher he is, the
worse your fall is going to be. You wait and see."

A fire ignited inside Trang's ribcage. Its heat spread to her tongue.
She tasted the poison of words that formed in her mouth. "Oh, now I
know why you're upset. I have a handsome boyfriend and you don't. For
the first time in your life I'm doing better and you can't stand it."

"Get out of my face!" Quỳnh walked away.

The Cost of Hope

Hồ Chí Minh City, 2016

Phong stood inside the Sài Gòn Post Office, waiting for Mr. Lương, who was posting a package. He'd hoped that his DNA samples could be mailed to America to speed up the process, but Mr. Lương said the samples had to be carried by hand, by someone who was traveling to the U.S.; Vietnamese customs considered DNA test kits to be medical products and would not allow sending by mail. Phong wanted to talk further to Mr. Lương, to find out more about DNA testing. He had many questions: What could go wrong? How long it might take? What else would the test results reveal apart from family members?

The post office was busy at this hour, and Phong noticed two white foreigners standing near him. Dressed in jeans and a blue T-shirt, the man was tall. The woman was chubby, with blond hair that glowed like gold and silver. A Vietnamese man with a scar slashed across his left cheek accompanied the foreigners. He pointed toward the large portrait of Hồ Chí Minh on the wall and said something. The foreign woman chuckled but the foreign man frowned and looked away.

Just then, Mr. Lương made his way across the hall toward the small group. "Thiên! I haven't seen you for a long time," he called out, shaking hands with the Vietnamese man.

Thiên? The name sounded familiar. Thiên. Ah, Phong remembered now. It's the name of the contact person in Tôm Sờ-Mít's newspaper advertisement. So the white man could well be Tôm Sờ-Mít. Phong studied the foreigner. He looked old enough to have been in the war.

The white man was now staring at Phong. Their eyes locked. Phong registered some heaviness on the foreigner's face, the heaviness of someone who had to carry a burden larger than himself.

The foreigner looked away but turned toward Phong once more. Something told Phong he had to talk to the man. If the man was Tôm Sờ-Mít, Phong could ask about his time in Việt Nam, how it was looking for lost family members. In addition, the drink seller had said American men who came back looking for their children would be able to help him.

Phong stepped toward the foreign man. His heart thumped as furiously as a freshly caught fish jumping on dry land as he took off his hat. Surely the white man could now see his Black American features. "Hế-lô," he said, "mai nêm Phong. Ai em sân A-mé-ri-cần sấu-chờ." His children had helped him learn these English sentences by heart in the hope that he could communicate directly with the visa officer, but he'd had no chance.

The man shook his head and said something that sounded like "Só-ri?"

"Mai nêm Phong. Ai em sân A-mé-ri-cần sấu-chờ," Phong repeated, desperate for the foreigner to understand him. But the man was turning to his wife, who was telling him something. Phong tried to understand her but could only catch one word, "phôn." She gestured toward the entrance, as if wanting to leave.

Phong had been drowning for so long, he couldn't let a possible buoy float away. He turned to Mr. Lương and Mr. Thiên who were sharing a joke about eating phở and rice, laughing at the clever ways Vietnamese men distinguished sex with their wives as "eating rice" while sex with their mistresses as "eating phở."

He interrupted them. "Eh . . . please help tell this foreign man that my father was an American soldier and I've been searching for him."

Mr. Thiên narrowed his eyes.

The woman was raising her voice higher, pointing toward the exit. The foreign man looked at Phong, saying something—his words were bees buzzing into Phong's ears. He turned to the Vietnamese men, but their faces bore no compassion.

He looked at the foreign man. "Mai nêm Phong. Ai em sân A-mé-ri-cần sấu-chờ," he said slowly, hoping that he'd placed the right accent on each word. How hard was it to get two sentences right?

The man exchanged words with Mr. Lương. Phong strained his ears. They must be speaking about him since they were glancing at him. The woman threw her hands into the air, looking upset.

Finally Mr. Lương turned to him. "The gentleman here wanted to know what you were trying to tell him, so I translated what you said, that your name is Phong and you are the son of an American soldier. He asked how you know for sure."

"Sir . . ." Phong held the white man's gaze and gestured at himself. "Look how dark my skin is, my curly hair, my beard . . . They are the proof that I'm the child of a Black American soldier. Besides, I'm one meter eighty. Vietnamese don't get that tall."

"But your mother must have told you something about your father, no?" the white man asked, and Mr. Lương translated.

"Sir, I don't know my mother, either. I was abandoned in front of an orphanage."

As Mr. Lương interpreted, the woman exclaimed something. She spoke in long sentences and started walking toward the entrance.

"Son of a bitch." Mr. Thiên snarled his teeth at Phong. "You just poured more oil onto a fire. Now that woman thinks we are colluding to scam her."

"Huh? What scam?" Phong said, but Mr. Thiên had already taken off, running after the woman.

Phong turned to the foreign man. "Sorry, Sir. I didn't want to upset anybody."

"Ah . . . it's not your fault," the man said via Mr. Lương's translation. "My wife forgot her phone at the hotel and wants to go back to get it."

The foreigner and Mr. Lương exchanged words.

"He asked if I knew you." Mr. Lương said. "So I told him about your DNA test, that you're truly looking for your father. He said you're the first Amerasian he ever met, and he really wants to talk to you. He doesn't have time now, but he's staying at the Ma-chés-tịch Hotel. Can you see him tonight? At nine o'clock?"

"Yes, yes . . . Of course!" Phong felt as if he'd won the lottery.

"My name is Đan. See you tonight at the lobby of my hotel," the foreigner said before hurrying out of the post office.

◈

PHONG HAD EXPECTED to see the drink seller when he returned to Lê Duẩn Boulevard, but the pavement where her cart had stood was empty. He hoped she hadn't fallen sick. What a pity he couldn't tell her the good news about Mr. Dan wanting to talk to him. She'd have been able to coach him about the right questions to ask.

Noon was approaching, but outside the American Consulate, a handful of people still waited patiently. He searched but Quang the visa agent wasn't among them. He had the crook's phone number but calling wouldn't help and would cost money.

His throat burned; his stomach rumbled. More than nine hours until he could see Mr. Dan. He should have asked for an earlier meeting, but Mr. Dan had been in such a hurry to go after his wife.

He was checking for his wallet to make sure his money and ID card were still there when someone touched his arm.

"Brother, are you applying for an Amerasian visa?" A man with sunglasses and tattoos glistening on his neck asked him.

Phong quickened his footsteps. There was no way he'd allow another visa agent to cheat him.

"Wait, Brother." The man followed him, whispering. "I have something that you might want to see. It'd make a great addition to your visa application."

His visa had already been denied. No random Vietnamese person could help. He pressed forward. As he turned the corner, the man caught up with him.

"Brother, have a look!" In the man's palm was a photo.

An old, faded picture. In it, a dark-skinned man in a soldier's uniform smiled broadly, his arm around the waist of a Vietnamese woman.

"He looks like you." The tattooed man pointed at the photo with his dirty fingernail. "He could be your father."

This was surely a trap. Still, Phong held up the photo. The couple evoked in Phong a strange yet welcomed feeling, that his parents might have been happy together, that he might have been a love child. The woman's smile looked so genuine, it shone like springtime in her eyes.

"Five million đồng and you can have it." The man took back the picture.

"Hey . . . Let me have a closer look."

"Enough looking," the man said as he slid the photo back into his breast pocket. "This is a rare find. I'm doing you a favor by selling it to you so cheaply."

"Five million? I can't even dream of having such money, Brother."

"No money, no honey." The man grinned. "Think about it. It'll be your ticket to America."

"How?"

The man looked around, then lowered his voice. "American people, you know . . . they need proof. Your proof is right here." He patted the pocket. "Just say the woman is your mother and the man your father. Say that your mother gave you the picture before she died . . . or something like that."

"Ha. You think Americans are stupid?"

"Listen to me. If you don't try, how do you know that it won't work? No pain no gain, my friend. This picture, hard to find. You want it or not?"

"May I look at it once more?" Phong held out his hand, wanting to touch the couple's happiness again. For reasons he couldn't explain, he'd like to have the photo. Perhaps just to stare at it, to imagine how his father and his mother had been. Where had the photo come from?

The man pushed his sunglasses higher on his nose. "Five million đồng cash. Money handed over, the porridge will be delivered."

"Tell you what. My visa agent cheated me. Quang. You know him? If you help get my money back, I might be able to—"

Laughter rolled from the man's thick throat. He yanked his sunglasses off his face, glaring at Phong with bloodshot eyes. "You son of a bitch. Create trouble for Quang and the next thing you know . . . you'll be gone." He made a slitting gesture across his neck.

Phong shook his head and walked away. He wasn't afraid, not really. He'd been in enough street fights to know that he was hard to beat. But he had to be careful, for in this city he was alone.

◈

PHONG SAT DOWN on a bench at the 30/4 Reunification Park, waiting for the time to pass until he could see Mr. Dan. Sunset had arrived, spreading golden light on top of rustling trees. As he cast his eyes around him, he rose to his feet. Quang and the tattooed man were on a bench not too far away, going through some papers that looked like a U.S. visa application. A woman and a girl stood by; their faded, simple clothing told him they were from the countryside. Heat rose to Phong's chest. The two men were conspiring to deceive those less fortunate and taking their hard-earned savings without remorse.

Phong went to the girl and the woman. "Be careful with them," he said, "they cheated me."

"Shut your fucking mouth." Quang stood up and took a swing at Phong. As Phong stepped back, he shifted his weight onto his right foot, and swept his left foot against Quang's closest ankle. As the visa agent fell sideways, Phong brought his knee up into Quang's face. Quang lay sprawled on the ground, screaming in agony.

"You son of a bitch," the tattooed man hollered. He ran to a patch of blooming marigolds and grabbed a large rock.

A loud whistle. Two security guards came running toward them.

The tattooed man dropped the rock and helped Quang up. Both men threw hateful glances at Phong, cursing him.

"Stop cheating others, or else you'll suffer from bad karma," Phong said. He'd wanted to demand that Quang return some of his money but knew he wouldn't have a chance. He considered following the two agents out of the park and beating them up; he knew he could win, but the police might arrest him. He gathered the papers and gave them to the shaken women who were hiding behind the trunk of a tree.

"I was suspicious of those men," the older woman told Phong later at the tea stall from across the street, after Phong had shared with them his visa experiences. "But my daughter was certain they could arrange for her to marry someone in the U.S. so she could migrate there. They asked for a lot of money. They said we could sell our land . . ."

Phong turned to the young woman who was bending her head, as if in shame. He poured more tea for her. "It's good that you haven't given those guys any money," he said, his voice gentle. "If you agree to a fake marriage, your visa might be denied and you might be banned from entering the U.S. forever. Believe me, you don't want to make the mistake I once did."

◈

PHONG GAZED AT the grand building, which he knew as Cửu Long Hotel. Cửu Long meant "nine dragons" and the hotel deserved its name, for it looked magnificent with its domed windows on the ground floor and balconies that curled above the street like halves of the moon on upper levels. Why had the government allowed the hotel to change its name to Majestic—which, when pronounced by Mr. Lương, sounded like Ma-chés-tịch—a word so foreign, so meaningless to Vietnamese like Phong who didn't know English well? Hadn't they said they fought the war to get rid of foreign invaders?

Phong smoothed his clothes, combed his hair and beard with his fingers. He'd found a public bathroom, washed his face, and rinsed his mouth. Still, he wished he could have taken a shower and changed his clothes. His white shirt had been stained from sweat and dust. His pants appeared crumpled. But he hoped that once he touched the grandness inside the hotel, his life would be transformed. Mr. Dan looked sincere and he sensed the man would help him.

At the hotel's entrance, he approached a young man dressed in a black-and-white uniform. "Hey Elder Brother, may I go in? I have an appointment." The doorman was younger than him, but he used a respectful title.

"Appointment with whom?" The doorman looked him up and down.

"Mr. Đan and his wife, they're Americans."

"Full name? Room number?"

"I don't have it, but Mr. Đan told me to be here at nine." He looked through the glass door. Several people stood inside, but none of them were the people he'd met at the post office.

The doorman frowned at him, then flashed his broadest smile at an approaching Westerner. Bending, he opened the door for the white man. Phong turned away. He felt that if he were white, he could enter this hotel without the need to answer any question.

A car rolled toward the entrance. Mr. Thiên sat behind the steering wheel. Mr. Dan stepped out, holding a large painting with both hands.

The doorman rushed to Mr. Dan, who handed over the painting and helped his wife out of the car. She stepped down, several large shopping bags in her hands. As their eyes met, the smile on her face vanished.

"Phong," said Mr. Thiên via the half-open car window, "go with them inside. I'll park the car and come back."

Mr. Dan patted Phong on the shoulder, telling him something.

"He thanks you for coming, Uncle." The doorman translated, then opened the door for him. Phong couldn't believe how much a hand-shake with a foreigner had elevated his status.

Inside, the air was cool and smelled of jasmine flowers. Piano music floated in the air. Impressive chandeliers hung from the high ceiling, radiating their light onto the paintings, stained glass panels, furniture, and decorations, most of which bore the royal color of gold. Countless orchid flowers bloomed from a center table. Phong wished that his wife and children were here to witness how lavish life could be, and to be a part of it.

Mr. Dan gestured toward some ancient-looking brocade armchairs. As Phong sat down, he touched the rosewood armrest. The wood-work was exquisite, brown as honey, carved with birds and flowers. He wished he could learn how to make furniture like this.

Phong smiled at the woman who sat next to Mr. Dan across the table, but her eyes were fixed on her fancy phone. Her black dress must be made out of real silk and her sandals real leather. Her husband was dressed in jeans and a T-shirt, but they must be made in America and cost a fortune. The couple's skin looked pink and well nourished. Of course they had to be rich to stay in this luxurious hotel. One night probably cost enough to feed his children for three whole months.

A man approached, gave Mr. Dan a menu and asked Phong what he'd like to drink. Phong shook his head. He couldn't afford anything from this hotel.

The woman said something. The waiter nodded, gathered the menu and walked away. It seemed Mr. Dan and his wife weren't ordering anything either. Phong's heart pounded. He'd hoped for a long talk with Mr. Dan, during which he could tell him everything about his life and ask for help, but it looked like he wouldn't have time. Damn this woman. Why did she have to be here, dampening his spirit with her sullen face?

The doorman had placed the painting on a chair. Mr. Dan lifted the wrapping paper, revealing a golden rice field being harvested by farmers. He nudged his wife and said something. She nodded.

"Tranh đẹp quá." Phong gestured toward the painting and gave it a thumbs-up.

The woman watched him.

"Tôi cũng làm ruộng như vậy." Phong pointed at himself, then toward the farmers. To make himself understood, he stood up, bent his back, pretending to harvest the field.

Mr. Dan smiled and exchanged words with his wife, whose face softened.

This wasn't as bad as Phong had feared. He recalled the English words his children had taught him. "Ai pham-mờ," he said. He pointed at his chest, repeating, "Ai," then toward the farmers, "pham-mờ."

Mr. Dan said something that sounded like "Du pham-mờ?" He gestured at the farmers, then Phong.

"Đúng, đúng rồi." Phong beamed. He couldn't wait to tell his children how much their English had helped him.

The woman nodded and exchanged words with her husband. Now that she no longer appeared to be upset, Phong appreciated her fine facial features. Her high nose, porcelain skin, big eyes, and well-shaped face resembled those of Western women who often appeared on advertising billboards for Vietnamese beauty products.

"Looks like you're doing well without me." Mr. Thiên sat down next to him.

"Oh, so good you're here, Uncle." Phong breathed out a sigh of relief.

"I was just trying to tell your friends that I'm a farmer, like the people in the painting."

"Yes, we got that," Mr. Dan said, through Mr. Thiên's translation. "Thanks for coming here to see us today, I really appreciate it. By the way, this is my wife, Lin-đà."

"My name is Tấn Phong. It means 'strength from thousand gusts of wind.'" Phong hoped the foreigners would be impressed by the special meaning of his name, but they showed no reaction. Perhaps Mr. Thiên hadn't translated it right.

"How long have you worked as a farmer?" asked Mr. Dan.

"More than ten years, Sir. I also grow vegetables, I raise fish, and I make furniture. And you, are you really from America?"

"Yes, we are. From a city called Xi-át-tồ." The man clasped his hands together, leaning forward. "What sort of furniture do you make?"

Phong smiled, appreciating Mr. Dan's interest in his life. "I make simple furniture for street sellers." He thought about the tables and chairs stacked high at the back of his home. He hadn't been able to sell anything for months. Street sellers these days preferred plastic products, cheaper and easier to carry. He took a deep breath. "I'd like to build bigger furniture, like cupboards and wardrobes, using wood like this," he said, patting the armchair, "when I get to America." He had to mention his American dream. Reaching that dream was the entire purpose of him being here.

The woman said something.

"She wants to know why you want to go to America. You already have different types of jobs here," Mr. Thiên translated.

"Madam . . . I have to do many things because none of them earns enough money to feed my children and pay for their schooling. As for America, I need to go there, for my children." He handed the woman the photo of Tài and Diễm. "Look how beautiful my kids are."

The woman stared at the picture.

"My children are bullied at school, Madam. Because of our skin color, people think we're dirty, low class. Because I'm the child of an American soldier, some people consider us the enemy."

Mr. Dan flinched, his head bent low.

Phong cleared his throat. It had been a while since anyone had said his family was related to the enemy, but he had to make his case. "Sir, Madam . . . I live in Bạc Liêu. I come to Sài Gòn this time to apply for a visa with the American Consulate. I must bring my wife and children to the U.S. It's our right to emigrate. Unfortunately, our visa application has just been rejected." He needed to find a way to tell the Americans to help him.

The woman frowned.

"I am very sorry to hear," said Mr. Dan. "In the post office, you said you grew up in an orphanage?"

"Yes . . . I was just a newborn when I was abandoned outside an orphanage's gate. I didn't have any papers with me. But you can tell by my physical features that I'm related to a Black American."

"Your orphanage . . . where was it? Were there many children? Was it difficult for you there?" Mr. Dan leaned forward again.

"It was in Hóc Môn, an hour by car from here I think . . . Yes, there were many children, Vietnamese and Amerasians. Sister Nhã and two other nuns took care of us. . . . I wish I could stay there but when I was three years old, Communist troops took over the orphanage. We had to go to the New Economic Zone up in Lâm Đồng Mountains. There, I worked in the fields with Sister Nhã. We didn't have enough to eat. It was very . . . very hard." He wanted to say more but was aware that he had to stop for Mr. Thiên to translate.

"The kind nun who took care of you . . . where is she now?" Mr. Dan said.

"She died when I was twelve . . . After that I lived on the streets for many years."

Mr. Dan looked as if he was about to cry. "I am so, so sorry."

Phong closed his eyes. The pain from his past dug into him, like the sharp claws of a mud crab. "I didn't want to beg, so I tried to find a job. I thought I could work as a waiter or dishwasher but shop owners just laughed at me, saying their customers would run away because of my dirty-looking skin. Others just wrinkled their noses. Luckily, I met a bus driver. He let me work as his assistant."

Mr. Dan apologized again, as if it was his fault. Then he said, "You mentioned you've been searching for your father. How?"

"I just did my DNA test, Sir."

The woman cleared her throat. "You told us your visa application to the U.S. was denied, did you try to leave previously?"

"Yes, Madam. I applied once before, in the nineties, but they didn't give me the visa either."

Instead of interpreting, Mr. Thiên asked, "Why couldn't you get a visa then? With your facial features, it should have been very easy for you to leave."

"I didn't have enough papers, Uncle. That's why I'm applying again. Please understand my situation . . . I really need to get my family to America, to give them a future."

Mr. Thiên translated. The woman looked at her husband, opened her palm and said something that sounded like, "Xi? Ai thâu du." Phong looked at Mr. Thiên, wanting to understand her, but he reacted as if she'd uttered nothing.

Mr. Dan didn't answer his wife, either. He looked at Phong and said something.

"So you grew up in Sài Gòn? How come you ended up living in the Mekong Delta?" Mr. Thiên translated.

Phong felt himself sweating, even though the air was cold. The way these people attacked him with questions, it wasn't different from the police or visa officers. He wanted to explain how the Khuấts had driven him out of Sài Gòn and to Bạc Liêu, but that would reveal his effort to bring strangers along with him to America. Instead he said, "My job on

the bus took me to Bạc Liêu. There, I met my wife. Her name is Bình."
The thought of his soulmate lifted Phong up. He smiled. "She can be
stubborn at times but is the kindest person I know. The best mother to
our two children. We have a good family now. We work hard but life is
tough. Sometimes my kids don't have enough to eat."

"I'm sorry but I have to ask . . ." The woman straightened her back.
"If you get to meet your father, what would you want from him?"

"I want him to know that I've missed him so much over the years."
Against Phong's will, tears welled up in his eyes. "I want him to meet
my children and my wife, and I want him to be our family."

"But you also want him to sponsor you to America, right?" The
woman asked.

"Yes . . . it would be wonderful, Madam. We have no future here.
People despise us. We don't belong."

The woman turned to Mr. Dan, repeating "Xi? Ai thâu du." Then she
said something very long, from which Phong only caught the sounds of
"sờ-cam" and À-mé-ri-cà.

He turned to Mr. Thiên, but the guy had his eyes on the entrance
door as if wanting to leave.

Everyone was silent. The piano music kept playing, each note hammering Phong's temples, making his head spin and his hands grow
sweatier. The scented air was suffocating.

He swallowed. He had to try harder. "Sir and Madam, please . . ." He
twisted his fingers. "I'd be grateful if you could help me find my father.
The American Consulate said if I have proof that my father was a soldier here, I could go to your country. Perhaps you could talk to the visa
officer? They'll listen to American people like you—"

"They're just tourists here. They don't know anyone from the consulate," Mr. Thiên interrupted Phong.

"Uncle . . . please . . . these people are very interested in my life.
Perhaps they'd want to help."

"Interested? Help? Ha! No way. They're selfish, self-centered, and
ignorant. They wanted you to dig up your past to satisfy their curiosity.

They don't really care about you nor me. They live privileged lives and they consider us dirt."

Phong glanced at Mr. Dan and his wife. It was a good thing the foreigners understood no Vietnamese. Did they pay Mr. Thiên to be their tour guide? If so, they'd made a foolish choice.

Across the table, the woman shook her head as she exchanged words with her husband. They both looked upset. Phong wanted to get out of there, but he said desperately, "Uncle Thiên, could you translate what I said? Please tell Mr. Đan and his wife that my family would be thankful for their help."

"I said it's not the right thing to ask," answered Mr. Thiên coldly.

When the couple finished arguing, Mr. Thiên told them something very short. He didn't mention the word "À-mé-ri-cà" at all, so for sure he wasn't translating what Phong had said.

The woman reached into a backpack, took out a stack of Vietnamese đồng and pushed it across the table.

"She's sorry about your situation, but there's nothing they can do," Mr. Thiên said. "This money is for your children, to help with their school fees."

Phong stared at the money. Each bill was fifty thousand đồngs. The stack looked like it was at least ten bills—nearly twenty-five dollars. The money would help a great deal. His mind told him to take it yet his heart said that if he did, the woman would think he was a scammer, and she wouldn't want her husband to help him.

"Thank you, Madam, but I'm not here to beg for your money," he said as he pushed the bills back. He gave the woman his best smile and looked her in the eye. "To be able to get to America, I need to find my father, and I don't know how. Please . . . could you and your husband talk to your friends about me? Or perhaps you could contact some veteran associations in America and tell them about my case. Someone must know someone who knows my father. Please . . . my father might not have much time—"

"Phong, I can tell them you don't want the money, but I can't insist that they help you," Mr. Thiên interrupted him again.

"Please, could you translate?"

Mr. Thiên sighed but told the woman something. Again, he didn't mention the word "À-mé-ri-cà" at all. The woman frowned. She returned the money to her backpack. The words that rolled out of her tongue sounded as cold as those uttered by the visa officer.

"Too bad you don't want her to help your kids, but that's the best she could do. She wishes you the best of luck," said Mr. Thiên.

The woman stood up, telling her husband something.

Mr. Thiên rose to his feet. "Phong . . . they've had a long day and they're tired. Let's go now."

Go? No! Mr. Thiên the gatekeeper had blocked out the most important questions Phong wanted to ask. "Please, Uncle," he said. "Mr. Đan said he wanted to know how life was for Amerasians, and I have many things to tell."

"Believe me, helping you is the least of his concerns right now. He has his own shit to deal with." Mr. Thiên fished his phone out of his pocket and played with it.

Across the table, the couple was arguing again. Their rising voices and their flushed faces sent an icy feeling down Phong's spine. Mr. and Mrs. Khuất had argued like that after hearing the news of their visa application. And they'd blamed Phong.

"Are they upset because of me, Uncle?" Phong whispered.

"Not really. Giận cá chém thớt." Mr. Thiên shrugged.

Ha, angry at the fish, they hack on the chopping board. So the couple was blaming Phong even though he wasn't the problem.

"How long have you known them, Uncle? Perhaps you could convince them to help me after they've resolved their issues?"

"Thankfully not long. I'm their tour guide since yesterday, but today's my last day working for them."

The woman was raising her hands high into the air. Mr. Dan told her something, reaching for her shoulder, but she broke away from him, heading toward the elevator.

Phong was glad the woman was leaving. How could Mr. Dan, who appeared to be kind and gentle, put up with such a spoiled, arrogant woman—someone who caused her husband to lose face in front of others? Bình would behave better. If they had a problem, she'd talk to him behind closed doors. She wouldn't vạch áo cho người xem lưng—lift her husband's shirt so others could look at his naked back.

He turned to Mr. Dan, hopeful that the woman's departure had given him the chance for a man-to-man talk.

Instead of sitting down again, Mr. Dan stretched out his hand and gripped Phong's. He said, slowly, "Ai em só-ri."

Phong's eyes blurred. What he needed was help, not an apology. "Tôi xin ông, hãy cho tôi cơ hội hỏi ông vài câu hỏi," he said in Vietnamese, begging the American to give him a chance to ask some questions.

Mr. Dan withdrew his hand. Without a single glance at Mr. Thiên, he hurried after his wife.

Watching the couple disappear, Phong felt as if a snake had bitten him in the face. The muscles of his cheeks twitched. He'd waited the whole day, for what? To satisfy the American man's curiosity about the suffering he'd endured? Now he'd have to spend another night at the park. How stupid of him to have rejected such a large sum of money.

Mr. Thiên was texting on his phone. Phong hated the guy but had another question for him. "Uncle . . . I saw your name in the *Tuổi Trẻ* newspaper. Are you the one helping your friend Tôm Sờ-Mít find his Vietnamese girlfriend Lan Lan?"

Mr. Thiên looked up immediately. "Yes. So?"

"Mr. Tôm Sờ-Mít . . . is he here in Sài Gòn? Can I talk to him, please?"

"He left last week." Mr. Thiên dropped the phone into his breast pocket. "I have to go . . . Here's my business card. Call me tomorrow night. I'll write down your details. If I have a Black client searching for his child, I'll look into your case."

"But Uncle—"

"Look, I've had a bad day and I don't need your shit now. Call me tomorrow, okay?" He hurried to the entrance door.

Phong gripped the business card. Thiên means "Heaven" but the guy should go to hell; he only wanted Phong's personal details for his future business.

As Phong tore the card into pieces, his fingers tingled with satisfaction. He'd memorized the guy's phone number from Tom Smith's newspaper notice and now he pulled it from his memory. He jumbled the number around so he would no longer remember it. He didn't have space in his mind for such a terrible man named Thiên.

The Laughing Buddha

Sài Gòn, 1969

I t poured the day Trang moved into the apartment with Dan. They left the windows open and stayed in bed looking out at the silvery blanket. The wind rushed in, trembling on Trang's skin as Dan peeled off her clothes, gently. They made love to the murmur of rain.

After he'd rolled away from her and his breathing eased, she circled her finger on his stomach. She felt like the rain had brought him to her and he was a part of the water, pure and heavenly. Now that they were together, she believed the war could no longer touch them. "I am very happy," she told him. She truly was. She didn't know what being married was like but she felt Dan was her husband. From now on, she wanted to take good care of him.

"I'm very happy, too. Very . . ." He pulled her closer.

She rested her head on his forearm. The air was cool and he was warm. She could stay like this forever.

When her eyelids grew heavy, she told herself they hadn't unpacked. Gingerly, she pushed herself up and covered Dan's chest with his shirt.

"Have a nap, em . . ." Dan's voice was raspy.

"I need to go market." She looked around the empty apartment. Bags of belongings scattered on the floor. Unpacking could wait, but a home wouldn't be complete without an altar. She needed the Laughing Buddha's blessings. He'd brought her luck and she must continue to pray to him.

"Market?" Dan rubbed his eyes. "You want to buy food? I've got some chocolate in my bag . . ."

"I'm not hungry." She kissed his forehead.

"I am, for my delicious mangoes." He grabbed her breasts, which hung before him.

"You bad boy." She slapped his buttocks and got out of bed. She pulled her dress over her head.

"You go now?" He sat up. "May I come along?"

"You? Market?"

"Why not?" He put his jeans on, hopping on one foot. "At least I can help you carry."

She combed her hair. If Dan joined her, her neighbors would find out, and the news could spread to her village. Hiếu would know, but she no longer cared about him. Compared to Dan, Hiếu was a coward: he'd never dared to confess his feelings to her.

She hadn't received any news about Hiếu and wondered if he'd been drafted. Hiếu's father had sold their buffaloes and cows to pay for the bribes required to help his son escape the draft. But she'd heard that no young man could stay away from the army forever. With the fire of war burning, it needed more men as firewood.

"Don't look so worried." Dan smoothed the wrinkles on her forehead. "I'll leave first . . . the back door . . . Where should I wait for you?"

She looked at the smile in his eyes and realized that during this turbulent time, propriety wasn't important; love was.

"We'll leave together," she said. It was risky, but she was feeling excited to show off her man.

The market was overflowing with activity. Everyone was getting on with their lives despite the war.

Dan held her hand as they browsed stall after stall. People turned their heads, looking at him, whispering. Trang had wanted him to be a secret, but now, she felt pride surging through her. She wanted to shout out to the world that Dan was her boyfriend.

They stopped at a fruit stand. "This looks strange." He picked up a rambutan, its long hair nesting against his palm. "You sure we can eat it?"

"The red color lucky." She squeezed the fruit lightly, testing its firmness. She needed to buy five types of fruit, in five different colors, for the altar.

"Where did you find him? He is so *very* cute." The seller—a middle-aged woman—asked Trang, studying Dan.

"How do I ask for a price?" Dan nudged Trang.

"Bao nhiêu một ký."

He turned to the seller. "Bau nhiu mut ki."

The woman laughed out loud. "For you . . . one dollar per kilo."

"Năm chục đồng một ký, dì ơi," Trang bargained.

"Nam chuc dung mut ki, zi oi," Dan repeated.

The seller snorted and shook her head. She pushed a small bamboo basket into Dan's hand. "Pick what you want . . . You're too adorable."

They came back from the market lugging a wooden altar, a ceramic Laughing Buddha, bags of fruits, bunches of ancestor money made from joss paper, flowers, and incense. At home, Trang taught Dan how to set up the altar, how to arrange the fruits onto a plate, how to pray with incense, and what to say as they burned the ancestor money to send it to the dead. Kneeling next to Dan, Trang whispered her prayers to the Laughing Buddha, asking him to protect Dan and keep his helicopter safe.

They started unpacking their bags, putting their clothes into the closet. Before it was done, Dan grabbed her by the waist, throwing her onto the bed.

In the middle of the night, they woke up and reached for each other. Dan was gentle and loving. When she worked at the bar, Trang's body tensed up with fear whenever another man touched her, but it had learned to trust Dan. It had discovered the ability to relax, surrender, and demand pleasure. It knew how to sing under Dan's touch. It taught Trang that when she was with Dan, she could forget about her own problems. No responsibility to her parents. No trace of shame. Only the overwhelming feeling that she was entitled to happiness. And she felt the passion between her and Dan was fueled by their mutual sense of being stranded between intimacy and strangeness, dream and reality, safety and danger.

When she woke up the next morning, Dan had put money into her purse. She understood that she could use it to buy food for both of them, to pay for water and electricity. And she understood that she could keep whatever was left. For that she was thankful.

Dan told her he was being transferred to another unit and would be away more often. She was anxious. Did being away more often mean he would be doing more dangerous missions? When she asked him, he just smiled and told her not to worry. She cooked a lavish meal, and as they ate that night, she explained why it was important to take off one's shoes before entering a home, how one should invite older people to eat first, and how to hold chopsticks.

After dinner, he sat on the floor, next to a bucket of water. As she massaged soap into his hair, washing each strand, he told her about his family. He came from a city called Seattle. He had a sister, and he missed his mother very much.

Dan must love her. Why else did he tell her about his family? He never mentioned a wife or a girlfriend and she was sure he had none. She felt no need to ask; she trusted him to tell her the truth because he seemed so open.

Curfew time was approaching and he had to go back to the base, but she hung on to him. "Don't go." She had no idea what exactly he'd do on his missions and she didn't want to know.

"I'll be back, em."

"Remember, you fly high. No joking."

He nodded. "I fly high. No VC can get me."

The following morning, Trang was so restless; she went out. Her feet were heavy as if she were lugging buckets of water. She passed Hân's former building. Hân had found herself a boyfriend and moved with him to Đà Nẵng.

She knocked at the door of Quỳnh's apartment. Quỳnh's roommate opened it, let her in and climbed back into bed.

"Wake up, Sister. Come have breakfast with me." She shook Quỳnh's arm.

Quỳnh turned away. Her face was smeared with makeup. Her breath stank of liquor.

The room was as quiet as a book no one had read. Trang studied each piece of furniture, each item of clothes, knowing how much history was held within it, just like an unopened page. She lay down next to Quỳnh. She gazed at her sister's bony shoulders but didn't dare touch them, knowing how much Quỳnh needed sleep. She'd apologized to Quỳnh after their fight but the distance between them was expanding, a river swelling during the rainy season. Trang would have to cross that river to be close to her sister again, but she feared her secrets would drown her. She wondered what secrets Quỳnh kept.

What was her Má doing at this time of day? She must be feeding Ba breakfast or working in the field. She must be sad that her daughters hadn't come home for a visit. There'd been regular reports about attacks by the VC along the highway to Kiên Giang, but people were still traveling. She should bring Dan home and introduce him to her parents. They'd be delighted to learn that such a wonderful man had fallen in love with their daughter.

She just hoped that Dan stayed safe.

She opened her eyes to see Quỳnh staring at her. The light, streaming from the window, was blindingly bright. The heat told her it was probably noon.

"Everything alright?" Quỳnh asked.

"Everything perfect." She smiled.

"Your boyfriend, he still treats you nice?" Quỳnh turned onto her stomach, resting her cheek on her palm.

"I'm his princess."

"Ha, tell me then, how much does he pay you per week?"

"It's not about money with him, em."

"Of course it has to be about money first, that's why we are here, chị Hai. Don't let him fool you." Quỳnh sat up. "Remember that on top of the rent, electricity and water, he has to give you at least one hundred dollars per month. All soldiers must do that to be able to keep a girl to himself."

Other bar girls had talked about this rule, but how could Trang ask Dan? Besides, she stayed with him because it made her feel good; their love was purer than money. She got out of bed, rolled her hair into a bun. "Come, let me treat you to bún thang."

Over steaming bowls of noodle soup cooked with chicken, pork, and dried shrimps, she avoided mentioning Dan and gossiped about other bar girls.

Afterward, Trang went to the Hollywood. She pretended to be sick, running several times into the toilet to vomit, coughing constantly and so hard that she was told to go home. She passed by the market, bought a ripe, large, and thorny red gourd fruit. Back at her kitchen, she extracted the fruit's red flesh, marinated it with rice wine and salt, then mixed it with the sticky rice she'd soaked the night before. She steamed both with coconut milk. In front of the Laughing Buddha, with her forehead touching the floor, she prayed for Dan's safety. After the three sticks of incense had burned out, the door clicked open. Dan stood against the evening.

She rushed to him and enveloped him in her arms so tightly she was sure he wouldn't be able to get free. He ripped away her pajamas and pinned her to the wall. With her clinging onto his waist, he made love to her urgently.

Later, on the bed, he tugged a lock of hair behind her ear. "Your Mekong Delta . . . beautiful. I see it from the cockpit of my helicopter, em."

Cóc-pít? Was it the place where Dan sat when he flew his helicopter?

"You keep safe." She caressed his lips. "You alway come back to me."

"You bet." He rolled her onto him.

She kissed the muscles of his chest, then moved her mouth lower. "You stay still. You close eyes."

His chim was sleeping when she reached it, but it soon got up and grew.

"Oh, baby, where did you learn that?" he groaned.

She grinned. A few days earlier, she'd found a book with photos of a Western couple in the bar's changing room. The couple was giving each other pleasure in ways she hadn't known about. The expressions on their faces told her that sex wasn't dirty and evil the way her work had made her believe. Sex was one of the greatest gifts someone could give his or her lover.

When it was Dan's turn to give her pleasure, she closed her eyes and let the music of her body lift her up and bring her to faraway places so she could see the bluest mountains, the most enchanting clouds and the brightest stars.

Later, they ate dinner in bed, naked. The sticky rice melted into her with its deliciously fragrant salty-sweet taste. She fed Dan the soft grains, laughing as he bit into her fingers. The war was raging outside, people were dying, but here in her apartment, she felt like she belonged to a world of peace, of safety, protection, and complete trust. She was astonished that she could love a person beyond their language, skin color, and nationality, and that love was stronger and more powerful than any war. Love overcame fears and threats.

When Dan came back next time, he gave her a most special present: the sensitive plant. She'd described to him her rice field, how much she missed it, and now he brought her a piece from the countryside. As she watched the plant timidly open its leaves inside his C ration can, she felt herself blooming for him, too.

She had brought along from home a diary and now she penned her happy feelings on the pages. She translated her favorite love poems and read them to Dan. She wrote her own poems, too, not about love but about a world of peace where kindness and compassion grew and blossomed, its light overtaking the darkness of wars and violence.

Dan's schedule was hectic, and he wasn't allowed to leave Tân Sơn Nhứt as often as before. She missed him like a rice field missed the rain, like the sea missed its waves, like the stream missed its fish. She was hungry for him, and for his love. But she noticed as the weeks went by that he was becoming more quiet, distracted, lost during his short and occasional visits. She tried to convince herself it was normal, that couples ran out of things to talk about. She wanted to know what he'd seen or done during his flights but it was a forbidden topic.

One evening Dan came by, looking tired and withdrawn, answering her questions in mumbles. She tried to brighten the mood when they were eating dinner by telling him a funny story she'd heard at the bar. She was halfway into it and giggling when he dropped his spoon and stared at her, his face reddening. "Are you fucking other men?" he asked.

She flinched. His words cut into her, sharper than a knife. "Of course not. I loyal to you, anh."

"Stay home then. You need money? Take it!" He threw his wallet onto the table.

Of course she needed money. Her parents' debts were still to be paid. Since moving in with Dan, her income had been slashed to less than a third. If Dan had really wanted to help, she would have accepted it, but the way he behaved was so arrogant, she felt heat rushing to her forehead.

She put down her chopsticks. "You need to trust me like I trust you. I do nothing bad. I don't go with men to private place." She would never depend on him for money. She had to stay independent, save for her education. Besides, what would she do all day at home when he was away?

"If you want to work, find another job."

"I tried, remember? I told you how hard it is." Since meeting Dan, she'd been determined to find employment at an office. She'd spent weeks writing job applications, to no avail. She hadn't gotten a single interview. There were too many unemployed people and the fact that she hadn't graduated from high school didn't help.

"Then try harder." Dan walked away from the table, leaving behind his half-eaten bowl of phở.

He didn't come for several days after this, and she blamed herself. She went over the argument they'd had countless times, telling herself that it was just a misunderstanding. But she sensed that it wasn't. Quỳnh's words echoed in her mind like a curse. *They're all like that at the start, but once they own you, they'll drop their masks.*

The next time he turned up, she showed him the many job advertisements she'd cut out of the newspapers and explained that she'd had no luck. Instead of listening to her, he picked up the *Sài Gòn Daily News* that she'd bought that morning. He stared at the article about an alleged Việt Cộng attack at a café in Sài Gòn, printed on the front page. He gazed at the photos of two Vietnamese men and a woman, their bodies mangled, bloodied. Suddenly he ground his teeth, then began tearing the newspaper into shreds.

"You okay, anh?" she asked him later, after she'd finished sweeping the torn paper into a corner.

"How can you even ask that question, given everything that's going on outside?" He went to the toilet, slamming the door behind him.

She looked at the torn pieces of paper. The illusory world she'd built, that she'd believed existed, had crumbled. How naïve of her to have thought that her relationship with Dan would save them. Dan was right. She had been pretending that things were normal, when she should be angry about the war and sorrowful about its victims.

When Dan came out, he sat down next to her on the sofa. He muttered words of apology, pulled her into him, and buried his face into her hair.

"Tell me what's going on, anh? Did you see things during your flights that upset you?" she asked later, after they had finished making love and she lay naked in his arms. When they first met, he'd told her that his helicopter only transported passengers, but she wasn't so sure anymore.

He flinched as if she'd just splashed boiling water onto him. He jerked his body away, got up from the bed, and put on his clothes.

"Anh . . . please . . . you never talk to me anymore."

"Be careful with your questions," he glared at her, his belt jingling as he buckled it. "You don't want me to think that you're an undercover VC, do you?"

Fear ran through her veins. She opened her mouth but words were glued to her throat.

He left the bedroom, only to return to tell her that he was kidding, that he was sorry she hadn't gotten his joke. By the time she was dressed, he'd gone, leaving some money on the table. She was seeing a pattern in his behavior. He would come to her distracted, nervous, and his temper would explode at something she said or did. Later, he would apologize, act tenderly, become again the man with whom she had fallen in love. Other times, though, he would remain quiet, brooding, but would cling to her as if she was keeping him from drowning.

She wanted to reach out to a friend who had an American boyfriend, who could help her understand Dan's erratic behavior. But her friends all worked at the Hollywood. They would tell Quỳnh, and Quỳnh would insist that she leave Dan.

She sat on the floor, staring at the palms of her hands. She'd believed that Dan wouldn't be pulled into the vortex of war, but now it seemed obvious that he was already in the middle of it. She imagined him roaming above her village's rice fields, that the dead bodies scattered under his helicopter were those of her parents and her neighbors. She broke down crying.

Later, she knelt in front of Buddha, holding the sticks of smoldering incense above her head. She prayed for Dan, for his innocence to be protected. She prayed for him to remain the gentle boy she'd met, the person she'd fallen in love with. She prayed for her parents, her sister, and everyone she knew. She prayed for the monster of war to disappear.

The following week, she opened the door to see Dan with a grim look on his face. He brushed her aside, went to the fridge, and stood next to it, drinking one can of beer after another, talking to himself, swearing. When she served dinner, he stared at the bowl of tomato soup, cupped his palm against his mouth, and vomited, right there onto the floor.

"Don't cook anything red!" he screamed as he washed up in the bathroom.

She stared at the soup, made from ripe tomatoes she'd sautéed with finely chopped shrimps. Perhaps the color resembled blood—blood that he'd seen or blood that he'd caused to spill. She shuddered. He was bringing the war into their apartment. Now she had to fight it head-on.

During his subsequent visits, the gulf between them grew larger and deeper. He stopped trying to speak or learn Vietnamese. All he did was eat, have sex, and sleep. He'd once enjoyed listening to her read aloud in bed but now violent sounds of American rock music replaced her voice. He drank constantly: beer, whiskey, and other hard liquors whose names she didn't know. He smoked cần sa, calling it "grass." There was no longer light in his eyes, just darkness.

Even his skin smelled different. It smelled of death and anger. She'd loved the taste of his mouth but now it stunk of tobacco and liquor, just like the men who frequented the bar. She'd imagined their love to be pure and delightful, like the sensitive plant's flowers, but despite her efforts, the plant had withered. Picking up the shriveled leaves, she felt as if her dreams had shattered, too.

"I do nothing bad, em. I don't kill anybody. Do you believe me?" Dan told her one day, as he was leaving the apartment, his hand already on the door's handle.

She bit her lips. She had a thousand questions that demanded answers. "Stay and tell me more, please . . ."

"I can't." He shook his head and looked at her with desperation. "I need you to trust me, that I do nothing bad. Not on purpose."

She gazed at his face. There were worry lines grooved into his forehead and dark pouches under his eyes. It seemed he'd grown ten years older in the past months. A lump rose to her throat. "Yes, I trust you, anh."

He took her face into his hands and kissed her. The most tender and passionate kiss.

When he was gone, she paced the apartment. She'd heard his call for help. He was sinking and she could be his lifeline. Maybe she'd never get the chance to be a doctor, but here was a chance to save someone.

She tidied the apartment. She went out and bought a recipe book for Western dishes. She would show it to Dan and asked him what he wanted to eat. She came up with plans to spend time with him outside the apartment, to remind him of the fun they used to have. Not just markets, there were museums, parks, theatres, and cinemas. She would borrow a motorbike for them to ride around town.

But when Dan came, he shook his head at all her suggestions. He stared at the colorful pages of the cookbook as if they were blank. "Just make whatever you want," he said.

He no longer complimented her cooking. He seldom smiled. He'd disappear for days, and when he visited her, he sat with his chair against the wall, his eyes on the door. He no longer ate on the street with her. He'd never carried weapons before but now a handgun was his companion.

On her way to work at the bar, Trang often came by Quỳnh's apartment to pick her sister up. One day, she found her sister curled up against a corner of her room. The night before, Quỳnh had gone for a long-time with a soldier, who gagged her, tied her to the bed, and hit her.

"Stay away from such men, em . . ." Trang told Quỳnh, wincing as she applied eucalyptus oil onto the black and purple bruises on her sister's arms.

"It's like they are possessed by devils," Quỳnh said.

"Who?"

"Those soldiers . . . The newly arrived ones are civilized. But when they go to the battlefield, it changes them."

Trang nodded. She'd seen it happening with Dan. "I've been thinking . . . violence is a poison. When you commit violence or witness it, it rots you."

"Yes . . . That's why I fear those men, but I also feel sorry for them. . . . I mean, they think they come here to help us, but they're making things worse. The bombings, the killings . . . all of that horror is being returned to them."

"But the Việt Cộng aren't any better. They're brutal, too. . . . I wish all of the fighting would stop."

"What will you do when the war ends, chị Hai?"

Trang inhaled the strong scent of eucalyptus into her lungs. The scent of her mother's love. The oil had always been the first thing her mother used whenever she and Quỳnh had a flu, a stomachache, a headache, an insect bite. "I want to go home with Ba and Má," she said. She no longer wished to be a doctor. She was failing her first patient. She would rather return to being a rice farmer, bringing seasons of life to her field.

"Yes, home . . ." Quỳnh said, her eyes distant.

Once again, Trang asked Quỳnh to move in with her. Dan had stopped spending the night at the apartment for a while now so Quỳnh could surely sleep there. But Quỳnh shook her head. "It's him who's paying the rent, I don't want anything to do with him." Quỳnh didn't know about Dan's erratic behavior. Trang had told her sister that Dan only transported people and wasn't involved in any fighting, but Quỳnh still didn't trust him.

At least Quỳnh agreed that she wouldn't go into private rooms with her customers any more. She was popular enough to earn a decent income by just entertaining men at the bar. They'd managed to pay more than half of their parents' debts. In a couple of months, they'd be free.

But it was getting harder to earn money at the Hollywood. Many GIs were boycotting bars that overcharged them and gave their girls Sài Gòn Tea without whiskey. While Trang tried to charm her customers into buying her drinks, she would think about Dan.

Dan, though, seemed to be so lost in his own world. He made love now as if she wasn't even there.

When he didn't visit for three entire weeks, Trang went to the base, looking for him. The longest he'd been away before was one week, for his R & R, to Taiwan, and he'd let her know in advance about his trip. At Tân Sơn Nhứt, she asked the armed guards about him but was told to go away. She feared he'd been killed.

She prayed to her Buddha every night. Then one morning, as she was washing her clothes, Dan stumbled in, drunk. She hardly recognized him: white bandages covered the top of his head. His left hand was in a cast and he limped. He'd lost so much weight, his cheeks were hollow. His eyes darted around constantly. He refused to let her touch him. He didn't answer any of her questions. He gave her some money, just enough for the rent, and left in the same taxi that had brought him to her.

The next time he visited, it was raining. He sat on the bed, his head in the cradle of his arms, his knees to his chest. As the rain hit the window, his body jumped, as if each drop were a bullet.

"No need afraid. Rain is music, anh." She hugged him from his back. "À ơi . . . trời mưa bong bóng bập bồng, mẹ đi lấy chồng con ở với ai," she sang quietly, a lullaby to the rain's rhythm. That night, she sang him countless lullabies, and he wept.

His injuries healed, and he went on missions again. He visited her from time to time, and their sex life resumed.

One day, she wasn't home when he turned up. He came to the bar to get her; when he walked in, she was drinking Sài Gòn Tea with a new customer. Back at the apartment, she was making her way to the bathroom when he grabbed a chair.

"You were having such a good time with other men. You whore." He flung the chair at her.

She ducked as the chair whizzed over her head, hitting the altar.

Watching the Laughing Buddha shatter into pieces, her legs gave way under her. "Oh Heaven, oh Earth," she cried, kneeling, knocking her forehead on the ground. "Please forgive us, Buddha, forgive—"

"Shut your fucking mouth!" Dan threw his can of beer at her. It hit her forearm, bounced off the wall, spattering liquid onto the floor.

She ran into the bathroom, locked the door, and pushed her body against it. She trembled. Buddha would be angry at Dan. Buddha could punish him, bring bad luck to him and to her for being with him. Nobody could avoid karma.

Dan continued to ramble. She heard the sounds of furniture being knocked against the wall. "Death is our business and business is good," he shouted, over and over. On his last visit, she'd seen the phrase written on his T-shirt. She'd asked him what the English words meant and he said, "It's who we are, you dumb cunt."

Tears ran down Trang's face, rinsing away any doubts she'd had. If she stayed with Dan, she could end up dead. He was lucky to have her and if he didn't know it, it was his loss. Unlike other bar girls who brought clients to their beds as soon as their boyfriends went on missions, she'd been faithful. Unlike other women who demanded expensive gifts and monthly allowances, she'd hardly asked Dan for anything. How stupid of her to think that he loved her when he didn't even know her real name. She knew his from his dog tags. Not Dan but Daniel. Daniel Ashland. But he'd never even thought to find out her name.

She took down the iron rod from which the shower curtain hung. Even though the rod was no match for Dan's gun, she had to defend herself.

Things became quiet. Dan started to weep. After a while, he knocked at the door. "Baby, I am so sorry."

"You get out! You leave!"

"What?"

"I don't need you. You go now. You called me a whore. Fuck you!" She'd never said that word out loud before, but once she did, she realized it didn't sufficiently express her anger. "Đù má mày! Mày chửi tao thì tao chửi ba má mày. Tao chửi tổ tiên của mày đó!" She ranted in Vietnamese, cursing Dan's parents and ancestors. If Dan understood, he would kill her, but she no longer cared. She would prefer to be dead than to be insulted by the man she had shared her life with like a wife. How stupid of her to have trusted him. She had cooked for him, served him, given him her body and her mind, only to see him flick her away as if she was a mosquito.

"Honey, please . . . I swear to God I'll never, ever behave like that again," Dan told her through the door.

"You liar, you go away!" She gripped the iron rod tighter. Dan was no longer the gentle boy she'd known. Whatever he'd seen and done was rotting him.

"Baby, I need you. I'm a wreck, you're the only one who can help me. Please, would you help me?"

She shook her head. As he broke into sobs, her grip on the rod eased. She slid onto the floor, tears rolling down her face. She recalled the first moment they met, the joyful memories they'd shared. With her blurry eyes, she saw her enemy: the war. It stood between her and Dan, like a gigantic monster. It was laughing at her, baring its teeth. If she gave up her fight, it would swallow her whole.

She opened the door, sat down next to Dan and embraced him.

After their tears had dried, he asked her to wash his hair. She understood the silent plea under his words. He needed her to wash away all the smoke and the death he'd seen underneath the blades of his helicopter. Wash away his sins.

"Your helicopter down? What happen?" she caressed the big scar on his leg.

He nodded, then stared into the distance, unblinking.

◇

SEVERAL WEEKS LATER, she woke up, nauseated. She dashed into the bathroom and vomited.

"Your stomach hurt?" Quỳnh's voice said. She had come over for a bowl of late-night rice porridge, which Trang had served with salted white radish and century eggs; after the meal, the two sisters had curled up in bed, talking about old times, and Quỳnh had ended up spending the night.

Trang gagged and threw up again.

"It can't be your delicious food, I feel fine." Quỳnh lowered herself down next to Trang on the bathroom's floor. Her brows knitted in concentration as she pressed her fingers against the main veins on Trang's throat, under her jaws, as well as on her wrist. "Your pulse," she gasped. "It's racing. Oh Heaven and Earth!"

Trang pushed herself up. She grabbed a towel and dried her face. "What?"

"You're pregnant, chị Hai." Quỳnh cupped her mouth with her hands.

"No, you're wrong." They'd always used condoms, but Dan had recently refused. He said he felt nothing with the rubber on. To avoid getting pregnant, Trang had started taking pills. But as Dan came by so rarely, she'd stopped the pills and washed herself after sex. She'd done it before. She hadn't gotten pregnant. She couldn't be pregnant now.

"Oh Heaven, oh Earth." Quỳnh's face was pale, drained of blood. "I told you to be careful, didn't I?"

"Why are you so paranoid? Perhaps I'm sick with the flu or something. Besides, if I'm pregnant, Dan will take care of me. He loves me."

"You're such an idiot! These American men, they only want sex. They want sex and nothing else, you understand?"

"*Shhh.* You want the neighbors to hear?"

"You'd better not be pregnant." Quỳnh held up Trang's wrist, pressing her fingers against Trang's vein again. "Oh Heaven and Buddha," she whispered, "I can see the blood vessels on your neck. I can read it in your pulse. You're truly pregnant." She buried her face into her palms and howled; her cries painful as those of an animal being butchered.

Trang rushed to the sink and threw up.

On the bed, she shook Quỳnh's shoulder. "Em, don't you think you might be wrong?"

Quỳnh looked up, her eyes red. "I learned how to check a pulse from dì Vinh the midwife. She let me practice on her customers. I have no doubt you're carrying a child, chị Hai. You'd better tell Dan about it."

Trang brought both hands to her stomach. A child? She hadn't wanted it, but perhaps it was for the best. Dan had said he needed her. A child would help him forget about all the troubles of this world. During the previous months, whenever they went out, he'd often beamed at small children, complimenting them on how adorable they looked.

"I'll tell him soon." She pulled up the blanket, covering Quỳnh's chest and hers. "Let's get some more sleep. I'm tired."

She closed her eyes. Dan might have become hot-tempered, but he cared about her. Since that big fight, he'd behaved better. She felt the warmth of a new life sprouting in her stomach. Her baby. Her baby would be beautiful, inheriting her and Dan's best features.

She couldn't wait for Dan to come back, to tell him the fantastic news.

◇

Trang counted each minute, until six days later, when Dan appeared at the bar. She ran to him. "News, I have news," she shouted above the music.

He looked around, eyeing some soldiers.

"Anh, you not hear me?" She tugged at his arm.

"What?" He faced her. His hair was unkempt, his eyes were red and cloudy as if he hadn't slept for days.

"I have news. Good news." She clutched his hand, pulling him outside.

On the pavement, away from the bar's entrance, everything was quiet. A peddler approached them, two baskets filled with mangoes and guavas dangling from a bamboo pole balanced on her shoulders. "Ai mua ổi mua xoài không?" she sang.

Dan leaned against the brick wall, lighting a cigarette. She coughed, fanning the smoke away with her hand.

He blew more smoke, eyeing a girl in a miniskirt who was walking past them.

"Dan." She waited until he turned back to her, then took his hand, placing it on her stomach. "Baby. We have baby, anh."

His eyes widened. "What the fuck?"

"Baby. Em bé. I'm pregnant. We have child, anh."

He snatched his hand away from her stomach as if he'd touched a burning coal. He dropped the cigarette, grinding it slowly with the tip of his right shoe.

"Your baby." She reached for him.

He lifted his head to look at her.

She had anticipated this moment and imagined many possible reactions from him: he could be overjoyed; he could be cautious; he could be upset.

Never had she imagined what happened next: she saw fear cross his face. As she stood there, stunned, he turned, and without a word, walked away from her.

◈

"WHAT DID HE SAY?" Quỳnh asked when Trang returned inside. The bar was busy as usual; too many girls were drinking, chatting, and laughing, as if it wasn't their own lives they were gambling with. How stupid of Trang to have placed all of her bets on Dan; how naïve of her to have believed in the wonders of love.

Trang turned to her younger sister. The hope in Quỳnh's eyes pained Trang; she realized how much Quỳnh had cared about her and wanted to protect her all along. With trembling lips, she faked a smile, avoiding Quỳnh's gaze. She'd dried her tears and hoped Quỳnh wasn't able to read her worry. "Oh, he's very happy," she said. "He assured me he's going to take care of me and our child."

"You're lucky, chị Hai." Quỳnh let out a big sigh, embracing her. "Tell him you need money to prepare for the baby's birth. If he doesn't give you his dollars, ask for PX stuff. Radios and watches are selling well these days. And liquor."

Trang nodded. In the beginning, Dan had given her a few things from the military post exchange, but he hadn't brought her anything for a long while. Standing in Quỳnh's arms, Trang rested her tired bones against her sister and wished to travel back in time, to the days when she sat with Quỳnh under the banana plants waiting for their father. At least the waiting had been filled with hope.

She didn't know what to do. In no case would she end her pregnancy: this baby was the fruit of the love between her and Dan. She had to nurture that love.

Dan might be upset because the news was so shocking. When she saw him next, she'd say she didn't need extra money from him. She'd continue to work until she was ready to give birth.

She told herself that everything would be all right, but something twisted in her stomach. Since the incident with the chair, she'd replaced the altar and bought a new statue, but every time she prayed, she sensed the Laughing Buddha was no longer listening.

Three days later, she came home to find an envelope on the table. Only Dan and her sister had other keys, and Quỳnh had been with her all day. The envelope was stuffed with money. Money, but not enough for the time she'd spent with Dan. She waited one week, and then two. She went out to Tân Sơn Nhứt, but the guards wouldn't let her onto the base. She understood it now: Dan was too much of a coward to face her.

Back at the apartment, she sat staring at her stomach. She realized that her involvement with Dan, just like his country's involvement in Việt Nam, was a mistake. Both caused irreparable damage, leaving the Vietnamese to clean up the mess.

She lifted the mattress, and as she touched the envelope Dan had left behind that she'd hidden there, she flinched. These American bills were the reason that women like her were despised. She'd sold herself for these dollars and now they no longer meant anything. She lit her stove, wanting to burn the money, but extinguished the flame. She would need it to take care of her baby.

War and Peace

Hồ Chí Minh City–the Mekong Delta, 2016

D an pulled the duvet to his chest. It was morning. Linda was sitting on the other side of the bed. She'd been up for ages writing postcards to her friends and reading her guidebook. It must be the jet lag. They hadn't talked since leaving Phong in the lobby and returning to their room the night before. He was relieved she was no longer accusing Phong of scamming them into helping him get to America. And she was no longer threatening to go back home.

Yesterday, when she left him at the post office, he'd hurried after her, but she'd refused to look at him. She didn't talk to him in the hotel elevator. Once inside the room, however, she had yelled, "You asked Thien about GI kids and guess what? One shows up and tells you what a hard life he has. He looks poor, and he wants to go to America. It's a scam. They want to take advantage of you!"

He'd tried to convince her that Phong sounded genuine, but she asked whether he knew enough Vietnamese to understand what was really going on. She brought up Kim and challenged him about honesty and truth. As she wept, he gave her Edith Hoh's business card. "Your Dr. E. . . . She told us to call in case of a crisis, remember? If this isn't a crisis, I don't know what is."

Linda dialed the number straight away. It was already 10:15 p.m. in Seattle but Dr. Hoh was both patient and helpful. She listened to them both, advised them to keep talking to each other. She told Linda it wasn't uncommon for veterans to conceal their past; one of her clients had discovered her husband's Vietnamese child only after the husband had passed away. Dr. Hoh made Dan promise to be honest with Linda from then on and to have Linda's agreement on decisions regarding his search for Kim.

They talked for over an hour, and Linda gradually calmed down enough to agree to continue the city tour in the afternoon, and to meet Phong in the evening.

Dan curled his body into a fetal position inside the duvet. He wished he could have talked to Phong more, but he'd promised Linda to speak to him only in her presence. What a terrible life Phong had had. He hoped Kim hadn't left his child outside an orphanage somewhere.

When Phong mentioned his longing for his father, he'd wanted to pull the younger man into his arms. He'd been afraid that his child would blame him, but he saw in Phong so much yearning, hope, and determination that overwhelmed any blame.

He needed to talk to Phong again, see what he could do to help—maybe he could share Phong's story with his veteran friends, some of whom were connected to other vets online. What a pity he didn't have Phong's phone number, otherwise he could ask a hotel staff member to arrange for another meeting and help translate for the conversation. Thiên sucked as a translator; he was being a jerk and it had been clear the guy wasn't translating parts of the conversation and Phong had looked frustrated.

The clock on the bedside table now showed 7:18 a.m. Linda started texting on her phone. She must be telling her friends about the fights she'd had with him. Those women must be cursing him for ruining her holiday. He closed his eyes and turned his back to her. Regardless of Linda's admonitions, he intended to go ahead with his search. There was no way he'd allow her to control his life. If she worried about ads in newspapers and on TV, he'd go for DNA testing; it'd be more private.

Dan wished it was still night so he could get some more sleep. His body ached. He could feel the imminent attack of a headache. He reached for the bottle of water he'd left on the bedside table.

"All that time I was thinking he was a scammer, but he didn't even take the money I tried to give him," Linda suddenly said.

He choked on the water, and coughed to clear his airway. He turned to her. "You mean Phong?"

She nodded. "I told Jenna about him and she sent me some links to articles about GIs' kids. So I did some more research—"

"What did you find?" He sat up.

She gave him her phone. On the screen was an article published in the *Washington Post*, entitled "Legacies of War." As he read, his eyes teared at the story of Võ Hữu Nhân finding his American family after forty-six years; he learned about Amerasians' struggles. The article ended with a story of an Amerasian man, Nguyễn Thành Trung, who said that if he ever found his father, he would ask just one question: "Why did you leave me here?"

Dan stared at the question. If he told his child he had just been twenty years old, scared as hell, would his child forgive him?

Linda moved closer and they looked at more stories online, so many stories: Of Amerasians' desperate search for their parents, of fathers rejecting their Amerasian children, of American vets traveling back to Việt Nam to find their kids, of happy reunions, of heartbreaks.

As he read, he hoped for a glimpse of light that would lead him to Kim and his child. But there was nothing about the Hollywood Bar nor the two sisters who'd worked there. From the phone, strangers stared at him; strangers who could well be his family.

He couldn't believe he'd ignored this for so long. Over the years, sometimes it had crossed his mind that he should search the internet. But he'd resisted the urge. He'd buried the past and decided that it would cause him more pain to dig it up again. He'd tried to convince himself that Kim and his child were better off without him, and that the child wasn't even his.

"This whole thing is so messy." Linda pulled up an article. "Have a look . . . It's about a woman who didn't want to be found. Her family was destroyed because her GI came back looking for her. She was married and hadn't told a soul about her past."

Dan had imagined the family Kim had, and her children, but not the consequences his search for her might bring. What if Kim wanted nothing to do with him? What if he could crash the life she'd worked hard to rebuild by finding her?

A ding on the phone. "That's probably Jenna." Linda took her phone back. She read the message, then looked up. "She wants to give us some money so we can buy some books and clothes for Phong's kids."

The hotel's phone rang. Dan reached for the receiver.

"Good morning, Sir . . . I'm calling from reception," a male voice said. "Mr. Thiên is here. He would like to talk to you alone, without Madam. He asks if you can come downstairs."

"I'll be there right away." Dan put the phone down. Yesterday morning, when Thiên said he would quit, Dan had snickered. He hated the guy, and felt glad never to see him again. But in the afternoon, as they continued the city tour, he could see how helpful Thiên was to Linda. He was accommodating to her requests and enabled her to get good deals at the Bến Thành Market, the tailor, and art galleries. Dan thought Thiên had probably changed his mind about quitting. After all, the guy was earning good money from this trip, and probably also commissions from all those sales. But Thiên being so early couldn't be good news.

He pulled on his jeans. "It's Thien."

Linda looked at the clock. "The tour starts in an hour. Or am I wrong?"

He zipped up his fly. "He wants to talk to me . . . alone."

"What? Another secret you guys want to hide from me?"

"No more secrets, I promise. I'll tell you what he says."

Linda frowned. "Something is going on. Yesterday you two behaved as if you despised each other. I was the one who had to beg him to translate for your meeting with Phong, remember? Now that I think about it, he was pissed when you shouted at him in front of the post office."

"Let me go deal with it, okay?"

She yanked at the curtain, opening it wide, refusing to look at him.

◇

STANDING IN THE hotel's reception lounge, Thiên slapped an envelope onto the table. "Money you paid me in advance." He dropped the hundred-dollar bill onto the envelope. "Good luck with finding your girlfriend."

Dan wanted to gather the money, tell Thiên to fuck off, and go upstairs, but he couldn't afford to upset Linda even more. If he let Thiên quit, Linda would explode. Thiên had booked all their hotels, arranged for transport and activities for the whole two weeks.

He sighed. "Let's sit down and have a talk, shall we? Mr. Thien . . . you've helped a lot of vets, you know how much pressure I've been under."

"No vet is as rude as you. You talk down to me, treat me like shit. I already told Duy and Như I cannot help you. I don't care that your wife is their friend. If you need a guide, ask reception."

"I thought you were professional, but you dump your customers during a tour? Don't forget you're the one who started all this trouble. You got drunk and told Linda."

"I told your wife your secret, I know. . . . I didn't mean to. But I'm glad she's upset. She should be very angry. Because of you guys, we lost the war. I was fighting my ass off, and here you were, having a good time with your prostitute, getting her pregnant." Thiên clucked his tongue. "All those years, people said we lost because we Southern Việt soldiers were coward, but the coward ones are you. You fucked our women and you don't dare accept responsibility."

Thiên's words hit Dan so hard, he was blinded with anger and couldn't acknowledge some of the truth. "Oh, come on," he said. "Don't tell me that you guys were all angels. I saw with my own eyes how some of you behaved. As for losing the war, ask your corrupt, incapable former leaders . . . If someone were to blame, it's them."

"Ha, at least they stayed and fought," Thiên responded. "We were here fighting when you ran off, went home to your mama, remember? You left us here so the Communist had fun with us. Yeah, they had fun. They put us in reeducation camps. I spent five years in those prisons. Five years and they still call me Ngụy. That means illegitimate, you think that's fair? You think it's fair when they still treat me like the enemy but they welcome you back? You're their rich tourists now. You're their friends. I served your damn war and now I serve you."

Dan thought of his dead friends. There was no way that he and his comrades should be blamed for the shit the Vietnamese had done to each other. It was their civil war. Thiên had suffered, but so had millions of Americans. He was too tired and had no time for another argument. Linda could come down any minute. "Okay, I hear you," he said. "Can we just sit down and have a civilized conversation?" He wished the receptionists would stop glancing at them from across the lobby.

Thiên shook his head but threw his body onto an armchair.

"Mr. Thien ." Dan leaned across the table. "I'm here to make amends, and I need your help. Please . . . Linda was looking forward so much to this trip. You've been really helpful to her and I appreciate that very much. I know that I've been moody, but from now on I'll try to keep my emotions in check."

"Oh yeah? I not sure your drama is over yet. Now your wife knows about Kim, what are you going to do? You forget about Kim to make your wife happy?"

"Linda is a compassionate person. She'll come around. She'll understand that I need to look for Kim and my child." As Dan uttered those words, he wondered if searching for Kim would be the right thing to do even if Linda agreed.

"If you want my advice, I say you ignore Linda. Women can't pee higher than the top of grass blades."

"Sorry? Women what?"

"They can't piss high. That's our proverb. Women cannot think big. So, are you man enough to look for your child, or are you afraid of wife, crawl under her skirt?"

"Of course I want to find my child—"

"Yeah, that's the right thing to do." Thiên sat up. "Everyone needs a father. A child with no father is a home without its roof. That's our proverb, too. Because you want to search for your child, I'll help you. But if you shout at me again, we're done, understood?"

"Okay, but I need you to remember something." Dan looked Thiên squarely in the eye. "I was an officer here. You can advise me but there's no way I'll accept being told what to do."

As the words left his mouth, Dan wondered why he felt the need to express his authority over a person whose help he needed. Besides, he'd spent decades trying to escape his military title.

"Yeah, I know you were an important guy." Thiên snorted. "But don't expect me to salute you. For four years, I was a Marine Captain."

Dan blinked. Up to now, he'd thought of Thiên mainly as a tour guide. He hadn't stopped to consider the battles Thiên had fought, the men Thiên had led, the sacrifices Thiên might have made for those men. "Where were you stationed?" he asked. "With your rank, I think you could have immigrated to the U.S. if you wanted to?"

"I was in Huế and Quảng Trị." Thiên stared at the table between them.

Dan shuddered. Those areas sandwiched between the North and the South had been soaked in the most blood. Despite their distance from Sài Gòn, he'd had to fly there occasionally on missions. He remembered picking up bodies near Huế. Intestines spilling out of open abdomens. Faces half blown off. Shredded limbs. The weight of the dead would pin his helicopter down as he tried to lift it off the ground. The smell of blood would cling to him even after he'd washed himself. The redness of it.

"With my years in the camps afterward," Thiên said, "I qualified for the Orderly Departure Program, but my mother didn't want to go. She said she was born here, she must die here. I'm her only son, how could I have left my mother behind?"

Dan looked at Thiên, at his gray hair and many wrinkles. The Vietnamese had suffered so much and had to make such difficult decisions. He recalled the stories he'd read, about families separating themselves onto different boats as they escaped Việt Nam to ensure at least someone would survive.

"I still have nightmares about those times, you know . . ." Thiên squeezed his forehead. "About Huế and Quảng Trị, the camps, the years after my release when I had no rights as a citizen . . . But I'm better off than my dead comrades. There's no memorial for them here. Some graves of my friends were destroyed, dug up." Thiên's scar twitched. "You American vets have benefits, paid by your government. We have nothing. You have a wall in Washington, but we aren't acknowledged there. We fought for you, alongside you, yet you pretend we don't exist."

Dan sat in silence. In his subconscious, he'd brushed aside the stories of ARVN veterans like Thiên. On his bookshelves there was no book written by any ARVN veteran, either.

Thiên looked at his watch. "Oh . . . I have to bring granddaughter to school." He stood up.

Dan gathered the money, gave it to Thiên. "You can't quit now, please . . ."

Thiên sighed, stuffed the money into his backpack and slung it over his shoulders.

"Hold on," Dan said, "I still owe you. Our bike ride the other night, and your overtime." He gave Thiên fifty dollars and walked Thiên to the entrance. "Let's go to your wife's shop later today, I think Linda would like to meet her, too."

◈

NHÂN'S SHOP OCCUPIED the living room of the house she and Thiên owned. The building was tiny, situated within a maze of winding alleys, but it was neat: the rooftop and balconies were filled with pots of healthy-looking lemongrass. Up close, the plants looked like razor grass, but their use was versatile. With Thiên translating, Nhân explained the health benefits of lemongrass: it could cure a cold, stomachache, cough, or diarrhea, and help boost digestion. According to Nhân, the Vietnamese often surrounded their gardens with lemongrass bushes to keep mosquitoes and other insects away.

Dan and Linda went with Thiên's family to dinner at a street restaurant where chicken, beef, squid, prawn, okra, and eggplants were marinated with minced ginger, chili, and lemongrass and grilled on coals right in front of them. Sitting there, surrounded by locals, listening to them chat in their own language, Dan recognized something unique about Sài Gòn that had survived the war: the charm of its people, their incredible energy and resourcefulness. In his nightmares, the city was war-torn, ravaged with violence like the day he'd left it. Now, seeing it thrive brought him a sense of peace and consolation. He was starting to understand why other vets had said the return trip had helped them.

◈

LINDA LOWERED THE car window and snapped pictures of the emerald rice fields rolling alongside the road that led to the Mekong

Delta. The wind lifted her hair, wafting a refreshing scent of lemongrass Dan's way. She'd used the shampoo made by Nhân and said she should have bought more.

On a rice field, two farmers stood opposite each other, holding long pieces of rope, swinging a bucket to scoop water from a stream onto a field. In another field, a boy was riding a water buffalo, his body a mere mark of punctuation on the great sentence of the animal. As Linda waved and took photos, the boy threw both hands into the air, beaming.

Dan told himself he should print Linda's photos from this trip and display them around the house. Perhaps the smiling child could replace his dreams of buffaloes and boys with their bodies ripped apart.

Yesterday, when Linda took a nap after their morning tour and before visiting Thiên's house, he'd gone to the hotel's business center. He needed to know more before he could decide whether to look for Kim and his child. An online search for "Hollywood Bar, Saigon, 1969" yielded no results. Plenty came up when he looked for "Bars, Saigon, 1969," but there was nothing about the Hollywood. The information he found led him to more stories about Amerasian children. There was so much for him to read and learn.

Now, lush fields and gardens soothed his eyes. He couldn't believe he was venturing into the heart of the Mekong Delta again. On his first mission here, he'd been amazed by the many shades of green from rivers, lakes, crops, and forests glistening below his helicopter; it wasn't until later that he'd let himself see, among that green, the many shades of black and brown: scorched villages, burnt forests, deserted fields, bomb craters, and scattered bodies of people and animals.

He studied the thatched-roof houses surrounded by ponds and gardens where chickens and pigs wandered. Kim and his child could be living in one of them.

Their car approached a small town and traffic slowed.

"Mr. Thien, is your phone on? We wouldn't want to miss Phong if he called," Linda said. "My friend Jenna keeps asking if we've talked to him yet."

Thiên held up his phone. "Maximum volume, Madam. Last night, I asked him to call me today, but he hasn't."

"Too bad we don't have his address," Dan said.

"We won't be far from his hometown. If he call, we can visit him."

Dan nodded, feeling grateful for Thiên's help, thinking about Thiên's struggles. Thiên's only son was divorced. Like many, he worked as a construction worker in Saudi Arabia, leaving his only daughter for Thiên and Nhân to take care of. Dan had been astonished to learn from Thiên that hundreds of thousands of Vietnamese were working overseas as laborers. Thiên's former daughter-in-law was in Taiwan taking care of an elderly Taiwanese man. She hadn't seen her daughter for several years.

Thiên and his family would have had a very different life if the winning regime had acted differently. Thiên said that in the late eighties, his son had passed the university entrance exam but wasn't allowed to study. Many children of former ARVN soldiers had experienced various forms of discrimination, some of which continued today. So strange, because everybody seemed to welcome returning American vets.

Linda cocked her head. "Is that a market? Can we stop to have a look?"

To their right, sellers and buyers were gathering on a dirt path that cut into the main road. "Great idea," Dan said. Since last night's adventures around Thiên's neighborhood, he was excited to experience more of the local life.

Thiên parked. Linda handed Dan his cap, put on her sun hat.

The market was bursting with activity. Vendors squatted behind bamboo baskets brimming with vegetables, metal trays piled with meat, buckets filled with flopping fish, wriggling eels, or crawling crabs. Not far away, women stood behind pots of green plants and yellow and pink flowers.

Linda pointed her phone at Dan. "Say hello to our friends," she beamed. He waved back awkwardly, realizing that she was doing a livestream on her social media. Thiên had gotten her a local SIM card with internet connection.

When Linda moved her camera onto Thiên, who was bargaining with a sweet potato seller, Dan continued on the dirt path. The happy look on people's faces and the sound of their language reminded him of how much, at first, he'd adored the way of life here. If it wasn't for the war, he'd love to come back regularly with Linda once they retired. They could escape the wet, cold Seattle winter to bask under the sun here, somewhere near the beach. The year-round warm weather of South Việt Nam would be good for Linda's arthritis.

He ventured deeper into the market, and found himself in the middle of a crowd. People were speaking loudly; some were almost shouting. The breeze that had welcomed him at the market entrance had disappeared, leaving him alone with the sun's intense heat. Sweat started to trickle down his neck and forehead. As he passed the meat vendors, the smell of blood nauseated him. He had to go back to the car. He looked for Linda but couldn't see her. A cold feeling ran through his body. He imagined the VC, their faces smeared with mud, appearing from surrounding rice fields and pulling her away.

Several bells clanged. He turned around. Three bicycles with bamboo cages piled high approached. More than a hundred chickens were imprisoned inside the cages, their eyes black, their mouths gasping. Some were squawking, fighting for a place to stand, their feathers fluttering into the air. The bells continued to clang. "Tránh ra. Tránh ra," a rider shouted at the women whose baskets blocked his path. The shouts drilled into Dan's temples.

He gazed at the bicycles and saw himself staring down at them from his helicopter. "Those motherfuckers," Rappa was screaming into the intercom, "they're carrying ammo!" On the trail that zigzagged through the forest, a line of gooks were bicycling. As his helicopter neared, those on the ground looked up at him. They dropped their bikes, ran for cover, but the trees around them had been burnt by napalm, their charred branches grasping at the sky. *Ack-ack-ack-ack-ack. Ack-ack-ack-ack-ack.* The gunner and the crew chief's M60s coughed fire. As his aircraft lowered, Dan blinked. The dead looked young. Too young. They lay motionless on the ground, their bodies punctured by bullets. Blood had soaked their white shirts, which glistened under the sun. His eyes searched frantically for weapons. None. Next to him Reggie McNair was staring through the plexiglass, his mouth working silently, his hands white-knuckled on the cyclic pitch control.

"Oh fuck! They're wearing school uniforms. Oh fuck!" Rappa cried, standing by the helicopter's door, next to his M60.

"It's their fault they ran from us. Their own damn fault," Hardesty said.

"NO . . ." Dan howled and the corpses sat up, became the row of vendors who were smiling, chatting to each other, bargaining.

He walked to a tree, knocked his head against the trunk.

Noise rose around him. Sellers called out their wares. A child laughed.

Someone pulled his shirtsleeve. An old, toothless woman. Her mouth caved in as she smiled. She made a drinking gesture, offering him something with both hands: a cup of water.

He shook his head and walked away. He didn't deserve kindness. Not from Vietnamese people.

He focused on his breathing. In and out. In and out. When would this end?

"Are you okay, Sir?"

A young man stood in front of him, his worried-looking face framed by a pair of square glasses.

"Yeah, thanks." Dan turned to go back to the car but Linda appeared, her phone in front of her.

"Smile for the camera." She snapped a photo of Dan and the young man.

"Oh, you caught me off guard." The young man laughed. "I bet I look terrible," he said, his white shirt blotched red with blood as he touched his exposed intestines.

Dan closed his eyes, shook his head, and turned away. He tried to control his breathing. In and out. In and out. As his tremors eased, he pulled his cap lower. That day many years ago, coming back from the mission, his crew chief had filed a report of ten enemies killed and five probables. Dan had said nothing about the children lying dead on the forest floor being counted as the enemy. As he lifted his chopper, he'd caught a glimpse of their school bags tethered to the back of their bikes.

How had the parents of those children coped? How could one cope with the pain of losing a child?

Opposite him, a boy was kneeling, arranging ears of corn onto a mat together with his mother. The boy looked the same age as the children he'd helped murder.

He wanted to kneel in front of the boy, take him by the shoulder, look into his eyes and say he was sorry.

Linda was still talking to the young man in glasses.

Thiên appeared. He lifted several bags high up, beaming. "My wife loves food from the countryside. Oh . . . that rice over there looks good. Give me another minute, please."

Thiên squatted down in front of a bamboo basket heaped with white grains. How lucky for the guy, Dan thought, that he could get so excited about such everyday things.

The sun burned down on Dan as he waited. His throat was dry, sweat soaking the back of his shirt. He edged next to Linda, hoping she'd notice that he wanted to leave.

"Now . . . tell me where you learned your English," Linda was asking the young man. "I think you speak it better than me."

"No way." The man laughed. "I learned it at university, and I hope you have no problem understanding me, since I'm an English teacher."

"You are? That's wonderful."

"I am between my classes. I teach at the local primary school." The man patted the black case he was holding.

Dan reached for Linda's arm. "Can we please go?"

She turned to him and gasped. "Are you okay?"

"A heat stroke can be dangerous, Sir," said the man. "I think you should sit down. Come to my house for a cool drink?" He gestured across the rice fields toward a low house nestled in a garden filled with tall trees.

"Thanks, but I'd rather get to our hotel early," Dan said. They still had a long way to go and he didn't want to travel in twilight or the dark. Not in the Mekong Delta.

"It's no trouble at all, Sir. Really."

Linda squeezed Dan's hand. "Come on. Didn't you say we came here to experience the authentic Vietnam?"

As they left the market together with Thiên, Dan gazed at the rice fields. A breeze blew, sending ripple after ripple across the vast green. He let his vision fill with the rolling waves as his breath slowed.

◇

THE YOUNG MAN introduced himself as Thanh. His house, with its sloped roof of red tiles and wooden pillars, looked like a sanctuary. Thanh unlocked the door. As they took off their shoes and entered, the soothing scent of incense welcomed Dan. The sight of a family altar greeted him: a high table laden with plates of colorful fruits, two vases of radiant white and yellow chrysanthemums, a row of ancient-looking portraits, and a blue ceramic holder from which sticks of incense smoldered, their perfume both enchanting and mysterious.

"Today is my grandmother's sixth death anniversary," Thanh said. "My mother is out shopping. You should see how many dishes she'll be making. . . . But we'll need plenty of food. Many of our relatives will visit us tonight."

Dan recalled how Kim had cooked and prayed to her grandparents on their death anniversaries. She'd believed that the dead could return to enjoy the food, and that incense smoke could help the living communicate with those who'd passed away. Dan wished he could believe in it, too.

"Meet my father." Thanh led them toward a man who sat in an armchair in the living room. Thanh bent down, telling the man something in Vietnamese.

The man looked up, his eyes blank. As they shook hands, Dan studied the man's haggard face. Was he in pain? He sat with his back hunched, his feet on the armchair, his knees against his chest.

"How are you doing today?" Dan asked. Thanh translated, and the man's face lifted. His smile was as timid as a child's.

"Nice to meet you," Linda said and the man gave her the same facial expression.

"What happened to him?" Thiên whispered as they sat on low chairs around an equally low table on the other side of the living room, near the altar. Thanh had opened a window and a cicada chorus streamed in, punctured by the chirping of birds.

"He lost his memory a few years ago, Uncle. I think the English word is 'Alzheimer's'?" Thanh turned on the standing electric fan and a breeze rushed to Dan, easing the heat that had clung to him like a tight shirt.

"Yes, Alzheimer's . . . I'm so sorry," Linda said.

"He doesn't know who I am, nor my mother." Thanh sighed, and the pain in the young man's words cut into Dan, deep in his gut. Dan had witnessed such pain when he came along with Bill and Doug to visit Bill's mother, who had been living in a care facility and also suffered from Alzheimer's. Every time Bill visited his mom, he would bring along a photo album of their family to remind her of the life she'd had, of the children and the husband who loved her.

Dan turned and gazed at Thanh's father, who was sitting there, silent, as if frozen in time. He wished he could tell the man about his wonderful son, who'd bestowed kindness to strangers and brought them home.

On the table was a bamboo tray holding a blue and white ceramic tea pot surrounded by matching cups. Thanh poured some dried tea into the pot. "My father doesn't remember anything from his past, except for one thing." Thanh shook his head. "His walk through Trường Sơn Jungle during the war."

"You mean he was a Northern Communist soldier?" Thiên asked.

"Yes, Uncle . . . He fought in some major battles. Quảng Trị, for example. We're lucky he survived."

Dan exchanged looks with Thiên. Quảng Trị was the blood-soaked province where Thiên had commanded his troops, where Dan's comrades had released countless bullets, rockets, and bombs to clear the way for him to pick up the dead and the injured.

How would the man react if he knew his former enemies were visiting his home?

"What's your father's name?" Dan asked Thanh, desperate to get to know the older man as a person.

"Nguyễn Văn Khoa."

Thiên filled a glass with water and brought it to Nguyễn Văn Khoa. He knelt down so they were both at the same level; he talked to Thanh's father, his voice gentle, as if speaking to a dear friend.

"I'm sorry . . . about what your father had to go through," Linda told Thanh. "How long was he in the army?"

"Eight years." Thanh poured steaming water from a large thermos into the teacups and rinsed them; slender white strands of steam whispered up his hands. "My grandma had already set up an altar for him, crying every day for her dead son. And then he came back."

"Your grandma believed he was dead? Why?" Linda asked.

Dan looked up at the portrait of the elderly woman on the altar. She wore a black áo dài and a calm smile. He thought about the vicious memories snarling beneath that serene demeanor. He thought about his mother.

"It was terrible, really . . ." Thanh poured tea into the cups. "Her neighbor listened in secret to a Southern radio, which often broadcast a list of Northern soldiers killed. One day, they read my father's name, his home village, and date of birth. My grandma hadn't heard from my father for a long time, so she believed it was true. Later, once he returned, my father said the radio must have gotten the list from a former comrade in his unit who had deserted and joined the other side."

Dan shook his head. There'd been a psychological war going on with dueling radio broadcasts. During his time in Sài Gòn, he'd sometimes listened to broadcasts from North Việt Nam, read by a woman called Hà Nội Hannah. She always brought the most terrible news about the war, announcing American units that had supposedly been wiped out, encouraging American servicemen to defect. It had been difficult to know what was true. When Hà Nội Hannah said that the American Army had massacred hundreds of civilians in a hamlet in Central Việt Nam, he'd thought it was all exaggeration and propaganda. But upon his return to Seattle, he read about the horrors of Mỹ Lai, which were confirmed by the Mỹ Lai court-martials.

"The ironic thing is," Thanh's eyes were distant, "during his years as a soldier, my father used to listen to a Southern radio channel. It was forbidden, but he did it because the radio aired classical music just after midnight. He would lie there in complete darkness on his hammock in the jungle or in an underground shelter, his small portable radio pressed against his ear while his comrades were sound asleep. The music saved him."

The teacup radiated its fragrance in Dan's hands. He stood up and walked toward Nguyễn Văn Khoa, a man he and his comrades would once have called a gook, a dink, a slope. They'd used such names not just on a man like him, but on many Vietnamese, even the ones fighting on their same side, like Thiên.

Dan blew on the tea to make sure it had cooled down before giving it to Nguyễn Văn Khoa. The man received the tea, took a sip, and put it on a chair next to him.

"Your wonderful son made it. It's good, isn't it?" Dan said, and Thiên translated.

The man looked out the window. Only silence was in his gaze.

"I tried but couldn't get him to talk," Thiên said.

Back at their table, Thanh poured more tea for everyone. "He was the best father," he said. "He built this house with his own hands, but now it's hard to get him to do anything. . . . I really miss him. When he came home from the war, you know what he brought along from the South? Books. He said he'd seen people burning them and he stole some."

"Books were burned? When and why?" Dan asked.

"After the war," said Thiên, "the new government said certain books were evil. So all types of books, deemed to be 'đồi trụy và phản động'—'decadent and anti-Communist'—were destroyed. Books written by writers in the South, translated books . . ."

"That's terrible," Dan said. For a reader like him, burning books was an incomprehensible act, and most people who didn't even read would fight for the right to open any book they chose. Those in power feared free minds, and nothing unlocked thinking like literature.

"Where were you during the war, Uncle? Did you have to fight?" Thanh asked Thiên.

"I was with the ARVN. Your father and I . . . we could have killed each other." Thiên rubbed his scar.

Linda had stood up to take a group photo, but she sat down as she heard this.

"Does it still hurt, Uncle?" Thanh said.

"Nah, but it painful here still." Thiên put his hand on his heart.

Thanh shook his head. "What the poet Nguyễn Duy wrote is so true. At the end of each war, whoever wins, the people lose. Even though my father has Alzheimer's, he can't get rid of the war. Sometimes he wakes up in the middle of the night, screaming."

"Has he been able to receive any kind of counseling? He could be suffering from PTSD," Linda said and Dan studied Nguyễn Văn Khoa, wishing he could do something for the man.

"I haven't found anyone who could help him," Thanh replied. "I read plenty of research in the U.S. about PTSD and trauma, but little research has been done here, nor do people pay much attention to mental health. My father is suffering from trauma, this I'm sure of. He can't be in a room with a ceiling fan for example. The fan's spinning blades would terrorize him and remind him of American helicopters."

A shock jolted through Dan's body; he had lost faith in God but he now felt God had led him here, to this conversation. "What did your father tell you about helicopters?" he asked.

"He said helicopters were his worst enemy, that there were so many of them. They appeared out of nowhere, any time, day or night. They dropped soldiers to hunt him and his comrades down. Twice, he was chased by helicopters that tried to shoot him . . ."

Dan looked at Nguyễn Văn Khoa. Had the man once been under the blades of Dan's chopper? Had the man tried to shoot up at him?

Dan turned to Thanh. He didn't want to reveal his past, but he owed it to this young man who had shown him nothing but kindness and honesty. "I'm so sorry," he said. "Your father, I . . . it was unlikely we were in the same battle, but I was a helicopter pilot here in 1969. I was stationed at Tan Son Nhut."

Thanh's jaw dropped. "You flew helicopters?"

"My husband's task was to rescue injured soldiers." Linda interjected. "He didn't fly helicopters that shot people."

The children were laid out in a row, as if lined up to go to class, surrounded by the brown earth, stained with red blood. What could he say to Thanh? He and his crew hadn't slept for over two days, flying mission after mission, adrenaline screaming in their veins. The land below tried to kill them. Not soldiers, not VC, not AK 47s or recoilless rockets or Quad 50 machine guns, but the land itself. The endless green of it. That morning they had watched it spit up green tracers that raked another helicopter. The Huey, filled with troops, burst into flames, fireballing into a jungle-thick hill. The day before, another chopper had gone down, caught in an American artillery barrage someone hadn't called off in time. He could still see the scratches in the metal of the 155-millimeter shell a split-second before it slammed into and obliterated the chopper.

It made no sense. The reasons they were there. The reasons for them to fly, their eyelids held open as if by invisible wires piercing their skin. "Gooks," his gunner had said. "If they're dead, they're VC. No sweat, GI."

Would that serve as apology enough to Thanh? To Kim? To the children he had helped murder? To the child he had left here?

"I'm really sorry about what happened to your father," Linda told Thanh. "The war ruined too many Vietnamese lives, Cambodians, Laotians, and Americans, too. My husband still wakes up screaming sometimes. You may not believe what I am saying"—her voice was filled with tears—"we're here to offer our apologies, and to make amends."

Thanh wiped his eyes with the back of his hand. "Then I have to do something, for all of us." He hurried to the altar, ignited a match, lit sticks of incense, and raised the smoldering incense high. Dan stood up, his head bent; he prayed for innocent lives lost, for bleeding wounds to heal, for those who had been wronged to be able to forgive. When he opened his eyes, Thanh had led Nguyễn Văn Khoa to the table. Once the elderly man had sat down, Thanh reached for Thiên and Dan's hands, putting them on top of his father's. Thanh spoke in Vietnamese, in long sentences that sounded like prayers. Nguyễn Văn Khoa began to tremble. Thiên, too. Dan's body started to shake; he sensed he had been allowed to live just so that he could witness this moment when a child of war brought former enemies together. The spicy-sweet smell of incense embraced them, and Dan felt so many other dead and wounded Vietnamese and non-Vietnamese gathering around them. His crew members Ed, Neil, and Reggie were there, along with the children they'd killed. All were holding hands, praying for each other, praying for peace.

◇

LINDA SAT NEXT to Dan on a stone bench in the garden, under the shade of trees. Birds chirped above their heads and butterflies flittered on a branch of yellow flowers close by. Inside the house, Thiên and Thanh were deep in conversation.

"Isn't Thanh incredible?" Linda said.

Dan nodded. He'd written down Thanh's email and phone number, with a promise that he would arrange for Dr. Hoh to talk to him.

"When Thanh prayed, I joined him too." Linda looked up to a green canopy, as if searching for answers. "I found myself thinking about Phong and his family. . . . Thanh and Phong . . .they've both inherited our horrible war. Remember what I told Thanh in there? That we're here to make amends. I must honor those words."

Dan was on the edge of tears. He shook his head against it.

"What is it?" Linda asked.

"All of it. This place. I'm not sure, but I think it's near the site where my helicopter went down . . ."

"Where you got injured?"

He nodded. He hadn't wanted to tell his mother about the crash, but the army had notified her when he was in the hospital, so of course Linda knew.

"Are you ready to talk about what really happened? It may help," Linda said.

He kissed her hair. He'd put up tall walls between himself and Linda. He needed to break them down.

She placed her hand on his.

He stared at their hands, covered by age spots. He wasn't sure how many years they still had with each other, holding hands like this. He took a deep breath.

"It was October twelfth, 1969," he said. "That afternoon, my crew and I were tasked to pick up a Long Range Reconnaissance Team, or LURP as we called it. They'd radioed us the location and said everything was clear." He focused his eyes on the rice plants beyond them. "I approached the landing zone, not knowing that it was surrounded by a large number of VC."

Linda gripped his hand.

"I almost made it when all hell broke loose. While our men were being butchered on the ground, my helicopter was hit by AK-47 rounds. Mortars and rockets exploded all around us. If one of those had struck the Huey, we'd have been destroyed. The LZ was so narrow, the trees so tall, I wasn't able to lift the helicopter up quickly. And it was raining so hard . . ." He closed his eyes. He hadn't been at his best that day. Kim and he had had a terrible fight the previous night about something trivial. He'd thrown his bottle of beer at her, hitting her head. He'd left to go back to Tân Sơn Nhứt without making up with her and ended up tossing and turning the whole night.

"Then?" Linda looked at him.

"Both my gunner and crew chief were killed almost instantly. My copilot called for air support as I tried to get us out of there. I thought we'd make it back to the base but our engine had taken such bad hits, we crashed shortly after. I don't remember how we went down, just that when I came to, my copilot . . . he was dead too." He couldn't tell her that Reggie McNair had been trapped in his seat with a tree branch piercing his chest.

Linda clasped her palms against her mouth.

"All these years, I've wondered why I deserved to live. It was me . . . I was responsible . . ."

"It's not your fault. It's not!" She whispered. "Don't think about the people who died, think about those you rescued, please . . . Remember David who visited us the year after your return? He told me you risked your life to save his. And Tom, who still sends you a card every Christmas."

He loved Linda for trying to save him, for being here, for listening. In telling her about the crash, he'd hoped to lift the weight off himself.

But it was still there, still contained in what he couldn't bring himself to tell her: the school children he had helped slaughter—there was no other word—two weeks to the day the men he mourned crashed and burned. Maybe it was not his fault. Maybe it was what Kim would call his karma.

The weight of those dead children. The weight of the child he had abandoned.

How to Be a Mother

Sài Gòn–Hóc Môn, 1970

Trang paced back and forth in the room she shared with Quỳnh and two other girls, her hands on her eight-and-a-half-month swollen stomach. Her brown bag of clothes sat on her bed. She hadn't packed any of her books, which piled up next to her pillow. She'd spent a lot of money on them and what a waste. It was their fault she had allowed herself to daydream, to believe romance existed, to be convinced that women could overcome anything life threw at them. They were the reason she saw life in color, when she should have seen it in black-and-white all along.

How stupid of her to have fallen for Dan. Without him, she and Quỳnh would've been able to pay their parents' debts *and* save enough for their future by now. Dan and this baby were the worst mistakes of her life. She should have listened to Quỳnh and gotten rid of the baby. Buddha would have understood and forgiven her.

Their two roommates, Đông and Nguyệt, were sitting on the other bed, playing cards. They worked at Paradise, a bar where Trang and Quỳnh found a job after the Hollywood had been closed down during one of the government's anti-prostitution campaigns. Trang liked Paradise better even though it didn't pay as much: it didn't have a back room.

Quỳnh had gone out to borrow a motorbike to take Trang to the house of Đông's cousin in Hóc Môn, around forty minutes away, where Trang would give birth and hand over the child to a nearby orphanage.

Trang looked toward the window of the room she was in. It was on the third floor and the wooden panels were shut, but Sài Gòn's noise still squeezed in. A mother was scolding her daughter, the bells of cyclos jingled down the street, and a peddler called "Who'd like to buy some steamed cassava?" The distinctly raspy, nasal voice of Khánh Ly singing "Cát Bụi" by Trịnh Công Sơn issued from a radio: "Hạt bụi nào hóa kiếp thân tôi, để một mai tôi về làm cát bụi."

How true. Everyone came from dust and would one day return to dust. Life was transitory, after all. Trang had thought about returning to dust. It would be simple. She would plunge into the Sài Gòn River. The fast current would sweep her away, pulling her down into an abyss of dreamless sleep. But if she did that, what would happen to her parents and her sister?

After Dan left, she could no longer afford the apartment he'd rented for her. She moved back with Quỳnh. As her pregnancy became obvious, she stopped working. She stayed inside and hid herself from curious eyes. And now, she was about to go out on the street.

She glanced at her stomach. She looked and felt like a pregnant buffalo. For sure someone would notice her on the street, and the news might travel to her parents. She thought about her mother bending over her father's bed, cleaning him and changing him. Her father had fallen sick again. He couldn't walk, the doctors had been wrong. He was scheduled for another surgery.

How would her parents react if they found out about the baby? She shuddered at the thought. Several years before, in her home village in Phú Mỹ, a mother committed suicide after her daughter had died giving birth. The daughter was unmarried and the villagers' malicious whispers were too much to bear. If Trang's parents knew about the pregnancy, they'd surely blame themselves; perhaps they wouldn't survive such a shock.

Sweat slid down Trang's neck. She'd heard frightening stories about childbirth. She hated this baby. She wished it would disappear.

She had considered going to a hospital or a medical clinic for her delivery, but then she would have to present her papers, which had her address back home. And she would risk meeting people who knew her parents or relatives.

Someone pulled her arm. Trang looked up to see Đông, her roommate. "Bồ tèo," Đông said, "come and talk to us." She took Trang's hand.

Trang sat down on her bed.

Đông handed her a glass of water. "Drink up. It's hot out there."

"The midwife, are you sure she's capable?" Trang asked.

Đông nodded. "She's *very* experienced. She used to work at Hóc Môn's maternity hospital and retired recently. She delivered my elder sister's baby. My mother always said that when I give birth, she'd want Mrs. Yến to be the midwife."

"You really think it's a good idea?"

"You're the one who should decide, Trang," Đông said. "Since you're so terrified about your parents finding out, having Mrs. Yến as your midwife is a good option. My cousin Ngân's house . . . it's just down the road from the midwife's. The best thing is that the orphanage is close by."

Trang nodded. Quỳnh had been to Ngân's house, she said it was simple but comfortable enough; she'd also met with the midwife and talked to the nuns at the orphanage, who were willing to help. Trang held back tears thinking about all the women who were reaching out with helpful hands while no man did so much as lift his.

Đông and Nguyệt went through the contents of Trang's bag again: a few sets of clothes, a washcloth, lots of dark-colored underwear, a toothbrush, ten pieces of soft, white cotton fabric for diapers, and two sets of baby clothes—one blue and one pink. Đông and Nguyệt had brought these clothes for the baby. No one knew whether the baby was a boy or a girl, and Trang didn't care.

Đông went downstairs and came back quickly, panting. "Quỳnh's here. Let's go."

Trang put on her sun jacket and her cloth hat.

Đông walked ahead with the brown bag while Trang followed, descending the stairs at the back of the building. Her bulging belly was hindering her view of the steps. She held on to Nguyệt's elbow.

Soon she was out of breath. She gestured to Nguyệt and they slowed down. Reaching the ground floor, she tried to control her breathing. She snuck a look and caught a glimpse of her landlady's back. She ducked and pulled the hat's rim lower. The radio was still on, broadcasting news of a VC attack in Thủ Đức, on the outskirts of Sài Gòn. She shivered, thinking about the village Quỳnh was about to drive her to. She knew it was in Hóc Môn but didn't know whether that was in the same direction as Thủ Đức.

She squeezed through a tiny door and into the back alley. From beneath the brim of her hat, she could see a sagging Honda 67. Quỳnh sat in the front; a food bag had been secured to the motorbike, between her legs. Đông tethered Trang's belongings to the back with rubber cords.

Trang climbed onto the bike, her belly squashed against Quỳnh's back. She placed her feet on the footrests and held on to her sister's waist with both hands. Her pants felt so tight, she feared she'd faint. This baby was the cause of all her trouble. Once it came out, she wouldn't give it a name. She wouldn't look at its face. She'd give it to Quỳnh and ask her to take it to the nuns immediately.

❖

"Thu Hoa ơi, Thu Hoa ơi," Trang called her daughter's name. With both hands, she lifted the baby to her face. Hoa was asleep. Sunlight leaked through the closed window and lit up her fair skin, hazel hair, and high nose.

"Why do you have to look so American, so much like him?" Trang said to her two-day-old infant. Hoa was light in Trang's hands, the blue shirt was too big for her, and the cloth diaper that Trang had wrapped and tied around her bottom hung loose.

A rattling came from above her head and Trang shrank, looking up. The VC could be hunting for women like her. She imagined black muzzles piercing through the layers of coconut leaves, coughing out fire.

Trang held her baby tight against her chest. With her heart hammering against her rib cage, she quietly got up from the bamboo bed and stood next to a rattan clothing cabinet in the corner, her hand clutching her weapon—a hoe, which she'd found in the front yard. She wished that Ngân was home, but Ngân had gone to her parents' to help take care of her sick mom.

Outside was nothing but empty fields. Ngân had said American airplanes had been spraying some type of chemical. Since then all the crops just withered and died. "My father told me it's stuff to make leaves fall off trees, so their soldiers can see the VC more easily." Ngân had sighed. "The war doesn't just kill people, it robs our livelihood and destroys nature."

Silence, then the squeak of rats. Trang let out a sigh of relief. She got back to the bed and gently lowered her daughter onto the straw mat. She admired Thu Hoa. The curled fingers. The small hands, already dotted with mosquito bites. The chubby legs and the little toes. Every part of this baby had come from inside of her. It was a miracle that she'd given birth to such a perfect human being. Perfect except for the mosquito bites. She blew on the red dots, blaming herself for not being careful enough.

Hoa stirred, turning her face toward Trang, her mouth opening, searching. Trang unbuttoned her shirt. Her chest ached as the milk started to flow. Hoa's hand reached up and met Trang's hand. Trang held on to the tiny fingers, lifting them to her nose. They smelled like flowers. She cried into them.

She'd been so sure about giving Hoa away. She'd told Quỳnh to go and prepare the nuns at the orphanage for the baby's arrival. With each passing minute, though, the bond between her and Hoa grew stronger, as if Hoa was becoming a part of her body again.

Hoa sucked hard; she was hungry, and so was Trang. She still had some cooked rice in the kitchen, but nothing to eat it with. She hoped Quỳnh would come back soon with food. But then Quỳnh would want to take the baby away. Trang's chest grew heavy, just thinking about it.

The heat, the slant of sunlight, and the wailing of cicadas told her it must be early afternoon.

Hoa released Trang's breast, opened her mouth and started to fuss.

"Don't cry, don't cry," Trang whispered, switching her to the other breast.

Again Hoa drank greedily; droplets of sweat lingered on her forehead and Trang bent, kissing them away. She caressed Hoa's hair. How fine the strands were. As fine as Dan's hair. Where was he now, and did he have any regrets? How would he feel if he knew how beautiful his daughter was?

Weeks ago, she'd been to Tân Sơn Nhứt again, looking for Dan. The guards there, armed with rifles and cold stares, had told her to leave. After lingering outside the airbase for several hours, she saw one of his friends. She ran to him, asking for Dan. "He's packed up and gone home. That lucky bastard," the man said, staring at her swollen stomach. He ignored her questions, waved for a taxi, and left.

Hoa's lips were moving more and more slowly. They stopped, then moved again. Trang looked out of the bedroom, toward the house's entrance.

◈

TWO DAYS PRIOR, Trang was on the mat and in terrifying pain when she heard the baby's first *oe oe*.

"Trang, feed her." Mrs. Yến put the baby in Trang's right arm. The baby was as slippery as a fish and as small as a cat, her skin wrinkled. Yet in Trang's embrace, she stopped crying. She opened her lips as the midwife guided Trang's nipple toward the infant's mouth. As the baby sucked, Trang felt tiny heartbeats against her chest. A strange sensation overcame her and suddenly her tears came. Her pain eased and calmness spread through her. She had a daughter. A daughter!

While the baby ate greedily, Mrs. Yến wiped her clean. Quỳnh didn't touch the baby. She dropped the pink dress onto the bed and stepped away.

Mrs. Yến taught Trang how to wrap and tie the cloth diaper around the baby's hip. "When you hold her, always support her back and neck. They're very weak right now. Oh, and before I forget, you should get up as soon as you can and move around. Drink plenty of water, otherwise your constipation will be worse than labor pain."

Trang caressed her daughter's face. Her skin was as soft as rice powder.

Mrs. Yến wiped Trang's thighs with a towel. "Such a large baby, and you don't have a tear. You did well, really well."

Trang smiled. It had been a long time since anyone told her she was good at anything. She hoped Quỳnh heard it, but her sister was at the door, listening for outside noise.

The midwife pulled the blood-soaked towels off the bed and put them into a bag. She folded a piece of cloth diaper and placed it inside Trang's underwear. "You'll bleed the next few days, but it's normal." She lifted Trang's hips and slid the underwear on.

Trang felt overwhelmed with gratefulness. "Cảm ơn dì."

Mrs. Yến nodded. "I have to go."

Quỳnh let her out of the house. Trang gazed at the creature she was holding. How wonderful that she could stop the baby from crying by feeding it. She sensed the baby knew who her mother was. And look, the baby was falling asleep on her breast, her long eyelashes fluttering.

Quỳnh sat down next to her. "Are you hungry, chị Hai? I have some sticky rice."

Trang shook her head. "Water, please."

"I have something better." Quỳnh rummaged in her bag for a small carton of milk. Trang drank and smiled at Quỳnh. How lucky she was that her younger sister had arrived in time. The pain had started early that morning, when it was still dark out. As daylight came, it became almost unbearable. But Trang dared not go to the midwife, fearing she'd meet the VC on the road. She was on the floor, digging her nails into her palms, hoping the midwife would come check on her as she'd promised, when someone reached for her. Through her tears, she saw Quỳnh. She hadn't even heard her younger sister, nor the motorbike. Quỳnh told her to stay calm and ran for the midwife.

Trang wanted to thank Quỳnh but her eyelids were as heavy as bricks. "I think I'll sleep a little." She was still half naked but didn't care.

"Of course. You must be exhausted."

Trang gazed at the baby once more before sleep drifted her away.

◆

She woke to rays of sunlight slicing across the room. It must be late afternoon. Hoa was still sleeping soundly, her head resting on her arm.

"How do you feel?" Quỳnh's voice said. Trang looked up to see her younger sister sitting next to her.

"Much better."

"Good. Ready to go?"

"Go where?"

"The orphanage."

Trang turned to the baby. The corners of the rosy lips were lifting, as if smiling. In her pink dress, Hoa looked like a lotus flower.

"She is too small," Trang found herself saying. "Give me another day, please. She'll be stronger then. I just want to make sure that she lives."

"She will. As I said, the nuns at the orphanage take care of newborns all the time. And I can't wait another day."

"Then come back tomorrow . . . please."

"Sister, do it now! The more time you spend with her, the more difficult it'll get."

Trang gazed at the baby again. She'd had a good rest, and her head was clear. She knew what she wanted. "Just one more day, please, em."

"It'll cry, and the neighbors will hear."

How annoying that Quỳnh was calling the baby "it," the same way she'd refer to an animal.

"Not if I feed *her*," Trang said. "Don't you think it's a miracle that I have milk for her? I actually have milk!"

Quỳnh stood up. She stomped her feet; as if this could release her anger. She paced the room. Trang looked around and realized that her bags of clothes and food were gone.

"Chị Hai, snap out of this, won't you?" Quỳnh shook her head. "I can't do this any longer. I'm damn tired. I can't keep supporting you like this. You're my older sister, you're supposed to take care of me."

"I know, and I'm sorry." Trang noticed how skinny Quỳnh had become. All those long motorbike trips must have been exhausting. "I'm forever grateful to you, em. I know I've been selfish, but what I'm asking is one more day, just one more . . ."

"If you care for me, you wouldn't have done this. You've wasted too much of our time." Tears rolled down Quỳnh's dusty face. "More and more girls have come to the city since you stopped working. You can't believe how difficult it is now to get a guy. And at our bar, we're fighting for each customer, like dogs for a bone."

"When I'm back, I'll help you fight." Trang smiled. "Women are fat after giving birth, but I'm still slim, you see? Just my boobs got bigger.

American men will like that." She lifted her breasts, bobbing them up and down.

"What I am saying is . . ." Quỳnh reached for her bag. "If you care for me, you'll let me take the baby to the orphanage. Now!"

"Please, em . . . I told you, and I'm begging you again. Just one more day. I want to make sure that Hoa will live."

"I hate that name. And I hate him. I hate him for destroying us."

"Quỳnh, please."

Quỳnh held out her arms. "Give it to me. The nuns will take good care of it. Better than you ever can."

Trang held on to the baby tight. "No! Just one more day, I beg you."

Quỳnh rolled her palms into fists and beat them onto the floor. She went out and brought back Trang's belongings. She left for Sài Gòn without a word.

Trang drifted in and out of sleep that night. As soon as the baby made the slightest noise, she was up, feeding her. Throughout the dark hours, she reached for the baby's chest and nose, time and time again. She feared her daughter might stop breathing.

The next day with the baby passed in a flash. How different it was compared to the previous week, when each day seemed like a year. Trang discovered that when the baby turned toward her, her mouth opening like a bird, she was hungry. When the baby kicked her legs, she was happy. When the baby gazed at Trang with her brown, innocent eyes, the world stopped moving and nothing else mattered.

For the first time in Trang's life, a human being depended on her entirely and she could satisfy its every need. Her day was occupied with feeding Hoa, putting her to sleep, changing her diapers, and humming lullabies. And she found herself telling her daughter the stories she'd read. She knew now that to live without imagination was only to exist, and to be without books was the greatest punishment.

◇

HOA WAS SOUND ASLEEP. Trang rocked her slightly, then laid her down on the bed. She got up, twisting her body. Her bones creaked.

She was about to go to the bathroom when a noise came from the front door. She knew it wasn't Quỳnh, as she hadn't heard the motorbike. She raced to the baby, picked her up, and hid behind the rattan cabinet, one hand gripping the hoe.

Sound of a key. The door was pushed open and light rushed in.

She blinked, trying to recognize the person who'd appeared before her. The door quickly closed.

"Trời ơi," a low voice said. "You're still here?"

Trang let out a sigh of relief. She released the hoe. "Dì Yến . . ."

"How's she doing?" The midwife opened her arms to receive Hoa.

"She drinks a lot and sleeps plenty." Trang smiled.

"She's *adorable*." Mrs. Yến admired the baby, who now opened her eyes. Mrs. Yến clucked her tongue. "Oh you cutie, you cutie . . . All of us Vietnamese want to have your high nose. We want your white skin. Are you giving me some? How about giving me some?"

Trang smiled, delirious that the midwife agreed with her: Hoa must be the most beautiful baby ever born.

"Such a good little girl." Mrs. Yến handed Hoa to Trang and pulled a tiny flashlight out of her shirt pocket. "Does it still hurt?" She examined Trang's lower lip. "I've never seen a girl as brave as you. Giving birth without a single cry. You were biting your lip so hard, I was afraid a piece would fall off."

Trang winced.

"It looks bad. You don't want it to be infected. Tell your sister to get some medicine."

Trang nodded. She hoped her lip would heal by itself. She'd burdened Quỳnh enough.

The midwife lifted the baby's shirt, examining her. "She's quite healthy. You're doing a great job."

"Really, Auntie? I wasn't sure."

"Trust yourself. Look, the umbilical cord is drier, so that's excellent. Just let it be. It'll fall off by itself." The midwife put the torch away. "All is good. I don't think you need me anymore. Anyway, I'm going away for a few days. The Black Virgin Mountain. I take my mother there every year to pray."

"Auntie, this baby, I . . . I don't know what to do."

"Her father, try to find him."

"My sister and I looked everywhere, Auntie. His friends said he's gone back to America."

"Without telling you? What a bastard."

Tears stung Trang's eyes. She hated Dan for being such a coward. He had disappeared from her life as soon as he heard about the pregnancy. As much as she resented him, it broke her heart. She realized that she'd been deceived all along. Dan must have had a girlfriend or a wife in Seattle. One time he'd been drunk and thrown up all over himself, she had helped him change and, as he slept, washed his jeans. Inside the pocket, she'd found a picture of a blond, beautiful girl. At the back of the picture were the words "I love you. Come home soon." She asked him about it as soon as he woke up and he mumbled that it was his sister. She was surprised that a sister could tell her brother "I love you," but he acted annoyed, saying that it was a normal thing for American siblings to say. Now, upon reflection, she knew that he'd lied.

"I wish I could help you more, Trang," the midwife sighed. "But please, think about the orphanage or find somewhere safer than here." She cocked her head and listened for outside noise. "I must go. Sorry."

Trang pushed a rolled-up bill into the midwife's hand. "Thanks for everything, Auntie."

The midwife returned the money to Trang's pocket and reached into her own. As she undid the buttons, a delicious aroma rose up. She gave Trang two golden bananas.

"I'll never forget what you've done for me." Trang held on to the fruit, letting the woman's kindness be her pillar. "If you change your mind about visiting, I'll be here . . ."

The midwife avoided Trang's eyes. She gazed at the baby. "Good luck, little angel." She walked toward the door, opened it, and disappeared.

Trang heard the clicking of the lock. She tasted salt on her lips.

❖

HOA RELEASED TRANG'S NIPPLE, her eyes wide open, innocent, joyful. As Trang gazed into those eyes, all her worries became lighter, then vanished. What else mattered when she could hold her precious child in her arms? Outside, the wind sang. A bird chirped, as if declaring that life was beautiful and worth living.

Trang laid her daughter on the bed, and Hoa looked up at her, the corners of her lips lifting.

"Oh, you want me to talk to you?" Trang clucked her tongue. The baby's eyes lit up, her legs kicking.

Trang buried her face into the baby's scent and tickled Hoa with her nose.

"How about a bath? I think you would like a bath, wouldn't you?" Next to the bed was a water jug and a wash bucket, and Trang poured water onto her washcloth. She wiped her baby gently, from face to neck, from chest to back, from hands to feet. Hoa waved her arms and kicked her legs, looking more and more excited. Trang cleaned the hands, each finger, thighs, each toe. She turned the baby to her side and cleaned her back.

She hadn't known there was so much pleasure in taking care of a little human being.

After dressing Hoa, she picked her up and fed her. Hoa quickly fell asleep.

Trang reached for her bag again. At the bottom, under her clothes, she found an envelope. Inside was the picture of her and Dan taken at the zoo. She stared at his face. She'd waited for him to come back and rescue her, but now she knew she was the only person who could save herself and her daughter.

◈

THE ENTRANCE DOOR OPENED; Quỳnh snuck in, closing it behind her. A cloth bag dangled from her hand. Trang's stomach rumbled at the smell of food.

"You okay?" Quỳnh glanced at the baby.

"Yes, em. Thanks for coming." Trang smiled, her lips trembling.

Quỳnh gave Trang a container. "Stir-fried noodles. Sorry I couldn't manage to get anything else . . ."

"It's perfect." Trang put the box down. "Quỳnh, I've made up my mind."

"About what?"

"I'm bringing my baby back to Sài Gòn with me."

"Are you crazy?" Quỳnh's eyes widened.

"I'm more sure about this than anything in my life." Trang held Hoa to her chest. "I can't abandon my girl. I won't do it." Once they got to Sài Gòn, she'd find an ugly nickname for her daughter, to protect her from evil spirits. For now, the baby looked too beautiful, too precious, she could not bear to associate her with something hideous.

"How about our parents? Have you thought about them?"

"It'll be a shock, I know . . . but they'll get over it," Trang said. "I'll explain and they'll understand. They love me so they'll support me." If she abandoned her baby, Hoa could become one of the Amerasian children who scavenged at markets. There was no guarantee that the orphanage would be there forever, not when the Southern government was so corrupt and in chaos, not when the Communists had been gaining strength, winning battles, convincing many Southerners that they were more organized and capable of liberating Việt Nam from foreign domination.

"The Việt Cộng would bring trouble to our family." Quỳnh shook her head.

"The war will be over soon, em. I don't have to bring Hoa to our village until then. I've worried about our parents, but I need to live my life. This baby is mine. No one can take her away from me."

"You've gone mad," Quỳnh said. "How are you going to raise her, huh?"

"Heaven gives birth to elephants, Heaven will give birth to grass," Trang said, quoting a proverb. "There'll be a way. I don't want a life without my daughter by my side." The words filled her with pride. She couldn't believe it'd taken her so long to make up her mind. Of course she was going to raise Hoa. She was going to have to work hard, but being a mother was the best thing she'd ever experienced.

She showed Quỳnh the money that Dan had left behind. "This will help in the beginning."

"You're fucking crazy," Quỳnh fumed. "This baby is going to destroy your life, and mine, too."

Trang stood up. With Hoa in one arm, she started gathering her belongings.

◈

THE SUN WAS hiding behind a curtain of cloud when Trang climbed onto the back of the motorbike. She clutched the baby against her chest with one arm, the other hand wrapping around Quỳnh's stomach. Quỳnh had been angry but she seemed convinced that Trang would change her mind once they were back in Sài Gòn. As the motorbike started to move, Trang held the baby tighter, using her body to absorb the bumps.

Quỳnh was driving faster and faster. Hoa slept soundly in Trang's arms.

Trang made the calculations in her head. They'd paid most of their parents' debts. She'd resume her work at the bar in a week and the money would help pay for a babysitter. Hoa wouldn't need much during the first months, except for her milk. In Trang's village, mothers had raised many children by themselves, it shouldn't be too hard for her to do the same. And save. She'd save ferociously, and resume her studies one day. She would never, ever let a man distract her from her plans again.

A breeze came. Trang took a deep breath, packing her lungs with the cool air. She bent, feeling her daughter's tiny face with her nose. What a wonder that she'd given birth to such a beautiful human being. And Hoa smelled so good, just like a lotus. A gift from Buddha.

At a checkpoint, Quỳnh stopped the bike.

Two military policemen searched their belongings, including everywhere on the motorbike. They must be looking for mines; there had been attacks on this road.

The third soldier tossed his chin at Trang who stood by the roadside, her daughter sleeping in her arms. "How old is this baby? Where're you bringing her?" he asked.

"Three weeks old, Brother." Quỳnh smiled seductively at the young man. "The poor baby, she's got terrible diarrhea. We're bringing her to a doctor. Please, let us go before she wakes up and starts crying . . ."

"Doctor or not, you need to be searched."

"Sure." Quỳnh winked. She took off her T-shirt, exposing her bra. "See, I have nothing on me." She turned around once and put her shirt back on. "My sister doesn't need to be searched, please! If you do, that monster of a baby would wake up, and I can't stand her crying."

The soldier glanced at his comrades who were busy checking under the bike's seat. "Do that again," he grinned.

◈

"SEE WHAT I had to do for you and your little devil? Are you happy now?" Quỳnh said as the motorbike roared.

"I didn't ask you to. It was dangerous . . . And don't call my baby that, please . . ."

"She's the cause of all this trouble!" Quỳnh gave the bike extra gas and it jerked forward. "You should at least thank me for getting us out of there. They could have kept us much longer. Don't you know how dangerous it is to travel in the dark?"

Trang looked down at her daughter, who still slept so peacefully in her arms. She was glad she had given birth at Ngân's house, for it had allowed her time alone with Hoa. In the silence offered by motherhood, all her fears had gone quiet, and she had been able to hear herself, loud and clear, and feel the bravery passed down by the generations of women before her. Hoa was a continuation of her dreams, hopes, and a love for life she had thought she'd lost. She smiled at her daughter and cast her eyes across the road toward a grove of bamboo. The graceful trees stood as if in meditation, as if violence could never touch them. A flock of storks rose high, their fluttering wings penning poetry onto the sky.

They entered Sài Gòn and neared a military complex. Trang leaned forward. "I'm thankful to you, em, more than I can ever say. I promise when—" A zipping noise interrupted her. It sounded as if a giant had just whistled.

Trang bent, shielding Hoa. "Careful!" she shouted. A blinding light flashed. Quỳnh turned around, opening her mouth as if wanting to say something to her sister when an explosion smashed into the bike, sending it into the air. Screams escaped Trang as her whole body curled around her baby. Heaven and earth tumbled. Pain seared through her and everything blackened into ink.

Finding a Needle at the
Bottom of the Ocean

Bạc Liêu, 2016

"What do we type into the computer for the search?" Bình said, sitting squashed against Phong on a chair. Diễm stood behind them, her hands on Phong's shoulders. Tài knelt on the floor.

They were in an internet café filled with young people renting computers by the hour. Each machine was shielded by flimsy wooden partitions, and Phong only needed to look to his left to see a young man scrolling through pictures of naked women. Women with skin as white as milk and breasts as big as pomelos. To his right, a boy, barely older than ten, was playing a game, his gun coughing out fire, cutting down figures of humans as if they were useless frogs. The victims' screams tore into Phong's temples.

"Let's start with something simple." Tài typed into the computer. "American father . . . searching . . . for . . . Amerasian . . . child." He pressed a key and the screen was filled with images and words.

"So much information," Diễm gasped. "We're stupid not to know."

"You call your parents stupid?" Bình glared at Diễm. "How could we have known without any internet, and without anyone telling us what to look for?"

"That's why I've been saying we need a smartphone." Diễm threw her hands high into the air.

"Hey!" Tài whistled. "This looks interesting." He pointed at an image of a man with dark skin and curly hair. "It's a movie about Amerasians finding their parents."

Phong settled in to watch as the computer screen blanked, then revealed the curly-haired man. Wearing a thick, old jacket, he was standing on a street empty of people, lined by low brick houses and barren trees. The camera zoomed onto the man's face. His nose was tall, his skin dark, and his eyes so sad, they looked like bottomless ponds.

The man told them that he'd been living in America for twenty-five years, and that he'd spent most of his free time searching for his parents. He'd spent thousands of hours on the internet and talking to people. He'd done DNA tests. He'd received help from kind people including other Amerasians, American veterans, and even strangers, but so far, no good news. He feared that his parents had either died or didn't want him. Walking on a snowy street, shivering in the cold, the man joined a white Amerasian. Together, they rummaged through large metal trash cans. "I can't speak much English and it's been impossible to find a job," the man said. "I'm still lucky, though, since I get to stay in a homeless shelter. The things that I gather from the trash, I sell to other Vietnamese. The money isn't much, but it helps me buy the things I need, like a good meal, a beer, some cigarettes."

"Enough!" Phong shut his eyes, covering his ears with his palms. He hadn't imagined such a life for trẻ lai in the U.S. Somehow he'd been sure there were no poor people in this country he'd been dreaming about.

"This is a lie. It's not possible," Bình said, her voice quivering.

"It's a documentary made by a famous TV channel," Tài protested. "The story must be true."

Phong leaned toward his son. "I'll tell you what it is: propaganda from the Communists, who've always tried to stop us from leaving."

"Whatever you say!" Tài punched the keyboard and the documentary disappeared. The computer screen was again filled with images and words.

"You take over now, Diễm," Tài told his sister, standing up. "Whatever I do is wrong. Whatever I do isn't good enough . . ."

Phong rose to his feet, reaching for Tài's arm. "Son, my reactions . . . it's just that . . . the story is just too shocking for me . . ."

"How about me, huh? You think I wasn't upset watching it?" Tài's voice rose above the sounds of gunfire from the computer next to them. "I actually dreamt about us finding your parents, that I had grandparents who loved me. Now I know it was just a stupid dream." A tear rolled down Tài's cheek.

"Haven't you heard that dreams can come true sometimes?" said Diễm. She pointed at some words on the screen. "This article is about someone who found her father."

"Read it to us, Daughter," Bình said.

Diễm clicked. The computer screen changed and a picture of a middle-aged woman and an older man appeared. They both looked like white Americans. Diễm started reading. Tracy Trần, the woman, was adopted from an orphanage in Sài Gòn and brought to America when she was five. For the last ten years, she tried to find her father. She had nearly given up hope when her DNA test led her to her father's brother.

When her father heard about her, he didn't even know he had a daughter in Việt Nam.

Phong had closed his eyes to avoid the words that filled the screen. But Diễm's voice was too soft, almost drowned out by the noises around them. Unable to hear her, he opened his eyes. The sharp little points and barbs of the letters scraped across his vision.

The screen became blurry. The chair under him turned into the wooden chair of his first grade class high up in the mountains. Five boys, three of them older and from the third grade, were surrounding him. One pushed a piece of paper filled with words toward his face.

"Read these!" a tall boy said, tapping on the paper.

"I can't." He stared desperately at the corridor outside, searching for help. It was empty. All the teachers and other students had gone home. He wished to see Teacher Nương, who had been kind to him, but saw no one.

The boy ran his finger under some words. "Read this out loud. 'Con lai mười hai lỗ đít.' Read it now!"

He bit his lip, his head shaking. He would not call himself an Amerasian with twelve assholes.

A hard smack landed on his left cheek, another on his skull. Fire exploded in his vision. He screamed in agony.

"You stupid half-breed. Repeat after us! 'Con lai mười hai lỗ đít.'"

He sobbed, clutching his head with his palms.

"You should learn how to read, Stupid. Now, repeat after me." A boy yanked his hair, forcing him to stare into another piece of paper. "'Phong's mother was a prostitute. She spread her legs for the American imperialists.' Read it!"

Phong bit his lip so hard he could taste blood.

The words were brought closer to his face, so close that they blurred. "Read it!"

He closed his eyes.

"How stubborn you are! You filthy son of the enemy."

Someone stamped on his foot. The pain was hot, running like an electric current to the top of his head. He screamed.

"If he doesn't want to read these words, he must eat them," a boy said, and the others cheered.

"Eat them, eat them!" they chanted.

Phong faced the words. He refused to acknowledge their meaning. They were nothing unless he spoke them. Under his eyes, the words began to twist and turn. They turned into gaping mouths, cackling at him. They grew out of the paper, like snakes. They grasped his arms and legs, pulling him to the ground.

The floor was cold under his back. The boys towered above him. Hands forced his mouth open. The paper was rolled into a ball, pushed against his tongue. He tasted the bitterness of words. He gagged.

"Chew and swallow, or we'll piss into your fucking mouth!"

With tears running down his face, he ground the words between his teeth. The words slithered into his stomach, spreading themselves onto his limbs. They were laughing, their shrill cries penetrating his brain.

"No!" he jerked back. The classroom ceiling spun into the computer screen in front of him.

Phong covered his eyes with his palms and shot to his feet. He ran for the door. People were blocking his way, their eyes glued to computer screens, their hands punching keyboards.

"Let me out!" he screamed.

◆

PHONG SAT IN the cool shade of a shop's awning, his family around him.

"You okay, Ba? What happened?" Diễm knelt beside him.

"The ghosts . . . they haven't released your father." Bình fanned Phong with her hat. "We need to find a good shaman."

Phong shook his head. Bình believed that shamans could drive away the evil spirits that possessed him. Over the years, she'd invited to their home three different shamans who performed ceremonies on Phong. They'd smoked his house to drive away the invisible ghosts. Nothing had helped. Phong knew there were no ghosts, just the bullies who continued to burrow deep inside his bone marrow. He wished he knew how to control his bad memories.

"You need a drink, Ba? Should we bring you home?" Tài asked, sitting on his haunches, worry carving deep lines into his young face.

Phong's eyes teared. "Let us go home." He reached out for Tài's strong shoulder and let his son pull him up. As they started walking toward home, a strong wind gusted. A vendor cried out as the wind flung several of her newspapers across the street. Diễm and Tài ran, catching the pages, putting them together.

"Look, Ba, Má," Diễm suddenly called, pointing at a page. "A search notice. From an American!"

◇

STANDING ON THE PAVEMENT, under a large phượng tree, away from shops and people, Tài and Diễm both held the newspaper. Red petals scattered around their feet and yellow leaves flittered through the air. From somewhere inside the rough tree trunk, cicadas vibrated their songs into the thick, hot air. There had been nights Phong stayed up with Bình and his children under moonlight, watching cicada nymphs emerge from under the earth, crawl up onto tree trunks, shed their nymph skin, and transform themselves into cicadas. He'd told his family Sister Nhã's tales, tales that explained why only male cicadas could sing, and why only from their abdomens, not from their mouths or chests.

"What does the notice say?" Bình asked impatiently, fanning the children with her hat.

"Let me read it," Tài tried to yank the newspaper away from Diễm.

"I can do it better than you." Diễm tickled Tài under his armpit. Tài yelped, releasing his grip.

"Ready?" Diễm looked at Phong. As he nodded, she cleared her throat. "Đan, a helicopter pilot based at Tân Sơn Nhứt in 1969, is looking for Kim. Đan met Kim at the Hô-li-gút Bar on Trương Minh Ký Street. Kim told Đan she was from the Mekong Delta. If Kim would like to talk to Đan, please call Mr. Thiên."

Phong couldn't believe he was hearing Mr. Dan's name and that crook Thiên's number again.

"Is Mr. Thiên the same person helping Tôm Sờ-Mít?" asked Diễm, looking at Phong.

"Yes . . . that's him. Please . . . read the notice once more."

"My turn." Tài tickled Diễm in the stomach until she dropped the paper. He laughed, picked it up, and started reading. Once Tài was done, Phong shook his head. Everything made sense now: Mr. Dan's unusual behavior, his curiosity about Phong, his wife's anger.

"This Mr. Thiên . . . his name and number keep appearing in front of us," Bình said, turning to Phong. "The universe is trying to tell us something, anh. It's no coincidence. We should call him."

"Of course it's a coincidence. He's just an agent, a crook . . ."

"Why do you always think that people are out to get you?" Bình stood with her hands on her hip.

"Can you blame me, after everything that's happened to us?" Phong said, then turned and headed for home.

"Ba." Diễm ran after Phong. She took his arm and shook it, the way she always did when she begged for something. "I think we should call Mr. Thiên. This American . . . Mr. Đan . . . he could be your father."

Phong almost laughed. Hope was a dangerous thing.

It'd taken him years but now Phong realized he had to be a cicada nymph. He must shed his past, to be free, to transform himself into a new person—someone calm and happy. His son had been right. They should forget about it all: the visa application, the search for his parents.

It wasn't worth it to relive the trauma of his past and drag his family down with him. He should accept life as it was, raise his children, take good care of Bình.

"Come on." He smiled at his family. "Let's go home. Throw away that paper. That American man is not related to us; he's a white man. I know, because I met him last week in Sài Gòn. And I don't want to see him ever again."

The Past and the Future

Mekong Delta, 2016

In the car, Dan studied Linda's knees. They were still swollen, and he felt as if Linda's pain was his, slow and burning. He took out the Bengay cream, massaged it onto her knees, and she let out a sigh of relief. They had been walking a great deal, up and down the steps of Khmer temples in Sóc Trăng and around a village known for its ceramics. In another village, they'd learned how to make rice paper and coconut candies. The trip had energized him and Linda in a way he hadn't imagined. It made them curious about the world again, brought out their creative sides, and gave them activities to enjoy together.

But the weight he'd felt became heavier since yesterday, when they visited an orphanage where he'd met children affected by Agent Orange. Some had missing or crooked limbs. Some had gigantic heads. Some were unable to speak and could only make gurgling sounds. As Linda embraced a young girl whose head was twice the size of her chest, he went out to the garden and wept. He recalled the times when he'd accompanied C-123 Provider aircraft from Operation Ranch Hand on their spray missions. He recalled the many color-coded drums at Biên Hòa and Tân Sơn Nhứt Airports. Drums marked with orange, green, pink, purple, blue and white stripes. Much later, he would learn that these stripes gave these so-called Rainbow herbicides their names: Agent Orange, Agent Green, Agent Pink, Agent Purple, Agent White, and Agent Blue. Like his peers—but not his damn superiors—he was ignorant of the effect of these chemicals, but still, he should have asked questions. He should have known anything that killed plants would kill people. Or worse.

Later, inside the orphanage, when he held the children and gave them the toys Linda had bought, he kept thinking that he could be the cause of their suffering, and that one of those children could be his grandchild.

Leaving the orphanage, he'd felt angry with himself. He should have returned earlier, done something. Thiên said many veterans had come back. They volunteered at orphanages, helped build schools and hospitals. There were veterans who settled in Việt Nam, even retired here.

Last night, during the follow-up counselling session with Dr. Hoh, he'd told her about Thanh, Thanh's father, Thiên, the orphanage, and the fact that many people here didn't have access to psychological support. "Then we really need to do something about it. Let me find out how," Dr. Hoh had said. She'd noted down Thanh's number and promised to call him.

A mobile phone rang.

Linda sat up, rubbing her eyes.

"It's an unknown number," Thiên said, glancing at his phone.

Dan hoped the person who called was Kim. The seat pocket in front of him held three issues of the *Tuổi Trẻ* daily newspaper, with his search notice for Kim printed on them. He and Linda had had a long talk with Thiên; they had agreed that a brief newspaper notice would be safe: Kim could reach out if she wanted to.

Thiên cut through lanes and pulled over to answer the phone. Dan cocked his head to listen. Thiên spoke rapidly. With the phone against his ear, he reached under the front passenger seat, retrieving his backpack. He held up the itinerary, read from it, then scribbled something down.

"He's speaking to a woman," Dan told Linda, and could see how nervous she was. He held her hand in his. If Kim answered his ad, their lives would never be the same.

Thiên finished his call and turned around. "It's Phong's wife."

"Who?" Linda and Dan asked in unison.

"Phong . . . He was with his wife and children when they saw your search notice. His wife just called. They don't know Kim but they'd like to talk to you."

"We need to talk to them, too," Linda said.

"We're heading in the direction of their hometown. I asked them to go to our hotel tonight."

"We should pass by some shops, buy books for the children—" The phone's ringing interrupted Linda.

Thiên answered, turning to look at Dan. His eyes were wide with surprise.

"Who is it?" Dan mouthed, but Thiên shook his head and kept talking while writing on the itinerary.

Dan's throat prickled with nervousness. He looked out the window, at the stream of vehicles. While people were moving on with their lives, he felt mired in his past.

Thiên finished talking. He stared at the phone before putting it down. "A woman. . . . She read the notice and wants to meet us in person. I asked if she was Kim but she wouldn't say." Thiên turned to Dan. "She said she knew you. And she remembers that you come from Seattle."

Linda brought her palm to her mouth. "The notice didn't mention Seattle. It could be her."

Dan sat back in his seat. He didn't think he had told any other

Vietnamese woman he was from Seattle, he'd only told Kim about his family. But he could be mistaken. It'd been a long time ago.

"She gave me her address. She lives in Cần Thơ—it's about an hour away. Remember the big city we passed, the one with the huge bridge?"

"Why don't we call her back?" Linda told Dan. "I'm sure you can tell if it's her, after some questions. We could lose two hours of driving . . . and this traffic is giving me a headache."

Linda was right. They had to be cautious. Yesterday two women had called. One claimed to be Kim but wasn't able to answer the most basic questions. She said she had to work at the bar because her whole family had been killed by bombs. Another woman was certain she was Dan's daughter. She said her psychic feelings told her so; she didn't believe the Vietnamese couple who'd raised her were her parents. Thiên had called her on video chat and confirmed that she looked 100 percent Vietnamese, and the woman couldn't show any proof that she was adopted. Afterward, Thiên admitted that he sometimes received phone calls from people who claimed they were related to Americans.

"I don't want to drive back, either," Thiên said, his eyes on the chaotic traffic. "But something tells me the woman is real. She refused to answer questions. She said she had things to tell Mr. Dan, things that can't be discussed on the phone."

◈

THE CAR HAD taken them to the outskirts of Cần Thơ, to a residential area, green and quiet. Houses lined up along the road, their doors and windows opened as if ready to welcome faraway guests. Dan half expected Kim to be standing outside waiting for him, but there was hardly anyone on the street.

It may not be her, Dan told himself as fear and nervousness pinned him to his seat.

He had imagined seeing Kim again countless times, each time with her reacting differently. And now all those possible reactions were running wild in his mind: she rushed to him, telling him how much she'd missed him; she slapped him, screaming he'd killed their child; she introduced his child to him, pushing their grandchildren gently toward him; she told him coldly that she'd given their child away and didn't know where his child was.

He wasn't sure he was ready to face Kim. He wasn't sure this wasn't a big mistake.

"Hey . . . it's going to be okay," Linda said. "We're here to make amends."

He pulled her into him, overcome with gratitude. The day that he went to Việt Nam in 1969 was also the day that Linda became a soldier, and she hadn't stopped fighting. He had to make sure whatever happened next would not wound her.

The car slowed, then stopped. Thiên checked the address. "We're here."

Dan blinked. They were in front of an impressive entrance gate, framed by yellow bell flowers. Thiên drove through and into a spacious yard. Dan clambered out of the car to find himself in front of a large brick house with a deep blue door and matching window frames; a pristine, brilliantly white Vespa was parked outside.

Thiên called out a greeting. No answer. Dan snuck a look inside the house through a half-opened window and saw pots of white orchids, as well as polished wooden furniture. He continued looking on his tiptoes, but didn't see anyone.

To his right, a mother hen was busy scratching under a grove of banana plants, clucking for her chicks to come. Above the chicken hung three huge banana flowers, red and magnificent. Dan hadn't been aware of their beauty until this trip, when he saw them displayed in restaurants and hotel lobbies. His favorite dish was now banana flower salad, thinly sliced, tossed with shrimp, mint, and roasted peanuts. Behind the bananas was a garden filled with lush trees, from which many types of fruit dangled: mangoes, papaya, grapefruit, durian, and jackfruit. A marble table and two long benches stood deep inside the garden under a shady mango tree.

"Lemongrass!" Linda exclaimed, and Dan cast his eyes across neat rows of vegetables and saw tall bushes that ran along the garden fence.

"We need to tell Mr. Thiên's wife." Dan squeezed Linda's shoulder. Thiên called out again.

This time, the house's door opened and a woman appeared. She made her way toward them, across the veranda and through the yard. Dressed in black pants that rippled when she walked and a light blue shirt that glowed in the afternoon light, she was slender. When she neared, Dan bowed his head in greeting, then studied her face. She looked to be in her sixties. Though she wore no makeup, he could tell that she'd once been beautiful. He searched for a small scar above her right eye, but couldn't see one.

Without a glance in his direction, she spoke to Thiên.

"She invites you take a seat," Thiên said. As they walked to the marble table, the woman headed for the gate. She closed and latched its solid wooden doors. Dan was anxious to ask his questions, but the woman went back inside the house. Whoever she was, she appeared to be well-off. This was certainly not a scam.

"Is it her?" Linda whispered, fanning herself with her notebook.

Dan sat down next to his wife. "I don't know." Perhaps Kim had skillfully covered her scar.

Dan's gaze stayed fixed on the house. Perhaps the woman wasn't the one who'd called. Perhaps Kim was inside, figuring out how to deal with him now that he'd shown up with Linda.

It was quiet, except for the chicks' chirping and leaves rustling. What a beautiful sanctuary, Dan found himself thinking. If Kim lived here, he would be glad for her. In all the times he'd imagined this moment, Kim had been poor and desperate. Only now did he realize that she might even be more well-off than him.

He turned to Thiên, who shrugged.

Finally the woman came back, carrying a lacquered tray on which a ceramic pot and several glasses rattled. At the table, she poured a golden green liquid into the glasses. Her nails were painted light pink and a large diamond twinkled on her right hand. She said some long sentences and Thiên smiled.

"She knows Americans love soft drink," he translated, "but she prefers to make her own, from boiled corn and pandan leaves."

The woman distributed the glasses around the table.

Dan took a sip. The liquid was cold, fragrant, and tasted refreshing. "It's really good. Try it," he told Linda, who nodded but didn't pick up her glass.

The woman sat down next to Thiên. Her hands, placed on the table, started to form fists. For the first time, she looked at Dan. Their eyes locked. He shuddered when he caught the glint of hatred in her expression.

Thiên said something and she nodded, exchanging words with him. They spoke for a short while.

"I introduced you," Thiên told Linda. "She asked if you're Mr. Dan's wife, and I said yes."

Dan shifted in his seat. Sweat rolled down the back of his shirt and his hands were damp. He opened and closed his mouth. He wanted to ask his many questions but feared he would say the wrong thing.

The woman talked to Thiên.

"She welcomes you, Madam Linda, to her home," Thiên said.

"Please thank her for having us," said Linda.

"Thanks for the drink." Dan smiled nervously at the woman. "Do the corn and the pandan leaves come from your garden?"

Thiên translated and the woman's lips curled up. But she didn't smile. She told Thiên something. Her face remained cold and her hands were still clenched.

"She said it's a pity she can't speak English anymore. Many years

ago in Sài Gòn, she spoke some," Thiên said. Dan wondered if Thiên
had translated correctly because the woman didn't answer his question.

The woman looked at Dan and said something. He could make out
the words "Seattle" and "Tân Sơn Nhứt."

"She wants to confirm that your name is Dan, you're from Seattle,
and that you were a pilot at Tân Sơn Nhứt Airbase in 1969," Thiên said.

"Yes, that's me." Dan looked at the woman, met a fire in her gaze,
but didn't avert his eyes. "Are you Kim?" He couldn't believe he needed
to ask. Wouldn't he recognize Kim after having been so profoundly
intimate with her?

"You met Kim at the Hollywood Bar. Correct?" the woman said,
and Thiên translated. She referred to Kim in the third person. Perhaps
she wasn't Kim, but one of the women who'd worked at the bar.

"Yes, I met Kim at the Hollywood," he said. "She used to call her
mama-san the tiger madam." He smiled as Thiên translated. He hoped
the woman would smile, too, but her face remained cold.

"And later you rent apartment for Kim?" the woman continued to ask.

"Yes . . ." Dan nodded. The question made it clear that the woman
knew him, which was good, but it must be inflicting pain and humiliation on Linda. He turned to his wife. "I'm sorry you have to listen to
this. I already told you . . . about renting the apartment."

Linda nodded. She stared at the table.

"Where was the apartment? You remember?" the woman asked.

"Around fifteen minutes' walk from the bar. I can't recall the street's
name . . ." Dan rubbed his palms against his jeans. He hated it that they
were so sweaty.

Thiên translated, and the woman refilled Thiên's glass.

"Mr. Thien," Dan said, shifting in his seat, "please ask if she's Kim."
He wished he'd spent time refreshing his Vietnamese. It wouldn't be
too difficult for him to learn simple phrases such as "Are you Kim?,"
"Where is Kim?," "Take me to Kim." All his life, he'd expected people

from around the world to know English, to translate their life experiences to serve people like him. Why should they?

Thiên told the woman something, with the word *Kim* in it. Once again, the woman's lips curled up, but she didn't smile.

"She said you met her at the bar," Thiên said. "She knew you well."

"What bar? The Hollywood?"

Without waiting for Thiên's translation, the woman nodded.

"You knew me well? And you knew Kim?" Dan gazed at the woman. He wished the language barrier between them would disappear.

The woman stayed silent. Behind her, under the grove of banana plants lit up by their red flowers, the mother hen was spreading her wings, protecting her chicks. Dan reached out for his wife's hand. Whatever truth he discovered next, he was determined not to let it hurt her.

After a long while, the woman looked up. "Yes, I know Kim well," she said. "My name is Quỳnh. I am Kim's sister. We worked at the same bar."

The words stunned Dan. He'd never thought about finding Kim's sister first. He didn't remember much about her, except that she'd disliked him and refused to talk to him.

Quỳnh looked at him. Her fists on the table relaxed, then tightened again. Her face became flushed and her lips trembled. As she spoke, each word that came out of her mouth sounded heavy, as if she was spitting it out.

"You remember that when you left my sister, she was pregnant?" Thiên translated. "She was pregnant with your child."

"Yes . . . I am so sorry." Words tumbled out of Dan's mouth. "I was young and irresponsible . . ."

"Young? My sister . . . she was just eighteen when you ruined her life. She trusted you and you were a coward! Do you remember this?" A tear rolled down Quỳnh's cheek. She reached into her shirt pocket and handed Dan a black-and-white photo.

Dan stared at the faces of the couple in the faded picture. It was him and Kim at the zoo. They were standing next to each other, laughing, happiness alive on their young faces. He hadn't even touched her by then; he'd been determined to stay loyal to Linda. But later, the impact of the explosion outside Kim's apartment had shaken him. In a moment of vulnerability, he had kissed Kim. That kiss changed everything.

He'd denied it, but now, looking at the picture, he knew the feelings he had for Kim were real. They had found each other, and clung to each other amid the hurricane of war. Both had been torn from their families, both trying to do their best. Together they had erected a safe haven that protected them both. At least for a short time.

A sob escaped his throat.

"You had this picture taken at the zoo," Quỳnh said. "You swallowed your promise to be there for my sister. Why did you leave her when she was carrying your child? Why didn't you come back earlier? What do you want from her now?"

"I'm so sorry . . ." Dan said. "I can't explain my past mistakes, except that I was irresponsible. But I'm here now, to meet my responsibilities as a father. Please . . . tell me where Kim and our child are." Dan looked into the house. He could only see the orchid flowers. Their white petals were so pure; they reminded him of Kim when they'd first met.

"My sister, her real name is Trang." Quỳnh took the photo back. "Her name means graceful, elegant."

"Trang . . ." Dan whispered. "Trang." He held on to the table. He didn't know much about the woman with whom he'd fathered a child. He hadn't even cared to ask for her real name, or her full name.

"Trang gave birth to a beautiful daughter and named her Thu Hoa," Quỳnh's voice trembled. "Thu Hoa means Autumn Flower."

"Thu Hoa . . . Autumn Flower," Dan repeated. He turned to Linda. "I have a daughter . . . a daughter."

Tears welled up in Linda's eyes.

"Please, where is Trang now? Where is Thu Hoa?" Dan stood up.

Quỳnh rose from her seat. "You want to see my sister? Come with me."

◇

THE VERANDA WAS built from shiny ceramic tiles, decorated with the images of rising phoenixes. Following Quỳnh, Dan and Linda left their shoes on the front steps.

Inside, the living room was spacious, furnished with a wooden sofa, a coffee table, and four armchairs. A large glass cabinet displayed many types of exquisite-looking fabrics. On a long stand sat a large TV, surrounded by framed pictures of a young couple and their two children. Next to a door that opened into a corridor stood a small wooden altar. Dan's heart leaped at the sight of the Laughing Buddha. "Kim . . . Trang," he called. He gazed at the corridor, hoping for a shadow, a movement. Perhaps Kim was bedridden. It wouldn't be rare for people her age to be sick. Perhaps she'd been injured during the war. He would not let himself think about the other possibility.

The woman turned and Dan saw an ancient-looking wooden cabinet, inlaid with mother of pearl. On top of the cabinet stood three incense bowls, a vase of flowers, a bottle of liquor, and a plate of fruits. Behind them were three framed pictures, their details obscured by the offerings.

The woman struck a match, lighting up sticks of incense. As the incense smoldered, she held it above her head, saying something.

"Elder Sister Trang," Thiên whispered his translation, and Linda clutched Dan's arm. "Dan and his wife are here to see you. Come back and say hello to them. Come back, Elder Sister . . ."

Dan stepped closer to the altar. He saw Trang's diary. The diary from which she had read her favorite poems to him, as well as her own poems. She had penned her dreams, her hopes, and her longing for peace between those worn covers. And now, she was looking at him from one of the framed photos. Her eyes were still filled with hope, as if she never ceased to believe in him, and in a better future.

Revenge and Forgiveness

Cần Thơ, 2016

Standing in front of the altar, Quỳnh looked at Dan. He was kneeling, wailing her sister's bar name, "Kim! Kim!" as if he didn't know her as a real person. His face was scrunched up, wet with tears. He was crying, but it was too late.

On the altar, Trang smiled from her photo. She was still beautiful and full of life. If she hadn't died, Quỳnh's life would be different now. She wouldn't have to stay awake night after night, thinking that it was she herself who had killed her own sister by forcing her to go to Hóc Môn, and by driving the motorbike on that road.

Dan bent lower, hitting his fists against the floor. Quỳnh brought her palms to her ears, trying to block out his cries. She'd witnessed enough sorrow, she could no longer burden herself with someone else's, especially when that person was her worst enemy.

Dan stood up and got closer to the altar. "Trang, Trang!" he called. The sound of her sister's real name was sharp against Quỳnh's blurred mind. She felt as if Trang had just died, her body bloody on the road, her head torn open.

That day, kneeling by the roadside, Quỳnh had wished she had perished along with Trang. Gone was her best friend, the pillar of her strength, someone who always believed in the goodness of people. Gone was her only sibling, who had cheered her on, had always picked her up when she felt down. She'd never told Trang that she loved her, and she regretted it.

Quỳnh looked at Dan through her tears. *If you weren't such a coward, my sister would have survived*, she thought. She wanted to hurl these words at Dan. The vicious words that she'd repeated to herself like a mantra last night. But she saw the sorrow in Dan's eyes, and knew how much he'd suffered. "It was a mortar attack," she told him. "We were traveling on the road . . . Trang was holding your newborn baby."

"NO!!!" Dan howled. Linda reached out to him, held him tight, and sobbed into his shoulders.

The sight of the shaken couple was too much for Quỳnh to bear. "I need to be by myself for a while," she told Thiên, and hurried outside. In her garden, she stood with her face against the rough trunk of her jackfruit tree and wept.

She didn't know why the mortar had taken Trang's life but spared hers. And she kept wondering whether the things she'd done after Trang's death were right or wrong.

Never could she imagine that Dan would come back looking for Trang and their daughter. She'd seen Dan's search notice when it first appeared in the newspaper. She immediately tore it to shreds. She cursed him, screaming, "How dare you? What do you want from my sister?"

In the days that followed, she burned incense and asked Trang what to do. She'd wanted the incense to flare up, as a sign, and when that didn't happen, she prayed to Trang, asking her to send a message via an owl's cry, or a sudden gust of wind, but nothing. She tossed and turned during the nights. This morning, she received her newspaper delivery and opened it. There it was, Dan's notice again, staring back at her. He refused to go away. He refused to give up. She crushed his message into a ball. It was then that she decided she must meet him, to condemn him and tell him he'd killed Trang.

She'd practiced time and again the harsh words she wanted to fling at him. Words that would be knives that would slice his heart open and leave it bleeding. But she couldn't do it, for she felt she was responsible for her sister's death, along with Dan. And now, the truth about Dan's daughter would be his biggest punishment.

She dried her tears. She shouldn't feel sorry for that bastard. He deserved it, after what he'd done or failed to do.

"Toi xin loi," someone said, and she turned around.

Dan walked to her. He reached for her hand, bringing it to his face. His tears were hot, as hot as hers. His face was trembling hard, as hard as hers.

She raised her other hand and hit him in his chest. "I hate you, why don't you go away!"

He nodded as if he understood her.

She launched both fists at his chest. "Why don't you hit me? Slap me! I'm guilty, too. I killed my sister."

Dan put his hands on her shoulders and said something. Something soft and sorrowful. Something that sounded like an apology. Then he pulled her to him.

With her face resting on his chest, she wept. She wept for Trang's unrealized dreams and hopes. She wept for her parents. She wept for herself. And she wept for Dan and Trang's baby.

◈

From across the marble table, Dan was silent. His shoulders drooped, as if the regrets were piled high onto them. When he looked at Quỳnh, his eyes were brimming. "I'm so, so sorry," he said via Thiên's translation. "It wasn't my intention to bring harm or pain to your family."

Quỳnh stared at her drink. It was empty, as drained as she was. She feared the many questions that Dan would ask. It had been a lifetime since she spoke about her past with anyone. She'd tried to bury it deep into the marrow of her memory, but it refused to sleep.

Linda refilled the glass and handed it to Quỳnh. "I can't imagine what you've had to go through. I'm so sorry."

Quỳnh drank the water and let her gaze rest on the banana flowers. She'd tried to recreate the garden her parents and Trang once loved. She burned incense for them often, offered them food, and invited them to visit her. She felt their spirits and knew they were never far away. She hoped her cousin was taking good care of her family home. Even though her birth village was a part of her being, after her parents' death she had to detach herself from it. She'd moved to this neighborhood, more than a hundred kilometers away, where nobody knew her. She'd needed a new identity, a fresh start to life.

"The pictures in your living room," Linda asked. "Are they of your family?"

Quỳnh nodded, studying Linda. The woman's features radiated kindness. Linda had to have a generous heart to be here with Dan. Was she married to him when he was with Trang? Did Trang ever know about her?

"Yes, my son," Quỳnh said. "He lives in Sài Gòn with his wife and two children." Thinking about Khôi and her grandchildren sustained Quỳnh. They were the pillars of her life. Khôi had called her the day before, saying that he was driving his family down for a visit. They would be spending the entire weekend with her. She couldn't wait for her house to be filled with their laughter and footsteps. They would cook together, eat, play cards, climb trees, pick fruit, harvest vegetables, and fly kites. Even though her maid, Phúc, had a long list of things to do, Quỳnh had told the woman to take the afternoon off. No one should know about Dan and Linda's visit. She would do anything to shield Khôi from the trauma of her past.

"Your son looks like a fine young man," Linda continued, as if trying to console Quỳnh with her words, "and his children are adorable."

Quỳnh nodded. She was proud of Khôi, who was a lecturer in business and economics at a public university in Hồ Chí Minh City. He often used her company as an example for his teaching. His son and daughter, four and six years old now, revitalized her.

It had taken Quỳnh many years of hard work to build up her business, but she'd done it. She had to prove herself again and again by pushing against sexism, deeply rooted in such proverbs as "đàn bà đái không qua ngọn cỏ"—"women can't pee higher than the top of grass blades" or "đàn ông nông nổi giếng khơi, đàn bà sâu sắc như cơi đựng trầu"—"when naïve, men still seem as profound as a deep well; when thoughtful, women are no deeper than a flat-bottomed betel leaf container."

People in her province now called her Cô Ba—Auntie Number Three. None of them knew her real name, nor her past. In their eyes, she was simply a successful businesswoman, a key supplier of cloth to tailors in the province. They envied her frequent trips to India, Bangladesh, and China. They admired the unique materials she brought back. Recently, retailers from different provinces in the Mekong Delta had been calling her, wanting to get hold of the batik she'd been importing from Indonesia. Two years ago, she'd stood at the Mayestik Market in Jakarta, in awe of the exquisite designs and low prices of batik. She knew the long pieces of cloth, with stories embedded into each design, would be perfect for Vietnamese áo dài. She'd enjoyed working with the artists there, incorporating Vietnamese elements into her orders.

"I am afraid to ask," Dan said, tears still in his voice, "but please do tell me, what happened to my daughter?"

Quỳnh bent her head. It seemed as if yesterday that Trang stood in front of her, her newborn baby against her chest. "I'll bring my baby back to Sài Gòn with me," Trang had said, "I will raise her."

Quỳnh sighed. "You should know that my sister loved your daughter very much," she told Dan. "We'd planned to give Thu Hoa to an orphanage, but once the baby arrived, Trang refused to do it."

Thiên translated, and Dan nodded and said, "Yes . . . that sounds exactly like her."

It was difficult but Quỳnh took a deep breath and described the motorbike trip to Hóc Môn, Trang giving birth, their fights, the journey back to Sài Gòn, the guards who stopped them, and the explosion.

"Oh God, it was all my fault!" Dan clamped his palm against his mouth. "Please . . . don't tell me that both Trang and my daughter . . ." He couldn't finish the sentence.

Quỳnh brought her hands to her eyes, as if blocking her vision now could stop her mind from recalling Trang on the road: her face covered by blood, her body motionless, curled around her screaming baby. Even in her death, Trang had protected Hoa.

"My sister died saving her daughter," Quỳnh said. "It was truly a miracle that Hoa didn't suffer any injury." Quỳnh recounted how loud Hoa had screamed when her mother was put into the ground by those who lived near the explosion site, brown dirt blanketing Trang's feet, then body, then face. Hoa calmed down only when a nursing mother offered her milk. "That kind woman . . . her name was Phương . . . I met her at the medical clinic where I was treated for my broken ribs." Quỳnh stared at the back of her hands, at their blue veins. Like the blood that rushed to her heart, her memory was gushing back to the image of Phương, a tired-looking mother who lay on a bamboo bed, one hand embracing her newborn son, another hand caressing Hoa's back as Hoa greedily drank from her breast. "Phương lost her own mother to the war so she bonded with Hoa instantly. . . . She said there was no deeper sorrow than losing one's parent to violence." Quỳnh would never forget how Phương hummed a lullaby to Hoa, and how the tenderness of Phương's voice silenced everything else: the screaming in Quỳnh's heart, the piercing pain of her broken ribs, the thundering airplanes above her head, the shells that exploded in the distance. In that sacred and rare stillness, Quỳnh caught a glimpse of a future for her niece.

"When Phương told me that she had two sons," Quỳnh said, "and that she'd been yearning for a daughter, I offered . . ." She paused. "She kept Hoa."

Dan flinched, his eyes opened wide in shock.

"I'm sorry, but I had no choice." Quỳnh returned his gaze. "I had no means to raise your daughter. And there was Hoa's chance for a real family: a mother who loved her, a sibling her age . . ."

"Are you . . . are you sure the woman kept Hoa?" Dan asked.

"Yes . . . I gave her all the dollars you'd given Trang, and she promised to take good care of Hoa. Her husband, Thịnh, was there, too. At first he said they couldn't feed so many mouths, but I begged him to save Hoa. I told him about Trang, our parents, my demanding job. He agreed . . . on one condition . . ."

Dan looked at Quỳnh, unblinking. Quỳnh had despised him so much, she had thought that seeing him in pain would bring her satisfaction. But now she knew the suffering of someone else could not possibly be the source of delight for another, and that revenge, however successful, would not be able to resurrect the dead.

"What condition?" Dan leaned his whole body forward, as if his life depended on her answer.

"Thịnh said he would agree for his wife to bring Hoa home if I gave them, *only them*, the right to be Hoa's parents, that I would not try to take Hoa back, that I would never contact them again. He said he wouldn't want to see his wife fall in love with Hoa, only to have Hoa taken away from her."

Dan covered his face with his hands, as if not wanting Quỳnh to read his feelings. She wouldn't be surprised if he resented her, or even hated her. But it was he who had abandoned Hoa first.

She had agreed easily to Thịnh's request. She blamed Hoa for Trang's death. She had wanted Hoa to disappear. Looking back over the years, Quỳnh knew she'd made a good decision for her niece. It was her last act to honor her sister: she'd found not just a mother for Hoa, but a whole family.

"I gave them my promise," Quỳnh said. "After the war ended, though, I wanted to check on Hoa. I needed to know that she was okay. Unfortunately I didn't have her new family's address or full names. I asked at the clinic where we'd met, but they had lost the records. I visited surrounding areas and asked about for Hoa, but no one knew."

Tears trailed down Dan's cheeks. "It's all my fault. How can I ever find my daughter?"

Linda held Dan in her arms. "You should do a DNA test," she told him. "Maybe Hoa grew up wondering about her parents because she looked different from her siblings. She might be searching for you."

"Yes, Hoa looked like a mixed person," Quỳnh said. "She had a high-bridged nose like her father. I'm not sure, but I think her eyes were brown, like Trang's. And she had hazel hair."

"Do you happen . . . to have a photo of Hoa?" Linda asked.

Quỳnh shook her head. "There was no chance for photos."

"Sister, we need your help to find Hoa," Thiên said, opening his notebook. Dan also started to take notes. "Please tell me what you remember."

"I can tell you everything I can recall, on one condition." Quỳnh looked around the table, at everyone. "You won't reveal my identity. You can't publish my picture, my address, my name . . . You can't tell anyone about me or this meeting."

"Of course, Sister. We respect your privacy," Thiên said.

"It's more than that," Quỳnh said. "It's my life."

In the world she'd rebuilt for herself, esteem was everything. Over time, the designs of her clothing products had gained prestige; her clients associated them with grace, luck, beauty, and class. The fabrics she curated and distributed were not for daily wear, but for weddings and special occasions. If people found out she'd been a prostitute or that she'd abandoned her own niece, and more, the news could crash her business empire.

The person she worried about most, though, was Khôi. Like everyone else, her son was ignorant about her past, which served him well. His family history was being investigated because he'd applied to become a Communist party member—he had to, in order to become the head of his department. He'd worked hard toward his goals, and she wouldn't allow her past to ruin his opportunities.

"Please don't worry," Dan said. "Any search notice will only mention me as the father, and Mr. Thien as my friend who helps me. And we will be very careful, to protect Hoa and her family."

Quỳnh nodded. "You can publish my sister's full name: Nguyễn Thị Kiều Trang, and Hoa's full name: Nguyễn Thị Thu Hoa." She waited for Thiên to finish helping Dan and Linda write down the names before continuing. "Hoa was handed to her adopted parents on August twenty-eight, 1970." Quỳnh described in details the location of the medical clinic, in case Dan wanted to visit it himself.

"How about Hoa's date of birth? Any special features?" Thiên asked.

"She was born three days before, August twenty-five. As for special features . . ." Quỳnh closed her eyes. She hadn't really looked at Hoa. She hadn't wanted any attachment to the girl. "Sorry, I can't remember."

Thiên picked up his phone and typed. "Let's see . . . if Thu Hoa published any search notice."

Quỳnh knew the answer. She'd googled her niece's name countless times.

Linda started looking, too. After a while, both she and Thiên shook their heads.

Dan turned to Quỳnh. "May I ask . . . did your parents know about the baby? How did they cope with Trang's passing?"

"They didn't know . . . And about Trang, I told them she'd gone to America."

"You were able to convince them?" Linda asked, surprised.

"I hope so. . . . I said Trang had found herself a nice American boyfriend, that he'd been sent back to America, and at the last minute arranged for her to come along. Later on, I imitated my sister's handwriting in letters that I attached to mine. I explained that Trang sent her correspondence via my Sài Gòn address, that it might get lost if sent directly to our village. In those letters, I described how happy Trang was, that her in-laws loved and respected her. If my parents had any suspicions, they didn't tell me. They died a few years later. My mother went first; her doctor suspected she'd had a heart failure; my father shortly later, I think he didn't want to live without her."

"At least you gave your parents some hope when they were still around," said Dan. "I'm so sorry."

Quỳnh looked away. She couldn't tell Dan, but he was the boyfriend in those fake letters. He'd taken Trang back to Seattle and married her. The first letter was incredibly difficult for Quỳnh to write, but eventually she looked forward to escaping into the imagined life she'd created for Trang. A life where her sister could live in peace, study at a good university, and become a doctor. Those letters had given her hope, too. Hope for a life without wars. Hope for a life where women were respected for their intellect and treated equally.

"I saw the beautiful fabrics in your living room," said Linda. "I guess they have something to do with your or your husband's job?"

Quỳnh nodded and told Linda about her business. She'd started it by chance, five years after the war, when she was a maid for a family who owned a tailor shop. There, she noticed that customers often asked to buy materials but the shop hardly had any designs. When Quỳnh told her employers she could travel to Chợ Lớn Market in Sài

Gòn and bring back samples, they weren't too enthusiastic. But whatever she brought back sold well, and before she knew it, other tailors sought her out. She didn't have any real competition in the beginning. It was during the subsidized economy where free trading was prohibited. Smugglers like her could be arrested and all products confiscated, but her experiences in Sài Gòn enabled her to negotiate her way out of difficult situations, and her knowledge of the black market helped.

She told them briefly about her ex-husband, their thirty years of marriage. She didn't mention the reasons he'd left her for his mistress: her fear of sex and her panic attacks, all stemming from her time before the war's end. She talked at length about her son, Khôi, who loved American music and films. Khôi often visited her with his children and his wife, an architect who designed and helped build Quỳnh's house. Recently they were insisting that she come and live with them, that she had enough staff to run her business, but she knew she could never live in Sài Gòn again. There, every street corner, every tree, every house was a reminder of Trang and of the many secrets Quỳnh had tried to forget.

◆

THE SUN WAS setting as they said goodbye. A part of Quỳnh wanted to ask Dan and Linda if they would like to stay for dinner. It would be a normal thing to do, to show hospitality to faraway guests, but she wasn't ready to have Dan sit inside the house like an old friend. It would be too much of a betrayal to Trang, after what he'd done.

"You take good care, please." Dan held her hand in both of his. "Mr. Thien will call you right away if there's any news of Hoa. And don't hesitate to contact us at any time." He'd given her their home address as well as phone numbers.

In Dan's tears, Quỳnh saw his plea for forgiveness, but she wasn't able to give it. Not before she could forgive herself. People said that time healed, and more than forty years had passed, but for Quỳnh, her pain and guilt were bottomless.

She reached for Linda. They hugged. When they let go, Quỳnh said, "If you find Hoa, please be her mother, on my sister's behalf." Strangely, she felt a bond with this woman, someone whose language she didn't know, but perhaps grief was their common language.

Tears rolled down Linda's cheeks. "I will . . . I promise." She embraced Quỳnh tight.

"Thank you, Brother," Quỳnh told Thiên, "for translating, and for helping Dan to find my niece." She wished she'd had time to get to know the man whose scar and sorrowful expressions throughout their conversation told her that he'd been haunted by the monster of violence, too, and he'd been fighting to get rid of it.

Thiên gave her his business card. "I wish I could have done more, Sister. Call me whenever you think I can help."

Sweetness and Bitterness

Bạc Liêu, 2018

Sitting on the veranda of his home with his dog Mun sleeping at his feet, Phong picked up his guitar and played "Chiếc Khăn Piêu," a song by Doãn Nho, inspired by the colorful lives of ethnic people up north. It was a love song, set against the majestic Tây Bắc region, and its lyrics empowered him. He was thrilled to be able to try different musical instruments. While the đàn sến could accompany Bình when she sang the cải lương songs, his guitar and flute could get his children to sing along, and even get up on their feet and dance.

Two years ago he had decided to give up on his visa application, as well as the search for his parents, and the decision liberated him. Like a bird no longer imprisoned by its cage and who could now rise up into the immense sky, he gained an overview of his life and saw that he was a complete human being even without his parents. He was the one in charge of his destiny. And he was destined to build his life here in Bạc

Liêu, not in a faraway country. "An cư lạc nghiệp," people often said, and it was true. When his home was settled, his career prospered.

His work in the rice field was still backbreaking, but his carpentry business had taken off. He'd learned new designs from several carpentry workshops and could tailor his cabinets, wardrobes, beds, chairs, and tables to meet customers' requirements. Mr. Dan and his wife had lent a hand by sending 2,500 U.S. dollars. "This is not just from us, but also from our friends and my sister," Mr. Dan's letter had said. Phong had used part of the money to build a simple tin-roofed shed next to his house, which served as his working space. He had no shop, but his customers had been telling others about his work and the competitive prices he offered.

Tài and Diễm had each written back a thank-you letter to Mr. Dan and Mrs. Linda, in which they enclosed pictures of the dog lolling her tongue next to their secondhand computer, Bình smiling next to her motorbike, and Phong grinning while holding his toolbox. In recent letters, the children had talked about Phong teaching carpentry skills to Khmer youth and to the children of his Amerasian friends. Even though they were oceans apart, Mr. Dan and Mrs. Linda had become a part of their lives: over the video calls, Phong was able to see their house and garden and showed them the renovations he'd done in his own home: a brick floor, a new roof, as well as the seasons of vegetables he and Bình had been growing.

The results of Phong's DNA tests had come back a long time ago, confirming his Asian, African, and Caucasian heritage: 47.66 percent Asian, 39.58 percent African, 12.76 percent Caucasian. He had stared at the numbers and imagined the many secrets, heartbreaks, and betrayals underneath the statistics. He was happy not to dig any deeper. More than a year ago, Mr. Thiên had brought a DNA test kit on one of his visits and wanted to take another sample from Phong, saying he could send it to another company in America. Phong had shaken his head. He was content with his life.

Mr. Thiên turned out to be kind and helpful. He'd been helping quite a few Amerasians and had connected Phong to a group of anh chị em lai—Amerasian brothers and sisters, as Phong called them—who lived in Sài Gòn or were scattered throughout the Mekong Delta. Phong had attended a few of their get-togethers and learned that he was one of the luckier ones: he had a job, healthy children, and a hardworking, dedicated wife. Most other anh chị em lai had worse problems: living in small rented rooms, unable to pay their bills, struggling to find stable employment because they were illiterate. Some had harmed themselves, and Phong was pained seeing the cigarette burns and razor slashes on their arms and legs. Two men had cut off one of their fingers during drunken rages. "Self-harm was our way to tell others that we suffer, but nobody helped," one of the men had told him.

Most anh chị em lai whom Phong met lived on the brink of time, waiting for the day they could leave for America, believing that their lives were not here, not now, but somewhere ahead of them. They shared with Phong stories of successful Amerasians in the U.S.: how some of them had become famous singers, business people, restaurant owners, writers. Phong admired the people in these stories greatly, knowing the challenges they'd had to overcome—challenges still endured by many. He had met three Amerasians who had been deported back to Việt Nam by the American government: they'd gotten entangled with the law and were imprisoned.

The life experiences of anh chị em lai Phong knew sounded so unbelievable that if he hadn't heard the tremor in their voices and seen the frustration in their eyes, he'd think that their stories were fabricated, cooked up by writers in the novels that Diễm and Tài raved about.

One particular story that stuck with him was that of Hồng, a white Amerasian woman whose mother had given her away to a friend when she was a baby. The mother showed up a few years ago and handed Hồng an American soldier's dog tag, her father's. Hồng was elated and began her search. With the help of a group of American veterans, she received happy news. "When my father came to Sài Gòn to meet me, I cried so much," Hồng had told Phong. "My father cried, too. He said he hadn't known I existed. He'd had a short-term relationship with my mother. He said he loved me and wanted to sponsor me, as well as my husband and kids to America. At the American Consulate, we were told we needed DNA tests. And you know what happened when our test results came back? They didn't match! My mother had fabricated the whole story about the dog tag. When she gave it to me, she said that once I found my father, I had to sponsor her over to America." Hồng fumed. "Even if your parents find you, be careful, Phong. Don't fall for their words easily, because words can be the most dangerous traps. If they only start looking for you now, you must ask why. Are they feeling old and lonely and need a caretaker?"

Phong knew well what it meant to be scammed.

He finished his song. Mun was up, her tail wagging. "You hungry yet?" Phong sat on his heels, picked Mun up, ran his hand through the dog's white fur, laughing out loud as Mun licked his face, her tongue warm and rough. He walked, with Mun in his arms, into the kitchen, with its window open to the rice field at the back of his house. There, he mixed leftover rice with stewed fish and gave it to Mun. He watched with a smile as she devoured the food. He hadn't wanted a dog, thinking it would cost too much, but his children had brought Mun home, given her to their mother, declaring it Bình's birthday gift. They called the dog Mun, which meant "Black as Velvet," a brilliant name for a white poodle.

Phong gave Mun some water, then headed back into the shed. He was on lunch break but was anxious to continue his work on the desks for Trương Định School. A recent storm had caused a building to collapse and he wanted to deliver the furniture earlier than promised so that students could return to their temporary classroom.

The heat radiating from the shed's tin roof surged to Phong as he stepped inside. The two finished desks looked good, and so did the shelf where his carpentry tools were neatly arranged: hammers, planes, saws, drills, mallets. He was glad his students had followed his instructions and stayed organized.

At his workstation, he planed a piece of wood the size of a desk's surface. As the shavings curled and coiled into rolls, his mind was filled with thoughts about Mr. Dan. That evening two years ago, he'd sat in the lobby of Tài Lộc Hotel, stunned as Mr. Thiên told him that Mr. Dan's daughter had been given away three days after her birth.

Mr. Dan's search for his daughter had revealed that Hoa's mother had died, and Phong knew something like that could happen to him if he continued his search.

The sound of an engine drew his attention. He looked through the shed's open door to see Bình riding the motorbike across their front yard. Two large canvas sacks towered on the back of the bike—fertilizer for their rice plants. These days Bình worked in their field and also took care of the paperwork for his carpentry business.

He hurried outside to help his wife unload the sacks.

"Mr. Thiên called," she told him, breathless. "He said he couldn't reach you. He asked me to tell you to call him right back." She handed him her mobile phone. "He said he'd found your mother. She did her DNA test recently and the results matched with yours."

"What?" Phong laughed. Either Bình, Mr. Thiên, or fate must be joking with him.

"Apparently your mother is very excited. She's coming here to meet you. This afternoon."

◈

PHONG SAT IN Chiều Mơ Café, two streets away from his home. Because of Hồng's story about her cheating mother and her warnings about being careful, he hadn't invited the woman who claimed to be his mother to his house. The café was a popular meeting venue and he could see why. Yellow Tonkin jasmine flowers hung like a curtain above him and soft music floated through the air. A standing electric fan sent a light breeze to his table, where a woman sat opposite him. Fair-skinned. Perfect makeup. She was dressed in long pants and a silk shirt, the pattern of which reminded him of the clothing worn by the royal family in Huế.

The woman had arrived on a fancy motorbike, with cloth gloves covering her arms and a mask on her face. Like a typical Vietnamese woman, she was protecting herself from getting brown and now, looking at her skin, Phong was certain she'd used whitening cream. That must have been why she rejected him in the first place: he was too dark to belong to her world.

Mr. Thiên had said the woman was his mother, proven by the results of their DNA tests. "I've sent the written report to your son's email," Mr. Thiên had said on the phone. But Phong's son was on a school camping trip and would not be back for three days. In the meantime, the woman had been so eager that she'd traveled two hours to reach Phong's hometown.

Phong had imagined this to be the happiest moment in his life, but his mind was clouded by doubt. The woman in front of him bore no resemblance to the mother of his imagination. She wasn't weeping, she didn't look like she had suffered or been tormented by her decision to abandon him. On the contrary, she looked as if she'd enjoyed a good life. He felt a lump of resentment rising to his throat.

"How's Bình? How are Tài and Diễm?" The woman asked about his wife and children, casually, as if she'd known him all her life and had just gone away for a short holiday. She had a strong Mekong Delta accent. Mr. Thiên had said she didn't live too far away from him, but refused to reveal more, saying that she'd tell him herself.

"They're all fine." He avoided her eyes by flipping through the menu, even though he knew what to order. The café was quiet, just the sun roaming free through the leaves. There was nobody sitting near them since it was sunnier. Everyone crowded on the other side, under the shade of large bàng trees.

A waiter arrived. The woman ordered a cà phê sữa đá—iced coffee with condensed milk—and Phong did the same.

The woman cleared her throat once the waiter had left. "Son, I'm sorry it's taken me so long to find you . . ." She called him "con trai"— Son—and addressed herself as "Má"—Mother—as if it was the most natural thing.

Phong held up his hands. "Wait . . . how can we be sure?" He avoided using "you" in his sentence, since "you" would need to take a form of address: Má for Mother, Dì or Cô for Auntie, or Bà for Madam. Calling her Madam or Auntie would be awkward. As for Mother, he'd made that mistake once before.

"You mean the DNA results might not be correct?" The woman dabbed the sweat on her forehead with her handkerchief. "Yes, that could happen. Let's verify our details then. How about . . . could you tell me . . . where you grew up and the year of your birth?"

"Phú Long Orphanage. I don't know my birthday, but I was abandoned in the front of the orphanage in February 1972."

He stressed the word "abandoned" and the woman flinched. She brought her hand to her face and the sight of her rosy fingernails made the lump inside Phong's throat expand. He thought about Bình's callused hands, the fingers discolored by hard work. The only time Bình had had her nails painted was on their wedding day. Bình had wanted their wedding to be perfect, but her parents hadn't come. They hadn't come because of this woman, who had thrown him away, only to appear more than forty years later pretending that things were all right.

"Má . . . Má xin lỗi." The woman called herself Mother again, offering her words of apologies. "Do you remember the name of any nun from your orphanage?"

"Of course. Sister Nhã raised me. She loved me like a mother. But she died early, when I was twelve."

"She saved you, I know. And I am grateful," the woman said. "Did Sister Nhã tell you how you arrived at Phú Long?"

"I should be the one asking questions," Phong said, determined not to be cheated again. "So. . . how did I arrive?"

The woman recoiled at the harshness in Phong's voice. But she quickly regained her composure. "You were wrapped in a blanket and put into a bag."

"A bag, imagine that!" Phong's voice was louder than he'd intended it to be. "And where was the bag left?"

"It was . . . hung onto a branch of the Bodhi tree outside the orphanage."

"How cruel," Phong said bitterly. "An animal could have gotten to me first. I could have lost an arm, a leg, an eye . . ."

"No animal could have gotten to you, Son. I was there. I watched you until Sister Nhã came . . . And do you know why I placed you under the protective branches of a Bodhi tree? It is said that a Bodhi tree has the power to chase away sorrow and bad luck. And as I entrusted you— my baby—to the tree, I was hoping that Buddha would protect you, because He achieved enlightenment under the Bodhi tree." The woman stopped speaking as soon as the waiter neared their table, holding a tray. He placed two cups of crushed ice onto the table, followed by two tall glasses with metal filters dripping coffee into sweetened condensed milk. Last came two small glasses of trà đá, thinly diluted green tea mixed with ice cubes.

Phong watched the coffee drip slowly. His life had been like this, each major event a gradual slow drop.

"Phong . . . I'm sorry that you are upset. I deserve it," the woman said, and he looked up to see a tear slide down her cheek. "I'm quite certain that you are my son. The DNA. Phú Long Orphanage. February 1972. Sister Nhã."

"Quite certain doesn't mean one hundred percent. Is there some proof, a picture?"

The woman shook her head. "I didn't have any means to take pictures. But I know another thing only your mother would know."

Phong looked at the thick layer of coffee that had escaped the filter, covering the layer of condensed milk inside his glass. Sweetness and bitterness. Perhaps the woman was telling the truth, after all. He waited.

"I said I was quite certain. And I need to confirm this, to be absolutely sure." The woman swallowed. "Do you happen to have a large birthmark on the right side of your chest?"

Phong stared at the woman. Slowly, he lifted his shirt. A birthmark, the size of a palm, glistened on the right side of his chest.

◇

THE WOMAN STARTED sobbing in front of Phong. Heat gathered behind his eyes. He blinked and distracted himself by taking the coffee filter away from her glass. He stirred her coffee, mixing it with the condensed milk before filling the glass with ice. He pushed the glass toward the woman. He did the same with his coffee, yearning for a sip of the fragrant liquid, but felt he didn't deserve it. He didn't know why he couldn't reach out and console his mother. All those years he'd wanted her tears, wanted to know she cared about him as much as he missed her, and now she was giving them to him.

Only Sister Nhã and Bình had seen his birthmark. He'd always worn a shirt in front of others, including his children. He considered the birthmark to be a mark of shame. He'd imagined his mother's disgust as she saw his birthmark for the first time.

"I am so, so sorry"—the woman choked for a moment—"for not being able to raise you."

"What were the reasons then? And why look for me now? Why not sooner?" He was aware that he sounded impolite, but he couldn't call her Má yet. A woman earned the title Mother not simply through the act of giving birth but from years of raising a child, from sleepless nights when the child was sick, from many meals and conversations they shared, from the joy that doubled in her presence and the sorrow that lessened with her being there.

The woman reached for his coffee and stirred it even though he'd already done so. She acted as if she was desperate to do something for him. She gave him the glass. "Son, in answering your questions, may I tell you a story?"

Phong frowned. This wasn't the time for stories, this was real life. Sister Nhã had said stories could save him, but they hadn't. He'd seen how people had twisted stories, turning them into propaganda. Once, on the public radio, he'd heard a Vietnamese novelist declare that writers had blood on their pens; too many writers had encouraged people to go to war by glorifying it. Too many young men and women had died because they believed in the stories dreamt up by writers.

He was tempted to say no to his mother's request but thought better of it. She'd no doubt prepared for this meeting. Her story must be a way of answering his many questions.

"I hope your story won't take that long." He drank his coffee. "I need to get back to work . . ." He didn't want to say that, on the other side of the café, his wife and daughter were waiting. They'd insisted on coming along.

The woman nodded and cleared her throat. "Once upon a time, during the war, there was a girl. She lived in Sài Gòn. She had a Vietnamese boyfriend but he'd broken her heart. To cheer her up, her friends took her out dancing. At the club that night, she met an American man and danced the night away with him. He was an administrative officer, not a combat soldier. His name was Tim. Tim had been in Việt Nam for a few months, was stationed in Kon Tum but was on leave in Sài Gòn."

Phong looked at his mother. Her eyes glowed as she mentioned Tim's name.

"The girl was amazed how much fun she could have with Tim on the dance floor, how much of herself she could let go." The woman beamed. "The girl had never thought she could be friends with a Black man, but Tim changed that. He proved to her that he was a gentleman, and compared to him, her ex-boyfriend was . . . shit." The woman gave a small laugh. "The day after, Tim invited the girl to a fancy French restaurant in the center of Sài Gòn. They had a most delicious meal. Tim managed to communicate with the girl despite their language barrier. They talked about anything and everything. Tim had several days in Sài Gòn, and they spent all that time together. They connected like soul mates. Just as he was due to return to Kon Tum, Tim lifted her hand to his lips and asked the girl to wait for him."

The woman didn't look at Phong. She gazed at the palm of her hand, as if her fate had been written on it. "The girl tried to resist her feelings, knowing that Tim wouldn't stay in Việt Nam for long, that he would be going home after his tour, and that he could be killed at any time. But her heart was stubborn. She fell for Tim anyway, and Tim for her, too. He returned to Sài Gòn often, as often as he was allowed. He loved her passionately, insanely. When the girl became pregnant," the woman paused, " . . . when she was pregnant, the girl was afraid Tim would walk away from her and never look back. Most Americans behaved like that then. But . . . Tim was different. When he found out, he celebrated. He picked her up, twirled her around until she became dizzy. He said he was the only person left in his family. He had no siblings and his parents had passed away. He promised to the girl that at the end of his tour of duty, he would marry her and bring her to America. The girl kissed Tim and told him she loved him. She had every reason to believe his words. He had always kept his promise."

Phong shook his head. The story sounded like a fairytale, too good to be true.

"Tim longed for a family and loved their unborn child. He used to press his ear against the girl's belly, hoping to hear the baby; he sang

the baby many silly songs. When the girl was six months pregnant . . .
Tim was meant to come and take her to the doctor. They'd decided
that she'd give birth at Từ Dũ Hospital, the best in maternity care. The
girl was very excited. She imagined their beautiful child, their future
together in Los Angeles, where Tim was from. She waited for Tim . . .
but he never came. A few weeks later, the girl received a letter from Kon
Tum where Tim was stationed. The letter was from a friend of Tim. Tim
had told the person about the girl, and now he was writing . . . to inform
her . . . that Tim had died from an enemy attack. He died while working
in his office, processing payroll for his comrades. The friend ended the
letter with the sentence: 'I'm so sorry.'"

The woman tried to hold back her sobs. The sorrow in her eyes was
so deep Phong had to look away, not wanting to be drowned by it. The
sorrow was so real, he had no choice but to believe her story. A shiver
ran through his body. Could this Tim be his father? If so, his father had
died. Oh, Heaven and Earth.

The woman choked. "The girl was devastated. She hugged her swollen belly and cried for three days and three nights. When she could get
up, she wrote Tim's friend a letter. She begged for his help. She waited,
but no news. She wrote several other letters but never received any
response. She didn't want to believe that Tim was gone. She gathered
all her money and traveled to his base camp in Kon Tum. There she
learned that Tim had truly died, and his body had been sent back to
the U.S. She returned to Sài Gòn, desperate. She lived with her friends
then, but no one could help her. They were all working, struggling with
their problems, struggling to survive. When hope had abandoned her,
she received a notice from the post office. Somebody had sent her one
hundred dollars. The name of the sender was left blank. It must have
been from Tim's friend. The girl wept. The money wouldn't be enough
for her to raise the baby. Her parents lived in the countryside and knew
nothing about her pregnancy. Her village was controlled by the Việt
Cộng and she couldn't bring the baby of a Black American there."

The woman clutched her mouth with her palm, trying to stop cries from escaping her. Her shoulders shook. Her mascara was running down her face, leaving black trails on her cheeks. Phong stayed rooted in his seat. He should offer her a tissue or his words of condolences, but he was unable to move.

The woman closed her eyes. "The girl wanted her baby to stay in her belly so she could protect him from all the cruelty of this world, but he arrived after nine months. He was such a beautiful boy, just like his father. His eyes were bright, his eyebrows very dark, his hair curly, and he had a big birthmark on his chest. In addition to this birthmark, he also has a smaller birthmark on his left thigh."

The world stopped spinning. Phong struggled to breathe. When he managed to fill his lungs with air once more, pain seared through him.

The woman sobbed. "The girl didn't want to give her baby away, but the whole world was against her. She had no means of bringing him up, she couldn't offer him protection. So she had to make one of the most difficult decisions of her life. . . . She wrapped her son in a blue blanket. With a sedge bag in one arm, her baby in the other, she went to Phú Long Orphanage, where she knew the nuns were kind and there'd be enough food for her son. She knew it'd be safe for him to be there. Safe from the American and the Việt Cộng attacks."

"The girl would forever remember that night. . . . It was a dark, dark night. There was no moon, no stars. Holding her son in her arms, she sat in front of the orphanage. She fed him until he was very full. She sang him lullabies. She whispered that she loved him very much. When her son was fast asleep, she rewrapped the blanket and carefully placed him into the sedge bag. She hung the bag onto a branch of a Bodhi tree. She didn't want any animal to get to him before a nun did."

Phong bit his lip so hard, he tasted the saltiness of his blood.

"The girl waited in darkness, punctured by flickering fireflies, until her baby cried. As Sister Nhã went out and lowered the bag, the girl wanted to run to her and take her baby back. The baby was her last reminder of Tim. The girl had loved Tim and knew she should be taking care of his son. But she had no choice. She looked on as Sister Nhã brought the baby inside and closed the gate."

Phong gripped the table. He needed to hang on to something. This was the same story that Sister Nhã had asked him to remember by heart. It had helped lead him to his mother, but shattered him at the same time.

The woman cried into her handkerchief. After a brief moment, she regained her composure. "The girl felt empty once she had no more baby. She returned to Sài Gòn, worked hard and earned money to send back to her family, who needed her help. She missed her son and thought about him every day. But she knew she couldn't give him a future. She traveled back to the orphanage many times. She stood outside and gazed into the front yard. There, she saw her son crawling, and as he grew up, she watched him play with his friends, jumping and laughing. He was beautiful. He looked healthy. He had a good life. She wouldn't be able to give him that. Toward the end of each visit, she would cry until she was emptied of tears. She always returned to Sài Gòn without saying hello to the boy. She was ashamed of herself and thought she didn't deserve him."

Phong's palms rolled into fists. What bullshit. There were no excuses for a mother to abandon her son and let him grow up an orphan.

The woman sighed. "For a mother to maintain her distance from her child was a most difficult thing. But the girl was comforted by the fact that her love for Tim was alive. Her son was thriving and she sensed that her sacrifices were worth it: he had a better life than what she could ever give him."

Sacrifices? How could his mother attribute the terrible things she'd done to sacrifices? Didn't she know how much he'd suffered? He'd become the dust of life because of her. There was no virtue in that.

"By April 1975, the girl saw so much death around her that she decided her son was most important. She had to raise him herself.

She sold the few things she owned and travelled to the orphanage. She planned to bring him some place where the Communists wouldn't cause them any trouble. But she couldn't get to the orphanage for several weeks: the roads were blocked, and there was no transport available. When she finally managed, the war had ended. Soldiers swamped the orphanage's yard. She asked around for the whereabouts of her son and the nuns, but no one knew."

Phong shook his head. Whatever this woman said about wanting to raise him was a lie. He had stayed at the orphanage for more than three years and she didn't approach him once. Not once. And why hadn't she ever met Sister Nhã, to at least thank her for taking care of him?

"The girl left the orphanage, not knowing where to go," the woman continued. "She kept looking for her son and found out about an evacuation program called Bấy-bì Líp. She hoped her son had been able to go."

What bullshit about Operation Babylift, Phong thought to himself. His children had looked it up on the internet and told him about the program: it'd evacuated around 2,500 children, a small fraction of the many tens of thousands of orphans in South Việt Nam at that time. The woman had ruined his life, and now she appeared out of nowhere, to tell him his father had died?

"The girl has punished herself for what she did," the woman said, trying to hold back tears. "She's an old woman now, but every day, she yearns for her son. She hopes that he'll sympathize with her situation. She's afraid he thinks she doesn't love him. But she does . . . she's always loved him, with all her heart. She didn't want to give away her baby, a baby conceived by love and born from her flesh and blood."

Phong's mother leaned forward, reaching for his hand. "Son, I am so sorry . . . I hope you can forgive me. The things I had to do, they were terrible. But please understand . . . I had no choice."

At her touch, Phong flinched. He snatched his hand away. He closed his eyes and shook his head. "I don't believe you." He said each word clearly. He called her "bà" and addressed himself as "tôi," as if they were strangers. "Every word you just said is a lie! My father is not dead until you can show me proof otherwise."

"Phong . . ." She reached for him again but he shifted his chair away from the table.

"Show me a picture of my father then. A picture with you and him in it!'

"I'm sorry, Son. We never took pictures."

"Ha, I knew you'd say that. How about letters? You said his friend wrote you a letter from Kon Tum."

"Yes he did, and Tim wrote me when he was alive, too. But I burned everything as the war ended. . . . I was stupid. Like many people at that time, I was afraid of being punished for being linked to Americans."

"Oh how convenient!" Phong said, even though he knew many people had destroyed their papers.

"I understand your doubts, Son, and it's good you're being careful. But let me assure you that only your mother would know about your birthmarks. And the sedge bag, the orphanage . . ."

Phong glared at the woman. He hadn't expected to be so angry at his mother once he found her. "You said you came back for me many times? That was a lie. Sister Nhã would have seen you. She said no one looked for me."

"But Phong . . . she didn't know I'm your mother. I spoke to her twice, before I was pregnant. I'd visited the orphanage, on behalf of somebody else. That's how I was sure she would take care of you well."

"If you knew Sister Nhã, why didn't you hand me over to her yourself? Why abandon me like that? What if an animal got to me first?"

"As I said, I was there to watch you, Son. . . . I guarded you from afar, until Sister Nhã brought you inside. As for the reasons of me not asking Sister Nhã myself . . . I can't explain. I was not thinking straight. Tim had died and I could hardly make it through the days—"

"I don't care about your stupid reasons!"

"Phong. Má xin lỗi con. Má xin lỗi!"

"You say you're sorry? If you were, why didn't you look for me? It's been a lifetime since you abandoned me. I was beaten, abused, rejected, put in prison."

"Son . . . believe me, I've longed for you throughout these years. But I was sure you'd left for America. I thought you'd be better off without me."

He shook his head. "I tried to find you because people told me you'd thrown me away because I was ugly and I wanted to prove them wrong. I tried to find you because my friends had mothers and I had none!"

"What those people said is not true, Son. You are beautiful and it broke my heart, having to do what I did." She reached out for him again but he leaned back.

She sighed. "I understand how you feel, Son. I hope you can believe me, but if you don't . . . there is someone you can ask. That person knows how dire my circumstances were during the war."

"You mean Mr. Thiên?"

His mother swallowed hard, then shook her head. "No . . . an American. Mr. Đan. You're friends with him, Thiên told me."

"How the hell did you know him?"

His mother put her palms against her face. In her silence, he heard motorbikes roaring on the road outside, as loud as the screams of someone who had just lost his father.

When his mother looked up, tears had filled her eyes. "Mr. Đan . . . he . . . he was my sister's boyfriend, back in 1969. My sister . . . her name was Trang."

Love and Honor

Bạc Liêu, 2019

"Grandma . . . what are you thinking about?" A soft voice pulled Quỳnh out of her reverie. She had been remembering a rainy night in 1970 when she'd walked the streets of Sài Gòn alone, after her sister's death. She shuddered, reaching out for Diễm, and held her granddaughter close. She wished she could lock the gate to her past and throw the key away. At the same time, she wished she could talk to herself—the young girl of eighteen—and tell her not to lose hope, because despite feeling like she'd died along with her elder sister, she would survive and would never let anyone look down on her, ever again.

"Grandma, will you sing for us?" Tài nestled against her, and Quỳnh wished she had found Phong sooner; she loved being the grandmother to his two wonderful children. She was lying on Tài and Diễm's bed in their home, inside the cocoon of a white mosquito net. Tài and Diễm were already teenagers who no longer needed lullabies to lure them to sleep, but still, they asked Quỳnh for songs or bedtime stories every night during her visits. As if they, too, wanted to make up for lost time. As if they needed her as much as she needed them.

Quỳnh embraced her grandchildren in each arm. The warmth of their bodies calmed her turbulent mind. It had been a year since her reunion with Phong, but the reality felt as fresh as a rice field that had just received seedlings.

"À à ơi . . ." Her voice rose against darkness. "Gió mùa thu mẹ ru mà con ngủ năm canh chày, là năm canh chày thức đủ vừa năm hỡi chàng chàng ơi, hỡi người người ơi em nhớ tới chàng em nhớ tới chàng . . ." She sang louder, as if to declare that she had a voice, and nobody could erase it.

That day at the café, when Quỳnh revealed her connection with Dan, Phong was stunned. He had blinked, stayed silent, then shook his head. "You're worse than I imagined," he said. "You've ruined two lives instead of one. What kind of an aunt are you, to give your niece away, after Hoa's mother had just died?" He flung some money onto the table for his coffee before hurrying out to the street. She was sure she would lose him forever, but a few minutes later, Diễm ran toward her, calling "Grandma! Grandma!"

Now, on the bed, she kissed Diễm's cheek, inhaling the girl's scent. Earlier in the evening, she'd rubbed coconut oil on her granddaughter's hair to be able to comb it, and was astonished at the healthy glow of Diễm's skin, the unique beauty of it. For many years, Quỳnh had spent money on whitening cream like so many Vietnamese women she knew, and on sunny days never left her house without covering herself from head to toe. Now she could see Heaven had blessed people with their different skin colors, and regardless of their differences, they were beautiful in their own ways.

"Grandma, that's a really romantic song." Diễm giggled. "Do you think about Grandpa Tim when you sing it?"

The word "Tim" sent a knife through Quỳnh's mind. She swallowed. "Yes . . . of course. I used to sing him lullabies and he'd always fall asleep with a smile on his face." As Trang had often said, she'd launched the javelin, she had to follow its path.

"Tell us more about Grandpa Tim, Grandma," Tài asked.

The bedroom door was open and Quỳnh could see the altar Phong had set up for his father, from which three red dots peered down at her, like eyes of a hovering ghost. Even though Phong was a Catholic, he followed the Vietnamese customs of ancestor worship. He had burnt incense for his father before going out with Bình that night to a cải lương play. He prayed to his father so often, whispering Tim's name. Every time Quỳnh saw her son do it, she wanted to scream.

"Grandpa Tim really didn't have any family left, Grandma?" Diễm nudged her.

"Well . . . he was the only child. His parents died young. He was so lonely that he joined the military, to seek companionship." She caressed her grandchildren's backs. "Now . . . close your eyes and dream of something sweet, darlings. You have school early tomorrow." The more she loved them, the more she feared their questions.

"I don't like school," Diễm said. "And I hate some of my textbooks. They say American soldiers were bad, they were killing machines. When we read those passages in class, I can feel my friends staring at me."

"Oh . . . I'm so sorry." Quỳnh hugged her granddaughter tighter. "Don't feel like that, please. You should feel proud about your grandpa, not ashamed of him. Remember that he wasn't a combat soldier? He wasn't involved in any fighting. He was an administrative officer who helped a lot of Vietnamese, actually. He processed paperwork and payments that enabled the rebuilding of houses, medical clinics, and schools in Kon Tum."

Quỳnh wondered if she should go to Diễm's school and talk to her teachers. Atrocities did take place during the war, but they weren't just committed by the American side. What purpose did it serve anyway to teach children about hatred, to continue glorifying victory while not acknowledging the human costs on all sides?

"Grandpa Tim would want me to study in America, don't you think?" Diễm asked. "Schools there would surely be better."

"Shut up," said Tài. "Don't stand on one mountain and say the next is more beautiful. America has its problems, too. You know there's tons of racism there too, right?"

"Tài, no harsh language, remember?" Quỳnh tapped her grandson on his shoulder. "It's true that each country has its own issues, and it's up to us to live our lives the best we can, wherever we are. . . . As for studying overseas, if you are keen, we can arrange it, but perhaps at university level, not before." Some of Quỳnh's friends had been sending their school-aged children and grandchildren to boarding schools in the U.K. and the U.S., and although Quỳnh could afford it, she wanted Diễm and Tài to stay close by. She needed to see them often, now that she'd found them.

"Something is going on with my father . . ." said Tài. "He's become restless again. He's thinking about doing another DNA test and register the results with a larger company to have a better chance of finding Grandpa Tim's relatives. He said Grandpa Tim must have had aunts and uncles who might have children. Now that he's with you, he feels luck is on his side, Grandma."

Shock jolted through Quỳnh's body before settling into the pit of her stomach. So heavy, it pinned her down onto the mattress. She'd just found Phong, Bình, Tài, and Diễm, and now she risked losing them again. It had taken her nearly two years since meeting Dan and Linda before deciding that she would embark on a search for her first son. There were many reasons that changed her mind: Khôi's secure position at his university, a traffic accident that nearly killed her, her retirement from the daily operation of her business, and the repeated nightmares. Never had she imagined that Phong lived so close by.

The day her taxi had been hit by a container truck—the driver squashed beyond recognition, while she lost consciousness and found herself many hours later in an emergency room in a full-body cast— was the day she realized she'd been given a chance at redemption. She realized that if she could turn back time, perhaps she would raise Hoa and Phong herself. The rumors about the Communists' punishments hadn't been true, they didn't burn those with permed hair nor chop off painted fingers. She knew no women who were imprisoned simply because of their sexual relations with Americans. Tiên, a woman from her bar, decided to raise her Amerasian child and they'd been left alone. It was true that some mothers were interrogated and sent to the New Economic Zones, and others were asked to report to their local police stations for months, but there were no mass executions.

She had reached out to Thiên after the accident. He immediately organized the DNA test for her. Finding Phong had been a miracle, and afterward she'd traveled to Sài Gòn and taken Khôi out for dinner. At his favorite Japanese restaurant, she had told her second son the same story she'd told Phong. She was talking about Phong's wife and kids when Khôi threw his serviette onto the table. His chair scraped against the floor as he stood up. "How can you tell me now that your life and mine have been based on lies?" he said, then walked out, leaving her with two full plates of sashimi and sushi that neither of them had touched. He stopped talking to her for many weeks. Now, even though he brought his family back home occasionally for a visit, he asked her not to mention Phong. He refused to meet his half brother, even during the New Year. A few months ago, he'd sent her a text: "I worked hard to help you with your business. I was there for you throughout the years. I traveled with you on many overseas trips and translated for you, remember? When it comes to inheritance, don't forget that he is not entitled to anything!"

Phong didn't yet know about the text regarding inheritance. Khôi stood to inherit plenty of money, but Quỳnh knew now that she would be giving a share of it to Phong as well.

Phong had visited Quỳnh several times at her house, together with his wife and children. She'd taken them to her shop, explained her business to them, and introduced them to her staff. She hosted a dinner for them, to which she invited her relatives, friends, and neighbors. Her story about Tim seemed to have amazed people, but they were more interested in Phong's life, in his experiences at the reeducation camp, in what it was like to be an Amerasian. "Your story should be made into a movie or written into a book," someone had said, and she could only laugh at that.

Quỳnh was grateful that Phong seemed to have forgiven her. She'd wept when he called her Mother for the first time. It happened during their third meeting, her first time visiting his home. She'd brought along canvases, paints, and brushes, and spent the afternoon having fun with Tài and Diễm. They decided to paint Mun the dog, and the end result looked so much like a bear that Mun barked at the painting. As her grandchildren doubled over with laughter, Phong had leaned toward her, saying, "Cảm ơn Má." He'd thanked her with not just his word, but also his smile.

Phong had told her to give Khôi time, and that he didn't want to cause any tension between his mother and his younger brother, but as months passed and Khôi continued to avoid him, Phong must have felt hurt and disappointed. He almost never expressed it to her, though, as if life had tested him enough to make him patient with its struggles. But how long would his patience last?

"What have you been thinking, Grandma? Didn't you hear my question about the DNA test?" Diễm nudged her.

Quỳnh blinked. "Oh . . . I was just . . . recalling Mr. Dan's last letter. When did he say he and Mrs. Linda are coming back?" She didn't want to talk about DNA tests. Not to her grandchildren, who were too young to understand that the results of such tests may not just reveal family relations.

"They'll be back this September, Grandma," Diễm said.

"I wouldn't mind listening to you read the letter again. You did such a great job translating it, young man." Quỳnh patted Tài on his arm. Tài was taking an intensive English course and used Dan and Linda's letters to practice his language skills. Hardworking and ambitious, Tài would graduate from high school in a year; he planned to study computer science at an international university in Hồ Chí Minh City.

"Ah, I'm glad you asked, Grandma," Tài said cheerfully, "because I improved my translation." He got out of the mosquito net and Diễm switched on the light.

As Quỳnh sat on the bed, her back leaning against the headrest, flanked by her grandchildren, she thought about the milestones of their lives that she had missed: their first words, their first steps, their first day at school. She wished she'd been there to pick them up when they fell down, dry their tears when they sorrowed, and double their laughter. She wished she'd been able to color their childhood with joyful memories, the way she'd done for Khôi's children. She needed to do more to bring Khôi and Phong's families together. She would go to Sài Gòn in a few days to talk to Khôi again.

That afternoon, as she worked with Phong in the garden, she had watched butterflies fluttering on squash blossoms. In the pink rose apples and green guavas around her, she saw reasons to believe that Khôi would change, the way the flowers and the fruits were maturing in front of her eyes. Once Khôi got to know Phong, he would be proud of his half brother—a survivor, a man who overcame all odds.

"Today I gave my teacher this new version of my translation, Grandma," Tài showed Quỳnh his notebook. "He said I stayed true to Mr. Dan's letter and managed to make it sound natural in Vietnamese."

"Your teachers are way too easy on you." Diễm snatched the notebook from Tài's hand. "Let me be the judge." She started reading aloud.

Dear Quỳnh, Phong, Bình, Diễm, and Tài,

Can you believe it, that this is the first time I am writing with Vietnamese diacritics? Looking back, I am amazed at how I always stripped diacritical marks from Vietnamese names and words, to make things look and sound easier. Forgive me for the many times I misspelled your names! My Vietnamese teacher highlighted the importance of Vietnamese tonal marks to me. He pointed out that by writing Tài's name as Tai, I called him "Ear" rather than "Talented."

Diễm clutched her belly, laughing out loud. She turned to Tài. "I'm going to call you Brother Ear from now on."

"Don't you dare!" Tài narrowed his eyes.

Diễm giggled. She turned back to the letter.

Linda and I are making a big effort to learn Vietnamese because we're returning this September. My sister will travel from Australia with her family and will join us in Hồ Chí Minh City. We are so excited and can't wait for you to meet her.

We still have a lot to do before the trip. We've been working with our psychologist, Dr. Hoh, to set up a charity to provide psychological support to people affected by the war and by Agent Orange. It's Mr. Thiên who gave us the idea, helps us with the paperwork and he will be the manager of our operations in Việt Nam. Isn't that amazing? We are grateful that our family and so many of our friends are joining hands with us.

Just three more months and we'll see you again! We are counting down each day and can't wait to visit your home. Linda is very excited to go fishing with Tài and Diễm, taste the delicious vegetables in Phong's garden, visit Bình's rice field and hear her sing, and learn how to cook from Quỳnh. We will test our skills with Phong's musical instruments, of course, but might not be brave enough to take up your offer to ride on a water buffalo!

Tài and Diễm: your English is getting so good; I hope one day I'll be able to write you letters in Vietnamese the way you are writing to us in English.

Bình: thank you again for sending Linda the áo dài dress. She still wears it to all our parties. Her friends are jealous and want tailor-made clothes, too.

Quỳnh and Phong: it's truly a miracle that you have found each other. It makes me smile every time I think about it. Your reunion enables me to believe in God again. I hope our family will be further extended when we find Hoa.

See you soon!

With many warm hugs from Seattle,

Dan (and Linda)

It was the second time Quỳnh had listened to the letter but she still found herself teary-eyed. She noticed how positive Dan sounded, how enthusiastic.

"Did Mr. Dan really write 'our family' in the original letter?" Diễm asked Tài. "Or did you make it up?"

"Make it up?" Tài snorted. "I had to show both the English *and* Vietnamese versions to my teacher, you dumbhead."

"Hey, no foul language, remember?" Quỳnh said sternly. "Of course Mr. Dan and Mrs. Linda are our family, for the many things they have done for us, and we for them. But more than that, we share a common history that bonds us together stronger than any blood ties.

"When you answer the letter," she told Tài, "could you ask how someone could make a donation to their charity?" None of her family members knew, but over the years, she had donated money to hospitals, pagodas, and orphanages. She'd had good financial fortune, and it was her duty to share her luck with others. And she hoped the psychologists from Dan's group might talk to Phong, who had told her about his past panic attacks.

"Please, Grandma . . . can I have Mun?" said Diễm as they settled into bed again.

"We're not supposed to have the dog in bed, but I'm sure Grandma won't tell," Tài laughed.

"Ah . . . That could get me into big trouble with your parents, but I suppose it's worth it." Quỳnh laughed along. Spoiling her grandchildren was not only her great joy, it was her job. Mun was half-sleeping in her basket when Quỳnh picked her up and brought her to Diễm. The dog smelled like a rose from this afternoon's bubble bath.

With the warmth of her grandchildren against her, Quỳnh sang one lullaby, then another, and another, until Tài and Diễm relaxed in her arms and their breathing became regular.

Quỳnh slipped from the bed and stepped out to the front yard. The stars were alive above her. They looked like Trang's eyes. Quỳnh brought her palms together in front of her chest and looked up. In the star's twinkle, she was reminded that her sister lived on—Trang lived on in the light that had given Quỳnh strength in her darkest moments.

"Thank you for helping me find my son, chị Hai," she whispered. "You arranged for Phong to meet Dan, then for Dan to find me. You brought us together." She bowed to the stars' light. People who died young are said to have supernatural powers, and she believed this now. She believed in the blessings of the dead, and the interconnectedness of life. And she believed that all stories relating to the war were connected, one way or another, by blood.

Looking up to the sky, Quỳnh saw Trang's face. She was still nineteen, forever young, forever beautiful. Before Trang's burial, Quỳnh had knelt down next to her sister. She'd wiped all the blood away from Trang's face, covered her sister's head with a scarf, took off Trang's torn clothes, and dressed her sister in fresh shirt and pants. "You are the most special angel," she'd whispered to Trang, trying not to cry, for she'd heard tears that touched a dead person would prevent him or her from having a peaceful departure from earth.

"Chị Hai, I know you're watching out for me, so please do more,"

Quỳnh told the stars. "Please convince Khôi to accept Phong. Please protect my secret. Please help us find Hoa."

She had prayed for Hoa often. She wished for Hoa to be at peace. She hoped that Hoa was loved by her adoptive family, who could make up for her parents' absence. She wished she could find Hoa one day, to tell her how profoundly her mother had loved her.

Quỳnh had loved Trang, too, even though she'd never been able to say it aloud. She'd realized the depth of that love in the abyss of sorrow she experienced after her sister's death. The sorrow that drove her to drinking, that made her undesirable to the men who frequented the Paradise Bar. After that rainy night when she was kicked out of the bar by her boss, she'd wandered around, wanting to take her own life. Another madam had plucked her out of the street, brought her to her brothel, Minh Anh, and pushed her into the arms of men.

The stars blurred as Quỳnh's tears started to fall. She cried silently: for herself, for Trang, for the countless young women whose lives had been nothing but firewood in the furnace of wars.

When her tears dried, Quỳnh stood up to go back into the house. She got a whiff of the incense's fragrance. She'd always loved the smell, for it represented respect, honor, and sacredness, but now she winced, for it reminded her of her lies.

Yes, she had lied to Phong. She had made up her story of romance with Tim so that Phong felt pride in his father and in himself. And now, she could see that the story helped her grandchildren, too.

Phong knew she'd worked at the Hollywood Bar. That part of the story she couldn't twist because it involved Dan, Linda, and Thiên, but she told him she'd quit after her sister's passing. Unable to find a decent job afterward, she said, she had sold tea and soft drinks on the street.

The truth was that at the Minh Anh brothel, she'd had to have sex with too many men to remember their faces. None of those men had told her their names. None had shown her any tenderness. She had merely been an object to them.

How could she ever tell her son the truth, that he wasn't the fruit of a love story but the product of prostitution, and that she didn't know who his father was? Phong's father could have been one of the men who had poked at her as if they were poking at dead fish, who had mocked the shape of her eyes, who had called her unspeakable names.

Inside the house, the three red tips of the smoldering incense were still hovering in darkness. Without thinking, Quỳnh stretched her hands and grabbed the incense. The embers sizzled into her palms. She smelled burnt flesh but squeezed them tighter, her heart hammering in the cage of her chest.

In the yard, she dropped the incense. She trampled on it until each stick became dust. With each stamp of her foot, she vowed that the darkness from her past would never touch Phong. She would never let her son know the seeds of his life had come from the depths of her humiliation. She loved him. Out of that love, she had planted the story of Tim and grew it until its fruit tasted sweet in Phong's mouth. She'd heard Phong telling others about his father with such pride and knew that the sweetness of her fruit of deception was not only real, it was necessary.

Tim was her secret and her fantasy, the name she'd picked out of a book of translated literature. She chose that name because it meant "the heart" in Vietnamese.

She had tried to kill Phong before he was born. She'd beat her fists against her stomach when she found out she was pregnant. She'd swallowed bowl after bowl of bitter herbal medicine.

Now, she was thankful that Phong had refused to let go.

In her decision to continue lying to her son, sometimes regret clouded her mind. Was she denying Phong's chance of knowing his father, and Tài and Diễm of knowing their grandfather and his family? "No!" She told herself firmly. It was not worth the risk of putting Phong through pain. Whatever Phong and his family needed from his father, she could provide for them. She could take care of them and love them more than any American could. And in a way, Phong had already found his American parents in Dan and Linda, who had become like grandparents to Tài and Diễm.

Phong had been looked down on by too many people, who had called him bụi đời—a child of dust. She must keep showing him, in every way she possibly could, that he was the child of love. She respected his decision to look for his father's relatives. In case he found them or his father, she would deal with the consequences, but for now, she would protect him.

She had tried to live an honest life, but the war had given her no choice. It had forced her to make up a version of herself that was acceptable to others. In a way, making up stories had been the basis of her survival and her success. Her lies had enabled her parents to go on living, and now her lies would protect her sons, their families, her business, and herself.

In her recent visit to her parents' home, she had unearthed a secret box she'd buried in the garden. The box contained the many letters she and Trang had written home over the years. Those letters hardly contained any truth, but they were beautiful to read. And upon rereading them, she saw how writing them had enabled not just herself but her loved ones to escape horror, and to experience the taste of another life. She was tempted to burn the letters, destroy all the evidence of her past, but decided instead to bring them home. They were safe now, buried deep under the earth, below the banana plants, below the flowers that hung like the red lanterns that once filled the village of her childhood during the Mid-Autumn Festival. The flowers under which she and her sister had waited, full of yearning and hope, for their father to return from the war.

She went into the kitchen, diluted a pinch of salt into a bowl of warm water and disinfected the burns on her palms. She swept the yard with a broom until there was nothing left that would betray her. She checked on her grandchildren and pulled their blankets higher onto their chests. Mun came to Quỳnh, her tail wagging, her wet nose buried into Quỳnh's arm. Quỳnh picked Mun up, taking solace in the dog's warmth. She tucked the mosquito net tightly around her grandchildren's bed. With tears in her eyes, she watched the still shadows of Tài and Diễm. She hoped her grandchildren's dreams were taking them to a peaceful world where humans were kind to other humans, so that no one needed to live with regret and sorrow.

Out in the yard, with Mun in her arms, she sat waiting for Phong, the stars and the moon bright above her head. There had been days when the starlight had been concealed from her eyes by clouds and storms. But she knew such light was always there. Bright and inextinguishable.

◈ AUTHOR'S NOTE ◈

I grew up in Southern Việt Nam, where during the late seventies and in the eighties I got a glimpse of the discrimination faced by Amerasians born from the wartime unions between American men and Vietnamese women. Over the years, I kept thinking about those Amerasians and hoping that life had treated them more kindly. In April 2014, I read a story that moved me deeply. Jerry Quinn, an American veteran, traveled back to Hồ Chí Minh City with an album of old photos, looking for his girlfriend and their son.[1] They had been separated in 1973, forty-one years earlier. Mr. Quinn's story made me realize the urgency to find their lost children that some American veterans, now in their sixties and seventies, were feeling.

Via an organization that helped unite Amerasians with their parents, I got in touch with American veterans who had been searching for their Amerasian children. I interviewed them and wrote about them for a national newspaper in Việt Nam. I got involved in real-life searches for family members. While I could help several people unite with those they were looking for, after more than forty years, I realized the

---

1   Sue Lloyd Roberts, "A US soldier searches for his Vietnamese son," *BBC News*, 26 April, 2014

complexity and the trauma involved. I also learned about the incredible challenges that Amerasians and their family members have had to face.

This novel, *Dust Child*, took seven years to write and is a result of my PhD research with Lancaster University. It fictionalized my real-life interviews, journalistic experiences, voluntary work with those impacted by wars, reading, and academic research. While characters are fictional, their life stories are inspired by real-life events such as the implementation of the Amerasian Homecoming Act as well as the buying and selling of Amerasians.

Dust Child also aims to demonstrate the effects of wars and armed conflicts beyond the resultant deaths and injuries: approximately 2,700,000 Americans served in Việt Nam during the war alongside and against millions of ARVN and Communist soldiers, most of them were young men, many of whom remain traumatized today. A sex industry, propelled by the American military presence, involved hundreds of thousands of sex workers—mostly young Vietnamese women who suffered their own forms of trauma and social ostracism. There was also a large number of bar girls, not all of whom were sex workers, and who often took their hostess jobs for many reasons, including economic hardship or displacement.

❖

MY WEBSITE (www.nguyenphanquemai.com) has a list of books, films, and resources for those who are interested in finding more about Amerasians and their family members. Some of these books include: Kien Nguyen's *The Unwanted*; Sau Le Hudecek's *The Rebirth of Hope: My Journey from Vietnam War Child to American Citizen*; Thomas A. Bass's *Vietnamerica: The War Comes Home*; Trin Yarborough's *Surviving Twice: Amerasian Children of the Vietnam War*; Steven DeBonis's *Children of the Enemy: Oral Histories of Vietnamese Amerasians and Their Mothers*; Robert McKelvey's *The Dust of Life:*

America's Children Abandoned in Vietnam; Aimee Phan's *We Should Never Meet*; Nguyễn Thị Thụy Vũ's *Mèo đêm (Night's Cats)*, *Ngọn pháo bông (The Tops of Fireworks)*, and *Lao vào lửa (Dashing into the Fire)*; Le Ly Hayslip's *When Heaven and Earth Changed Places*; Nguyễn Ngọc Thuần's *Cơ bản là buồn (It's Mainly Sadness)*; Nguyễn Trí's *Ma lực của cội nguồn (The Mysterious Force of Homeland)*; and Wayne Karlin's *Prisoners* and *Marble Mountain*.

I wrote this book to offer my prayers for a world where there is more compassion, more peace, more forgiveness and healing. May our planet never see another armed conflict.

❖ ACKNOWLEDGMENTS ❖

My deepest thanks to Amerasians, mothers and fathers of Amerasians, and all other participants of my PhD research project who shared with me their life experiences and allowed me to fictionalize their stories into this novel. Their names do not appear here, as I would like to protect their privacy and identity, but I bow to them with my deepest gratitude and sincerely hope their stories will continue to inspire humans to love other humans more so that this world can become a better place.

I am grateful to Lancaster University for giving me a PhD scholarship and, more importantly, a free world to grow my writing dream. I am very lucky to have been mentored there by the award-winning writers Zoe Lambert, Sara Maitland, and Graham Mort. At Lancaster, Jenn Ashworth, George Green, Eoghan Walls, Anne O'Brien, Inés Gregori Labarta, Margot Douaihy, and Tessa McWatt read early versions of this manuscript and gave me much-needed encouragement. Sincere thanks to the writer Wayne Karlin, who helped me sharpen my vision for both my PhD project and this novel.

My journey as a novelist in English would not have been possible without two women who have believed fiercely in me from the very beginning and dedicated countless hours of their lives to this book:

my literary agent, Julie Stevenson, and my editor, Betsy Gleick. To Julie, Betsy, and my team—Mae Zhang McCauley, Jovanna Brinck, Michael McKenzie, Stephanie Mendoza, Debra Linn, Travis Smith, Kendra Poster, Brunson Hoole, Annie Mazes, Katrina Tiktinsky, Anna Skudlarek, and everyone at Algonquin Books—thank you for lifting my writing up as if it were your own. My most sincere thanks to Christopher Moisan for *Dust Child*'s beautiful book jacket, Steve Godwin for the unique design inside this book, Chris Stamey for his good eyes in copy editing, and the wonderful people I am fortunate to work with at the Tuesday Agency, Workman Audio, Workman Publishing, Hachette Book Group, and Massie & McQuilkin Literary Agents.

To editors, publishers, and translators who have worked tirelessly to make my work available in many different languages: thank you for giving my writing such rich lives.

To writers, researchers, and filmmakers who have documented the Amerasian experiences as well as the impact of PTSD and trauma: thank you for informing my research with your work.

This book is a result of the very generous support from the Lannan Foundation, who awarded me the Lannan Fellowship in Fiction for my debut novel, *The Mountains Sing*. Prior to that, my poetry collection, *The Secret of Hoa Sen*, was published by BOA Editions as part of the Lannan Translations Selection Series. The kind and brilliant people at Lannan rarely advertise the impactful work that they do to support minority writers like me, and I would like to express my sincere thanks to the Lannan family and the entire team at the foundation and its volunteers. Special thanks to Patrick Lannan, Lawrence P. Lannan, Martha Jessup, and Penn Szittya.

Along my writing journey, I have been uplifted by organizations that are making significant impacts in promoting diversity in literature, two of which include the Diasporic Vietnamese Artists Network (DVAN) and the Dayton Literary Peace Prize. My sincere thanks to Viet Thanh Nguyen, Isabelle Thuy Pelaud, Sharon Rab, and Nick Raines.

I am lucky to be surrounded by a wonderful writing community and am indebted to several writers and friends who read earlier versions of this manuscript and offered their insightful comments: Đinh Từ Bích Thúy, Paul Christiansen, Karl Marlantes, Thiếu Khanh, Natalie Jenner, Robert Mason, Sofia Akel, Quyên Ngô, Steven DeBonis, Jimmy Miller, Trần Thị NgH, Elizabeth Griffiths. My heartfelt thanks to writers who read and provided their compassionate blurbs for this novel.

I am thrilled to be able to cite one of my most beloved Vietnamese works of literature, Nguyễn Du's *Truyện Kiều* (*The Tale of Kiều*), in *Dust Child*. There are many translations of *The Tale of Kiều* and I chose to quote from the scholar and translator Huỳnh Sanh Thông's beautiful and insightful translation (*The Tale of Kiều*, Yale University Press, 1983). Grateful thanks to Yale University Press for their permission.

The seed of my writing dream was sown in my childhood home in Ninh Bình, Northern Việt Nam, where my mother raised me with her lullabies and her storytelling. It grew in Bạc Liêu, Southern Việt Nam, where my father brought home many books and built a bookshelf for me with his hands. My parents never had a chance to go to university and worked days and nights to make sure my two brothers and I could continue to study. To my parents: Con cám ơn bố mẹ. Con yêu bố mẹ và biết ơn bố mẹ rất nhiều.

During the seven years (2015–2022) that I worked on this book, my family has been my pillar. To my husband Hans, my children Mai and Johann, my brothers, and my relatives: thank you for being the lush garden that surrounds me, protects me, enriches me, and nurtures me into the person I am today.

To readers, booksellers, book reviewers, teachers, librarians, book club leaders, bookstagrammers, and literary champions: thank you for being the wings that carry my stories farther than I could dare hope. I would not be here without you!

◇ QUESTIONS FOR DISCUSSION ◇

1. What did you know about Amerasians born into the Việt Nam War before you read this book? How do Phong's experiences influence your thoughts about the impact of wars on women and children? What could be done to prevent these situations?

2. Were you aware of the number of Vietnamese women who worked in bars that served American soldiers? Describe the nature of the trauma and social ostracism that Trang and Quỳnh faced. How did the experience influence the relationship between the two sisters?

3. Describe Dan when he first arrived in Việt Nam in 1969. Why was Trang first attracted to him? Trace how—and how much—the war changed Dan. Do you think wars have the power to change the moral character of human beings?

4. Which elements of Vietnamese culture described in *Dust Child* stood out to you?

5. Via the experiences of Linda and Thanh (the son of the Northern Vietnamese veteran who suffers from Alzheimer's), describe how war

trauma is inherited by family members. What have Linda and Thanh
done to help their loved ones cope with their trauma?

6. Discuss the ethics and complexity involved in the Amerasians'
search for missing parents. How do these ethical issues compare to
other instances of people searching for their birth parents or lost family members?

7. How does Phong demonstrate his determination to survive and pros-
per? Describe his transformation throughout the book.

8. Describe the difficult decisions that Trang and Quỳnh had to make.
What would you have done if you were in their situation?

9. What is Dan's initial motivation for returning to Việt Nam? Do his
reasons change during his trip? If so, how, and why?

10. In *Dust Child*, Vietnamese words appear with their full diacritical
marks in chapters written from the viewpoints of Vietnamese speak-
ers. These marks are necessary to interpret meaning: for example, in
Nun Nhã's name, *nhã* means "elegant," while *nhà* means "house," *nhả*
means "release," *nha* means "teeth" or "dental," and *nhá* means "to chew
carefully." In chapters written from Dan's voice, the diacritical marks
are stripped away. Did the use of diacritical marks affect your reading
experience? What do these two ways of representing the Vietnamese
language show you? Does Dan's understanding of the importance of
diacritics change?

11. In the novel, Quỳnh says, "She had tried to live an honest life, but
the war had given her no choice. It had forced her to make up a version
of herself that was acceptable to others. In a way, making up stories had
been the basis of her survival and her success." Can lies be necessary

for love, survival, and dignity? Were you surprised at Quỳnh's decision, and what do you think about her as a mother?

12. Which Vietnamese proverbs in the book are your favorites? Which ones demean Vietnamese women? Do you have similar proverbs in your culture?

13. Have you tried any of the Vietnamese food described in the novel? What would you like to eat and/or try to cook?

14. "Conversation about books represented the most intimate discourse. It revealed a person's values, beliefs, fears, and hopes. Experiencing the same books enabled people to travel on similar journeys and brought them closer together," Dan reflected in the novel. Do you agree with his statement? Has your book club enriched your life? If so, how?

Born and raised in Việt Nam, **NGUYỄN PHAN QUẾ MAI** is the author of the international bestseller *The Mountains Sing*, winner of the PEN Oakland/Josephine Miles Literary Award, the International Book Award, the BookBrowse Best Debut Award, and the Lannan Literary Award Fellowship for Fiction, as well as runner-up for the Dayton Literary Peace Prize. She has published twelve books of poetry, fiction, and nonfiction in Vietnamese and English and has received some of the top literary prizes in Việt Nam. Her writing has been translated into more than twenty languages and has appeared in major publications, including the *New York Times*. Many of her poems in Vietnamese have been composed into popular songs. Quế Mai is also a translator of ten books of poetry and fiction and has a PhD in creative writing from Lancaster University. She is an advocate for the rights of disadvantaged groups in Việt Nam and was named by *Forbes Việt Nam* as one of twenty inspiring women of 2021. *Dust Child* is her second novel. For more information, visit nguyenphanquemai.com.